# PRAISE FOR
## *She Walks These Hills*

"Sharyn McCrumb transforms mystery into astonishing literature. . . . her new novel is entertaining, suspenseful, and illuminating."
—*Cleveland Plain Dealer*

"A story of familial, cultural, historical, and legal intrigue . . . with thickening plot and subplots. McCrumb's writing succeeds. Descriptions feel exactly right. Point of view shifts smoothly. She allows the reader to visualize action that is not intrusively described."
—*New York Times Book Review*

"A lyrically written, emotionally charged evocation of present-day Appalachia and its population . . . will leave you both satisfied and hungry for more. . . . Sharyn McCrumb has few equals and no superiors among today's novelists."
—*San Diego Union-Tribune*

# Sharyn McCrumb

# SHE WALKS THESE HILLS

*Kimberly Bixler*
*Nov. 13, 1992*

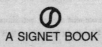

A SIGNET BOOK

SIGNET
Published by the Penguin Group
Penguin Books USA Inc., 375 Hudson Street,
New York, New York 10014, U.S.A.
Penguin Books Ltd, 27 Wrights Lane,
London W8 5TZ, England
Penguin Books Australia Ltd, Ringwood,
Victoria, Australia
Penguin Books Canada Ltd, 10 Alcorn Avenue,
Toronto, Ontario, Canada M4V 3B2
Penguin Books (N.Z.) Ltd, 182–190 Wairau Road,
Auckland 10, New Zealand

Penguin Books Ltd, Registered Offices:
Harmondsworth, Middlesex, England

Published by Signet, an imprint of Dutton Signet, a division of Penguin Books USA
Inc. This is an authorized reprint of a hardcover edition published by Charles
Scribner's Sons. For information address Simon & Schuster, 1230 Avenue of the
Americas, New York, NY 10020.

First Signet Printing, October, 1995
10  9  8  7  6  5  4  3  2  1

*To Gurney Norman,*
*the fox on the run*

I shall not leave these prisoning hills . .
Being of these hills, being one with the fox
Stealing into the shadows, one with the new-born foal,
The lumbering ox drawing green beech logs to mill,
One with the destined feet of man
                              climbing and descending,
And one with death rising to bloom again, I cannot go.
Being of these hills, I cannot pass beyond.

"Heritage"
James Still, *The Wolfpen Poems.*
The Berea College Press, Berea, KY, 1986, p. 82.
Used by permission.

# PROLOGUE

The woman had been running through the woods a long time. Blood crusted in the briar-cut on her cheek. Her matted hair, a thicket of dry leaves and tangles, hung about a gaunt face, lined with weariness and hunger. A shapeless, dirt-streaked dress that had once been blue gaped over bony wrists and sagged empty at the collarbone. She might have been twenty, but her eyes were old.

She was following the deer track that hugged the ridge above the river, moving silently past dark clumps of rhododendron, and always watching, looking back across the Tennessee mountains to see that no one followed her, looking down to make sure that the green river still curled around the hollows below. Sometimes she seemed to be no more than a pin oak's shadow, or a trick of light among the leaves at dusk, so colorless and silent was she among the trees. She seemed to hear nothing. She did not appear to feel the scrape of twigs across her face, or the chill of the evening breeze on the mountain. She looked only down and back. Down and back.

Nora Bonesteel stood under an apple tree at the

edge of her meadow, watching the woman pass by. She couldn't see her as clearly as she once had, but that could mean only that her eyes were dimming with age. For more than seventy years—when the air was crisp and the light was slanted and the birds were still— Nora Bonesteel had caught glimpses of the young woman following the deer track across Ashe Mountain.

She had been a child the first time she spied the running woman, and now she was too old to see her plainly anymore, but the woman on the deer path had not changed. She always ran along the same few yards of the woodland trace, looking down at the river and back at the blue mountains behind her. The path had grown over since Nora was a girl, and here and there a pine tree grew in what had once been smooth dirt, but the woman walked there anyway, no more heeding those new trees than she had the shouts of the child calling out to her. Nora had attempted to speak to her at first, before she understood about the Sight. She had tried to tell the grown folks up home about the poor raggedy woman in the woods, but they just looked at her and got all quiet.

Nora was ten before she realized that other people didn't see the things that she saw. Like when she saw the black crepe ribbons on the Millers' beehives, and asked who in the family had died, but nobody else could see those streamers. It was two days later before they saw them—not 'til after Aunt Effie Miller had passed away. Nora thought it out, and finally decided that most folks see only what is here and now, but that she could see what was and what was going to be. She didn't know why she was made different, but she figured that was the Lord's business, not hers, and if He wanted her to do something with it, He'd let her know. She learned on her own to keep quiet about things like funeral wreaths and cloth-draped mirrors until she touched them to make sure they were already there.

She stopped telling folks about the woman in the woods, but the vision still troubled her. Long before she found out who the woman was, Nora had tried to help this poor wayfaring stranger, but she couldn't make her hear. No matter how loud she shouted, the haunted woman ran on, always with the same cut on her cheek, the same leaves in her tangled hair. When Nora stood close to the path to try to touch her, she wouldn't be there at all.

As Nora grew older, she heard her Grandma Flossie tell the story of Katie Wyler, who had been kidnapped from her father's farm over in Mitchell County, North Carolina, by the Shawnee in the year seventeen-and-seventy nine. The Indian raiding party had taken Katie all the way to the banks of the Ohio River, but she had escaped and made her way back across hundreds of miles of wilderness to Mitchell County by following the rivers. It was a brave journey, but it ended in sorrow.

At sixteen, with an adolescent's love of tragedy and the arrogance of her youth, Nora had tried to save Katie Wyler. On an autumn evening, she had stood on the deer track overlooking the river, and waited for the running woman. "Go back to the Indians," young Nora called out. "You don't want to go home. Go back!" Without a pause or a flicker of expression, the running woman was gone, but nothing was changed.

Nora could still see her sometimes, when the air was

crisp and the light was right and the birds were still, but now she only watched from a distance. She no longer tried to help. Perhaps Katie was only an image of the woman who had run there, a mirage burned in the mountain air by weariness and terror. Whatever the truth of it, Katie Wyler had been gone a long time, and Nora Bonesteel was no longer young enough to think she knew all the answers. With age, Nora had come to accept the wisdom of a saying of another old woman. In a poke bonnet and a rustling black dress, Mother Jones, that implacable union organizer of coal country, had told her troops: "Pray for the dead, and fight like hell for the living."

# CHAPTER
# 1

My Lord calls me, He calls me by the lightning;
  The trumpet sounds within my soul: I have not long
to stay here.
. . . Steal away, steal away home.

"STEAL AWAY"

*August 1993–*

Hiram Sorley's feet itched, and he knew it was a sign. The doctor at the prison infirmary might call it dry skin from sweaty three-day socks or athlete's foot from the dank concrete shower room, but Hiram knew better. He had seen the flashes of lightning from the sealed window of his cell: another portent highlighting the message from the Almighty to him. He'd been getting the signs for days now. The Lord was trying to tell him something, and directly it would all be coming clear.

The window was long and narrow, like a church window, and the glow of the storm through black sheepskin clouds gave it the luminescence of stained glass. He sat down on his bunk beneath the window, with his palm-sized King James Bible cradled in his lap. Tattered by age and constant use, the Bible sagged at the spine, and the gold-leaf title on its cover had worn to glints of brightness in the lettering's deep grooves. In fine print beneath *Holy Bible,* the word *concordance* had lost its three initial letters, a source of amusement for the burly guard with yellow hair and yellower teeth. "Cordance," he'd said, catching sight of the prisoner's testament. "Looks like it says *cord dance*—the kind of high-stepping folks like you used to do inside of a noose. And that second *B* is almost gone out of Bible, which leaves you with *bile*. You know what *bile* is don't you, Harm? That's what dirties up your pants when you do the cord dance." He had laughed at his own wit. " 'Course we don't do our executing by rope in Tennessee no more, but I'd say you got a real gallows Bible there, Harm."

*Harm*. It wasn't even a nickname. It was just the way folks had always pronounced his first name, Hiram, in mountain dialect, a long "i" sound blending the two syllables into an aspirated breath: Harm. But to some of the younger inmates—those hoppers from Memphis, with their west Tennessee drawls and a lick of education—his name was a rich joke. They took to calling him that on purpose, and spelling it "Harm," because it struck them funny that a crazy old hillbilly should have such a malevolent name, while the murderers and child molesters from downstate answered to "Sweet Sam," "Snow," and "Cornbread." Those city cons—old at seventeen—would just as soon cut you as look at you, but their street names made them sound soft as a litter of barn kittens. They laughed at Harm, when they noticed him, but they didn't get in his face. Everybody knew that old Hillbilly Harm was on zap time, and didn't nobody mess with a zap-out, not even the guards.

He had been in prison a long time. So long that nobody even cared why he was there anymore. They just knew that he was not getting out. Harm was past sixty now, and although he was still lean with fine-chiseled features, his skin was as pale as a slate rock. He had been a long time out of the sun and wind. Some people

said Harm had shot some guy in a fight over moonshine; others said he had tried to rob one gas station
too many; the truth was, nobody remembered, and it
was no use asking Harm, because he was on zap time,
and didn't nobody ask him nothing.

Zap-timers are the ghosts of cell blocks. They start
their stretch like everybody else, enduring strip searches,
daily inspection of the cells, solitary time in the hole for
any infraction of jail law. Through all the dehumanizing
rituals of confinement, the inmates added their own in-
humanity to each other to fester the sores—other cons
getting in a prisoner's face . . . snitches signifying, looking for something to report or grist for the gossip mill
. . . lust-driven old-timers trying to scale the new fish—
all of it eating away at a prisoner's wall of self like a
trickle of water down a slab of concrete. Then one day,
the wall crumbles from one drop of water too many, and
the prisoner isn't there anymore. Physically he is present, same as always, still locked in his cell, still showing
up for chow, walking the yard—but somehow nobody
sees him anymore, or maybe they see him but they don't
*feel* his presence in their guts. He doesn't register. He is
on zap time. Now he can say any insulting thing he
wants to another inmate, and the provocation evokes no
outburst: a nervous laugh, maybe a shrug, where once
such words would have got his throat cut. Guards ignore
his most outrageous infractions. Let him walk into the
kitchen and reappear with a loaf of bread: they will
nudge each other with shit-eating grins. Within the con-
fines of the prison, such a man may seem free, but in
fact he is packed into an even smaller cell: that of his
own mind. Regimentation, antagonism, punishment—all

have become pointless, because a zap-timer no longer cares. Part of him went over the wall, and the rest of him doesn't even know it.

The word was that Harm was even crazier than your ordinary zap. The doctors said Harm had brain damage from decades of drinking jailshine brewed in somebody's toilet, and in the early eighties he'd been nearly throttled to death by a Nashville punk. When he regained consciousness a few days later, he never was quite right in the head. Everybody left him be. He was too old to arouse lust in anybody's loins, too small and ancient to be worth fighting with, and too zapped out to matter in the prison world. He kept to himself, in his own private year, and paged through his worn King James Bible. *Oh God, our help in ages past . . .*

The lightning flashed again, and the rumble of thunder seemed nearer this time. Harm knew it was the Lord, urging him on. Ask and ye shall receive. He'd learned Bible cracking from his mother's brother, Uncle Pharis, a long time ago in Uncle Pharis's cabin up the holler. Pharis truly believed that if your need was great, the Lord would speak to you through His word. All you had to do was think your question, open the good book, and point at random to a verse. Whatever it said was what the Lord meant you to do.

The Sorley clan did not have much use for religion, but the McCrorys, Harm's mother's people, had been strong in the faith. And Pharis had been outstanding, even among the Preaching McCrorys. Sometime around 1920, Uncle Pharis had gone into that new branch of fundamentalism born in the Tennessee mountains—the Pentacostals. Sometimes at meetings the Holy Spirit would descend upon Uncle Pharis, and he would begin to speak in tongues. Then he would open the door of the little sanctuary's pot-bellied stove, reach in and scoop up red-hot coals, and carry them in his outstretched bare hands from pew to pew 'til they were cooled down, praying all the while in a voice like falling water. Harm's uncle almost always knew what he ought to do without having to Bible crack to find out, but Harm felt that he himself walked among the godless, and the way was not always easy, so he checked with the Lord a lot, just to make sure he was traveling along in the path of righteousness. Besides, the feel of his mother's Bible took him back. It was the only thing the Sorleys hadn't sold to the antiquers, and surely all the home he had left. When he held it with his eyes closed, he could smell the lilacs that grew next to the porch up home.

Seasons didn't come behind the nicotine-stained white walls of Mountain City's prison, so Harm always imagined it spring—the locust trees shaggy with clustered white blooms, the wet woods flecked with bloodroot, and wild roses and honeysuckle flashing white among the chestnuts on the mountainsides. Harm's life had gone on after his boyhood in the holler, but he didn't care to think of anything or anyone farther along. Those memories blurred when he grabbed at them with his mind. He dreamed of golden fields of wild mustard, of snowmelt streams swirling around green trout pools, and of the taste of his mother's wilted lettuce salad topped with spring onions and bacon drippings. In his cell and in his dreams, it was always shining spring.

*My Lord calls me. He calls me by the lightning . . .*

And his feet itched. Itching feet mean you are going on a journey. Was that what the Lord wanted to tell him?

He hunched over the Bible in his lap, his right palm flat against the cover. He closed his eyes, willing himself to receive the wisdom to be imparted, and opened the book, pointing a trembling forefinger at the page. When it felt right, he opened his eyes to read the message from God.

Martha Ayers always jumped up when she heard the beep of the fax machine. It was a new addition to the sheriff's office, and the wonder of it had not yet worn off. Martha equated faxes with the telegrams of her childhood: the bearer of tidings so terrible they must be imparted without delay. She tried to assume a clinical detachment to the procedure—after all, the messages were never anything personal. But then, she knew almost everybody in Hamelin. Each newly reported tragedy would be official sheriff's business, but it would also affect her in some small way, and she would begin to grieve even before she knew who it was this time. Alerted by the sound signaling an incoming message, Martha would leave her dispatcher's desk to stand anxiously beside the machine while it clacked and sputtered out some new detail of bureaucratic law enforcement from Nashville.

"You don't have to *answer* the thing," said Joe LeDonne. "It's automatic."

Martha glanced at him. His feet were still propped on top of his desk, and he was still sprawled back in his swivel chair, watching her with a bemused smile. He was taking a break from county patrol in the Indian summer heat, with his brown tie askew, his uniform sleeves rolled up, and a frosty can of Pepsi held to his temple between swigs.

"Well, the message might be important," said Martha, resisting the urge to yank the paper out while the machine was still printing. "Otherwise, they'd just mail it, wouldn't they?"

LeDonne shook his head. "Not bureaucrats. We had a saying in the army: *hurry up and wait.* I figure the fax machine was just made for people like that."

She snatched up the finished dispatch, and scanned it quickly. "Looks like you're wrong this time," she told the deputy. "This is a message from the Northeast Correctional Center up in Mountain City, notifying us of an escaped convict. We need to be on the lookout for him."

"Well, not *we*, Martha," grinned LeDonne. "I don't reckon you'll have to worry about him, unless he stops in here at the office to ask for directions, but I guess we'd better tell Spencer and Godwin about it. What else does it say?"

She turned away, so that he wouldn't see the hurt on her face. LeDonne handled his own pain better than other people's. He hadn't meant to offend her by belittling what she did. It would never occur to him that she might not share his opinion of the job of dispatcher. She might bring up her injured feelings tonight after dinner, if he seemed relaxed enough to handle it, but she wasn't sure she could make him understand. People who have been shot at don't take desk jobs seriously.

"An escaped con," said LeDonne. Martha saw him

glance at the rack of rifles locked in place on the wall of the office.

"At least it wasn't somebody from Brushy Mountain," she said, keeping her voice brisk and professional. "Those are the ones I'd worry about, but still, I guess anyone who escaped can be dangerous. Mountain City is no country club. Let's see . . . It says here that the prisoner's name is Hiram Sorley. Never heard of him. This says that he was originally a resident of this county, so they think he might be headed this way."

LeDonne's smile faded. He pushed back from the desk and swung out of his chair, and his fingers brushed the butt of his pistol. His blue eyes were cold now, and all traces of amiability were gone. "They think he's coming this way? Who is he? Have we got a file on him?"

"I'll check," said Martha. "It says here that Sorley was doing life without parole. There's a description . . . Five feet seven . . . one hundred forty pounds . . . brown eyes . . . graying hair . . . sixty-three years old."

"Sixty-three? Must be a typo," said LeDonne, reaching for the paper.

"Aren't you going to tell Spencer?"

LeDonne looked at the closed door marked *Sheriff*, and then at the row of lights on Martha's telephone. "He's still talking. Maybe I'll just poke my head in and signal for him to come out when he's finished. You see if you can find a file on this guy."

Martha pulled out the S drawer of the filing cabinet of current cases. "Sanders . . . Seton . . . Shields . . . Smith . . . Smith . . . Spann . . . Stafford," she murmured. She pushed the drawer shut and said to

LeDonne, "Well, I've passed where he ought to be, even allowing for misfiling. I'll have to check the records farther back. The filing cabinet's in the storeroom." She flipped on the hall light. "Watch the phone for me, will you?"

LeDonne smiled. "And the fax machine, too?" he called out. He sat down on the edge of his desk and began to reread the message from Mountain City. He was composing a handwritten return fax asking for a photograph and more information when Spencer Arrowood emerged from his office, looking annoyed.

"Sorry to barge in," said LeDonne. When he had opened the door to the office a few minutes earlier, the sheriff had waved him away with an uncharacteristic scowl. Scowls were usually LeDonne's department. The sheriff, fair-haired, taller and leaner than LeDonne, had the pleasant gentleness of one who likes people and who has been treated well by most of them. He smiled easily, and he had a style of self-deprecating humor that generally deflated the wrath of his opponents. Like the deputy, Spencer Arrowood was an army veteran of the sixties, but he had spent his tour as a young lieutenant chasing paper clips around Germany. LeDonne, who had been an infantryman in a line company in Vietnam, sometimes wondered if the sheriff's sunny nature would have survived a tour in Southeast Asia, or if he would have come back with LeDonne's restlessness, his sullen distrust of humanity, and his impatience with authority and all things bureaucratic. But then, Spencer wouldn't have become a sheriff. The voters wouldn't have trusted him, and maybe he wouldn't have wanted the job. LeDonne didn't. Let somebody else kiss the local politicians' asses. He wanted to get rid of the local scum, and he didn't have to be polite to them. It wasn't combat, but sometimes it was enough.

"It's all right. That was Godwin. He's had another dizzy spell, and the doctor told him not to come in." He sighed. "I guess I'll cover for him four to midnight."

"I'll plan on taking tomorrow night," said LeDonne. "I wish he'd figure out what's causing this, and either get better or—or quit." It hadn't been what he'd started to say.

"If he quits, he loses his health insurance," said Spencer. "I just wish the doctors could figure out what's causing it. Still, I reckon we can put up with it a while longer. It could have happened to any of us."

"Well, I hope you have a peaceful night shift." LeDonne handed him the fax. "Looks like we might be having company from the NECC in Mountain City."

Spencer fished out his reading glasses and scanned the message. *"Harm Sorley!* I don't believe it. He must be older than God by now. He escaped?"

"So they say. Martha's in the back room trying to find the file on this guy. I take it you've heard of him?"

"Heard of him, yes. He was way before my time, though. I was probably away at college. Or maybe in Germany by then. Anyhow, Nelse Miller was the sheriff that put him away."

"What for?"

Spencer wasn't listening. "Old Harm. I thought he'd be out by now. Or dead, maybe."

Martha appeared in the doorway, waving a blue folder. "Found him!"

* * *

On Radio WHTN a Statler Brothers oldie from their Greatest Hits collection beguiled local listeners, while the afternoon disc jockey, Hank the Yank, readied his copy for five minutes of local news at the bottom of the hour. The show, part oldies and bluegrass, part commentary, with an occasional call-in, was billed as an auditory country store, where neighbors could tune in for a visit among themselves. The fact that the host was a carpetbagger from Connecticut might have guaranteed his solitude in the old days, but now that backwater Tennessee had a population of New Age pioneers, college professors, and retired flatlanders, his accent was less of a novelty. He had a way of making listeners feel that he could hear them, too, and he didn't preach political correctness at them, so they tuned in for the bluegrass, and found they liked Hank well enough to punch him in on the automatic radio tuner: second from the left, 85.3.

When the song trailed off into the instrumental finish, Hank twisted the volume knob and leaned into his voice mike. "And that last one was 'Tomorrow Never Comes,' some words of wisdom from Harold, Don, Jimmy, and Phil—the Statler Brothers—backed up by the Cowboy Symphony Orchestra. And that means we're coming up on local news time. For those of you who are passing through these mountains in search of fall foliage—and you're too darn early—your radio dial has landed on WHTN-AM, Hamelin, Tennessee. I'm your host for this afternoon's insurrection: Hank the Yank, a stranger in high places. A few years ago I got off the Appalachian Trail at Indian Graves Gap, and I just never made it back to Connecticut. If you've driven the Blue Ridge Parkway on an unclouded day, or marveled at North Carolina's mountains on film in *The Last of the Mohicans,* I don't reckon you'll wonder that I stayed. I built me a pine cabin on a flat place the size of a postage stamp between two ridges. I got this job. I couldn't get rid of this accent, but at least I learned how to pronounce things—Appa-*latch*-ian—so they let me stay. Right neighborly folks hereabouts, if you don't ask too many questions, or gloat about The War. But they're good people down here, and they'll help you if you're lost, so don't worry about that.

"Now that the introductions are out of the way for the tourists, the rest of us had better take a look at what's going on around here. Not much of it's good. That's what news is, though. All the stuff you'd rather not hear about, but curiosity gets the best of you. If it hadn't happened to strangers, it'd be gossip. So what's happening? The candidates for November's state senate race are going to be debating tonight in Johnson City. So there's your chance to see what they stand for, before you have to sit still for it for the next four years. I know it sounds boring, and you'd rather stay home and watch *Andy Griffith* reruns, but I think that's the gimmick in politics: being boring. Those who can stay awake for it get to run the world. Think about it, neighbors.

"On a more somber note, I'm sorry to have to tell you that Jamie Lee Montgomery, a sixteen-year-old from Rock Creek, flipped his car over an embankment on Route 23 late last night. Funeral Wednesday at Rock Creek Baptist . . . and a Wake County high school sophomore has been charged with the recent burglary resulting in the loss of three thousand dollars of equipment from the Elm Avenue Elementary School. Because he is a minor, his name is being withheld by the sheriff's department." Hank the Yank paused to let his listeners digest this bit of news. "You know, I was just thinking about that last song we heard, 'Tomorrow Never Comes.' The Statlers also sang a song about life getting complicated once you get past eighteen. I may play that in the next hour, for us to contemplate. But, you know, it seems to me that contrary to the Statler Brothers' musical opinion, the real complication in life is trying to stay alive and well-adjusted enough to make it past eighteen. Never mind what happens after that. Who's to say what success is anyhow? Why, back in Connecticut, my high school classmates think I'm famous 'cause you folks listen to me every day."

A sudden movement beyond the glass partition diverted his attention from the sweeping second hand of the clock. "Hold on a minute," he told his listeners. "I think Arvin wants me. He's waving a piece of paper at me. Y'all didn't get up a petition to have me replaced by a communications major from U.T., did you?—Well, come in, Arvin. You already broke my train of thought—Arvin is pitiless toward northerners. When I moved into my cabin in Banner Cove, Arvin came over and offered to plant me some wonderful kudzu vines by way of landscaping. I thought he was being quite neighborly until the next spring when the plants took over my yard. When they threatened to swallow my cabin, Arvin turned up and said he'd remove all the kudzu—for a price. He claims it's his standard housewarming gift—kudzu. Southerners pay him not to plant it in the first place, and he collects even more money from the rest of us when it engulfs the property."

He took the printed message from the sallow, bespectacled technician, whose fabled antics existed only in Hank the Yank's mythology. "Late-breaking news," said the deejay, switching to his serious mode as he scanned the tag line. "This just in, from the Northeast Correctional Center in Mountain City, Tennessee. Authorities there say that convicted murderer Hiram 'Harm' Sorley escaped from the prison sometime yesterday, and he is believed to be headed toward Wake County. The convict may be dangerous, and residents are urged to report any suspicious-looking persons to their local law enforcement personnel. Do not try to apprehend him, as he may be armed!" He looked up from the news release. "Well, that's a facer, isn't it, folks? Are they going to tell us what to look out for? Oh, here it is. The escaped prisoner is five-seven . . . weighs one forty . . . graying hair . . . brown eyes . . . age, sixty-three. *Sixty-three?* Tell me you made this up, Arvin."

Solemnly, the technician shook his head, and pointed to the fax machine.

"Arvin says it's on the level, folks. The message goes on to say that this Harm guy is originally from around here. Does anybody know about him? Give us the lowdown. You can call us toll free on the news line. We'll be back after this word from the folks at Chevrolet, who invite you to sit outside tonight, look up at the bright September sky, and listen to the Fords rusting in the twilight."

\* \* \*

On Ashe Mountain Nora Bonesteel switched off her radio, and stood staring out at the blue ripple of mountains that stretched away from the edge of her meadow. It was mid-September, still seemed like high summer, but for the sharp chill of the lengthening nights and the dulling of the asters as they shrank from the slanting light of a fading season. For now the landscape was still bosky: woods glowing deep green, fields bronzed with hay, and orchards apple-laden on the hillsides. Soon the autumn chill would turn the mountains to flame, shading each ridge a different color. When she was a child, Nora used to stand out in the meadow with Grandma Flossie, calling out the names of the trees by the color they turned the mountainsides. *Red for maple. Golden oak. Brown for the locust trees. Yellow hickory. Orange elm. Gold for chestnut.* She sighed, remembering the last. They were gone now, killed by a plant disease that swept the mountains sixty years ago. She had seen the last of them, and even in her girlhood they had been dying. The once-chestnut hills would be green now from the unchanging scrub pine, or a drabber shade as other trees grew among the bones of the great chestnuts. Autumn was paler now than it had been when she was a girl. To her it seemed that the whole world was diminishing, each year more stale and colorless than the one before. Even the winters were watery wearinesses, tepid compared to the howling blasts of wind-driven snow that she endured as a girl.

The century was going out like a lamb. The tunes all sounded the same; apples and tomatoes tasted like cardboard; church was a committee meeting; and even good and evil themselves had degenerated into timid good intentions versus intoxicated vandalism.

Not like the old days. She glanced back at the now-silent radio, in which Hank the Yank was no doubt continuing his recital of local happenings. *So Harm was out, and homeward bound.* Now, *he* was part of the vivid old days. Nothing tepid about the Sorley clan. They sailed through dust on washboard roads in their battered black coupes; costarred in every court docket posted in the county; and swaggered their way into oblivion, leaving a trail of blood and broken hearts in their wake.

Harm was the last of them.

She remembered who he was all right. But she wouldn't be calling the radio station to talk about it, even if there were phone lines strung up Ashe Mountain. It was a sad thing about Harm Sorley, dangerous as he might be. He was still the last of something, and she would hate to see him go, as much as she would hate seeing the last wolf, the last mountain painter, or even the last timber rattler blotted out of existence. It was a diminishing of sorts.

# CHAPTER

## 2

Will she, then, with fond emotion,
  Aught of human love retain?
Or, absorbed in pure devotion,
  Will no earthly trace remain?

#1047, "THEN COMETH THE END," CONDER

TENNESSEE METHODIST HYMNAL, 1885

# CHAPTER 2

"It feels good to get out of the office," said Martha, settling happily into the passenger seat of the sheriff's patrol car. "I get tired of sitting at that desk."

Spencer Arrowood smiled. "A few nights patrolling in January sleet would make you appreciate the comforts of the office."

"You don't accomplish much in this world by being comfortable," said Martha. "I believe in hard work. Deputies get a lot more respect than dispatchers. They get paid more, too."

Spencer made no reply to this. He concentrated on the road with perhaps more care than was required to drive thirty-five miles per hour down a residential street. He waved to a gaggle of boys on bicycles, and nodded to his constituents checking mailboxes or hauling groceries out of their cars. Finally he said, "I appreciate your coming with me on this. See how comfortable it feels, though, when you're doing the job, not just riding around sightseeing."

Martha turned to look at him. "And you see how well I do it."

"Well, Martha, I did bring you along, so I must have figured you were capable."

"You brought me because *you* didn't want to have to do it. You and LeDonne are just alike in that respect. You'd both rather wade through two gallons of blood and get shot at than to have to be comforting to some innocent citizen who's crying."

"It makes me sweat," muttered Spencer.

"I know it does. It's a lot easier to read somebody his rights and throw him in the back of the patrol car than to deal with pain you can't fix. You think listening is a woman's job."

"No. I just don't think I'm very good at it."

"Well, you'd better tell me more about this case then, so I'll know what I'm dealing with. You think she's likely to be afraid when we tell her? Want police protection?"

"I don't know, Martha. How would you feel if your husband were on his way back after twenty-odd years?"

"Depends. Which husband?" Martha shrugged. "I saw Leon Jarvis at the mall in Johnson City a while back. Didn't feel a thing. He was with his two daughters, and we all waved. I married him when I was twenty, and it didn't last long. No kids; no possessions worth arguing over. Now he's more of a stranger to me than the people on 'The Today Show.' And Howard shows up at church a couple of times a year with his dearest mama. I just stay out of his way, like I would a dead skunk in the road."

"Rita Pentland might react either way. I hope she does."

Martha considered it. "Every time I see Rita Pentland she looks like she just stepped out of the beauty parlor, and her yard looks like she tends it with nail scissors, so if I had to guess at her reaction to hearing that an escaped convict ex-husband was on the loose, I'd plump for teetotal embarrassment. It'll be the talk of the Garden Club. She might head for Myrtle Beach until the whole thing blows over."

"Maybe we should suggest that."

She looked at him speculatively. "You seem awfully concerned about this, Spencer. And for the life of me, I don't remember Harm Sorley at all."

Spencer smiled. "We were town kids. I only heard about the Sorleys when I visited the kinfolks back in the holler. Besides, I doubt if you took much of an interest in crime as a teenager. And Harm wasn't much of a desperado—never made the FBI's most wanted list—but he sure gave the law in these parts a hard time. He had style."

Martha was reading house numbers. "Never mind the reminiscences. We're almost to the Pentlands. Are you gonna tell me what he did or not?"

Spencer swung the patrol car into a driveway flanked by well-tended azalea beds. "He did a lot of things over the years, but what finally got him sent away for good was killing his neighbor Claib Maggard with an ax. He'll be dead before he's ever eligible for parole, and his wife divorced him while he was in prison. Now you have to tell her he's coming back."

Rita Pentland had not been listening to the radio that afternoon. On bright September days she took to her garden, trying to coax a few more blooms from her bronze mums, a few more days of color from the last of her dahlias. She hadn't cared much about flowers when she was younger. She had grown up barefoot and tow-headed, on a farm set slantways in a narrow mountain holler on the North Carolina side of the ridge. Up on the farm, her mama had grown cabbage roses, but most of her time and energy for cultivation had been given to the vegetable garden, which had to feed eight of them, whether Daddy worked enough to buy them shoes or not.

After that, she hadn't lived in places where anybody had time to care how the yard looked.

It was only as she got older that she began to find comfort in tending garden flowers. Flowers didn't scratch up your house and then go off somewheres and die the way cats did. And they didn't sit back and judge you the way people did, on how you looked or what you had, or whether you gave them what they wanted. You always knew where you stood with flowers. They didn't pretend. Too much water, and they made their leaves turn yellow to let you know about it. Too little water, they'd wilt, so as to tell you they needed help. Not like people, who pretended all the time, and maybe didn't even know themselves what it was they really wanted. Flowers were safe to love. They'd even give you little warning symbols before they died, so you'd be prepared for it. Not like people, who just up and died without caring whether you grieved or not. Like Daddy had done. One hot morning, he was hale and lusty, plowing a furrow with the broom-tailed mule and singing "Do Lord" so loud you could hear him in the pump house— and by noon, he was pale as ashes on Mama's Jerusalem quilt, breathing his last. Rita was nine then, but she neither forgot nor forgave.

Flowers gave you more notice. And no matter how loud their colors were—blaze orange marigolds, deep purple petunias, red-and-gold Joker pansies—no one thought that bright flowers were in bad taste. You didn't have to be careful with them like you did with clothes. It was all right not to have beige ones. Flowers were comforting.

And now, of course, over the past ten years when they had been living on Elm Avenue, gardening had become quite important. She belonged to the Garden Club with several of her neighbors, two of the other commissioners' wives, and Dr. Stowe's second wife. Then gardening became something to occupy her time, and something proper to talk about. It didn't matter if you hadn't been to college if you could grow four-foot azalea bushes.

Euell liked for her to garden. He said that the beds of well-tended flowers around their ranch house gave the place tone, and showed the neighbors what respectable, responsible people they were. She'd come a long way, Euell liked to say. With her beauty parlor-styled hair, and her dresses of blues and beiges from Montaldos, and their carefully furnished house, couldn't nobody tell she'd started out as white trash. He'd saved her from that, and she knew it.

If you looked real close at the flowers, though, Rita thought—put your face right down and stared at those velvet petals, dark enough to swallow you—they looked just the same as they had in Mama's old ditch garden up home.

* * *

The assistant warden reread the fax from the Wake
County Sheriff's Department, and then he consulted
the Tennessee map on the wall of his office. Wake
County . . . It was possible, he supposed. The prisoner's
original residence was there, after all. Hamelin, a
whistle-stop on the old Clinchfield railroad line, lay
deep in a valley carved out by the Little Dove River and
surrounded on steep sides by the heavily forested
Unaka Mountains. The eastern peak divided Tennessee
from North Carolina, traversed by a drovers road that
had linked Morganton to Jonesborough for two hundred years. There weren't many ways in or out of Wake
County. If the prisoner got that far, someone should
spot him.

The Northeast Correctional Center faced Highway
67 in the unincorporated hamlet of Doe Valley (mailing
address Mountain City, about five miles up the road).
Between there and the village of Hamelin, to the
southwest, lay a large TVA lake and approximately fifty
miles of mountain wilderness, part of the Cherokee
National Forest all around it. It would be a long, ardu-
ous journey for an old man, but not inconceivable.

He picked up the telephone. Of course, the warden
had the dogs out, and they expected to have the prisoner back in custody within hours, but all the same, it
wouldn't hurt to touch base with the county officers.

"Wake County Sheriff's Office. LeDonne."

"Hello, Deputy. This is Charles Gault, assistant warden at NECC. I'm responding to your fax inquiring
about our escapee."

"How did he get out?"

"We haven't issued a statement regarding that at this time," said the assistant warden. "But I am authorized to give you information about the prisoner that might aid in his apprehension."

"I understand he's a local man," said LeDonne. "You think he might be heading this way."

Gault chuckled. "Not necessarily. I know you're in his home turf, but remember that we're ten miles south of the Virginia border and about the same distance from North Carolina, so he might be someone else's problem altogether."

"But, as you said, his home is down here, and he might very well come this way."

"He might try, but it's mighty rough terrain."

"Not if you steal a truck, Mr. Gault. Then it's less than a two-hour drive. Now, look, let's take it as read that this conversation might be a complete waste of time, but in case it isn't, I'd like as much information as you can give me about the prisoner, starting with whether or not you consider him dangerous."

"Well, officer, he's in for murder."

"I know. Some murderers make the best trusties. I'd let a first-offense wife killer baby-sit my kids if I had any. I need to know what kind of reputation Mr. Sorley has got in Mountain City."

There was a pause, and LeDonne waited it out. He was good at silences. Finally the assistant warden said, "Hiram Sorley—they call him Harm around here—is a little unusual. I'll tell you about him, and you can draw your own conclusions about the degree of danger."

"Go ahead."

"Harm came into the prison system in 1968 on a

murder conviction. I don't have any details on that right now."

"I can get that. It was in our jurisdiction. Go on."

"That conviction was his third felony, and apparently the judge down your way was fed up with seeing Hiram Sorley. He sentenced him to ninety-nine years in prison. He'd have to serve two-thirds of that before he'd be eligible for parole."

"A sixty-six-year sentence?"

"That's correct, Mr. LeDonne. Harm Sorley was duly assigned a parole date of April 2034. He was born in 1930."

"I guess Tennessee wouldn't have much to fear from a hundred-and-four-year-old ex-con. Why the long sentence? Did he kill a police officer?"

"No. But he was considered a habitual offender, and I gather he had no money or family clout, so I doubt if anyone tried very hard to appeal his case. Just another worthless hillbilly warehoused into the system. Sorley's original lawyer was court appointed. You know what *that* implies."

"Yeah. He's a throwaway."

"And according to his record, he wasn't considered enough of a bad-ass to make Brushy Mountain. He got sent to The Walls. That's TNP in Nashville."

"I know."

"He was transferred here to Mountain City when we opened in the eighties. We're medium security. He was getting pretty old by then. Fifty-something. Of course, in prison, thirty-five is old."

"Yeah, crime is almost as rough as pro ball," said LeDonne.

"And—let's see, Harm tried to escape from TNP a few times. That's hardly surprising, though. I haven't been with the prison system long, but I do know that mountain boys do the hardest time. They can't stand being cooped up in a concrete cell away from nature. It's not too bad in the winter, but every spring we see them come down with ulcers, headaches, back trouble, and depression. The infirmary pumps them full of tranquilizers, and that usually does the trick. Of course, some of them go crazy anyhow."

"And this prisoner?"

"Harm Sorley is delusional. The prison psychiatrist thinks he's an interesting case. Wrote him up for a medical journal."

"What's wrong with him?"

"Well, he's abnormally religious. Reads nothing but his Bible, and seems to believe in prophecies—things like that. That sounds innocuous enough."

"Not necessarily," said LeDonne. "There's a lot of smiting in the Old Testament. What else?"

"The inmates here consider him a zap-timer. That's someone who is so out of it that he doesn't care what he does anymore, and—"

"I know about zap time, Mr. Gault. Anything else?"

"Yes. A big one. According to our shrink, Harm Sorley has Korsakoff's syndrome."

Rita Pentland's eyes were wide with fright, and her face was as pale as her blond-rinsed hair. But they hadn't even stated their business yet. Martha could feel the older woman's anxiety—it was giving her goose bumps.

No wonder Spencer hadn't wanted to tackle this by himself.

They had found Rita Pentland on her hands and knees in the side yard, trowelling weeds out of a bed of yellow chrysanthemums. When she caught sight of the sheriff's khaki uniform, she jumped up, brushing dried grass off her gardening tunic, and stammered, "What's wrong? Is my husband all right?"

Martha opened her mouth to blurt out "He's escaped," but before she could find her voice, Spencer had answered, "Yes, Mrs. Pentland. Far as we know, Euell is down at his office right now, working up somebody's taxes. I'm sorry we scared you. Could we go inside for a chat, please?"

She doesn't know, Martha had thought then. Of course she doesn't. That's what we're here for. Law-abiding people always see a uniformed officer as death's messenger. She took one look at us and thought: car wreck. And husband to her was Euell Pentland, the stout, balding accountant she had been married to for more than twenty years. Martha saw them in church on the rare occasions that she went. They would be sharing a hymn book—he in his blue plaid blazer and white loafers; she, a tiny aging blond, in hydrangea-blue chiffon with a hat and veil. She even wore gloves. Hardly any women wore gloves to church anymore—not even the ancient ones—but Euell Pentland was a particular man. He had his standards. More than one of his fellow county commissioners had complained bitterly about Euell Pentland's pettifogging standards. They swore that his presence on the board tripled the length of the meetings.

Still making little noises of dismay, Rita Pentland led them up the front steps and into the off-white living room of her yellow-brick ranch house. "Euell isn't home right now," she said for the third time, motioning for them to sit down. "Can I get you—a dope?"

Spencer almost smiled, thinking how a city cop might react to such an invitation. You didn't often hear that old mountain expression for soft drink anymore. She had reverted to the mountain speech of her childhood out of nervousness. "No, thank you, ma'am. We can't stay long." He sat down rather gingerly on one of two cream sofas covered in plastic. A trail of plastic runners covered the champagne-colored carpet, between the sofas, the kitchen, and the front hall.

Rita Pentland looked about her as if in search of something to fetch or dust or straighten, but finally she perched on the edge of the matching sofa, poked at a loose strand of hair, and fixed them with an earnest gaze. "How may I help you, Sheriff?"

Spencer glanced at Martha. Here goes, she thought, taking a deep breath. "Miz Pentland, we received some information at the sheriff's department this afternoon, and we thought you should be made aware of it."

"Yes?" The woman was clearly bewildered.

"It's about Harm Sorley."

Her cheeks pinched in, and she blinked at them. "Oh, honey . . . he's dead, isn't he?"

"No," said Martha, wondering what emotions she was witnessing. "He's not dead. He has escaped from Mountain City."

Martha wasn't sure what she had expected from Rita Pentland. A scream perhaps, or even a genteel faint.

But the frozen look lingered on the woman's face, making her wrinkles look like spiderwebs against her ashen skin. She stared at them as if she were still waiting to be told the purpose of their visit. She said, "And y'all came to tell me."

"You were married to him once, weren't you?" said Martha.

Rita Pentland looked around her at the Ethan Allen sofas, the white-brick fireplace, and the trio of Chinese vases on the mahogany coffee table. "Oh, yes," she murmured. "But that was a long time ago. Did you think he was here?"

"No, ma'am," said Spencer. "But if he got this far, would he know where to find you?"

"I don't see how. He went to prison in 1968. I was twenty-eight then, but I felt so old. Like they had just thrown a blanket of dirt over my head, and I'd never get up. Chalarty was a little bitty young'un, and she cried for her daddy day and night. I remember we laid up in that old trailer, me and her, eating bread and tomatoes—that's all we had—and just a-wailing, both of us. It was the worst time."

"You divorced him when he was convicted?"

"Yes. He got sixty-six years without parole, you see. That means never. Never. Never." She was looking at a bowl of chrysanthemums, not at her visitors.

Martha glanced at Spencer, a look that said maybe we should go now, but he shook his head slightly, and motioned for Rita to go on. "Was he angry about the divorce, do you think? Or does he still think of you as—as—a friend?"

"I think he understood."

"But you haven't kept in touch?"

"Oh, Harm wasn't one for writing. Or reading, either, much. I thought we ought to just go on with our lives, best we could. And, of course, there was Euell—I never heard from him in all these years."

"And your daughter?"

"Chalarty—" She bit her lip. "Euell calls her Charlotte. I guess everybody does nowadays, but me. She's twenty-six. She's in graduate school at East Tennessee State, and my boy, Buck—Euell, Junior—he's in his last year at U.T. in Knoxville."

"You don't think Harm would try to contact your daughter, do you?" asked Spencer.

The woman blinked at them again. "I reckon she's done forgot him by now. We never do talk about him. She calls Euell her daddy, you know."

Spencer stood up, and offered his hand to her. "We won't trouble you any further, Mrs. Pentland. It was a long shot, and I'm sure you've got nothing to be concerned about, but we have to follow up every lead. I expect he'll be back in custody pretty soon."

"Does Euell know?"

"We haven't notified him," said Spencer. "If he'd like to discuss protection, tell him to give me a call. Not that I think it's necessary, but if it would make you feel better."

She shook her head. "I don't think Euell will be worried. He had a security system installed last winter."

When the door closed behind them, Martha said, "Did that help you any?"

"Process of elimination," said Spencer. "You did just fine, Martha, but I don't think we're on the right track.

It's been twenty-five years since Harm Sorley went to prison, and his pretty young wife has become an old lady he wouldn't even recognize."

"Maybe it worked for the best. Remember how poor she said they were? Now she lives in a nice ranch house with a respectable accountant, and Harm's daughter got a college education. I'd say they were lucky."

Spencer looked back at the Pentlands' stone porch—urns of red geraniums flanked the steps, and a newly painted green door gleamed with a brass lion's head doorknocker. "Well," he said, "maybe you have a point there, Martha. Poor old Harm could never have given her all this."

"Poor old Harm? I thought you said he was a murderer."

Spencer shrugged. "Some people said Claib Maggard needed killing."

It wasn't spring after all. That was his first surprise, being out in the world. It had been spring so long for him, and now suddenly it wasn't. There were traces of dead blooms on the laurels, and the corn was tasseled. Besides, the smells and the leaf colors on the oaks and maples were wrong. They were the dark green of late summer, not the gold-green of new growth in April. Harm wished he could roll around in a stand of meadow grass, and feel the sun on his face, but he had to keep hidden. The Lord promised deliverance, but He didn't expect you to be a graven fool about it.

He was crouching now in a thicket of laurels on a wooded mountainside, but it wouldn't shelter him for long. When he was a boy, hunting way back up in the hills between Unicoi and Roan Mountain, the old men would talk about finding a *rhododendron hell* sprawling down a woody ridge—acres of pink-flowered bushes growing so thick and tangled that a dog could lose his way in the dark underbrush, and starve to death, trapped in the branches. You could find fox bones around the roots, they swore, if you was to crawl in there far enough, but Harm was never that anxious to find out. He wished he could find him a rhododendron hell right now, though, because there were sure to be dogs on his trail, followed by men with rifles.

The ground was still damp from last night's storm, and the morning chill hung in the air, making mist of the mountains in the distance. It felt strange to be outside concrete walls. But it was clearly prophesied. After the call by lightning and the sign of his feet, he had checked one last time for the will of the Almighty—seeking Him out right there in the covers of the Book. And sure enough, the pages had opened to the Book of Isaiah, chapter 22, verse 17. There it was: *"Behold, the Lord will carry thee away with a mighty captivity, and will surely cover thee."* He remembered that much.

It had been just before the ten o'clock lockdown, so the electronic cell doors hadn't been activated yet. Prisoners could still wander around the pod until lights out. He'd piled up his pillow and clothes to make his bunk look slept in, and then he'd tucked the Bible under his shirt and slipped off down the hall toward the kitchen. Nobody had paid him any mind, any more than they ever did. He had gone through passageways to the kitchen, climbed into the garbage bin, and waited for deliverance.

He had fallen asleep. He had awoken in terror, just before dawn, when he felt the container rise into the air, and he felt himself plunging headfirst into a fly-studded mound of potato peelings, coffee grounds, and rotting food. He'd had to push away piles of slick lettuce and eggshells—cutting his hands on tin can lids—to make himself a breathing space. And more than once he'd had to swim clear of the crusher mechanism as it packed the garbage tighter to make room for the refuse collected at other stops.

He had made himself wait until he could recite all of Psalms 13, 87, and 102, his favorites, three times over, before he wormed his way out from under the mounds of kitchen waste and made his way to the back of the truck. It was dawn by then, and the storm had swirled on over the distant mountains, heading for Virginia. In the gray light, he could see the dark shapes of trees in full leaf, and morning glories growing on a line of fencing on the side of a two-lane blacktop road. He could smell mown hay and cow manure, and feel the moist breeze against his face. He didn't know exactly where he was, but he knew that home lay to the south-southwest, over the farthest mountains, and it would be a fair walk to get there, because he'd have to stick to the wildest country to keep safe, being hunted like he was.

He had started walking then across the meadow toward the ridge of pines that lay between him and the crown of mountains. He felt dizzy, and a little wobbly on his feet, but he reckoned that was from the hard ride out. After that, he walked most of the day, staying hid under the trees, trying to put as many miles of timber as he could between himself and civilization. So far he had neither seen nor heard any sounds of searchers. He thought he might risk a few hours of sleep under the rhododendron cover before he went any farther.

Harm Sorley stood up and squinted into the fading evening sunshine, knowing that he was a wanted man, and wishing to God he could remember what for.

Martha Ayers was out for her evening run with the Samoyed husky that belonged to Deputy Joe LeDonne. He called it Steppenwolf—but whether for the rock group or the Hesse novel, she'd never asked. Martha couldn't for the life of her see why LeDonne insisted on owning a dog. She never saw him walk it or play with it. He hardly seemed to notice that it was there, but the dog still stayed with him like a shadow, ignoring Martha even when she fed him. Despite Martha's attempts to win the husky's affection, Step continued to regard her with distant civility, standing patiently while she stroked his thick, white fur, and glancing at LeDonne—for permission?—before he'd eat what she gave him, or come when she called. He put up with her, she reasoned, only because LeDonne seemed to want her around. Martha sometimes wondered why she kept trying to make that animal like her. Same reason she never gave up on LeDonne, she reckoned. Whatever that was. There were a lot of similarities between Joe LeDonne and his dog.

The husky liked to run with her, though. On nights that LeDonne watched a football game on cable, Martha, in her gray sweat suit and running shoes, would clip a chain leash to the collar buried deep in Steppenwolf's fur, and together they would slip off into the darkness to outrun their boredom.

Martha wore headphones and a Walkman, trusting the dog to alert her to cars or strangers lurking in their path. Hamelin was a safe place to run, though. A passing skunk was about all you could expect in the way of danger. She inhaled the moist, heavy air of summer darkness. After a day behind a desk, it felt good to stretch her muscles, to feel her body shaking off the stiffness, the tension of the day's encounters. She thought she could run all night if she could just figure out what to do with her mind. The sight of the same old streets, and the endless loop of minor worries that dominated her thoughts made a poor accompaniment to an evening's exercise. Hence the Walkman. Sometimes she tuned to WJCW in Johnson City, and ran to the country beat of Randy Travis or Kathy Mattea, but tonight was too hot for sprints and pounding rhythm. Martha was content to trot along with Hamelin's own WHTN, while disc jockey Hank the Yank conducted his audio town meeting.

Tonight they were talking about the escaped convict.

"Talk to me, Wake County!" said Hank the Yank, in that teasing tone that made some listeners just itch to argue with him. "The Tennessee prison system says that Harm Sorley, one of our own, has declined to avail himself of any further hospitality at taxpayers' expense. In a word—he is out and about. So, tell me, folks—I'm new here—should we be locking our doors tonight, or what?"

Martha felt a tug on the husky's lead, and realized that she had come to a stop when she heard the radio's topic for discussion. This information could be important—who knew him, who still considered himself a friend of the fugitive. She knew that Spencer wouldn't be listening to WHTN. He was on patrol tonight, filling in for the ailing Godwin. Martha knew that she ought to pay attention to the broadcast, and she couldn't afford to keep running and risk interference with the signal. She sat down on a log at the edge of a vacant lot, stroking the husky's thick fur and watching fireflies drift past her, while she concentrated on the voices in her head.

"I have to answer the phones myself," the disc jockey told his listeners. "Arvin has gone out to fetch my dinner and his pocket calculator. He likes to bring me the coronary bypass special from Neva's Burgerland, and then he sits here while I eat it, figuring out how many notches my cholesterol just went up. Greasy burgers and onion rings sure taste good, though. I think my arteries are used to it—Whoa! A flashing light. Somebody wants to talk about something besides my health, I betcha. Go ahead, neighbor. Who am I talking to here?"

"This is Gareth Marsh from over in Banner Cove." It was the quavering voice of a man well past seventy. "And I remember Harm Sorley like I seen him yesterday."

"You *didn't* see him yesterday, did you, Gareth?" asked Hank.

"No. No, I have not seen Harm since—I believe it was nineteen and sixty-two—"

"But you knew him? Can you tell us something about him, Gareth? Is he dangerous?"

"Well, he was one of those Sorleys from back over in Mitchell County, and they were forever getting into scrapes with the law, but there wasn't any meanness in them. They just drank a tad too much, and liked to carry on. Some folks didn't like it much, but I never did see no harm in 'em."

"An outlaw *family?*" said Hank the Yank. "Imagine that. Maybe I should go out and rent *Deliverance* again."

"They could be good people if they liked you. I remember one time when my daddy was laid off from the Clinchfield railroad yard—it was around Christmas, but we didn't have no money, and we were living on the vegetables Mama had canned from the summer garden—green beans and cornpone made with water, every meal. I was about eight at the time. Harm was maybe thirteen. Well, one evening in he comes—Harm and his uncle Pharis what was a preacher—and they brung us a deer they had shot up on the mountain, so we'd have meat for Christmas."

"Christmas isn't hunting season, though, Gareth."

"We needed to eat."

"Well, we've established that Harm can hit what he's aiming at, haven't we? Gotta go, Gareth. There's another line lighting up. Thanks for calling in. Hello, caller—you're live, so keep it clean."

"This is Carver Jessup—"

"Carver—my man! How's that tree-climbing coon dog of yours? This fellow on the line is a local celebrity, neighbors. A hunting legend. Are you going to put that hound out to track the fugitive?"

"No. But I did recollect something about Harm Sorley, and thought I'd tell it. This happened back in the fifties. Harm was doing three months in the Carter County jail for assault and drunkenness—a little disagreement at a roadhouse. Anyhow, that fall the people over in Meadow Creek had a fright cave at Halloween to raise money for their volunteer fire department."

"What do you mean, had a fright cave? I'm a Yankee, Carver. I'm not *au courant* with the local customs."

"In Meadow Creek there's a natural limestone cavern that goes a couple hundred feet back into the mountain on the Wyler farm. Every October the community would put together a haunted house attraction in the cave. The young men and teenagers would dress up as vampires and werewolves, and they'd be situated at various lantern-lit spots along the path in the cave, so that you couldn't see them 'til you were right up on them. People would pay fifty cents and stand in line for an hour just to be scared. It made good money for the fire department, though."

"Okay, Carver. I'm with you now. Go on."

"That year, people kept coming out of the cave, and telling Wyler that the best monster in the cave was the bearded guy in the flannel shirt, brandishing an ax."

"That would get my attention," said Hank the Yank.

"Yeah, but it sure puzzled old man Wyler, 'cause none

of the volunteers was dressed up like that. Turns out
that it was Harm. He'd walked off a county road gang,
and was hid up in the hills. Just for fun he snuck into
Wyler's cave, and joined the play-acting."

"Waving an ax at people? This is *cute*?"

Carver Jessup thought about it. "Well," he said at
last. "We all thought it was funny at the time. That
happened years before he killed Claib Maggard."

Martha sat in the warm darkness listening to the old
men of the county remember Harm stories. She found
herself growing indignant on behalf of the sheriff's department, on behalf of law enforcement in general.
That man they were so fondly recalling was an escaped
murderer, and no one seemed to care. Harm was funny.
Harm had style. Harm looked out for his neighbors.
What about the murder? And if the county's favorite
convict actually made it home through the wilderness,
which side would those garrulous old men choose—the
fugitive or the law?

"Well, that's all the talk-time we have for this evening," said Hank the Yank. "News is coming up at the
top of the hour. Tomorrow night we're going to talk
about composting with the county agent, and the night
after that—if it's still news—we'll be taking calls on the
Harm Sorley murder trial, so search your memories,
neighbors. Meanwhile, Arvin's back, so we're going to
leave you now with a musical interlude while I eat my
dinner. For your listening pleasure, my favorite
philosophers—the Statlers, again—with 'The Official
Historian on Shirley Jean Berrell.' I think that song
speaks to us, neighbors. Especially the line that says

the only thing that I don't know is where she is right now. This is Hank the Yank, the official historian of Harm Sorley, saying: Harm, if you're out there, go with God."

# CHAPTER

## 3

How happy is the pilgrim's lot!
  How free from every anxious thought
From worldly hope and fear!
  Confined to neither court nor cell
His soul disdains on earth to dwell,
  He only sojourns here.

#1041, "THE PILGRIM'S LOT," JOHN WESLEY

TENNESSEE METHODIST HYMNAL, 1885

"Korsakoff's syndrome?" Dr. Eliot Caudill frowned at his erstwhile patient. "That, LeDonne, you don't have. This is not to say that you are totally sane, my friend, but if you are shopping around for a new and colorful disorder, my advice is to keep looking."

The Veterans Affairs Medical Center in Johnson City could pass for a college campus—wide green lawns under full-leafed shade trees and sedate brick buildings drowsing in the shadow of the mountains. It was built by the U.S. government in 1903 for army veterans who had fought in the Civil War—fought for the Union, that is; nobody seemed to know where the Confederate soldiers were supposed to die. But east Tennessee had never been staunchly pro-South. Their hardscrabble mountain farms would not accommodate slavery, and tariffs are of little concern to subsistence farmers. The idea of fighting to preserve someone else's wealth did not appeal to many mountain boys. Deciding which side to favor in the war varied from one family to the next, and the anger stirred by those differences generated feuds that lasted past the turn of the century. The Vietnam War, a source of moral conflict in middle

America, had been much less divisive here. Tennessee-ans, who had reunited their separate patriotisms by serving together in two world wars, faced Vietnam squarely, as a duty demanded by God and country. The conflict in Southeast Asia had cost nearly every moun-tain family a relative, only this time, they'd all been fighting on the same side, so grief could be shared rather than blame. It was mostly veterans of that war who occupied the facility these days. The local name for the V.A. hospital was Mountain Home.

Joe LeDonne made the half-hour drive from Ham-elin to Mountain Home most Tuesday nights for the meeting of the Vietnam Veterans Support Group; occa-sionally he and Martha attended the session for cou-ples. Today he had come on behalf of somebody else's problem. Since he had the morning off, he decided to tap the psychological expertise he'd become acquainted with over the years. Just because they weren't doing him much good didn't mean they didn't know their business.

"But you've heard of Korsakoff's?" LeDonne asked his therapist. "You know something about it?"

"I work in a V.A. hospital, don't I? This is like a wild-life sanctuary for Korsakoff's patients—an outdated term, by the way, but never mind. Most hospitals only see people with this disorder briefly while they're treat-ing them for something else, but we at the V.A. get to *keep* them. Now, are you going to tell me what this is about, or are *you* being Freudian these days?"

LeDonne hesitated. It felt strange to be sitting in Caudill's rat's nest office talking about someone else's problems. Did patient/doctor confidentiality extend to third parties? "It's police business. I guess I can consider you a consultant, though."

Dr. Caudill smiled. "You mean, pay me?"

"Nope. I'm only asking a question, not bringing you a patient. You can't very well treat him if we can't find him."

"Couldn't treat him, anyhow. Who is this guy?"

"Harm Sorley—that escaped convict from Mountain City. You may have seen it in the papers. He's originally from my jurisdiction. He's sixty-three, and he's doing about forty more years on a murder charge, so naturally we're a little concerned about his whereabouts. According to the spokesman for the correctional center, Harm Sorley has a medical condition called Korsakoff's syndrome, which they defined for me as: *the fugitive is a fruitcake.* I came over to talk to you, because I thought your explanation might be a little more specific."

"More specific, less picturesque. Korsakoff's is a form of brain damage—usually alcohol-related."

"The D.T.'s, you mean?"

"No. It isn't alcoholic dementia, which is actually more complex than this. Korsakoff's is a problem with memory—with learning new information. It's a condition characterized by hemorrhages around the third ventricle, and degeneration in the mammillary bodies—how technical do you want this?"

"I want effect, not cause. Tell me something about this disease that I can use."

"It isn't a disease. It's the result of some other condition, like alcoholism or head injury. The kind you're probably dealing with in your fugitive seems to come from a lack of vitamin B1 in people who drink. Actually, it's kind of interesting. The patient loses his recent memories. He becomes stuck in a certain time."

"The year he developed the condition?"

"Probably a lot earlier than that. I remember one case history where the patient thought he was back in 1954, just out of the army, and planning his future. He thought he was still nineteen years old. But he was about forty years past that. He lost all his adult life."

LeDonne considered it. "So, what happened when that elderly nineteen-year-old looked in a mirror?"

"He'd be shocked. Very upset that this wasted old fellow is himself. He might become confused, or agitated, but it wouldn't last long. He'd forget the entire episode as soon as he turned away from the mirror."

"How would such a person explain all the trappings of modern times? Color television, new cars?"

Caudill shrugged. "Tune them out, I guess. They don't do a lot of reasoning or questioning. If you asked them how come there's a color TV if they think it's 1954, they might be puzzled, but basically it wouldn't register. And there's a trick called *confabulation*, which means that the patient will invent memories to fill in what he doesn't remember. He will try to appear normal by remembering recent events—but he can't, so he makes things up to appease the person he's talking to. Someone with Korsakoff's can appear pretty normal to a casual observer—play cards, talk about the weather, remember their high school Latin, whatever, but the longer you converse with him, the more off-kilter things get. He can play a hand of cards perfectly well, but minutes later, he'll forget that he'd played it. And he'll give you a completely different answer to the same question the next time you ask. He can read the same page twenty times and not realize it. Forget people he's seen every day for months."

"Could Harm Sorley have forgotten what he's in prison for?"

"Sure. We've got guys in here who tell you a different war story every time you ask about their old injuries. They don't remember how they got them, so they make up something plausible. But I think I'm safe in telling you that your escaped convict is stuck somewhere in the past, maybe even before he committed the crime."

"He had a wife who divorced him twenty-some years ago, when he went to prison. She's in her sixties now, and married to a local businessman. Will he remember that?"

"Your fugitive may think he has a twenty-eight-year-old wife who is still very much married to him. That could be a problem, except that he wouldn't know where to find her, I guess. Would he know his wife if he saw her, I wonder? Probably not, but it's an intriguing question. Let me know, if you find out."

"I hope we catch him before it comes to that," said LeDonne.

"I don't know why you haven't caught him already. What's he been gone? Two days? Patients in the late stages of Korsakoff's tend to be very apathetic, and they can't formulate a plan, or even remember where they're going. Strange places make them anxious. Also, since I assume he is an alchoholic Korsakoff's, he'll get worse if he gets drunk while he's AWOL. He could start hallucinating, which can be dangerous. But I think if this guy is seriously affected with the disorder, you won't have to worry about him for long. Come deer season, some hunter will stumble over his body in the woods."

"You make me feel sorry for the guy," said LeDonne. "An escaped murderer."

"You should feel sorry," Caudill told him. "You may get this Harm fellow of the hills, but you'll never get him out of the past. He's got nowhere to go."

Sometimes when he had to teach an undergraduate lecture class, Jeremy Cobb would take off his glasses, so that the faces of the students became one gray blur, leaving him alone with his subject. He could tune out the adolescent boredom or hostility, while he contemplated the nuances of eighteenth-century America in simulated solitude. This summer he was teaching his first session of Appalachian history, filling in for the regular professor, whose notes had been left for his guidance. The course fitted in nicely with Jeremy's dissertation topic, which was why he had volunteered to teach it. He was by no means an expert on Appalachian history, but there was little chance of an undergraduate finding that out.

For today's lecture, Jeremy's eyeglasses went into his blazer pocket before he even entered the classroom, so that he had to squint at the numbers on the door to make sure he was in the right place. He went directly to the lectern, hoping that no one would ask him a question before class. It would break the spell that had been forming ever since he gathered up his lecture notes—not that he needed notes today. He had this story by heart.

Today's topic, the settlement of western North Carolina, would be filtered through a discussion of ethnohistory, Jeremy Cobb's specialty: the reflection of an era through the lives of the common people. As a Phi Beta Kappa from Cornell and now an almost-finished Ph.D. tackling his first instructor's job at Virginia Tech, Jeremy Cobb did not consider himself one of the common people of the present century (symbolized in his mind by Wal-Mart and bowling leagues), but he was enchanted by his vision of yesterday's proletariat, with their quilts, and their spirituals, and their jack tales. The poor were the people who mattered in modern scholarship: you weren't going anywhere specializing in dead white males. This study of little lives in great times was the subject of Jeremy Cobb's dissertation-in-progress, and of an endless succession of largely unsuccessful attempts on his part to imagine their dreary lives.

Odd that he should admire strength, endurance, and outdoor pursuits in his historical subjects, since he avoided all three in his own life. He preferred computers to sports, and his only hobby was reading. He didn't socialize much, either. While he found history's plain folk fascinating, individual sophomores nodding off in terraced rows of a summer-school lecture left him cold.

He turned toward the faceless audience and waited. When the gray blur stopped shuffling papers and murmuring to itself, he began to speak, fixing his myopic eyes on the green chalkboard beside the door, and transforming it into a mountain meadow. He finished his remarks on the French and Indian War, covered in several previous classes, and worked his way through a discussion of the politics of Cherokee chief Little Carpenter, the Cherokee War, and the futile efforts of Indians and settlers to come to terms over the land.

At twenty past the hour, he was ready to talk about the westward expansion into Indian territory. He would begin the topic with the story that obsessed him, the Wylers of western North Carolina.

"It is the year 1779," he told the class. "Picture yourself in the Unaka Mountains of western North Carolina, in a place that will become still-rural Mitchell County in 1861. But in 1779 it was an unbroken wilderness, without roads or towns. Seventeen seventy-nine. The American Revolution was progressing nicely, thanks to the aid of the French; Harvard was already one hundred and forty-three years old; and cities like Charleston and Philadelphia rivaled England in their elegance of architecture and society."

The bent heads in front of him scribbled furiously without looking up. He thought of a log cabin set down in a long pine-ringed meadow.

"The Unaka Mountains are a long way from anywhere, and while the rest of the country grew tame and civilized, that territory remained the province of the bear and the buffalo. It was Indian land, the common hunting ground of the Cherokee, the Catawba, and the Shawnee, all of whom lived elsewhere, but sent hunting parties there to stalk game. The Warriors Path went through there—it was sort of an Indian Appalachian Trail, except that it was for hunting and commerce between tribes. One of the oldest trails on earth, forged originally by the buffalo and other animals in migration or in search of salt, the Warriors Path went from the

Creek Indian country in Georgia and Alabama past the Cherokee settlements of Hiwassee, Tellico, and Chote, and divided near the present-day town of Kingsport, Tennessee, with one branch leading up through the Cumberland Gap. Settlers, like Daniel Boone, had also used the Cumberland Gap to come the other way, in migrations from Pennsylvania.

"The Indians' right to the mountain land was guaranteed by the Proclamation of 1763, made at the end of the French and Indian War, in which the Crown—the British were still calling the shots then—decreed that no white settlers could homestead in that region. But that protection of Indian rights ended when the colonies declared their independence, and the North Carolina legislature repealed the British law. They issued the first four land grants by December 10, 1778.

"The wagons rolled in."

For a moment Jeremy wondered if the students could picture them, and the spell wavered, but he fixed his attention on the images in his mind: ox-drawn wagons rolling through old-growth forests without underbrush. There would have been no tangle of bushes and brambles under that canopy of ancient oaks and chestnuts— the obstructions of the modern forest would come later, when the settlers began to clear-cut, making space and light for the lesser vegetation.

"Was it dangerous? Most certainly. But in 1779, what wasn't? A family was lucky to see half its children live to maturity. Bad weather at just the wrong time could wipe out a season of crops, so that starvation was always a possibility. And good land in safe places—like Richmond, Wilmington, Philadelphia—had been claimed a century earlier. But if you were sufficiently brave—or desperate—or if you didn't want well-to-do folk running your life, then there were thousands of acres of rich soil, surrounded by beautiful mountains. Mild climate; forests full of deer; rivers full of trout. It must have seemed like a risk worth taking.

"Thomas Wyler must have thought so.

"In the fall of 1778, he and his wife, Eleanor, put their children and all their possessions into a wagon, and set out from Salem, North Carolina, after hearing word that the state's attorney general, William Waight-still Avery, had been given a land grant to the Carolina mountain country. Avery wanted settlers to develop his investment. Any man who would build a cabin, clear some land, and raise crops would be deeded acreage for a farm."

At this point in the narrative, he always tried *not* to picture the pioneer family, because Thomas Wyler always began to look like Fess Parker on the TV series "Daniel Boone," flotsam from Jeremy Cobb's suburban childhood. Wyler's wife, Eleanor, was played by Dorothy McGuire, another image from western movies of his youth. Their daughter, Katie, had changed many times in Jeremy's imaginings, but she was always beautiful.

"They took the Yellow Mountain road, a trail from Marion to Spruce Pine, blazed in 1771 by the wagon train of James Robertson. The Wylers had three children who survived infancy. Young Tam, eight, named for his father; Andrew, five; and Katie, who was eighteen. She had been engaged to a young farmer back in Salem, but he took fever and died, so she went west with her parents. Most of this story comes from a memoir left by Andrew Wyler, who lived to be eighty-seven. The area came to be called Mitchell County in the year he died.

"The family settled on bottomland beside the Toe River in 'backwater' territory—which means that the land was west of the Blue Ridge Divide, so that the stream drained west back into Tennessee and eventually into the Gulf of Mexico, rather than forward through North Carolina and into the Atlantic. It's a river with an alias: in Tennessee it's the Nolichucky.

"They built a one-room cabin of rot-resistant chestnut logs, and shingled the roof with oak, a wood that splits thin and straight. Their beds were pallets on the floor. Later, they might have built bedsteads corded with ropes attached to the wood frame to support a mattress stuffed with rye-straw. They cooked in a kettle in the fireplace; made soap in it, too, from hog fat and hickory ashes. Whatever utensils they needed they carved from wood or deer horn. About the only thing they couldn't fashion themselves were iron and gunpowder, and they traded for those with beaver pelts and other skins from the game they hunted: fox, bear, deer, mink."

"Yecch!" said a young male voice from a back row. Jeremy, who didn't entirely disagree with those sentiments in a more modern context, merely nodded and went on.

"The Wylers' nearest neighbors were Talt Greer and his grown sons. By late spring, Katie was engaged to the oldest one, who was called Rab, short for Robert. Andrew Wyler says that both families were pleased about it, thinking that it would strengthen the bond between neighbors."

A hand went up in the middle of the classroom.

Jeremy said quickly, "Andrew doesn't say what Katie thought about it." The hand went down.

"On the morning of May 28, 1779, the Greers were working in their cornfield when they saw five-year-old Andrew Wyler, stumbling out of the woods, with blood caked across his cheek, and mud clinging to the rest of him. They ran to help him, but he waved them away, saying that a band of Indians had attacked the Wyler farm. He had been down by the river with Katie, he said, when they heard screams from the cabin. They saw dark men running toward the door. Andrew remembers starting to run back to see what was wrong, but Katie pushed him down in the weeds, and told him not to look up. Crouching beside him, she whispered instructions: *crawl down into the river, and try to make it upstream to the Greers. Tell them to bring their guns, Katie told him. Go quick. And don't you look back.*

"It took him an hour to get there—wet, bleeding from his run through the woods, and faint from fatigue and terror. But he wouldn't stay behind. When the four men saddled up to go and help the Wylers, Andrew went with them, riding behind Rab Greer, holding on to the saddle. *We could see the smoke long 'fore we could see the cabin,* he writes in his memoirs.

"The Indians—they reckoned it would have been Shawnee—were gone, and where the cabin had been, there was only the stone chimney and a few blackened logs. They found Eleanor Wyler in some bushes near the cabin. She had been scalped."

Here the twentieth century stirred in his thoughts, and he felt obliged to remind his students that scalping was also practiced by the white settlers, who paid a bounty for each slain Indian. In fact, according to an article by James Axtell and William C. Sturtevant in the *William and Mary Quarterly*, settlers paid Indians to scalp other Indians, and then to scalp other groups of European settlers. "Indians as Victims" was a later lecture. This was Katie's day.

"Thomas Wyler and his son Tam were also slain, and the family's rifles and horses were gone. Of eighteen-year-old Katie there was no sign." He glanced down and read from the photocopied page of Andrew's memoir: *"I sorrowed over the dead so much that I was scarcely able to take in anything else, but Rab Greer—he was in a feeze at not finding his betrothed. We searched the fields all the way to the river, and poked in the charred remains of the cabin, looking for a trace of her, but she wasn't there. We knowed then that the Indians took her away."*

A stirring in the audience made him look up from his notes. The students were standing in the rows, stuffing loose-leaf notebooks into a rainbow of backpacks. He glanced at his watch, and saw that his hour was up. He had misjudged his time. "We'll finish next class period," he said to the faceless blur marching past the lectern.

Martha took a last look at the departmental time sheets before stashing them away in the drawer of her desk. The situation was getting out of hand, and the sooner she tackled the sheriff about it, the better.

Martha had been dispatcher in the sheriff's office for

seven years, ever since she'd got tired of the low pay
and the monotony at the Seed and Feed. She had been
a classmate of Spencer Arrowood's in high school, but
they hadn't run in the same crowd, and she was sure
that their common background had little to do with her
getting the job. She knew him better now than she had
in school, and she found it hard to think of him as a
boss in the traditional sense. He wasn't much on order-
ing folks around, which seemed odd to Martha, because she'd always assumed that people who chose law
enforcement as a career liked to bully other people.
But Spencer was polite to everybody—even to criminals. He charmed the county voters, and he made her
feel like part of a team, instead of like an office flunky,
which was good, but sometimes his good intentions
were a liability, and then she figured it was her responsibility to set him straight. Like now. Still, it wouldn't
hurt to soften him up a bit before tackling him about
it.

With this tactic in mind, Martha waited until Le-
Donne went out on patrol before she slipped around to
Denton's Cafe and bought the sheriff a ham biscuit on
waxed paper to go with his mid-morning coffee.

"Uh-oh," said Spencer Arrowood, eyeing the offering
with suspicion. "What are you mad about now?"

Martha sighed. "For Pete's sake, Spencer. Can't I
make a gesture of Christian charity without you getting
all suspicious about it?"

"No. Now, if I eat this, will it constitute implied as-
sent to whatever it is you want?"

"I just want to talk."

"I'm listening." He reached for the grease-soaked paper, and broke off a chunk of biscuit.

She waited until he had his mouth full. "I was just looking at the time sheets. Even though his sick leave is used up, Godwin is down for full pay. You and LeDonne have been wearing yourselves out working his shifts."

Spencer shrugged. "Everybody needs help now and then."

"You need help right now. You've got your hands full as it is, and now there's an escaped convict to contend with."

"Oh, that's just Harm." He smiled. "I don't think he constitutes much of an emergency."

"Every time that phone rings it could constitute an emergency, and you're understaffed. Godwin isn't getting any better. They still don't know what's wrong with him, and they can't seem to stop the dizzy spells."

"It's a hell of a note, isn't it? He's not even forty yet."

"Yes," said Martha. "He's a good man, and I'm sorry for him. I hope the doctors find out what's wrong with him, and get him well again, but right now the fact is that he is not well enough to keep his job. He may never be."

"I know. I kept hoping that if we just bought him some time, the test results would show something definite. As it is, I have to make the call without knowing what he's got. But you're right. I have to let him go. We need a third man on patrol."

Martha said, "Not necessarily."

"But you said LeDonne and I were wearing ourselves out—"

"Not necessarily a *man*, I meant. Spencer, I want Godwin's job."

His grin of disbelief faded when he saw her eyes. "But Martha, we need somebody who can handle it."

"Handle what, Spencer? Talking to witnesses? I did that okay when we went to see Rita Pentland. Handle domestic disputes? All the studies say that women are better at that, because the suspect doesn't feel he has to fight them to prove his manhood. And as for the routine, I've been in this office long enough to know what the job entails. The rest I can get in the training courses."

"But I need somebody now."

"You'd have to train whoever you get."

"Well, but, Martha—"

"Maybe you object to having a woman deputy?" Her soft voice was cold as a cornstalk.

He balled up the greasy waxed paper, and tossed it in the direction of the wastebasket. "Can I think about it?"

"How long?"

"What would we do for a dispatcher?"

"I'll train somebody when I'm off duty. There's women in town who could use the work."

"What if we spend the county's money to send you to school, and then it turns out you can't do the job?"

Martha considered it. "All right. How about this? You hire me as a deputy on probationary terms. If in six months you're satisfied with my work, you send me off for formal training."

"And if you don't make the grade? Your old job would be gone."

She shrugged. "I'm offering to take risks. Let that be the first one."

"But Martha, the deputy's job could be dangerous!"

"Hell, Spencer. Women get beaten up by enraged husbands, gang-raped by drunken good ol' boys, and hunted like deer by serial killers. Being a woman is dangerous. I'm just asking you to give me a gun, and more money to make up for it."

The lecture was over, but Jeremy Cobb was still under the spell of the running woman. There were no pictures of her, and no descriptions from life, but he knew that she was his own age, and he always saw her very clearly—usually with long dark hair and a heart-shaped face with determined blue eyes that seemed to be staring far into the distance. In his mind she was like an image in stained glass, standing against a backdrop of mountains, green, then blue, and finally a purple one blending into the clouds on the horizon. Try as he might, he could not make her real. He had been thinking about her for months now, reading everything he could to put detail into his imaginings, but she would not live.

On the corkboard over Jeremy Cobb's desk was a red-and-blue-veined highway map of east Tennessee. The Cherokee National Forest and the Great Smoky Mountains National Park were represented by a wide swath of green along the North Carolina border, and the edges of the neighboring states were bright yellow. Jeremy's own addition to the map had been a series of red- and green-tipped pushpins set in a wavering line from north of Bristol, down the mountain chain, to nowhere-in-particular in western Mitchell County. Amazing to think that most of that land was still wilderness, even two centuries later. The mountains that Jeremy could see from the campus of Virginia Tech were part of a chain that ran south-southwest from New England to northern Alabama. Just a few miles from where he sat the Appalachian Trail snaked through the Jefferson National Forest, and made its way south-southwest into the Cherokee National Forest, passing within a few miles of Katie Wyler's home. Jeremy wasn't one for hiking, but he had driven much of the Blue Ridge Parkway, admiring the sweep of mountains, and the stark beauty of the rock cliffs towering above narrow forested valleys. This was her land. Perhaps if she were to come back, she would know it still.

There was a tap on the door, and his officemate Bill Linley appeared, wiping his glistening forehead with a wad of tissue. "I thought you'd be here," he said, moving Jeremy's bags off the chair and flopping down in it. "Dr. Schilder is lecturing in the auditorium in twenty minutes. They want the graduate students to fill up seats. I hope the air-conditioning is working in there. You're still mooning over that map, I see."

Jeremy nodded. "Not so much the map. I was thinking about Katie Wyler, though. I started my lecture on her today. Those pushpins mark the last leg of her journey. I keep trying to get a fix on her, emotionally."

"She's a dissertation topic, Jeremy. You sound like you want to date her. Or maybe you're going to try out for her role in the outdoor drama." He held up a restraining hand. "I know. There isn't one. All I'm saying is that I didn't have to use the Stanislavsky method to get into *my* thesis."

"You're doing MacKenzie King of Canada."

"Exactly. Sure, I could have held a séance and interviewed him for source material. It's the sort of thing *he* would have done. But instead, I'm swotting through the usual texts, and I'm not obsessing about the old boy. I don't have a sudden urge to build a picturesque Roman ruin behind my apartment building at Fox Ridge."

"But you're dealing with politics," said Jeremy. "My research is in ethno-history, and in that field it matters very much what people thought and felt, because it affected the transmission of culture. In the eighteenth century, a number of pioneer women were kidnapped by bands of hostile Native Americans."

"I think your Katie would have called them Indians," said Bill Linley. "When she was in a good mood."

"Indians, then. Some of those taken were rescued. In the southern mountains, it was sometimes with the Cherokee acting as go-betweens—but some of those settlers who were made captives—usually those taken as children—stayed and became members of the—"

"Tribe. Not 'ethnic group.'" Linley grinned.

"But after a couple of months as a prisoner, Katie Wyler took off by herself, hundreds of miles from home, with no supplies, and no experience as an explorer, and she walked home. How could she do that? How did she know where she was going from one day to the next?" Jeremy pointed to the row of colored pins dotting the map.

"You've read memoirs from the period, haven't you?"

"Of course. Katie's own brother wrote one, but not

until decades later. And in Massachusetts there was
Mary White Rowlandson—she and her children were
captured by the Narragansetts. But that was 1676—a
century earlier. She was ransomed and went to live in
Boston. Then there was Mary Jemison, taken by the
Seneca in 1755. She stayed with them, and her memoir, dictated to the local schoolmaster, wasn't published
until Jemison was eighty. And I've read *Indian Captiv-
ities* by Samuel G. Drake. All of that is going into the
thesis, but my main topic is Katie Wyler's captivity and
her journey home. How she managed it, and why she
would risk almost certain death in the wilderness to get
back. She must have known her parents were dead.
Naturally, she never wrote her memoirs."

"I remember," said Linley, nodding. "Sad story. But so
what? You've got documentation. You know where she
went. You can't interview any Shawnee, can you?"

"No, they're all dead. Or assimilated. Culture is a
fragile thing. I suppose I could go with what I've got,
but it doesn't feel right. I just wish I could find some
source that wasn't somebody else's opinion. Something
to make it real."

Linley glanced at his watch. "Time to go to the
Schilder lecture. Look, Jeremy, I think you're being
overly conscientious about this, but if you insist on trying to get into this pioneer woman's head, then you're
in the wrong place."

"Wrong place?" Jeremy squinted at his map.

"You'll never figure her out sitting in an office in
McBryde Hall. You need the insight that comes from
experience. You know that old saying about walking a

mile in someone else's moccasins. You've got the map of where she went. In what month was her journey?"

"Mid-September to early November."

"Perfect. You have a couple of weeks to get ready, and you're not teaching any undergrad courses in the fall term, are you?"

"No. I'm supposed to be working on my dissertation. You think I should try to follow Katie Wyler's route on foot? By myself?"

"No," said Linley. "I think you ought to drink more beer and quit obsessing about your research topic, but if you won't give up on it, then I think your only option is to get up off your ass and hit the trail."

"But I grew up in the city. I went to *computer* camp as a kid. I've never hiked in my life!" said Jeremy.

"Then you're bound to learn something."


Harm Sorley was tired and hungry.

He had woken that morning to find himself dew-damp and shivering, deep in the woods, and he had wondered what in Sam Hill he was doing out there on a hunting trip with no rifle. He didn't see any sign of the camp, either. He had tried to remember what he was doing out there, and whether he'd got separated from Uncle Pharis and his boys, and missed his way back to camp. But, if that was so, his gun ought to be with him, and he didn't see one. He must have drunk a few swallows more than his share of the McCrorys' corn liquor to get so addled. As he stood up, he felt his knees go wobbly.

Then he'd looked down at his clothes: blue dunga-rees with a white stripe and a blue work shirt, scuffed

brown boots. No jacket; no cap. He wouldn't go hunting dressed like this. Had he been doing his drinking at
a roadhouse, then? He reached in his back pocket to
see if he had any money, and found an ID card from
the Tennessee prison system. *Hiram Sorley,* it said. He
didn't read the rest. On a flat rock beside him was his
mother's Bible. Hell, it wasn't no hunting trip. He was
a fugitive. He must have lit out of the Wake County
Jail last night, and wouldn't Sheriff Nelse Miller be
vexed on that score?

Funny, though, Harm couldn't rightly remember
what he'd done, or how long his stretch was. Better not
get caught, though. Cell time was always bad, but
come harvest time and hunting season, it just wasn't
tolerable. And Rita would be missing him something
awful, her and the baby.

He looked up at the circle of green mountains wondering just where he was. None of it looked like his old
stomping grounds. Was he still on the Tennessee side
of the mountains, and would Nelse Miller be sending
searchers with dogs after him? He listened for the bay-
ing of hounds in the distance, but all was quiet.

He got up then, and washed his face in a cold, stony
creek. A wild apple tree provided a few scrawny fruits
for his breakfast, but he'd had to climb for them. Deer
had picked the lower branches clean. One apple,
wedged in the fork of the tree trunk, had a half-inch
slit on one side. A turkey peck. The downy speckled
feather of a wild turkey lay on the ground near the tree.
Harm took that one, anyway. Farther along he found a
vine of fox grapes, its purple clusters just ripened in the

autumn sun. He picked all the grapes he could reach, and gulped them down, seeds and all.

Now he sat in the sunshine, chewing the rest of the small, sweet apples, and savoring the feel of the woods. He felt like it had been a while since he'd been out in the wilderness. He must have been in jail a couple of weeks, he thought, to be so pale-armed. After a while, he reckoned he ought to follow the stream down the mountain where the farms would be. He needed something to eat besides wormy apples. Maybe if he found a farm he could figure out where he was. He might even have to steal some clothes if there was a line of washing handy: this gear he had on was prison issue, and he'd best get shut of it. He hoped he wouldn't have to hurt nobody to get it.

# CHAPTER
## 4

While dead in trespasses I lie,
   Thy quick'ning Spirit give:
Call me, thou Son of God, that I
   May hear thy voice and live.

#416, "While Dead in Trespasses I Lie,"
Charles Wesley

Tennessee Methodist Hymnal, 1885

Martha Ayers smoothed down the front of her new khaki shirt. She liked the reflection that looked back at her from the mirror: the new haircut that had cropped off the remnants of her last curly perm; the angular figure that looked better as she aged; and especially the badge that she'd shined up with Wright's Silver Polish. Godwin had let it get tarnished in the past few weeks, but she didn't fault him for it. He had other things on his mind these days, like doctors' appointments, and whether or not he was ever going to get well. She hoped he would. He wasn't a particularly bright or effective officer as far as she could see, but he had been nice enough as a coworker. She didn't want him and Betty to lose their little brick ranch house, or have to go on food stamps, but she couldn't help being glad for herself that she was getting a shot at his job.

Wearing the uniform of a deputy made her feel—taller. Suddenly she looked like someone that people would pay attention to. For the first time in her life, she felt important. *Maybe this is what it feels like to be beautiful,* she thought. *Only I had to find some other way to achieve it.*

Spencer Arrowood strolled out of his office, carrying his coffee mug and today's *Knoxville News-Sentinel*. "You *look* all right," he said a little dubiously. "Better than Godwin, I guess."

Martha nodded. "He was paunchy. Lean looks more authoritative, I guess."

"Maybe. But don't forget that Godwin had a lot of years on the force. You won't take his place any time soon."

"I know. All I want is a fair chance." She glanced down at the black belt encircling her narrow waist. No holster. "A fair chance and a gun, Spencer."

He sighed. "You're going to need training, Martha. Do you even know how to shoot?"

"Yes. Joe taught me a while back. He'd go out target shooting sometimes for practice, so I started going to keep him company. I can hit what I aim at. Ask Joe."

"I thought about it," said Spencer, reaching for the coffee mug. "Asking LeDonne, I mean. Since you two are—umm—"

"Lovers," said Martha helpfully.

"I thought we ought to clear this with him before you sign on as deputy."

"Why? He knows about it, but he's not my daddy. Do I need a *man's* permission?"

"Well, I just wondered how LeDonne would feel about it." The sheriff reddened. "I mean, he might worry."

"Like I do, you mean? You think he might sit home wondering if I've been shot down on a country road somewhere, or killed by a drunk robbing a gas station? Neither of y'all ever cared that I worried, did you?"

Spencer didn't reply. What she was saying sounded logical, but the fact was that he did have to consider LeDonne's opinion. In a department as tiny as theirs, there was no room for dissension or resentment. He resolved to have a word with his deputy in private.

"We were talking about guns," Martha reminded him. "I'll have a 9 millimeter Glock, like yours, right?"

He nodded.

"I thought so. Those aren't too hard to manage. That plastic construction makes them a lot lighter than the old pistols."

Spencer winced at the word *plastic*, but he didn't want to be diverted from the subject by a discussion of weapons technology. Besides, she was right, the Glock was light enough for her to handle without difficulty.

"I guess I'll need a Kevlar vest like LeDonne's, too. Body armor. How much do those things cost?"

"Now, *Martha*, slow down. You're not going to stroll out of here, get into a squad car, and play cops and robbers. For the first few weeks, you'll be going on patrol with me part of the time—observing. The rest of your duties will consist of serving warrants, directing traffic as needed, or providing funeral escorts, and typing up reports. And you can help me write a grant to pay for your training."

"Fair enough. When do we start?"

"How's the new dispatcher doing?"

"Well, Jennaleigh is right straight out of community college, and she thinks this job is as exciting as tightrope walking, but she's local, so she knows the area, and some of who's trouble and who isn't. I think she'll be all right."

Spencer smiled. "We're not exactly the NYPD around here. With any luck it'll stay quiet for the next week or so until she gets the hang of the routine."

Martha glanced at the clock. "She'll be here any minute. I've already gone over everything with her, and I've written her an instruction sheet and a copy of the ten-codes. I think she'll be fine with the radio. She listens to what you tell her."

"Okay, then. You can start patrol with me in a few more days."

Just as the dispatcher trainee appeared at the door, the phone rang, and Spencer picked it up. "Sheriff's office." He listened for a few seconds, said, "On our way," and hung up.

"Trouble?" asked Martha.

"Hold the fort, Jennaleigh," he said to the new dispatcher. "We'll be back." He turned to Martha, and nodded toward the door. "Ten-eighty-three in Painter Cove. Let's go."

Jeremy Cobb wondered if he looked as out of place as he felt in the Blue Ridge Trail Outfitters. He had never frequented such a place before. It had been a storefront to hurry past on his way to the bookstore for an antidote to the tedium of thesis research, or to Saxon's Fine Clothiers at sale time, when he restocked his wardrobe's supply of blue Oxford broadcloth shirts and khaki trousers, the uniform of the liberal arts graduate student. But now the wares of the backpacking outfitter *were* part of his research materials, thanks to Linley's bright ideas, his own misplaced enthusiasm for technicalities, and his adviser egging him on.

He looked doubtfully at the displays of tents and sleeping bags, at metal-framed backpacks, hunting knives, and camping stoves. He looked down at the list in his hand, containing a row of items followed by question marks, and other items scored through in pencil. It was no use making a list when you didn't have the faintest idea what you needed, and if you hadn't yet decided what it would be ethical for you to carry. Technically, to be faithful to his subject, he should be going out into the wilderness with no provisions at all, but Linley had pointed out that Katie Wyler had been better prepared for the journey than he was. She'd had the advantages of a life in eighteenth-century austerity and the tutelage of the Shawnee to prepare her for the rigors of the trail, while Jeremy knew himself to be the pasteurized, climate-controlled, mobilized product of a softer era.

The smiling young woman behind the counter looked like a fellow graduate student. She was probably working part-time to pay her living expenses, or to finance ski weekends to Canaan Valley. She looked like a skier. She looked like somebody who wouldn't need a list.

"Can I help you with anything?" She came toward him, quizzically polite. He *did* look out of place—you could tell that by her expression. He should have worn flannel.

"I'm going hiking. I may need some stuff. I'm kind of new at this."

She nodded. "Well, I'll be happy to give you any help I can. There are some easy beginner trails around here that—"

"No, I have to be gone a couple of weeks. I'll be hiking in upper east Tennessee."

"Cherokee National Forest? Are you doing part of the Appalachian Trail? Did the members of your group give you any kind of hand-out advising you on what to take?"

"Group?" He felt the sweat beading at the back of his neck. "I'm going alone."

Her smile vanished. "As a beginner? Why?"

Jeremy sighed, wondering if it would sound any more sensible when he explained it to her than it did when he told his dissertation committee. Probably not. "I'm doing a dissertation in ethno-history and this is part of my research project." He waited for her to nod and change the subject, but she just kept looking at him. "Okay, the subject of my research is an eighteenth-century woman named Katie Wyler, who was kidnapped by the Shawnee, and escaped from their village to find her way home across a few hundred miles of wilderness."

"Good for her!" said the clerk. Her name tag said Tresha.

"Well, that's debatable," said Jeremy. But he didn't want to get into it. "It was a remarkable feat for a young woman, finding her way from the Ohio River back to the mountains of North Carolina, with no compass and no provisions."

"*You're* not going to try it, are you?"

"No, of course not. I don't have that much time."

She eyed him critically. "Yeah, like a year to train for it. Hiking isn't like strolling through the mall, you know. There's still a lot of wilderness out there in the

Appalachians. And, despite the fact that it is the late twentieth century, you can still be killed by a bear."

Jeremy began to ease his way toward the door. The clerk's withering competence was making him nervous. Maybe he ought to postpone the search for equipment. First he could buy a book. Surely the campus bookstore sold hiking guides. Perhaps he could pick up some serviceable camping gear at Wal-Mart.

"Shouldn't I have a gun?" asked Martha. "You never know with a ten-eighty-three."

Spencer glanced at her, then back at the road. He was hurrying, but he had dispensed with the blue light and siren. No point in attracting a crowd, when you were trying to restore peace and quiet. "A gun," he said. "Martha, didn't you sit there in my office not two weeks ago and tell me that women were better in domestic situations than male officers because they could talk the suspect out of a violent confrontation?"

"All the studies say that's true," she said. "But if we're going up into Painter Cove to straighten out the personal problems of one of the Harkryder clan, then I'd like an M-16 and a flamethrower, please."

"At least the Sorleys had style," said the sheriff. "All the Harkryders have is rage, and an infinite capacity for the consumption of alcohol."

They had left the lawns and shade trees of Hamelin proper, taking the north road out of town, where the old white houses gave way to brick ranchers, and then to four-room dwellings with peeling paint. Now unmown fields alternated with unkempt yards, and stands of scrub pine separated mobile homes with white-washed truck tires encircling flower beds. Then there were no more homes. Ancient oaks and full-leafed maples formed a canopy darkening the road and the river that ran beside it. Massive thickets of rhododendron grew here in the cool shade of the forest. In another mile, the road would begin to climb toward the North Carolina state line, and, through an occasional break in the slope's curtain of trees, it would offer glimpses of the valley below.

Adam One, as Wake County's dispatchers called the sheriff's patrol car, was not heading for the mountain gap. As the main road emerged from the forest to scale the mountain, they would be taking a gravel side road that followed the river through another mile of forest before it, too, began its steep climb to the ridge top. It was a poorly graded one-lane road, treacherous in winter ice storms, impassable when spring rain turned the red dust to mud, and scenically uninviting the rest of the time.

Nobody took the road to Painter Cove unless they were Harkryders or they had to. The name might have sounded scenic to wandering tourists, but the locals knew that in this case the word *Painter* had nothing to do with artists or vistas worth capturing on canvas; nor did *cove* mean an ocean inlet. *Painter* was the old mountain word for panther, and in the mountains a *cove* was an inlet of flat land set at the juncture of two ridges. The early settlers named the pocket of land for the mountain lions that prowled the wilderness. They were rare now, but people still saw one now and again, or heard its curiously human scream in the dark. Most people left Painter Cove to the wild animals and the

Harkryders; opinion varied on which was the more dangerous.

They rode on in silence. Martha watched the tree trunks flash by until she could no longer glimpse the silver light of the river between them. Then she said, "What did you mean about the Sorleys having style, Spencer?"

"I was thinking of the stories folks used to tell about them. Didn't you ever hear about Dalton Sorley?"

Martha frowned. "I thought that was a bluegrass song. *Yonder stands Dalton Sorley with an Iver Johnson gun . . .*"

"You got the tune right," said Spencer. "I didn't think you could sing anything the Shirelles hadn't recorded."

"All I know is the chorus," said Martha. "Heard it when I was a kid."

"Anyhow, that's him. He was more than just a folk song, though. Back at the turn of the century, Dalton Sorley was either a hero or a one-man crime wave around here, depending on your point of view."

"Who was he?"

"He grew up on the Sorley farm over in Mitchell County, and he did some logging around here as a teenager."

"I mean, is he any kin to the Sorley that just escaped from Mountain City?"

"Uncle. I checked. Dalton was the oldest of a string of young'uns, and Harm was the younger of six, so despite the decades between them, they're only a generation apart."

"So what was Dalton Sorley like?"

"They say he could play the guitar, train dogs to do

about anything he wanted, and that he was a good enough trick shot sharpshooter to join a circus act. Nelse Miller had a picture of Dalton on an old wanted poster left by the sheriff before him. It was dated 1894, and in those days he was a handsome kid. One of those short, banty rooster types, with thick dark hair, and cheekbones that made you think Cherokee. I don't know if he was part Indian or not, but that's what I thought when I saw his picture. Remember Sal Mineo in that Disney movie *Tonka*?"

Martha nodded. "To bad old Dalton didn't go to Hollywood to be a bad guy."

"He lived too early to be in the movies. When he was still a teenager, he left here and went over into Virginia. Don't ask me why. Maybe he was traveling with a circus. Anyhow, he was arrested for some trifling offense—picking a man's pocket, I think—and they put him in a small-town jail, from which he promptly escaped on Christmas Eve. A deputy sheriff went after him, and wound up dead—shot with his own gun."

"Over a petty theft charge?" Martha's eyes widened.

"You're never safe, Martha. Remember that."

"Did they catch him?"

"Virginia didn't. He turned up in east Tennessee the following April, courting a girl called Sarah Maggard. The legend is that the two of them interrupted a tent revival service near Johnson City one evening, asking the preacher to marry them. They offered him a ten-dollar gold piece to perform the ceremony, but the preacher saw that they had been drinking, and tried to run them off, and somebody recognized Dalton and went for the law. There was a reward out for Dalton, of course, and you know how policemen feel about a cop killer. Anyhow, six officers went out to capture him, armed to the teeth, and they left instructions to have a coffin ready for Dalton Sorley because they were bringing him back dead."

"Times have changed," said Martha.

"Yeah. *We* got civilized; *they* just keep getting deadlier all the time. Anyhow, the lawmen split into three groups before they approached the scene, found the happy couple outside the revival tent near the horses, and supposedly they opened fire, killing a horse, but missing everybody else. Dalton dragged Sarah behind the horses, and started shooting back."

Martha tried not to smile. "What were the revival folks doing?"

"Crouching in prayer," said Spencer, grinning. "Dalton fired back, killed a Carter County deputy, and badly wounded the other. Then the second team ran for some trees to the left of the horses, and he took them out with two shots."

"What was he armed with?"

"Two six-shooters. We were the West once, you know. Cowboys, Indians, the whole nine yards."

"So he killed four officers in a couple of minutes." Martha did not sound enamored of this specimen of a folk hero.

"Killed three. The wounded fellow recovered. When Dalton tried to escape through the woods, he ran into the fifth member of the posse."

"What happened to number six?"

Spencer hesitated. "I hope he went for a doctor, Martha, but the fact is that not everybody manages grace in a firefight. You won't know if you can handle it until you're faced with it." He turned to look at her. "That's why I'm starting you off slowly in this deputy business. I don't want to get shot saving *you*."

"So Dalton Sorley shot the fifth man in the woods?"

"Tried to," said Spencer. "The man said later that Dalton was three feet from him and aimed that six-gun right at his heart, but the weapon misfired. Anyhow, it didn't go off. He said Dalton looked down at the pistol, and then he smiled up at the deputy, and said, 'Boy, the Lord must think a lot of you.' Before the deputy could gather his wits enough to fire, Dalton threw the gun at him, and disappeared into the woods."

"What happened to his girlfriend?"

"Sarah? A horse kicked her, but she was all right. They didn't charge her with anything. People said that if those police officers had asked Dalton Sorley to surrender when they first approached him, he would have gone peaceable, so that Sarah wouldn't be put into danger. But they didn't give him a chance. They wanted a showdown. This macho business gets people killed. It may be just as well that you don't have it."

"I'll remember that. So what became of Dalton Sorley?"

"They captured him the next day. He had stolen a horse and was on the road to the Maggards' farm to see Sarah. They put him on trial in circuit court, and people came from miles around to see it. They say that pretty girls brought flowers and homemade cakes to him in jail."

"How do you know all this?" asked Martha.

"When he was young, Nelse Miller worked as a deputy for an old fellow who had been a deputy when they caught Dalton Sorley. There's still people who knew people who knew him—or so they claim. He was sentenced to be hanged, and they were building the scaffold for the occasion when Dalton escaped again, taking two chicken thieves and another murderer with him."

"Another escape! Maybe he should have tried a magic show instead of a circus," said Martha.

"They upped the reward another two thousand dollars, and people started writing songs about him."

The radio squawked, and an electronic voice said, "Adam One, are y'all Code J?"

"Adam One, affirmative," said Martha in response to the dispatching code asking if all was well.

The sheriff laughed. "We're not even *there* yet, Jennaleigh! We'll keep you posted."

Martha was silent for a bit. Perhaps she was being too uptight about the job. After all, they had fewer murders in a year than Washington, D.C., had in a day, but the element of danger was still there, and that knowledge kept her solemn. She was afraid that Spencer might tease her about it, so she turned his thoughts back to the escapades of the long-dead outlaw. "I suppose they caught Dalton Sorley eventually?"

"Not for another two years. A few days after the jailbreak, some lawmen shot it out with him in the woods, and they put two bullets into him, but he wounded one of them, and managed to get away. He headed for the cabin of one of his brothers near Roan Mountain. The brother gave out that Dalton had died, and he was even showing people the wooden cross marking the grave of his outlaw brother, while all the time the brother was nursing Dalton back to health in his cabin. That settled things for a while, but then Dalton turned up two years later in Louisville, Kentucky, where he turned himself in for shooting a man in a poker game. He was using another name by then, but the authorities soon figured out who they had in custody, and they sent him back to Tennessee."

"And he escaped again?"

"Almost. He got to the roof of the jail, but he broke his ankle making the jump to freedom. The hanging was two weeks later, and they were afraid to postpone it. Dalton Sorley went up the scaffold on crutches. It was a public hanging—when would that have been? About 1898. People came from miles around to see the famous outlaw swing."

"People would," said Martha.

"Nelse Miller said the old lawman friend of his had been present at the execution. The fellow said that Dalton asked the crowd to sing an old Methodist hymn, 'While Dead in Trespasses I Lie,' and while they sang it, he stood on the scaffold smoking a cigar, and nodding in time to the music. When the singing stopped, he handed the cigar to the sheriff, and said 'I will you this.' Then they put the hood over his head and hanged him."

"They finally got him? I don't suppose the rope broke or anything?"

"No. And unfortunately it didn't break his neck, either. He must have lost weight in prison, and they misjudged the drop. Took him fifteen minutes to strangle, and the hood came off twice. The old lawman claimed he'd wake up in a sweat for years afterward seeing Dalton Sorley's eyes looking into his as he hung there trying to die."

"That's enough, Spencer! Not even the Harkryders deserve that—not most of 'em, anyhow."

"They're fortunate to be living in enlightened times," said the sheriff.

They had reached the mouth of Painter Cove, and Martha saw the ramshackle houses and rusting trailers clustered around the dead end of the dirt road. "Enlightenment appears to be in short supply up here," she said.

One advantage to being a radio celebrity was the fact that no one ever recognized you in private life. Henry Kretzer, the off-air persona of Hank the Yank, led a less flamboyant life than his listeners might have imagined. Although he did indeed live in the cabin he often talked about on his program, it was a modern pine and plywood structure, rather lacking in rustic charm. Once outside the recording booth, the amiable popular pal of the WHTN radio audience faded into a nondescript balding man whose friends were his books. He felt sometimes that his body was the bottle that imprisoned the genie, and that only a radio microphone could release the magic.

It was early afternoon, five hours before Hank the Yank's evening talk show would be back on the air, but tonight's topic was uppermost in Henry Kretzer's mind. The escaped convict had been a popular novelty issue with WHTN's audience. The fact that the fugitive was sixty-three added spice to the discussion. A dangerous young thug would have frightened female listeners, and it might have led to law-and-order harangues from aging conservatives. Hank the Yank hated shows that prompted self-righteous middle-class sermons.

Nobody knew what to make of Harm, though. He was a convict and a murderer, but he was also a senior citizen and a local boy, not without friends. He could symbolize the continuing vigor of the elderly—certainly a plus with Hank's over-forty constituency, and for east Tennessee natives he represented the triumph of the homeboy over the bureaucratic outlanders. For all the newcomers and yuppies in the area, Harm added the spice of manageable danger to an increasingly civilized segment of mountain wilderness. *Sure, we have Japanese restaurants and tanning salons,* Johnson City people could tell visitors, *but there are still bears and rattlesnakes in the woods, and even an escaped mountain man at large: old, but still too tough and wily for the law to catch.* Privately, Hank doubted that the law was trying all that hard to catch Harm. The telephone inquiries he'd made to the Northeast Correctional Center and to the local law enforcement departments convinced him that efforts to capture the escaped convict were at best perfunctory. One prison official had told him—off the record, of course—that Harm Sorley was old and sick, and that an understaffed facility, overcrowded with *really* dangerous criminals, had no time to spare on the senile wanderings of an ancient hillbilly. In a couple of months, when hunting season rolled around, some good old boy in camos would stumble across his body, and that would be the end of it. Until then, the prison official said, the "Hank the Yank Show" would be welcome to lead a broadcast manhunt, but, no, the NECC could not supply a guest spokesman to appear on the program.

Tonight's topic was the criminal career of Harm Sorley. There were old-timers who remembered the case, and some of them were bound to call in, but Henry Kretzer liked to be in control of the discussion, and that meant having the facts at hand. To that end, he was using his spare time to visit the office of the *Hamelin Record* to check their files for articles on the case. If that failed, there was always the trial record in the courthouse, but he hoped to find the facts in more palatable form at the newspaper office.

Henry stood at the counter of the otherwise empty *Record* office, wondering if he should ring the little bell or call toward the back room to let them know he was here. The sign on the glass-fronted door had said OPEN. Before he could decide on the least objectionable course of action, a lanky young man in horn-rimmed glasses appeared. "Sorry!" he said, smiling at the visitor. "I didn't hear you come in. I'm Jeff McCullough, the editor." (And everything else, he might have added.) "How can I help you?"

"I'm doing some research on local history, and I wanted to look at some old copies of your newspaper." That statement wasn't entirely false; it merely failed to be specific. He wondered whether to introduce himself as Hank the Yank. He decided not to do so unless it became unavoidable. People who had heard of him were invariably disappointed. "Do you keep bound back issues, or are they on microfilm?"

"It depends," said McCullough. "How far back do you want to go? The library has issues on microfilm dating back to the twenties. We keep bound copies here, but nothing that old."

"Nineteen sixty-eight."

"Let me check." The editor disappeared into the back room again, and emerged several minutes later with a large, yellowing stack of newspapers, bound together on a wooden rod. He set them down on a yard-sale dining-room table, and motioned for the visitor to sit down. "This should do it. I haven't checked to make sure all the issues are there, but we can hope for the best. Anything special you're looking for?"

Henry Kretzer stiffened. He knew the question was coming. In small towns, it always did. Well, it was public record. "I'm interested in the escaped convict from Mountain City. Harm Sorley."

Jeff McCullough nodded. "Oh, yeah. I heard about him. Maybe I should do a story on him. Local guy." He peered at the slender, nervous man. "You're not a relative of his, are you?"

"No," said Henry quickly. "Just an amateur historian."

"Just checking. Your accent isn't local, but it was worth a shot."

"Do you have an index to these?"

"Do I *look* like I have time to index back issues? I answer my own phone half the week." He grinned. "You're on your own, sir. And good luck. I'll be working in the back. If anyone comes in, just holler."

Hank the Yank began to leaf through the stack of papers. Because the *Record* was a small weekly, there were only fifty-two editions to search, each containing fewer than twenty pages. He decided to look at all the front pages first. Surely a murder case in Wake County would be front-page news. They didn't happen very often.

He was three-quarters of the way through the bundle before he found it: *County Resident Killed in Altercation: Rural Tragedy Strikes Maggard Family.* Beneath the three-column headline was a studio photograph captioned "Claib Maggard," showing the murdered man in suit and tie, glaring pompously off the page. Henry hoped it wasn't going to turn out to be a beer brawl. Pointless violence would dampen the effect of Harm's heroism in escaping the bureaucracy. He scanned the story.

According to the stilted narrative of the 1968 *Hamelin Record* reporting staff, Claib Maggard and Harm Sorley were neighbors—except that Maggard was a county magistrate, with a big white farmhouse, two hundred acres of pasture for beef cattle, an apple orchard, woodland, and a cornfield, while Harm Sorley's trailer perched on ten acres of cleared scrubland, on which he had a trailer, two goats and a half-Guernsey cow, and a flock of speckled guinea fowl. Henry could picture himself in the persona of Hank the Yank saying, "They were neighbors in the same sense that a flea and a dog are neighbors." He read on.

The article described Harm Sorley as "minor scion of the infamous Sorley outlaw clan," but noted that he had not been particularly prone to violence in the past. He had a criminal record studded with minor offenses, though, whereas Claib Maggard had been an upstanding citizen from a prosperous family. Henry wondered what Harm had thought of him.

On the evening of October 16, 1968, Harm Sorley turned up at Maggard's farm, angry, possibly intoxicated, and shouting threats. The witness for this was a stockman, who heard the sounds of an argument as he was going into the barn several hundred yards away. He did not hear what was being said, though, and claimed that he did not know the cause of the disagreement. Maggard had been chopping firewood when Harm Sorley appeared, and "authorities speculate" (as the *Record* phrased it) that Maggard put down the ax to converse with his irate neighbor.

Twenty minutes later the stockman came out of the barn, and found the butchered remnants of his employer. Maggard had been hacked to death with his own ax. Harm Sorley was gone.

Sheriff Nelse Miller immediately organized a manhunt to comb the surrounding area, and at daylight the next morning searchers found Harm Sorley, still wearing bloodstained overalls, hiding in a smokehouse on a nearby farm.

But why did he do it? What was the fight about? Hank the Yank needed to know. He flipped through successive editions of the newspaper, and found several articles related to the case (*Tests Show Blood on Overalls Matches Victim's*), but nothing suggesting a motive.

"How's the search going?" asked Jeff McCullough, tottering out of the back room with a stack of the *Record*'s current issue.

"I found the article reporting the murder, but I can't find any follow-up explaining the motive."

"No. There probably isn't one." He set the papers on

the front counter, and sat down in the second captain's chair. "See, in small towns people don't find things out from reading the newspaper. Especially not a weekly. Gossip takes care of most of the local news long before the paper comes out, and certain topics never make it into print at all. Anything that would upset a respected local family, for example, doesn't get published. Weeklies are about garden club meetings and birthday parties—not about rapes and suicides. They're like a time capsule, but it's sundial time: they count no hours but unclouded ones."

"So do you know more than you print?"

"Sure. But not about a 1968 murder case. I was in Cub Scouts back then in Asheville."

"There wasn't even an eyewitness to the crime. I'm not even completely sure he did it. How can I find out more?"

"The trial records will help some, but remember that law is a chess game. Total truth is not their object any more than it is ours. You could ask around."

"Who? The sheriff?"

"Spencer Arrowood wasn't sheriff when this happened. He may still have been in high school." McCullough thought it over. "Who's old, but sharp? Who would I ask?" He looked suspiciously at the stranger. "You're not from one of those tabloids, are you?"

"No. I'm Henry Kretzer. Hank the Yank. On WHTN." He shifted into his broadcasting voice.

"Yeah! I recognize your voice now. I thought you sounded familiar."

"I'm doing this escaped convict story on my show this week."

"Okay. Who would I ask?" McCullough's smile faded. "Let me tell you about Nora Bonesteel."

# CHAPTER
# 5

Their names are graven on the stone,
 Their bones are in the clay;
And ere another day is gone,
 Ourselves may be as they.

#670, "Dwelling Among the Tombs,"
Reginald Heber

Tennessee Methodist Hymnal, 1885

Martha looked at the decrepit collection of shacks and rusting trailers in a field of Queen Anne's lace and tall grass. "Do you know which place we're supposed to go to?"

Spencer pulled the car to the side of the road, and turned off the ignition. "You stay on the radio. I'll handle this."

"Women are better at domestic confrontations. Isn't that why you decided to bring me along?"

"I guess so," said Spencer. "I didn't think it through at the office. Now I'm afraid I might be putting you in a dangerous situation."

Martha smiled. "Want me to sign a release form?"

"Oh, all right. Watch me. I'll find out what's going on, and if it's not assault with a deadly weapon, I'll motion for you to come out. Otherwise, you stay put. Understood?"

Martha gave him a wry smile. "Ten-four."

She watched him unsnap his holster and walk slowly toward the cluster of shacks. He was keeping close to a couple of derelict car bodies rusting beside the road—in case he needed quick cover—but all was silent in Painter Cove. Martha looked at the desolation, and wished she could earmark her state tax money to help send the Harkryders to college, and buy them brick houses with carports. She didn't think they deserved such beneficence; she knew they wouldn't take it if it were offered, but without wishing them well in any way, she wished they'd stop being poor: first of all, because the Harkryders were a constant irritant and danger to the Wake County Sheriff's Department, and also because Martha knew that when people heard the word Appalachia, it was the Harkryders they pictured. Never mind that all the Harkryders and their ilk from every cove in Appalachia wouldn't fill up one slum in a major city, they were still the image of the region. Martha wondered why city people judged urban areas by their wealthiest inhabitants and rural areas by their poorest. It didn't seem fair, but it had always been that way, and even if the Harkryders got indoor plumbing and learned to talk like Dan Rather, she doubted that it would change anything.

Now, about twenty feet from the nearest door, the sheriff stopped to "hello the house," a custom necessary for the survival of trespassers in the South. You let the householders know you're coming, so they don't take potshots at you for trying to sneak up on them. Having announced his presence, Spencer leaned back on the hood of the disintegrating car, and waited.

"I wonder where the dogs are," thought Martha. There ought to have been at least six enraged hounds vying for the privilege of tearing Spencer apart. He seemed to have his attention fixed on a tarpaper shack with a sagging porch set up on concrete blocks. Its front door was not completely closed.

"Jennaleigh, are you there?" said Martha into the microphone. "Could you call LeDonne on the telephone, and ask him to stand by? I know he's not working this shift. Tell him *I said so!* Out."

Martha had been hearing about the Harkryders for years from Godwin and LeDonne. They seemed to be perpetual participants in bar fights, car thefts, and trafficking in controlled substances. The old-timers favored moonshine, but of course the youngsters were into drugs. She wondered what the problem was today— and who had summoned them. Surely there were no telephones in Painter Cove. What could make a Harkryder call the law?

The door to the tarpaper shack opened wider, and Martha saw an old man, hunched with arthritis, come shuffling onto the porch. He squinted into the sunlight, and motioned for the sheriff to come up. Although Martha could not see a weapon, she was relieved that Spencer kept the old man positioned between himself and the open door. When he reached the bottom of the steps, the old man tottered down to meet him, and they spoke quietly for a few minutes.

Martha noticed that faces appeared from time to time at the window, but their expressions were curious, not menacing. The one dwelling at which the curtains stayed closed, and nothing moved, was the battered blue and white mobile home to the right of the tarpaper shack. The old man kept pointing to it as he talked. That must be where the trouble was. She wondered why people weren't crowded around the trailer, waiting for something to happen. Almost any kind of tragedy drew sightseers. Were they afraid to get too close? She peered at the roll-out trailer windows, looking for the glint of a gun barrel.

The sheriff motioned for her to get out of the car. Glancing uneasily at the silent trailer, Martha eased out the driver's side, and walked to the porch as fast as dignity allowed. "What's going on?" she whispered.

"Female suspect in the trailer with a knife," said Spencer. "Threatening to kill an infant."

"It's Sabrina," the old man offered. "I told that boy not to marry her. She's got Melungeon blood. Ain't no telling what them folk will do, I said to him."

Martha nodded, inching away from the blast of whiskey that came with his words. The Melungeons were an olive-skinned people of uncertain origin who had lived in the northeast Tennessee mountains for generations. Depending on who you asked, they were a lost tribe of Indian, descendants of Portuguese explorers, or the offspring of runaway slaves. Nobody knew for sure, and mostly they kept to themselves. It would be pointless to preach tolerance to a Harkryder, especially since the object of his disapproval was now armed and threatening mayhem. She said, "Sir, this Sabrina is threatening an infant? Where are the parents?"

"Why, she's its mama," said the ancient Harkryder. "And her husband is my grandson Tracy. He's in there with her. I think he's hurt. She told us all to get away from the trailer, and I went and called you."

Martha looked at Spencer. "Do you know why she's doing this?"

"He says the couple had a fight," said Spencer softly.

"That's all the old gentleman is willing to part with in the way of explanation. Except that he claims she also killed the dogs."

As if on cue the old man tapped Martha on the arm. "Did you know she poisoned them dogs? Every durn one, she was so mad. I told him not to truck with her, and she a—"

"Yessir, I know," said Martha. "Look, Spencer, if all she's got is a knife—and I know you'll insist that I don't get too close—I think I ought to be the one to talk to her. It doesn't sound like she has much use for men right now."

"She could go after anybody."

Martha had thought out the answer to that one. "Look, Sheriff, you're armed. If I stay in sight, you can cover me. Would you rather go up there yourself, and depend on *me* for backup?"

She could see that the thrust hit home. "You don't go inside," said Spencer. "You don't let her get near you. I want you in plain sight at all times. I'll radio the rescue squad. I can cover you, but I still don't like it."

Martha walked away before he could argue further. She tried not to consider the possibility that Sabrina would have a gun. She'd bet there was at least one fire-arm somewhere in that trailer; no Harkryder man would be complete without one.

A feet few from the cinder-block steps, Martha called out, "Sabrina!" *Sabrina what? Oh. Harkryder, of course.* "Sabrina Harkryder! My name is Martha Ayers, and I came to talk to you." She willed herself to stand still, and to appear calm. She waited. Excessive talking is a sign of nerves.

"You're a cop?"

Martha saw a girl's face framed in dust on the trailer window. Her dark eyes narrowed as she took in the badge and deputy's uniform. "A lady cop?"

"That's right. We heard you were having some problems, and I came to see if I could help." Martha smiled up at her, wondering if this child could possibly be eighteen. "I hear you have a baby. Is it a boy or a girl?"

"He's a no-account male like his daddy." The sullen face was streaked with tears. She was running the blade of a butcher knife against the windowsill.

Martha glanced back over her shoulder. Spencer was talking into the microphone. "Sabrina, can you open the door and let me see the baby? I just love babies. And then we could talk." The girl hesitated, so Martha added, "I don't have a gun or anything. I'm a trainee."

"Yeah? Did you go to a school for cops? Was it hard?"

"It was okay." Martha wasn't willing to admit the extent of her inexperience. "How about you? Did you finish school?"

She shook her head. "I quit to marry Tracy. I didn't think I'd miss it. But I do."

"Lots of married people finish school," said Martha. "Come out here, and we'll talk about things you can do."

Sabrina Harkryder considered the offer. "I'll open the door an inch or two," she said. "You sit on the top step. If you try to come in, I'll hurt this baby."

"I'm sitting," said Martha, settling gingerly on a hot cinder block. She motioned for Spencer to stay back. He was frowning at her, and she knew he was wishing they could trade places.

A minute passed. The door opened wide enough for Martha to see a metal kitchen chair in the shadows. The ammonia smell of unwashed diapers mingled with whiskey and sour milk. Martha held her breath to keep from coughing.

Sabrina Harkryder appeared, looking like a child herself in a faded blue shift and plastic sandals. She sat down, with a sleeping baby curled into the crook of one arm, and the butcher knife clenched in her hand. "This is him."

"He's beautiful," murmured Martha. She was thinking, *Squashed red features; less than twenty-four inches long—probably only a few weeks old. It's breathing, though.* "He has your dark curly hair, Sabrina. What's his name?"

"Dustin Allison Harkryder."

"Allison?" Surely that was a girl's name.

"It's after Davey Allison, the race car driver. He got killed right before the baby was born. Tracy and me wanted to honor his memory." It was a precise little speech. She must have explained the name many times.

"Dustin Allison is adorable," said Martha. *Call the hostage by name. Make them a person, not an object.* "I know you must think the world of him."

The girl looked away. "He's all right," she murmured.

"Well, then, what *isn't* all right? Can you tell me?"

New tears streaked her dark face. "Tracy!"

"Is Tracy as young as you are? Sometimes young men have a hard time adjusting to being daddies."

"They sure like *making* babies well enough! And they don't care whether you feel like it or not!"

"Has he been hurting you?" asked Martha, still watching the knife. "You or the baby?"

Sabrina sneered at the question. "He's not around here long enough to bother. I got pregnant, so he married me, and I went and quit school and moved up here, and as soon as I started getting all fat and tired, he wouldn't give me the time of day! He was always off somewhere cruising with his buddies, staying out half the night. You know where he was the night the kid was born? At a damned Alan Jackson concert in Knoxville! He showed up at the hospital the next day with a rose in a mason jar, and a shirt pocket full of cigars saying *It's a boy*. I could still smell the beer on him."

"But that was—what?—six weeks ago? That can't be what this is about." Without being obvious about it, Martha was trying to peek past the kitchen chair into the darkened interior. Where was Tracy now?

Sabrina looked away. "After the baby come, I had stitches from where they cut me down there, so I couldn't do nothing, and Tracy kept griping about how he'd been without his rights for such a long time. So he went out and found some bitch to give it to him. He told me last night. Said he'd be back today to get his clothes and his stereo."

"So last night you poisoned the dogs."

"Yeah. I been up all night waiting for Tracy to get back, and getting madder by the hour. At first light I hid his guns so he couldn't do nothing to me when he came home, and then I put antifreeze in the dogs' food. They all eat together, so it was easy. I hated them dogs. They barked all the time and kept waking the baby up, and then I'd have to tend to him. *He* wouldn't."

"What happened when Tracy did come back?"

"Oh, he saw the dogs lying in the dirt with flies all over 'em, and he carried on about those damned dogs, and when I told him it served him right for two-timing me, he tried to hit me, and I took a swipe at him with the butcher knife. Cut his shirt and left a long scratch on his chest. When he saw he was bleeding, he hollered like a baby, saying I was a-goin' to kill him. Then he grabbed the bottle of Jack Daniel's, and locked himself in the bathroom. I reckon he's passed out by now."

"When did you say you might hurt the baby?"

"Oh, this morning when he first came back, 'cause I was so mad at him for spending the night with *her*. I yelled it out the window at him while he was outside wailing over them dogs." She stopped for a moment. The tears welled. "I didn't know what else to do. I kept thinking, if it wasn't for this baby, I could get shut of all this. But I'm trapped here."

"How did Tracy react to you threatening the baby?"

Sabrina shrugged. "Didn't seem to phase him none. Not like seeing the dead dogs did. But I thought if I kept saying I'd hurt the baby, maybe Tracy would take notice of me, and see how bad I was hurting. He didn't care, though. I reckon he loved them damned dogs better than us."

"Do you believe that?"

"Yeah."

"I won't argue with you," said Martha. "There's men that are like that, and if you say he's one of them, then I'll believe you. But if he did love those dogs better than you and the baby, then you've done all you can to hurt him. Cutting that baby won't add much at all to his pain, Sabrina. But it will break your heart."

Sabrina was crying hard now. She hugged the infant, and it woke up squalling.

"Give Dustin Allison to me," said Martha quickly, leaning forward with her arms outstretched. "You're too tired to contend with him."

She hesitated. "You gonna take him away from me?"

"No," said Martha. *Probably should, but won't. If the baby isn't hurt, and the husband's wound is superficial, social services will do some paperwork, and release the child back to the custody of the mother.* She glanced back at Spencer, who was looking more impatient by the minute. He couldn't hear what they were saying, and Martha was too close to the knife. According to Tennessee's domestic violence law, if one spouse has injured the other in a family fight, the offender must be taken to jail.

"I don't call the shots here, Sabrina, but I'll talk to the sheriff about it. He's a pretty nice guy. If he'll allow it, I'll take you and the baby to your folks' place for a couple of days until you can work things out. Can you handle that?"

The girl nodded, and held the baby closer. Martha looked at the knife dangling from the girl's hand. Maybe a more experienced officer would have made a grab for it, but Martha wasn't going to gamble with baby Dustin's life. She could talk this one out. She was sure of it.

"It sure would help me persuade Sheriff Arrowood to help you if you'd put down that knife." *Get the knife. Make her put it down.* "But you won't lose Dustin."

Martha held up her arms again. "Not unless you hurt him. Sabrina, I'll tell you this: you might have thought Tracy Harkryder was worth marrying, but I promise you, he's not worth going to prison for. He's not worth it."

Might as well be hanged for a sheep as a lamb, thought Harm Sorley, worming the first Vienna sausage out of the tightly packed can. According to the little card he'd found in his back pocket, he was a prisoner on the run, and although he couldn't seem to remember any details, he didn't reckon God meant him to starve to death.

He felt as if he had just woke up. Dimly, he was aware that something was the matter with him, because people shouldn't feel that way most of the time, and he did, but it wasn't unpleasant, just puzzling. By now he was used to sorting things out. Here he was, sitting beside a little rocky creek on a mountainside, stretching in the afternoon sunshine, and dipping into a gunnysack for things to eat. Inside the sack he could see he had crackers, a plastic tub of peanut butter, sweet pickles, and a can of corned beef that opened with a little key on the side.

Harm didn't reckon the owner of the cabin would miss the food much. He might not even remember what he had stored there, and the plank door had no lock, so maybe he didn't even care. Anyway, Harm knew that the Lord had meant that food for him, and that was why he had been given to find the hunters' cabin.

Harm had been walking a couple of hours when he'd

come upon the one-room wooden hut with no water or electricity, but there was a deer head on the wall over an old sofa, and a lot of hunting magazines on a side table. The furniture was coated with a layer of dust, but the food in the pine cabinet was still good. He wished he could have taken the jar of coffee and the cans of Bunker Hill beef stew and pork and beans, but he had no way of boiling water to make coffee, and he hadn't been able to find a can opener. The kitchen drawer held a couple of spoons and an old paring knife, which he'd pocketed, but no other utensils, which meant that the Lord didn't intend for him to take the extra provisions.

Harm figured it was a hunters' cabin, abandoned most of the year, and he'd been tempted to bed down there for the night, but a search party might think to look for him there, or the hunters might show up to do some serious drinking or a little out-of-season hunting, so Harm settled for a gunnysack of food, and went on his way. He didn't want to contend with gun-toting strangers, and him armed only with a paring knife. It wasn't much of a weapon, but it was better than nothing.

He looked at the meager collection of foodstuffs in his sack, and thought he had chosen well. The Lord would be pleased. The food he had taken was just about a day's worth of provisions, which was what the Good Book allowed for a traveler. He remembered that well enough. It was in the Book of Exodus, when the Children of Israel were sent manna from heaven to feed them in their wanderings in the desert. The Lord permitted them to gather only enough for that one day.

When they tried to hoard it, the manna rotted and bred worms. Harm had heard his uncle Pharis quote the scripture many a time when they were short on rations on a hunting trip: *And Moses said, Let no man leave of it 'til the morning.* The Lord was teaching His children to trust Him, Pharis would say. The Lord will provide. And sure enough, about the time they'd be down to their last smidgeon of beef jerky, one of them would catch sight of a deer, or leastways a rabbit, and they'd be eating good again. And Pharis would say, "We trusted the Lord, and He provided."

Harm looked with regret at the jar of peanut butter. If he couldn't finish it all today, he'd have to leave it, or the Lord might take it amiss. He saw a honeybee hovering in lazy circles above the stream. A bee hovering around your head meant good luck. His idea of luck would be to have some fresh honey to go along with that peanut butter. Pharis could have got that honey. He'd sit on the bank of a stream, still as a log in the shadows, and he'd watch bees coming in for water. By and by, he'd follow one a few yards into the woods. Then he'd stop there in the shadow of an old tree, and he'd wait for the next bee to fly past on its way back from the stream, and he'd follow it a ways farther. Pharis would keep that up for hours on end if need be, until finally he tracked those bees back to their hive. When he found it, he'd smoke them out, and take their honey. Sometimes he'd even capture the queen, and let the whole hive swarm around him until he got them home, where he'd put them in a white box in the backyard to be tame bees. Pharis was no more afraid of bees than he was of hot coals and rattlesnakes. But

Harm never wanted honey bad enough to waste half a day tracking it, and he never quite trusted the Lord to protect him from the angry hive.

By the time the bee drank its fill and drifted back into the trees, Harm had forgotten its presence. He must have been napping in the sun. He felt as if he had just woke up. Beside him was a gunnysack of food. He smiled at the sight of it. Rita always packed him a lunch when he went off in the woods. He looked inside. Peanut butter and crackers. His favorite. Of course, she knew that. He wished he had some honey to go with it.

"I can't believe Spencer let you do that," said LeDonne again. He lifted his coffee cup, and set it back down, untouched. "She had a knife."

"Sabrina Harkryder is just a kid, Joe," said Martha. She put her hand on his arm and forced a smile. "She wasn't dangerous."

"She could have been out of her skull on drugs for all you knew. You're not exactly experienced in these things. And I don't care how young she was: any woman who threatens her own son at knife point has to be crazy."

"She didn't know what else to do." Martha knew that it would be useless to try to explain the confrontation to Joe LeDonne.

He was coming on duty for the evening shift, and she was getting ready to go home. This ten-minute coffee break would be their only time together for the day. They were sitting on either side of Martha's desk, with the glass coffeepot on a trivet between them. Spencer had already left for home.

She had thought about Sabrina off and on for the rest of the day, and she'd finally concluded that despite her apprehension that morning, she had ended up liking the sullen child bride. At least Sabrina Harkryder wasn't the cringing battered wife who stayed around for years taking abuse from a no-good husband. *Like I was,* thought Martha. *I wish I'd had enough sand to fight back against Howard the first time, instead of blaming it on his drinking, or saying I'd have to learn not to aggravate him.* Young Sabrina might not live happily ever after with her man, but at least she'd showed him she wouldn't take any shit from him. And nobody had been seriously hurt—except the dogs. Martha figured it could have been worse. But it was no use saying so to Joe LeDonne, whose black and white world did not contain the color gray.

"And instead of locking her up and throwing away the key, which by the way is in accordance with the Tennessee Domestic Violence Law, you two bleeding hearts give her a ride to her mama's house!" He shook his head in disbelief. "I hope I don't have to spend the evening driving out to her folks' place when her husband gets out of the hospital and decides to continue the fight."

"I don't think Tracy Harkryder will want to contend with Sabrina any time soon," said Martha, trying to keep her voice neutral.

"Wanna bet?"

To forestall the "you-have-no-business-being-a-deputy" lecture that she could see coming, Martha changed the subject to another of her concerns. "You went to see Dr. Caudill at Mountain Home this morning, didn't you? What did he say about the escaped prisoner?"

"He's never treated him," LeDonne reminded her. "But if the individual really does suffer from Korsakoff's psychosis, Caudill thinks he won't last long." He gave her the highlights of his discussion with the VA psychiatrist.

"So, what are you going to recommend to Spencer about capturing him? An all-out manhunt with volunteers, or just follow up leads, or what?"

"I'd say we have better things to do, Martha." He smiled. "Like checking for expired county tax stickers on windshields."

"But he's an escaped murderer, Joe!"

"He's a sick old man who spent longer in jail than any two murderers nowadays."

"If he's crazy, he might be dangerous," said Martha.

LeDonne looked surprised. "You don't feel sorry for the guy?"

"For an old drunk whose mind is gone?" She shrugged. "Not particularly. He's no great loss, is he? I just hope he doesn't cause us any problems on his way out. I'll bet poor Rita Pentland is afraid he'll come after her."

LeDonne stood up and put on his cap. "It's time I was out on patrol. You know something, Martha? You might be tougher than I thought."

In the kitchen of her apartment in Johnson City, Charlotte Pentland turned on her radio. She used country music as background noise while she worked. On the table before her was the beginning of the first draft of her geology paper on the plate tectonics of Appalachia: *Before the Indians wore a path from north Alabama to the Cumberlands; before the pioneers followed the valleys westward: The first journey was the journey of the mountains themselves.* She had been struggling with the phrasing of the introduction, trying not to state as fact concepts that were still only theories. She must be decisive, but not impetuous. Charlotte had long ago decided that cute little blonds had to try harder than anybody not to be thought of as stupid. Her rural Tennessee accent would count as strike two with most of the world. One lab instructor used to call her "Elly May," as in Clampett. So she studied a lot, and smiled very little, and after a while people got used to the idea that Charlotte Pentland was no airhead. She wasn't using East Tennessee State to husband hunt, either. She wanted a Ph.D., not an M.r.s.

This paper was only a third of the grade in a three-hour summer graduate course, and all she was expected to do was parrot the results of other people's research in a cogent summary, but because the subject fascinated her, she wanted to do well. Sometimes she would drive up to the grassy balds of Roan Mountain or to the Beauty Spot above Erwin and look at the crown of encircling hills, marveling to herself that they had not always been there. Once the entire continent had been covered by a warm, shallow sea. That's where the salt licks came from. A little town called Saltville, less than fifty miles away in the Virginia mountains, had been a source of salt to animals, Indians, and settlers

for centuries. The salt deposit had been left there when
the sea dried up—how many million years ago? She
would try to imagine the same spot of land as the view
changed through the ages.

Geology made sense of the land just as history attempted to make sense of people, but history was
subject to a constant reinterpretation of facts that
Charlotte hoped geology would be spared. Once you
got past the literal interpretations of Noah's Flood
(quite a strain for some fundamentalist undergradu-
ates), there wasn't so much revision as there was sorting out new discoveries to see where that knowledge fit
into the puzzle. Charlotte found it exciting to learn new
facts about the familiar landscape. This would be her
specialty: the study of her mountain home. She made
that decision as a sophomore, when a geology instructor took the class on a field trip up to Roan Mountain,
and announced, as they clumped around him gazing at
the acres of grasses, sedge, and wildflowers moving in
the ceaseless winds: "Ladies and gentlemen, you have
now been to Africa." From then on she wanted to know
every secret of that ancient journey, and there were
only the rocks to ask.

As she flipped the pages of text, she realized that she
wasn't hearing music. The radio was tuned to a talk
show. She glanced at the clock. It must be Hank the
Yank on WHTN, she thought, but she knew that he occasionally played music, so she decided not to bother
to get up and search for a new station. After all, she'd
grown up in Hamelin. There might be some news
about folks she knew.

* * *

"Good evening to you, neighbors. You're listening to Hank the Yank on WHTN, in Wake County, Tennessee, where you can dial a wrong number and still talk, and where even our escaped convicts are senior citizens. Welcome to day three of the Unaka Mountain Crime Wave. Did anybody have any Geritol swiped off their windowsill last night?"

The disc jockey scooted his swivel chair along the counter in search of a tape. "And they still haven't found him, neighbors! The law in all its majesty—and presumably with helicopters and bloodhounds—has been unable to locate one old man who escaped from the NECC in a garbage truck! Neighbors, do you think they need a little help?

"Do you think a group of down-to-earth, hard-working citizens might be of some assistance to these poor befuddled bureaucrats? Well if you do think that, friends, you're in luck.

"I have been talking to the folks in charge of the prison, and they don't hold out too much hope of finding old Harm, so they have given me exclusive permission to head up a broadcast manhunt. So if any of you good people see an elderly man wearing a striped suit and a ball and chain, and acting suspicious—give us a call. We'll be your Electronic Neighborhood Watch.

"But—consider this, Wake County—do we *want* to catch Harm Sorley?

"We'll come back to that fascinating topic a little later on. Meanwhile, if you have any thoughts about Harm that you'd like to share with our listening audience, give us a call. And especially if you've been around long enough to remember what got him sent to jail in the first place. This doddering old guy that has outwitted the Tennessee prison system—what crime did he commit? Is he dangerous—or just *smarter than the av-ver-rage bear*?" The baby boomers loved it when he did cartoon voices from their video childhood.

"Talk to me, Wake County.

"And, in addition to discussing the crime, we'll be recording Harm *sightings*. Arvin went out and bought a topographical county map today up at the forest ranger's headquarters, and he'll be sticking pins in it so we can track the movements of our superannuated fugitive. So, if you see anything worth reporting, give us a call.

"While you're mulling over all that, I'll take a break from talking at you, and play you a song. I found one that was in keeping with the tenor of this program tonight. In fact, I think we ought to dedicate this tune to old Harm Sorley himself. Coming at you right now on WHTN—it's the legendary Charlie Waller and his Country Gentlemen singing—what else?—'Fox on the Run.'"

The phone-line lights went on before Charlie Waller reached the end of the first verse. Through the glass of his sound booth, Hank the Yank watched Arvin screen calls from the Wake County faithful. The scale map of Wake County was indeed mounted on cardboard and posted in a prominent position above the tape machine in the sound booth, but Arvin had not purchased it. Hank himself had stopped by the Forest Service office and requested a map. He had run out of time before he could make the drive out to Ashe Mountain to see Nora Bonesteel, but the newspaper editor had written directions for him. If the convict was still news in the next couple of days, he would go. By then he might need a new angle. The flashing lights on the phone indicated that the fugitive was still a hot topic with his listeners.

As the last strains of "Fox on the Run" died away, Hank swiveled the chair back to the telephone to take the first call. "This is Hank the Yank. Caller, you're on."

"I just wanted to say—" the voice was that of an elderly east Tennessee native. "Do I have to give you my name?"

"No, sir. I'll just keep on being Hank."

"I mean—"

"I understand." Hank was chuckling. It was a favorite comeback of his to reluctant callers. "Let's put it like this, sir. If you don't tell any lies or slander anybody, you don't have to identify yourself. Fair enough?"

There was a long pause. "Can you slander the dead?" the voice said at last.

"That's an interesting question. Do you believe in ghosts? They might get annoyed with you. *Can you slander the dead.* Well, caller, Arvin is shaking his head no," said Hank, without a glance in the technician's direction. "He says if you couldn't say harsh things about the dead, the supermarket tabloids would go out of business. *Elvis and Liberace Adopt Love Child.* I'm quoting from the checkout line, folks. Don't attribute that one to me. Now we have a timid caller here who's afraid of slandering the dead. Is this related to our escaped convict discussion, sir?"

"You said you wanted to know about the crime that sent Harm Sorley to prison. Well, I called to tell you.

He killed a man named Claib Maggard, what lived on the adjoining land from him. He hacked him to death with an ax."

"An ax murderer!" said Hank, sounding as if it were news to him. "Well, caller, those facts are a matter of public record, so you haven't slandered anybody so far. Keep going."

"It was said that they had a fight, and that Harm up and killed Claib Maggard in a rage."

"But there were no witnesses, were there?"

"I never heard tell of one. But Harm ran away, and the posse caught him next morning with blood on his clothes."

"Circumstantial. But then I guess Harm wasn't exactly an upstanding citizen to begin with, was he?"

"Why, no. He had been in jail a time or two for brawls and suchlike."

"And from what I hear Claib Maggard was a well-to-do farmer and a county official, wasn't he?"

"Well, he was that. And he also was the dirtiest thieving dog that ever drew breath. And I'd cross hell on a rotten log before I'd say a word against the man who killed him."

"I guess that's what you meant about slandering the dead, caller. But you've certainly got *my* attention. Can you tell us what was so bad about Claib Maggard?"

"I'm eighty years old, and I'm speaking from my own memory here," the voice quavered. "Back in the nineteen and thirties, when Claib was a young man just out of East Tennessee State, he got himself a job with the United States Forest Service turning people off their land and stealing their belongings. My people lost everything they had to his schemes, and I say killing him was the best day's work Harm Sorley ever did!"

"The Forest Service? Stealing people's belongings? You've lost me here, caller. Can you explain—hello? Hello?" The dial tone buzzed in his ear. Hank turned back to the microphone. "He hung up, folks. Now, I'm just a poor dumb Yankee, so can somebody please tell me what that irate old fellow was talking about? Is Smokey the Bear a bandito? Maybe the next caller can help me out. Hello. You're on the air."

"Hello. My name's Clarence." Early thirties. Gun-rack-in-the-pickup voice. Hank always tried to picture his callers. "I just wanted to say that it does my heart good to hear about that old man escaping from Mountain City all by hisself, and I hope they don't never catch him. Thirty years is long enough to stay in jail for killing, unless you hurt a child or something. I say, *right on, Harm!*"

"Well, there's a vote for the prisoner," said Hank. "Do you have any idea what Harm's motive was in the murder?"

"I reckon he was drunk."

"Yeah, maybe so, but why did he go see Claib Maggard in the first place? They don't sound like the type that would pal around together. Motive! Doesn't *anybody* remember?"

"You got me there, Hank."

"Well, thanks for calling. I'm going to the other line now. Yes, caller. What's on your mind?"

He heard a burst of giggles at the other end of the line. High school kids. The spokesman said, "I want to report a sighting of that escaped convict."

"You saw Harm? We got our first sighting, folks!" Hank had the tape already cued. He pushed Play and the blast of a cavalry bugler sounding *Charge!* filled the booth. More giggles from the phone line. "Okay, guys," said the disc jockey. "I'll bite. Where did you fellas see the fugitive?"

"Uh—he was at Watauga Lake stealing picnic baskets." Muffled laughter in the background. "He had on a b-bear costume. You be sure and tell the sheriff that, okay?"

"Tell the sheriff," said Hank, bemused, as he hung up. "All right. Sheriff Spencer Arrowood, if you're out there listening, there's a bunch of teenage jokers who would like you to spend your evening driving all the way out to Watauga Lake in search of an escaped convict in a bear costume, stealing picnic baskets. If you have nothing better to do than that, then I won't bother to lock my door tonight. Who's next?"

"Hello, Hank. Love your show." Middle-aged man. Middling drunk, but still compos mentis. "I'm a local boy with a long memory, and I just thought I'd tip you a wink. If you really want to know about the convict Harm Sorley, why don't you ask his wife? Her name's Rita Pentland now, and she lives right in Hamelin, acting like she's as good as anybody these days."

Hank the Yank disconnected the call, choking off the stream of malice. He thought back over the caller's statement. No FCC problem there: what he'd said was almost certainly true, and therefore public record, but he wished—not for the first time—that they had a time-delay on the broadcast, so that the spiteful drunk wouldn't have made it on the air at all. Hate calls troubled Hank, as did anything that reminded him that small-town life was less than idyllic. Much of the time his Norman Rockwell villagers didn't disappoint him, but an occasional acid-tongued cynic did slip through, despite Arvin's best screening efforts.

Another part of Hank's mind was wondering how best to go about following up on this lead. And where could he get the dirt on the Forest Service?

The radio in Charlotte Pentland's apartment was off now, and the books on plate tectonics lay forgotten on the kitchen table. After two tries, she managed to get her shaking fingers to dial her home number, and when the ringing stopped, she said, "Mama? It's me. It's Chalarty."

# CHAPTER
6

In the wilderness I stray;
My foolish heart is blind;
Nothing do I know: the way
Of peace I cannot find.

#400, "Wretched, Helpless and Distressed,"
Charles Wesley

Tennessee Methodist Hymnal, 1885

"So you're going to retrace the route that Katie Wyler took in her escape from the Indians? Cool." He looked like a St. Bernard in a headband, and his T-shirt said *Virginia Tech Hiking Club.* Jeremy had noticed the T-shirt in the third row of the class as he was beginning the final lecture on Katie Wyler, and he'd asked the student to stay behind after class to discuss a hiking project. The hulking junior, a Mr. Larkin, suggested that they confer at Burger King, since he had only an hour to eat before a three-hour afternoon lab, and in a grand gesture not often seen in university consultants, he had even paid for his own burger.

"Of course, I don't have much hiking experience," said Jeremy, toying with his fish sandwich, and wondering if he ought to admit that the sum of his experience was zero.

"Where you from?"

"Levittown, Long Island." He'd got used to hearing that question from Virginians, and to seeing an expression of pity cross their faces. He'd given up trying to defend suburbia. "I was in Boy Scouts," he offered. "Hiking isn't my natural avocation, but I am doing my dissertation on Katie Wyler, and since the route she followed is only about two hours west of here, it seemed a pity to waste the opportunity. I'd love to get the feel of her journey firsthand."

Larkin nodded. "Yeah. But it isn't going to be a pleasant little stroll, you know. Even two hundred years later, there's lots of wilderness in those mountains. A good bit of the wilderness is intentional, of course. Back in the thirties, the federal government set aside the Great Smoky Mountains National Park and the Cherokee National Forest to preserve the land." He laughed. "Lucky for you, huh? Otherwise you could be hiking from one motel parking lot to another. If you don't have much experience, you might want to use the Appalachian Trail."

"I looked at a map of the area. The trail doesn't follow the route she's supposed to have taken."

"True. Katie Wyler followed the Holston and the Nolichucky/Toe south from Virginia, didn't she? And I understand your wanting to keep to that exact route, but you know most of her trail will be on private land nowadays. It seems to me that if you have to knock on the door of every farmhouse along the way, it will break the mood. So will dodging Herefords and barbed-wire fences." Larkin smiled. "You should hear some of the hiking stories we get in the club."

"But you said that a lot of it is national forest land."

"Yes, but the Cherokee National Forest covers more than half a million acres. There are roads and towns dotted all the way through it. The government bought off a lot of homesteaders, but big chunks of inhabited land remain."

Jeremy frowned. After all these months of picturing Katie Wyler's home in an unspoiled mountain meadow, he would hate to find a convenience store parked in the middle of it. Assuming that he could locate the Wyler homestead at all, that is.

"How long do you plan to stay out?" asked Larkin.

"A couple of weeks. I'm not really sure."

"That can be a long time if you're not used to hiking. I hope you've made arrangements to check in with people from time to time, but still I wouldn't advise you to seek too much isolation."

Jeremy didn't argue, but he was thinking that Katie Wyler managed it quite alone, and living on grubs. Too much tameness would defeat his entire purpose.

"The reason I'm recommending the Appalachian Trail is that it's an approved, well-maintained route through the area, and there will always be people around to help you out."

Jeremy blinked. "People?" He had pictured himself basking in the solitude of a primeval forest.

"Crowds of them," Larkin assured him. "Remember that the trail sometimes parallels a highway through the valleys. I guess you've hiked the section close to here. Remember that the trail follows Highway 42 a good ways from New Castle through Sinking Creek Valley to Newport. You'll run into tourists at campsites, and other hikers along the way, too. Thousands of people each year try to cover the whole 2,146 miles from Springer Mountain, Georgia, to Mount Katahdin, Maine. I did it when I graduated from high school. Took me six months, but it was awesome."

Jeremy took a sip of his coffee while he contemplated people voluntarily trekking through two thousand miles of wilderness. To try such a stunt himself, he would not only have to be chased by Indians, he would have to be able to hear them coming.

"Of course, if the AT doesn't suit your purposes, there are lots of other trails through the Cherokee National Forest," said Larkin, happily unaware of the dismay he was causing. "Tell you what. I'll check my trail guides and talk to some of the other hiking club members. I think we'll be able to draw up a route for you to follow. I'll bring it to class Monday, okay?"

"It's very kind of you," said Jeremy. "I'd really appreciate the help."

"Okay." He glanced at his watch. "Gotta run to lab. One thing I'd better warn you about—you'll really need to bear bag to hike the Cherokee National Forest."

"Right. A bear bag," murmured Jeremy. But he wasn't planning to hunt.

"Some people put their food in the bear bag, and then leave soap and deodorant in their pack, forgetting that *anything* that has an odor has to go in the bag. That's my safety tip for the day. You won't forget?"

Jeremy promised to remember. He was going out for more trail supplies after his office hours. Perhaps the camping store sold bear bags. He would add it to his list.


LeDonne walked past the new dispatcher with the barest nod, and went into the sheriff's office. Spencer was doing the monthly reports, his reading glasses perched precariously on his nose.

"Afternoon," said the deputy. "Where's Martha?"

Spencer glanced at his wristwatch. "She should be providing the escort for the funeral of old Miz Albright about now. I thought I'd let her see some of the glamour of police work."

"Hope she doesn't arrest the pallbearers," grunted LeDonne.

"She is pretty gung ho about the job, but I think a dose of reality will lower her expectations. Tomorrow I'm putting her on a roadblock to do license checks." He looked up at LeDonne's unsmiling face. "Actually, I've been meaning to talk to you about all this. Martha seems to want this job awful bad, but I wondered how you felt about it."

"None of my business. You're the sheriff."

"You're next-of-kin, more or less," said Spencer, wishing he didn't have to get personal with someone as remote as Joe LeDonne. "I wondered if it was causing you any problems."

"If you mean do I like the idea, the answer is no," said the deputy. "Martha doesn't have the military background that we've got, and her weapons training has been of the tin-can variety. I think putting her out there in a uniform is asking for trouble."

"Remember that we average about one murder a year."

"That could change. Punks in Knoxville have got semiautomatic weapons. They could be here in an hour on the interstate."

"I know. But saying that something *might* happen in the future doesn't justify denying her a job today. She's been with this office longer than you have, and she knows the county residents. We could do worse."

"I guess."

"Besides, I'll be with her on any calls more challenging than funeral duty or license checks. She seems to be doing all right so far."

"She is," said LeDonne. "She keeps bugging me about that escaped convict, though. I reckon she thinks we ought to have a manhunt."

Spencer Arrowood smiled. "For Harm? What did the doctor at Mountain Home tell you about his disorder?"

"He thinks Harm is on his last legs. He has no memory from one day to the next, and he may start hallucinating. Somebody will probably find him asking for a handout at their back door, 'cause he's forgotten he's a fugitive."

"I hope so. I wouldn't want him to die out there in the mountains."

"It's warm weather yet, and he could still be a good ways north of the county. I don't think we have the personnel to worry about him."

"I agree," said the sheriff. "But I'm not going to go on Hank the Yank's talk show and admit that."

Nora Bonesteel never went to funerals, and no one ever mustered the courage to ask her why, but more than a few mourners occasionally looked around them at the solemn rows of tombstones in a churchyard, and wondered what old Miz Bonesteel would see if she did come. She never said.

While the mortal remains of Geneva Albright were being consigned to the earth of Oakdale Cemetery, Nora Bonesteel kept her vigil alone in her old friend's tiny cottage. They had been friends for sixty years and more, sharing a girlhood of church picnics and square dances in Dark Hollow, and losing touch at maturity, when Geneva married Hervey Albright and moved to Knoxville, where Hervey's dad owned a clothing store. Nora saw her old friend from one year to the next, when the Albrights came back to Wake County to visit Geneva's family. She had held the new babies, wrapped in the fleecy woolens knitted for them by "Aunt" Nora; she'd admired young Tessa's doll-babies and pretended to be *askeered* of the salamanders Hervey Junior found in the creek. She'd sent them each a card and a five-dollar bill for high school graduation, and now they existed for her only as store-bought Christmas cards from far-off places. They had long been strangers to Nora Bonesteel. She reckoned they had been strangers to their mother, too, after their college days, when jobs and new families took them out of Tennessee, diluting the kinship with city customs.

Neither Tessa nor Junior had understood why Geneva insisted on moving back to a hillside cottage outside Hamelin after Hervey Albright's heart gave out on him, but they had been secretly relieved. An ailing country mama had no place in their suburban lives. Their visits were seldom and perfunctory, but they were both here for the funeral, with their own teenagers in tow, all attired in dark, well-cut suits, and looking properly bereaved.

Nora Bonesteel supposed that they were doing the best they knew, but for Geneva Albright, it wouldn't have been enough. Geneva had been raised in the old ways, and she'd not be letting go of them at the end of sixty-eight years of living.

So Nora had turned up at Geneva's cottage early the morning of the funeral to offer her condolences. When the family got ready to leave for the church, Nora told them that she would stay behind in the cottage, reminding them that someone had to see to the food that neighbors would be bringing. There'd be people stopping by the house after the burying to pay their respects, and you had to be ready to offer them a deviled egg or a piece of pecan pie to show your hospitality on Geneva's behalf. She'd tend to all that, she told them. They weren't to worry.

When they had gone, Nora Bonesteel tidied the parlor and set the food and plates out on the table as she'd promised. She put the jar of honey away, so that no one would eat any without thinking. You didn't eat honey on the day of a funeral. That done, she turned to the more important duties of a death in the house. She stopped all the clocks in the cottage, and opened all the doors and windows. It was August; she could tell Junior and Tessa that she was airing things out before the company started arriving. She doubted if they would notice the tin cup of salt she set on the windowsill, and they might think that Geneva's silk scarf had fallen across her bedroom mirror by happenstance. She wouldn't tell them otherwise. They had been brought up as city children, so they weren't raised to know the old ways of attending to a death, but she reckoned Geneva would want her to do things right.

She'd have to tell the bees. Geneva Albright, who never outgrew her sweet tooth, had kept a hive of bees in the white wooden box at the end of the garden. When they were growing up, people called it a bee gum, and they fashioned homemade ones out of hollow logs for their domesticated bees. Now few people wanted the worry of bee gums, when store-bought honey was cheap and easy to come by.

Geneva's children wouldn't be wanting those bees, of course. They had been horrified that their mother would keep such dangerous creatures around the place, where one of the young people might get stung, but Geneva was too partial to her sourwood honey to care what her offspring thought, so the bee gum had stayed. Nora thought some member of the McCrory family might be willing to take the hive now. Long ago that old preacher Pharis McCrory had been a wonder for making friends with bees, and Nora thought the gift of bee lore might have been passed on to one of his descendants. She would have to ask her neighbors which McCrory might be glad to have Geneva Albright's bee hive.

But first she'd have to tell the bees about Geneva's passing, or else they would take flight, and no one would have them. She supposed that's why you didn't eat honey on the day of the funeral—so that the bees could mourn, too. Nora Bonesteel opened her knitting bag and took out the length of black ribbon she had tucked away there for the ritual. Holding it, she eased her way down the steep back steps and walked down the hill to the white box at the back fence. The mid-morning sun was hot on her neck, and the smell of ripe tomatoes reminded her that Geneva's garden had to be seen to as well. A few worker bees hovered in lazy circles over a patch of clover beyond the fence. They were still there, then. Nora walked slowly toward the hive, saying over and over as she went: "Stay pretty bees, and fly not hence. Geneva Albright is dead and gone."

She *was* gone. All through the sweeping out of the house, and all the rituals of mourning, Nora had no sense of Geneva as a lingering presence. She had felt alone in a house that was as empty as if it had never been lived in. That was good. It meant that Geneva had been ready to go, and that she'd got to wherever she was going. She'd had a long and mostly happy life, and when she'd died in her sleep one summer night, apparently she had left this world with no regrets. Nora was glad. It was good to see death as a release and a beginning, rather than as a tragedy. She saw too much of the sorrow that came with dying and not being ready to let go.

She could tell the bees that Geneva was gone, and that it was a glad time because she had gone somewhere else, and then the bees would stay. Nora didn't know why bees left if you didn't tell them of a death in the family, any more than she knew why the salt had to be set out or the windows open to the wind. But she did know that bees understood a lot more about some things than city people. She would offer her sympathy to Tessa and Junior, and all the help they wanted in seeing to the visitors, but there were some things she couldn't share with them, because they had lost the understanding of them.

As Nora Bonesteel tied the wisp of black ribbon to the nail on the lid of the white bee box, she wondered if there were any other deaths she ought to mention to the bees, or if those mattered. Perhaps the bees did not need to be told yet. The other deaths had not yet happened.

After leading Geneva Albright's funeral procession to Oakdale, Martha Ayers had parked the patrol car on one of the dirt side roads in the cemetery and directed traffic until the last of the cars was parked along the grass verge of the cemetery lane. As the service began, the undertaker walked over to thank her for providing the escort, and when he shook her hand, she was surprised to find a ten-dollar bill in the palm of her white glove. "It's procedure," he assured her with a somber smile.

Martha slid the note into her pocket and walked over to the canopied grave to join the mourners. She had barely known the Albright family, but she had seen Rita Pentland in the knot of people at the graveside, and she thought that this might be a good chance to see how Harm's ex-wife was bearing up. Martha had heard Hank the Yank's broadcast, making Rita's first marriage common knowledge to WHTN's listeners, and she wanted to reassure the woman that the sheriff's department was doing everything in its power to apprehend the fugitive. That wasn't strictly true, of course; Spencer and LeDonne treated the whole escape issue as an inside joke, but Martha thought it might not be so funny to a frightened woman who had gone on with her life, only to find herself haunted by an ex-husband who was supposed to be out of the picture forever.

Martha stood on the outer edge of the circle of mourners—though she wasn't sure "mourners" was the right term for this assembly. They were a dry-eyed bunch, mostly neighbors and fellow church members; even old Mrs. Albright's children seemed solemn but resigned to their aging parent's passing. It had been a quick, simple death; there were worse fates.

Martha wasn't close enough to catch the words of the graveside service, so she contented herself with looking around her. You could tell a lot about families from cemeteries, she thought. Or maybe you couldn't, unless you had known the people to begin with. The family plots of the Winslows and the Drapers had fine stone monuments, but no flowers on any of the graves. The difference was that the Winslows had all died out or moved away, whereas the Drapers had lost all their money two generations back, and blamed the folks under those fine tombstones for their present misfortunes. Lottie Jessup's grave had a full complement of plastic flowers adorning its flat bronze surface, but Martha knew for a fact that Lottie's daughter Frances put those flowers there, and that she and her mother had fought like two scalded cats until the day Lottie died, so it wasn't sentiment that decorated that grave— not unless you counted Frances's obsession with keeping up appearances. Maybe Frances thought that strangers would see that grave and think that someone had regretted Lottie's passing.

Martha looked at the marble angels from the twenties and the modern bronze plates set off by shrubbery, and wondered what she would choose to mark her final resting place. Not many people had the foresight to do their own choosing, though. Most of the time the headstone reflected the taste of those left behind. Many a marble angel was a monument to display the prosperity of a widower. The second wife, who outlived him, would end up with a more modest stone nearby. Martha wondered if family guilt could be expiated with expensive funerals.

At forty-five, Martha was still young enough to contemplate her own mortality in the abstract, so that the thought of her tombstone was a curiosity rather than a distasteful image. She didn't much care for bronze markers, but she didn't suppose she'd rate a six-foot marble angel, either. There was always cremation, which settled the matter cheaply and without a fuss, but that seemed like more oblivion than Martha wanted in an honorable death. She hadn't been to Sunday school in years, but her Baptist upbringing ensured that a corner of her mind would still picture Judgment Day as "that great getting-up in the morning," and she thought one ought to have a grave to get out of when the last trump sounded.

*Suppose I get shot in the line of duty,* she thought. She knew that the state police buried their own with great ceremony—with an honor guard of white-gloved officers, a twenty-one-gun salute, and all the trappings of a military funeral. She didn't suppose the Wake County Sheriff's Department could manage such splendor. In fact, if she didn't pick a slow day to be buried on, either Spencer or LeDonne would have to miss the funeral. She wondered if she ought to write down some kind of instructions for her surviving kin. Somebody ought to know that she liked headstones and hated plastic flowers. Now that she wore a badge, death seemed more than a remote possibility. She ought to write something down, just in case, and leave it where it would be found in case anything happened to her. In the passbook of her savings account, perhaps.

Someone brushed past Martha as she stood pondering her own mortality. She looked up to find that the graveside service was over, and people were beginning to wander back to their cars. Martha saw Rita Pentland near the casket, shaking hands with Laura Bruce, the minister's wife. Her husband, Euell, stood next to her, talking to Junior Albright, his jowls set in an appropriately solemn expression. He had abandoned his usual plaid sportcoat for the service, and wore a navy blue suit, which went well with his wife's beige coat-dress.

As they turned away from the graveside, Martha caught up with them. "Good afternoon, Mr. and Mrs. Pentland," she said. Martha knew Euell from his work on the county commission, but she felt that the occasion called for formality, and besides, she didn't like him well enough to want a first-name acquaintance.

Rita Pentland looked startled. "Oh!" she said. "It's you. Is there—" she looked around quickly "—any news?"

"Not yet," said Martha. "I just wanted to make sure that you were all right, and to tell you that we're doing everything we can."

Euell Pentland scowled. "Everything you can? Well, for my money you can start by arresting that lout who called the radio station last night and broadcast my wife's name to all creation."

Martha nodded. "Yes, sir, I heard that program."

"So did half the county," he replied. At his side, Rita twisted her hands, and looked as if she wanted to shrink out of sight. "It was invasion of privacy. What are you people going to do about it?"

Martha knew the answer. She also knew that the wisest response would be to refer the Pentlands to the sheriff himself, but she said, "Well, sir, we don't know who made the call. He didn't give his name. Even if we did know the caller's identity, what he said on the air was true, and probably pretty widely known already. I don't think there's anything we could charge him with, and even if we tried, you'd end up with even more publicity than you have now. I take it that publicity is the last thing you want."

Rita Pentland nodded. Her husband glowered.

"I'm sorry for your embarrassment," said Martha, speaking to Rita. "But we can't control the media, even if we'd like to sometimes. I just wanted to wish you well, and to say that I hope you aren't letting this frighten you too much."

"Do they know where he is?" asked Mrs. Pentland in little more than a whisper.

Martha shook her head. "I don't think there have been any reports concerning him. No sightings or anything."

"He's sixty-three years old," said Euell Pentland, reddening to his scalp line. "How hard can it be to catch him?"

"There's a lot of wilderness out there, Mr. Pentland," said Martha.

"My daughter—Chalarty—called me last night—" Rita Pentland began.

"Charlotte was terrified," her husband said, drowning out the twitter of her voice. "Terrified. She heard that program, and now she's afraid her mother will be killed. I want something done. Can we keep the public safe from convicts or can we not? Election time is coming."

"Yes, sir," said Martha, keeping her face expressionless. "Try not to worry, Mrs. Pentland. Well, I have to go now. I'm joining in the search out there." As soon as she heard herself say it, she knew it was true. Except that there was no search to join. Nobody had time to worry about the whereabouts of one addled old man lost in the woods, even if he might be a dangerous madman. But Rita Pentland was frightened, and Martha felt that protecting Rita had somehow become her responsibility. She had Joe's hand-me-down Glock pistol, and she could max out her credit card in Knoxville to buy the five-hundred-dollar Kevlar body armor. Then she'd be ready to conduct the one-officer manhunt for the escaped convict.

If she caught him singlehandedly, Spencer Arrowood couldn't say that she wasn't cut out to be a deputy. She'd see to it that she got enough publicity to keep her job. But she'd have to do her searching in her off-duty time, because the sheriff had made it plain that Harm was not anywhere on his list of departmental priorities, and LeDonne didn't seem to want the convict caught at all. Well, she wouldn't tell them what she was doing then. Let it be a surprise when she captured him.

"Hello again. Still doing research on the escaped convict?" This time Jeff McCullough recognized the awkward, balding man as the local talk show celebrity. It had been a slow morning for the newspaper, and because he was glad of the company, he offered Hank the Yank a mug of coffee and pulled up a chair. McCullough liked to time his coffee breaks to coincide with company.

Henry Kretzer accepted the coffee, spooning enough sugar into it to turn it to syrup. "Yes," he said, "I'm still sort of on the convict story. One thing seems to lead to another with that topic. Nora Bonesteel wasn't at home today, so I thought I'd come back and bother you. Thanks for the coffee."

"I give it away to anyone who'll drink it," smiled McCullough. "That lets out a lot of people. What can I do for you?"

"Did you happen to listen to Thursday night's show?"

The editor shook his head. "Had a school board meeting to cover. Sometimes I listen, though. It's great. How's Arvin doing?"

"He's as wild as ever. He put somebody up to calling in and requesting the 'song about the Japanese Embassy.' It took me three thirty-second commercials to figure out that they wanted me to play 'The House of the Rising Sun.'" There had been three studio technicians during Henry Kretzer's tenure at WHTN, none of them named Arvin. The latest one, a Chinese-American graduate student from East Tennessee State named Steve Huang, had at least inspired this latest tale, if he had not actually played the prank.

"You mentioned last night's show. Did anything interesting happen?"

"A couple of things. There was a bogus convict-sighting from some high school kids. But an old fellow who insisted on remaining anonymous phoned in, and he seemed to think that Harm Sorley did the community a service by killing his neighbor. From the way he talked, Claib Maggard sounded like the local villain instead of an upstanding civic leader. I'm still trying to make sense of it."

"He was before my time," said McCullough, "but I've never heard anyone mourn the loss of him. There may have been a few unfavorable remarks about him, but I don't remember anything specific."

"Nothing in the files?"

"I doubt if you'll find anything in the *Record* to enlighten you," said McCullough. "As I told you, we don't print much bad news."

"Printing!" said Hank the Yank, snapping his fingers. "That's another thing I wanted to ask you about. Do you print things here? Besides the newspaper, I mean?"

"You mean like stationery or yard-sale flyers? No. We don't even print the newspaper here. I take the paste-up to Johnson City once a week, and the print shop over there does it on their offset press. They do all the weeklies hereabouts. They also print posters, brochures, things like that. Why? Do you need something printed?"

Hank the Yank nodded. "Yes. I can't spend more than fifty bucks, because there's a chance that this Harm story will fizzle. They *might* catch him, but I doubt it. I'm gambling that they don't. Give me the address of the print shop."

Jeff McCullough fished out a business card from his desk drawers. "They give me extra cards for referrals," he said. "What do you need printed?"

Hank the Yank smiled. "Tune in next week," he said.

"Right now I have another question. One caller last night talked about the Forest Service as if it were a division of the SS. I couldn't figure it out. Are they bad guys around here or what?"

McCullough seemed to be cross-checking his mind for negative references to the Forest Service. Finally he shrugged. "Not that I know of. It doesn't ring a single bell with me. Maybe there was some incident a long time ago that the old-timers still remember. You might want to check with someone who knows the region from a historical perspective. To me, it's all county commissioners meetings and birth announcements."

"Who do you suggest?"

"Try East Tennessee State. Forestry department? No, I've got it! Appalachian Studies. Maybe you can get a professor to do a guest spot on your show."

"Maybe. Thanks for the help."

"Good luck. Hope your convict stays missing. I'd hate to see you do all this work for nothing."

"Even if they catch him, I'll probably keep looking into this. It's got me interested." The disc jockey smiled. "Wouldn't it be great if it turned out he was innocent?"

# CHAPTER
# 7

"Come back! this is the way!
  Come back! and walk herein!"
O may I harken and obey,
  And shun the paths of sin!

#586, "Gracious Redeemer," Charles Wesley

Tennessee Methodist Hymnal, 1885

"Afoot and light-hearted I take to the open road!" Jeremy Cobb proclaimed aloud to the encircling hills. Lines from Walt Whitman—he thought it an appropriate beginning to his journey. He wished he could remember what came next; something about a long brown path. He could stop and look it up in the paperback copy of *The Poems of Walt Whitman* he'd stowed in his backpack, but it would spoil the moment. Despite everyone's advice to travel light, Jeremy had tucked away several small volumes of literature—food for the soul—and a clothbound journal in which he intended to record his thoughts as he traveled.

He was on Highway 91 south of Damascus, Virginia, maps at hand, ready to follow the trail that would lead him south into North Carolina, and finally to the scene of an old tragedy in Mitchell County.

Early that morning he had made the hour-and-a-half drive down four-lane I-81 from Virginia Tech to the Glade Spring exit, and then he'd followed a two-lane blacktop the few miles south to the village of Damascus. *The road to Damascus.* That significance was not lost on him. This was to be a journey of revelations.

As instructed by the Tech hikers, he had parked his car at The Place, a shelter well known to experienced hikers in the region offering a free parking lot, patrolled by the local police. From here on, he would proceed on foot, finishing up in Hamelin, just over the Tennessee line from the Wylers' territory, in about six days. Despite Larkin's arguments, Jeremy had decided against hiking the well-traveled and well-marked Appalachian Trail, which he pronounced too civilized for his purposes. He would begin the Katie Wyler Memorial Journey on the Iron Mountain Trail, 17.8 miles through the Cherokee National Forest, heading more directly south toward Mitchell County. He would pick up other trails as he made his way down the mountain chain.

The first three miles of the hike followed Virginia 91 south, a tamer beginning than he would have liked, but he had no choice. His cue to leave the highway would be a stone and metal archway, marking Camp AHISTADI, a Methodist Church camp. When he entered the camp and crossed a footbridge, the trailhead would lie to his right. He was pleased to see that a rocky mountain stream paralleled the road. Perhaps that was one of the rivers Katie herself had followed. Was it a river, though, or only a creek? In Appalachia, you couldn't tell which was which by looking at the stream. "Rivers are judged on length, not width," Larkin had informed him. Anything that flows a hundred miles or more is considered a river, regardless of how narrow and shallow it looks.

He took a few tentative steps to begin the momentous journey, and found that he had difficulty keeping his balance. The pack was heavier than it had seemed in a living room try-on—of course, he may have added one or two items at the last minute—and perhaps he hadn't distributed the weight as evenly as he should have. He decided to stagger on a ways, though, instead of trying to fix it. It was important to him to get under way, before he lost the enthusiasm of the moment. After all, he told himself, the fifty pounds on his back in a Northface external-frame pack could be said to represent the burden of his overcivilized existence, an encumbrance that Katie Wyler did not have.

After all his talk to Larkin about authenticity and a scholar's scruples, he had finally caved in at the thought of a week in the wild, and he'd packed with a view to self-preservation and even comfort. His first packing effort had been a spartan load: kitchen matches; canteen and sleeping bag from the army surplus store; small first-aid kit; Swiss army knife; tin cup; and a Eureka Timberline A-frame tent, borrowed from one of Larkin's hiking buddies. That pack, with additional food, clothing, and odds and ends, would have weighed considerably less than his present load. He found, though, that contemplating a week of privation filled him with dismay; surely not the right spirit in which to seek enlightenment.

He decided to augment this meager survival kit with some of civilization's amenities: a wool blanket; candy bars; a water purification kit; a camp stove and extra fuel; some used paperbacks; and field guides to birds, flowers, minerals, and reptiles so that he could better understand his journey. Of course, he needed a Coleman lantern to read by. He threw in a dozen cans of chicken noodle soup and Dinty Moore beef stew, his

favorite apartment meals, and a can opener; a complete
selection of Backpacker's Pantry freeze-dried packaged
meals; and, in case this supply failed him, he added a
fiberglass fishing rod and some tackle, so that he could
catch his own food. He packed his travel kit of toilet
articles, including extra shampoo and deodorant; his
35mm camera and lenses; raingear; and perhaps a
dozen other necessities. Tied to the external frame of
his pack, along with the fishing rod, was the latest
amenity for the hiker: a solar shower, consisting of a
bag of silvery vinyl, which you filled with creek water
and hung in the sun. Several hours later, when the water was warm, you stood under the hose attachment,
and showered in civilized warmth, even in the forest
primeval. At least, that's what the packaging had led
him to believe. These additional necessities added at
least twenty pounds of extra weight to his original gear,
but he didn't see how he could do without any of it.

He did not mention these additions to Larkin, who
had displayed a concern for his safety that bordered
on insult. He would be fine. He was an educated man,
planning to hike in a "wilderness" dotted with villages.
He also didn't mention to Larkin that, despite everyone's
assurances that wild animals avoided humans and that
homicidal hillbillies were a Hollywood creation, he had
bought and packed a P-32—a six-round, .32-caliber
semiautomatic. He'd got it used for eighty dollars at the
Salem Civic Center Gun Show, but the dealer said that
it worked fine, and should be all he'd need in the way of
protection.

Jeremy doubted if Larkin would approve, but why
shouldn't he take what he liked? After all, if he became

discouraged and quit, he would accomplish nothing. Katie Wyler *would* have taken those things if she could have, he told himself. He had been a historian long enough to know that there was nothing noble about simpler times.

Jeremy felt sweat trickling into his eyebrows. It was hotter than he had expected. Already he wished he had worn shorts and a T-shirt, instead of jeans and his Cornell sweatshirt. He tried to remember just *where* in the pack his changes of clothing lay. His feet felt cramped and stifled in his thick socks and new work boots, but he didn't suppose he could dispense with them. This was snake country.

A car sped past him up the two-lane road, brushing him with hot air as it passed. He decided to keep walking. He wanted to get away from the road as soon as he could, and into the green darkness of the woods.

In a more contemplative mood, Henry Kretzer might have thought the drive up Ashe Mountain was beautiful, but in the heat of mid-September, he was more concerned with the well-being of his ancient Gremlin on the washboard road. The temperature gauge was edging above the middle mark, and he could feel the engine straining to make the grade. Perhaps on the way back down he could stop to admire the ripple of mountains, wreathed in the clouds that gave them their name: the Smokies.

It was a pretty enough place on postcards, but despite Hank the Yank's radio spiel about being lured here by the beauty of nature, Henry Kretzer was not an outdoorsman. He much preferred the electric cockpit of radio, where you made something come true by just describing it into a microphone. He liked the feeling of control, over the instruments, and over the listeners. After an ungainly adolescence as an outcast, he relished the new-found ability to make people like him by the sound of his voice. He still hadn't mastered the knack of doing it off-air, but at least for a few hours a night he had more popularity than he'd ever dared hope for. Only the prospect of keeping that enchantment could have lured him out onto a Tennessee back road, heading up a mountain into what he thought of as *Deliverance* country. Of course, they had their strange rural types in New England, too, but up there the violence of choice was suicide.

This rugged mountain road was a far cry from Johnson City, with its symphony and its trendy restaurants for the university crowd. He reminded himself that he was going to see an elderly lady, who was not likely to meet visitors on the porch with a shotgun. He hoped any of her neighbors whose property he might pass through en route were equally peaceable.

As he eased around the curve of the narrow road, he saw a bare outcropping of rock high up the mountain. "If this were New England, I'd swear that was the great stone face," he muttered, recognizing the profile of a man. That must be the rock formation that the locals called The Hangman. He couldn't remember why.

The needle on the temperature gauge had just reached the uppermost line of safety when he saw the mailbox twined with morning glory and labeled *Bonesteel* at the side of the road. He eased the car into an unfenced space on the right, in the shadow of an old barn, and scrambled out, armed with pen and note-book. Nora Bonesteel's white frame house sat in a mountain meadow a hundred yards downhill from the road. It seemed to perch on the edge of the hillside, separated from the valley below by streamers of clouds. As he stood at the gate looking out, he could see ridge after ridge of green mountains, fading to blue and pur-ple on the horizon. He wondered how anyone could live in such isolation. Or perhaps even the Johnson City apartment dwellers were equally remote from one another, but their surroundings allowed them to pre-tend otherwise. Here the solitude was undeniable. He shivered in the sunshine.

In the shadows of the front porch, someone moved, and Henry Kretzer realized that the old woman was watching him. He cranked up a smile, waved a greet-ing, and picked his way down the path to interview Nora Bonesteel. He wondered if she owned a radio, or if he'd have to explain who he was and why he wanted information about the county's past. It was too bad she didn't have a telephone. Hank the Yank was always more charming once removed.

"I know who you are," Nora Bonesteel told him when he reached the porch.

"You listen to the radio up here, do you?" he asked, a shade too loudly. "My real name is Henry Kretzer, but you go ahead and call me Hank." Perhaps he should have brought her something, like one of those Hank the Yank coffee mugs the station sometimes gave away as call-in prizes. Later he would ask himself *how* she knew who he was.

"I've just made fresh coffee," she said, holding open the screen door.

Ten minutes later, Henry Kretzer was sitting in Nora Bonesteel's parlor on the downslope side of the house, facing the meadow and, far below, the wide valley, a patchwork of green and gold seamed by a muddy river. The old woman had altered her ancient farmhouse by having most of the east wall replaced with floor-to-ceiling windows, so that the cozy furnishings of the sitting room were eclipsed by a vista of field and forest, with the blue mountains of North Carolina fading into cloud banks on the horizon.

Henry accepted the mug of steaming coffee, and told his hostess what a pretty view she had, but after a brief glance, he turned his back to the window and concentrated on the purpose of his visit. Nora Bonesteel certainly looked old enough to remember a three-decades-old murder, and she looked spry enough to be a reliable source, if she knew anything. She was a tall, spare woman who looked seventy in a well-preserved way. Her dark hair was peppered with gray, but her skin was smooth, and eyes shone a clear blue from the hollows of a fine-boned face. Something about her look of watchful composure told him that this was no simple country biddy to be jollied along. Henry Kretzer felt his palms sweat.

"I guess you wonder what I've come about," he said, taking another sip of coffee. Nora Bonesteel did not reply. "Okay, you probably know that I have a radio talk show on WHTN. Maybe you've heard the program?"

"Now and again."

"Well, a while back I started to do segments on an

escaped convict called Harm Sorley. He lived around here before he got sent to prison. He's supposed to have killed a prominent local man, Claib Maggard. I take call-ins on the show, and a couple of folks have called in to say that Claib Maggard was no great loss to the world, which is interesting. The trouble is, it was all a long time ago, and I can't find much information on the case. You know the *Hamelin Record:* good news or no news." He laughed nervously. "So the editor of the *Record* suggested that I come and see you. He thought you might be able to help." The speech had been more glib when he rehearsed it in the car, but he still managed to deliver most of it smoothly.

Nora Bonesteel was looking past him, at the meadow and the woods at the bottom of the slope beyond the fence line. "Why did he send you to me?" she asked.

"Well, because you're a lifelong resident of the county, and he seemed to think you had a good memory for local history." McCullough had also told him that Nora Bonesteel had a local reputation for being some sort of psychic, but Hank didn't want to get into any séance.

"A lot of folks remember Claib Maggard." Nora Bonesteel smiled. "You see, Mr.—Hank—around here we have families that have been here since Indian times, and so we tend to look on individuals as bearers of their family trademark, more or less."

"Isn't that a little judgmental?" He started to say *prejudiced,* but thought better of it.

"I don't know about judging," said Nora Bonesteel. "After fifty years and more, we just know how folks are, I guess. If you want to buy a good hunting dog, you go to a Jessup. You don't let your youngsters take up with a Harkryder, and as a rule you don't lend money to a Hollister. The Arrowoods are honest and book smart, but nary one of them has the knack for getting rich; never has had."

"Okay. So what about Harm Sorley, the escaped convict? Are the Sorleys all criminals?"

"No. It depends on what opportunities there are. The Sorleys tend to be brave and reckless, but that's not always a bad thing. It can take them different ways. Gary Sorley got a silver star in Vietnam—awarded posthumously. A couple of his uncles died in World War II, taking out machine-gun nests, or leading a charge against the enemy. Sometimes the world is glad to have Sorleys around, but a lot of other times, there just doesn't seem to be anything for them to do except make their own trouble and get caught in it."

"So you're saying that Harm was a warrior without a war, is that it?"

"He missed his war," said Nora Bonesteel. "He was too young for World War II, and he'd served his time and got out before Korea. I think he did some moonshining back in the fifties. The Sorleys most always had a still going somewhere back in the hills. But he was a good fiddle player, too, and he could sing a right smart tenor. Harm had a good measure of the Sorleys' reckless charm."

"Do you think he was guilty of murder?"

Nora Bonesteel looked away, studying the shifting cloud patterns against the dark hills. "I hope so," she said. "He's paid his life for it, hasn't he?"

Hank the Yank waited for her to say more, but she sipped her coffee and gazed out at the sun-dappled meadow. "Well, what about Claib Maggard?" he said at last. Why would people be so bitter about him after all these years? One caller said he'd rather—what was that colorful expression he used?—cross hell on a rotten log than to speak ill of Claib Maggard's killer. "What are the Maggards known for around here?"

"The Maggards . . ." Nora Bonesteel thought about it. "There's a phrase the Lord uses in the Book of Matthew: *fishers of men.* That about sums up the Maggards, in a terrible meaning of the phrase that Jesus didn't intend."

"You're not saying they were ministers?"

"No. More like human stockmen. They saw other people as fair game to be taken for their own use. They'd cheat their hired help, sell a spavined horse to a neighbor, or put up fences a few feet over the property line and hope the other fellow wouldn't notice. My daddy used to say that old Ira Maggard made his money during the War Between the States, selling spoiled beef to both armies."

"But I thought Claib was some kind of county official."

"It gave him power over people. He could find out who was having money troubles and see that their taxes went up accordingly. The Maggards bought a lot of their land at auctions for back taxes. As a local government man, he could also help decide whose land the new roads would take. People were afraid of him, but he prospered."

"I heard that he once worked with the Forest Service. One of my listeners seemed incensed about that. Does that make any sense to you?"

"My mother's cousin had a farm," said Nora Bonesteel, speaking slowly, as if she were remembering something long past. "It was over near Hampton, and it had been in the family since the late seventeen hundreds, when Samuel Tamson came over from Scotland, traveled from Pennsylvania through the Cumberlands to east Tennessee, and settled there. The land passed to his son, and grandson, and finally to Roy and Hannah Tamson about the time I was born. They paid the taxes on the land every year, but they never had bothered to get the deed changed out of Samuel Tamson's name. The land just passed from father to son, without anybody seeing the need for lawyers to be mixed up in it.

"In the 1930s the federal government got the idea of making the Cherokee National Forest in east Tennessee to preserve the wilderness, and in order to do that they had to acquire the land. Of course, people didn't want to sell. This was family land; it's who we were. But the government was bound and determined. One day two men showed up at the Tamsons' place, and one of them was a lawyer for the Forest Service. The other one was Claib Maggard."

"They wanted the land?"

Nora Bonesteel nodded. "They had a copy of the old deed, and they asked to speak to Samuel Tamson. When Roy explained that old Sam had been dead a century, and that no one had bothered to change the wording on the deed, the government men declared that land couldn't belong to a dead man, and that the government was taking it."

"Could they do that?"

"They tried. Then the Tamsons hired a lawyer from Elizabethton, and tried to fight the matter in court, but every time they argued a point, the government's lawyer brought up two new ones. Those lawyers finally said that the land described in the deed wasn't the same land that the farm was on, and the judge ruled in the government's favor."

"What happened to your cousins?"

"They got evicted. That was Claib Maggard's job, putting people off their land. Another thing he did was to bring antiques hunters around to the condemned property—for a percentage, that is. The antiquers would offer the evicted folks a dollar or two for a hand-carved cradle or an heirloom quilt. Priceless things. Mostly, the women didn't want to sell, even when Claib offered to throw in a new Sears bed or a store-bought coverlet to boot. Then he'd get the menfolk off alone and offer them a dollar and a pint of whiskey for the family treasures, and most often they sold. Hannah Tamson cried for a week when Claib Maggard took her mother's spinning wheel."

"Her husband sold it for whiskey?"

"No. Roy was a good man, but they had cut down some oak trees to have firewood for the winter, and Claib got the judge to fine Roy and his boys twenty-five dollars for destruction of government property. That was a month's salary for a laborer back then. He told them that they could either sell him their belongings cheap or go to jail. It wasn't much of a choice. Besides, they didn't have a home anymore. What good was furniture?"

"But surely the federal government paid the Tamsons for their land, or gave them another farm."

"No."

"Didn't anybody protest?"

"Who to?" asked Nora Bonesteel. "All the judges and congressmen worked for the government. Nobody cared if 'ignorant hillbillies,' like they called us, lost our land."

"But the government can't just take people's land for no reason, and leave them homeless!"

The old woman's smile was grim. "Mister," she said, "have you ever heard tell of Indians?"

"I could do a show about this," said Hank the Yank, full of journalistic knight errantry.

"It was too long ago," Nora Bonesteel told him. "All those families are scattered to the winds now. Some of them went to Cincinnati, some of them went to the coal camps, and some took to being sharecroppers on other people's land. Mountain people just keep keeping on. They are like the chestnut trees, crippled by the blight of civilization, but they still struggle to survive, best they can. They're not snuffed out entirely yet."

"And your cousins, Miz Bonesteel? What happened to them?"

Nora closed her eyes. "Roy shot himself. I saw it happen."

"You were there with him?"

"No," she said. She was looking out the window again. "I was about thirteen at the time, and I was down at the spring watching the salamanders, when the water seemed to get cloudy, and I saw Roy Tamson reflected in the water, like he was standing behind me on the bank. Then I saw him raise the pistol to his mouth, and I turned around to stop him, but there was nobody there. When I looked again at the water, it was clear again. That afternoon, when somebody came riding up to the house with the news, my Grandma Flossie and I were already baking the cakes to take to the burying."

Henry Kretzer shivered. "What an interesting story. Maybe you could come on my show sometime."

"I don't think so," said Nora Bonesteel.

"Well, you've been a great help. I can certainly see why people hated Claib Maggard. Did he take the Sorleys' land, too? Was that the reason for the murder?"

"The National Forest land was taken in the thirties," Nora Bonesteel reminded him. "Whoever killed Claib in 1968 must have had some other reason, don't you think?"

"Don't you *know*?" Even the police used psychics to solve crimes sometimes. He'd heard about it.

"No," she said. "I get a flash of a thing now and again, but it's not like watching the six o'clock news." She looked amused.

Time to go, he thought, wincing at her smile. Hank the Yank stood up. "Well, thanks for talking to me, ma'am. I guess I'll be going now, and—" He stopped. She was at it again. Watching those woods. "Miz Bonesteel, why do you keep looking out that window so intently?"

"I've been expecting somebody," said Nora Bonesteel. "Somebody I haven't seen lately."

* * *

Martha Ayers stifled a yawn, and tried to focus her eyes on the Forest Service map. She'd had a long day. She had ridden with the sheriff as usual, and he was seeing to it that she got experience in all facets of local law enforcement. They spent the morning operating a speed trap on the main highway, and he'd let her work the radar gun until he was sure she'd got the hang of it. He wrote the traffic tickets himself, though.

"It's always risky to approach a strange car," Spencer Arrowood had told her. "Even if it's just a traffic violation, you never know when you might encounter a violent individual wanted elsewhere for more serious offenses. Every year a lot of officers get shot trying to write a speeding ticket. So be careful. Watch how I do it. And don't get out of your car right away. Give them a minute or so to stew about it. That puts you in control."

They hadn't encountered any desperados on that traffic detail, but they nabbed a couple of early drunks, and one pompous civilian had claimed to be "good friends with the sheriff," apparently unaware that he had left the boundary of Unicoi County. They'd had a good laugh over that one.

After lunch—Martha insisted on Dent's so that she could have a salad—they ran a license check on the old road to Erwin. "Those county stickers on the windshield help pay your salary," Spencer reminded her. "And don't forget that a lot of drunks drive even after the court has taken away their licenses. This is a good way to catch them, before they hurt somebody."

The shift had ended at four, when LeDonne came on duty, so Martha went home to eat alone, and to do the laundry. She'd barely had a chance to say hello to him, because he had to start patrol. He asked how things went; she said fine; and then he was gone. He had seemed brusque with her lately, but Martha thought that was from worry. He'd get over it.

Now she was sitting at the kitchen table, with a half-eaten plate of leftover spaghetti congealing in front of the empty chair. She'd pushed it away, too tired to eat. The map was more important. Tomorrow she would have off-duty time during the daylight hours, and she meant to spend those hours searching the hills. She'd wear civilian clothes so as not to attract attention, but she intended to take her badge along in case she needed it. And the gun? Yes. Tennessee law permits any peace officer to carry a gun, on duty or not. "You're never completely off duty," Spencer Arrowood had told her. Well, she would take him at his word.

Early that morning, before they left the office on patrol, Martha had checked the communiques from other departments, and she knew that there had been no definite leads on the whereabouts of the fugitive. Some of the counties closer to Mountain City had reported a few petty thefts—a cabin broken into and food taken; a man's shirt and trousers missing from an outdoor clothesline—but whether Harm Sorley was responsible was merely conjecture. Martha had told Jennaleigh to get her a copy of any reports relating to the escaped convict, and the new dispatcher promised to see to it.

Martha looked at the tangle of lines on the map of the Cherokee National Forest, trying to decide which route she would take to get home if she were an aging convict. LeDonne insisted that the old man wasn't sane enough to make the journey, but Martha thought other-wise. He would remember the home of his youth, and that memory might be a strong pull for a man who wanted above all else to be safe. Besides, he had roamed those mountains all his life. If those memories were intact—and according to LeDonne they ought to be—he'd know how to find his way back. She'd bet anything that one way or another, Harm Sorley would make it back to Wake County. And when he did, she planned to be there.

Harm Sorley was walking down a two-lane road. He was wearing a flannel shirt whose sleeves slid down over his knuckles. He'd picked it up somewhere. He couldn't quite recall. The Lord provided. He carried a gunnysack containing an extra pair of trousers, some mismatched socks, five apples, some hickory nuts, and his mother's leather Bible. He was chewing on a birch twig, savoring the natural root-beer flavor as if it were chewing gum.

The man in the red car had asked him where he was going, and he'd said "Around Hamelin, Tennessee." The driver laughed at the way he'd said the name of the state: *Tenn*-essee, with the stress on the front of the word. That's how the old-timers say it, he'd said to Harm. I reckon you're from there, saying it like you do. But I'm going down past Morganton, which won't do you much good. I'm taking the back roads, though, for scenery. If I take you as far as Banner Elk and then let you off, you'll be farther along, though. Harm said that would suit him just fine.

The memories of that car ride and the friendly fat

driver were already sliding out of Harm's consciousness like drops of rain down an oily windshield. He was forgetting that the driver had asked him what took him so far from home. He had answered he was doing some logging in Carter County, and needed to get home.

Logging? said the driver. An old man like you?

Harm shrugged it off. The fat man offered him some kind of candy bar made out of cereal, and he ate it. Then he drifted into a light sleep, lulled by the smooth purr of the big red car. When it stopped, he woke up scared, seeing the fat, sweaty face of a stranger telling him to rise and shine. This is Banner Elk, said the man. The end of the line. You want to get off here.

He didn't argue. He saw that he was in a car, pulled off along the side of a road. He didn't know how he'd got there, or where he was, and he felt his heart race as he tried to find some clues to what was happening. The fat man wasn't wearing a uniform. He seemed to want Harm to get out. So he did. Harm gave a little wave as the car pulled away, leaving a puff of dust on the berm. And then the dust settled, the car was gone from sight, and his mind was clear again.

He walked quite a ways in the afternoon sun, seeing nothing he recognized. The mountains were spaced farther apart here than they were up home, and there were big glass buildings perched at funny angles all over the ridges. There was even a big square box of a building smack on the top of the tallest mountain. You could see it for miles in any direction, he reckoned. It was ugly. He wondered why somebody would do that to a beautiful mountain, but he thought perhaps it was a prison, and if it was, he would like to get sent there so he could look out at mountains.

Harm kept walking along the blacktop until he saw a road that led up a mountain. There were still a lot of houses around, and a sign said *Beech Mountain— Skiing*, but he could see forest farther up the slope, so he kept going.

He had walked another twenty minutes before he decided to rest. There were wooden houses with signs like *Real Estate* and *Tourist Information* up ahead, and he was becoming uneasy. He wandered away from the road and sat down under a tree beside the parking lot of a place that said *Ski Rental*. He was on his way somewhere. He was hungry. He reached into the sack, past the clothes and the Bible, and pulled out a Stayman apple. It was rock hard, not ripe yet. So it was earlier than October. Mid-September, maybe, he thought, looking at the full-leafed trees and the fields of goldenrod.

He might ought to ask the Lord what was best for him to do. Pharis always said that the Lord would guide you if you let Him, which Harm hadn't done very often, but now he was good and lost, and *Jesus, Savior, pilot me*. He threw away the apple core, and pulled out the well-worn Bible.

There was a card stuck in it. Harm pulled it out, and held it at arm's length in the sunlight, squinting to read the fine print. It was an identity card for the Tennessee prison system. He was a convict. Again the fear gripped him, and he looked down, as if expecting to find a shackle on his leg. But he was in strange country on a mountain road that was more crowded with buildings than a mountain road ought to be. If he was a hunted man, which seemed likely, he would need more solitude. He slid the card back into the book, and placed his palm on the cover. "Help me, Lord," said Harm Sorley. "I am lost in the wilderness."

With his eyes shut, he opened the book, and pointed to a verse. It was the seventy-eighth Psalm, verse 54: *And he brought them to the border of his sanctuary, even to his mountain, which his right hand had purchased.*

He looked up at the cluster of buildings, which proclaimed itself to be *Beech Mountain—Eastern America's Highest Community.* He and the Lord appeared to have different ideas about what constituted a sanctuary. But then he looked across the road, and saw two stone walls flanking an entranceway, and a big sign set up in the middle on a stone-walled flower bed: *Emerald Mountain,* and beyond that there was a little building with windows, like a sentry box, but no one was in it. When Harm stood up to examine it further, he noticed that the wall and the flower box seemed set up in the middle of nowhere. The pavement ended a few yards past the guardpost, and a graveled road led away into tall trees. He couldn't see any signs of habitation. That was good. He stuffed the Bible back into his gunnysack, and crossed the road. A sign on the left stone wall said *The Oz Road,* but there was nothing ahead except forest.

He figured that this was what the Lord meant by sanctuary, this Oz place. He shouldered his gunnysack and began to follow the graveled dirt road.

* * *

Joe LeDonne had finished his shift and set the department phone line to forward calls to the neighboring county until morning, but he didn't feel like going home. He was tired, no doubt about that, but the thought of Martha waiting up for him made him wish he had somewhere else to go.

It wasn't that he didn't care about Martha, it was just that she would want to talk, and while he had once enjoyed unwinding at the end of the day with coffee and conversation, things had been different lately. He used to regale Martha with tales of speeders stopped, or trailer-park disputes he had arbitrated, and she would listen in respectful silence, or murmur that she hoped he was careful. Now, she was apt to launch into an account of *her* day's adventures, and she met most of his responses with, "I know what you mean," followed by a rehash of one of her own encounters with drunks or speeders. Her new attitude made him edgy. He couldn't relax when he was edgy.

It was nearly midnight when he pulled into the parking lot of the Mockingbird Inn. It was a pretty quiet beer joint most of the time, not like the strip-club drug hangouts on Knoxville's Clinton Highway. Going to one of those dives would just be another duty shift, but he knew most of the regulars in Hamelin's bars, and they knew him. There wouldn't be any trouble tonight.

If he drank one beer, maybe he could unwind enough to go home, and if he took long enough, maybe Martha would be asleep by the time he got there. She was on day shift again tomorrow.

The place was nearly empty, as he'd expected on a weeknight. A couple of old boys without jobs nursed beers at the counter while they watched a late-night show on the wall-mounted color set above the glassware shelf. LeDonne took the booth in the corner, so he wouldn't have to make small talk with them. He signaled the waitress, mouthed the word *beer*, and settled back to wait for it. He was almost tired enough to sleep here. He closed his eyes, willing his back muscles to unknot.

"Rough night, huh?" Crystal Stanley, the Mockingbird's younger waitress, was eyeing him sympathetically. She set a mug of Coors in front of him. LeDonne, who had developed a taste for dark, strong beer in the army, would have preferred Bass or Guinness, but try finding that this side of Knoxville. At least it was cold.

"It wasn't too bad," LeDonne told her. "Business as usual, even for the people I wrote citations to. They had all been stopped for speeding before."

"How could you tell?"

"Because none of them tried to tell me what a saint he was. They all argued, of course, but none of that *Officer, never in my life have I received a ticket* crap." He grinned. "Of course, I ran a license check, so I knew anyhow." He looked up at her: maybe twenty-four, blond hair showing mousey-brown at the roots, and a face that might be pretty without that sullen, wary expression. It occurred to him that Crystal had probably had a rough night, too. Maybe a lot of them. She wasn't a hooker, though. LeDonne made it his business to know things like that in Wake County.

"How about you?" he asked her. "Everything go all right here?"

She shrugged. "It was crowded during the game, but

about eleven business slacked off. I shouldn't be glad, 'cause I need the tips, but my feet sure hurt."

"Why don't you sit down? Those guys at the bar look like they've had enough, anyhow."

"Okay, if you want me to," said Crystal, glancing back at the loafers on the stools. She eased into the pine booth opposite the deputy. "Maybe I can stay for a couple of minutes."

LeDonne sipped his beer. "Sure," he said. "Why not? I'm in no hurry."

# CHAPTER
# 8

Before the hills in order stood,
    Or earth received her frame,
From everlasting thou art God,
    To endless years the same.

#667, "O God, Our Help in Ages Past," Isaac Watts

Tennessee Methodist Hymnal, 1885

More than two thousand years ago, in an Appalachia called the Alps, the ancestors of the mountain people had forged a hearth culture that spread in the succeeding centuries to other mountain ranges throughout Europe. They settled in Germany, Scotland, Ireland, Wales, and Cornwall, always seeking high ground wherever they wandered. Always the flatlanders thought them strange and backward, because they'd rather live poor and free in the beauty of mountains than grow prosperous in the fertile lowlands or the sprawling cities. There's a word for *hillbilly* in the language of every country with highlands—even in Vietnam, where it's the Hmong who are thought a bit peculiar by their plains-dwelling countrymen.

Some of Europe's long-lost mountain cousins migrated from Ireland, Germany, Wales, Scotland, and Cornwall to seek new lives and high mountains in the New World. When they met up again in the eighteenth-century culture stew that was the American frontier, they didn't know they were kin. Scholars who studied culture came later and pointed out the family resemblances: a superstition, a fiddle tune, or an old quilt pattern traced the family tree back across the ocean to the ancient tribe of Celts.

Mountains, too, have a lineage. That spine of towering rocks that rises in Georgia and ends with the sea in Nova Scotia, the Appalachian Mountains have long-lost kinfolk on the other side of the Atlantic. The bloodline that marks that kinship is a vein of a green mineral called serpentine that snakes an intermittent trail from Georgia to Newfoundland, and then appears again in the western extremity of the Caldonides in Ireland. From there the traces stretch though Scotland, Wales, and England, turning northward through the Shetland Islands, with a branch touching Greenland, and another line crossing Scandinavia to end in the Arctic Circle. The Precambrian rocks of Newfoundland and those of the Caldonides in Ireland match: once, so many millions of years ago that not even fish existed yet, these mountains were together. The soapstone bowls carved by America's eastern Indians and the steatite spindle whorls used by Viking weavers were talc-stone drops of mountain blood from kindred hills.

Perhaps when the pioneer descendants of those ancient Celts halted their covered wagons, looked up at the green mountains of Appalachia and felt at home, they were more right than they knew.

As she drove along the winding mountain road, Charlotte Pentland glanced at her mother, who was staring intently out her window at the alternating woods and fields, punctuated by rock cuts through the ridges, where the road builders had dynamited their way from one valley to the next. She wondered what her mother was seeing—a landscape for old memories, perhaps? It was not what she saw.

Charlotte's years as a geology major had changed the face of every landscape for her. She felt like a Cherokee tracking game by signs on a trail. The mountains left their own traces through unimaginable stretches of time. Now when she drove through a narrow pass between the mountains, she looked for fault lines, the shifts in the varying layers of rock. Here a thrust fault had moved a layer of Chilhowee sandstone over a dark band of micaceous shale; there a steep hillside of apple trees indicated a surface soil of the Unaka variety, dark brownish loam two feet deep over a bedrock of either gneiss or granite. Which would it be in this case?

"Gneiss," Charlotte guessed aloud.

"Yes," said her mother, smiling. "I do like a nice tart apple come fall. My grandaddy had an orchard of Jonathans that was the pride of the county for apple-pie making. One of those Jonathan pies took the blue ribbon every year at the fair. Those trees are bearing well this year."

Charlotte Pentland did not explain that *gneiss* was the metamorphic rock underlying the sandstone in the eastern part of the county. She didn't want to see the hurt look that invariably came to her mother's face after such misunderstandings. "Well, I never had much chance to get educated," Rita Pentland would say. "But it's real good that you know stuff like that, Chalarty." Sometimes, though, she did try to explain things to her mother in simple terms, just so there would be something to talk about. She didn't want to discuss the drive they were now taking, and she understood even less about her mother's motives than her mother understood about the Honaker Dolomite Formation. She tried to think of something to tell her about the land.

"These are some of the oldest rocks in the entire region," said Charlotte.

"All rocks are old," said Rita, still studying the landscape.

"Yes, compared to us, but the basement complex here in eastern Wake County—that means the rocks underneath everything else—started out as deposits of shale and sandstone nearly a *billion* years ago."

"Started out as shale? I thought a rock stayed a rock. What are they now?"

Charlotte had it by heart. "Rocks that change are called metamorphic. Heat and pressure transform them over the years. Around here some ancient deposits of sandstone or shale were changed over time into rocks called schist and gneiss. Gneiss, with a G; I think it's German. And then there's some gabbro and granite, which are igneous, and they trickled through the other rocks as molten lava and then hardened when they cooled."

"We had some Germans living up in Brummett's Cove when I was a young'un," Rita said. "Folks called them Dunkards."

"You can see black gabbro and banded gneiss on the top of Roan Mountain." Charlotte didn't want to be drawn into a conversation about family memories. "Now, look at the red-brown rock on your side of the road, up the hill. That's the Erwin Formation of Chilhowee sandstone. It's deposited right on top of the

Precambrian Ocoee rocks, which are so old they don't contain any fossils."

"Deposited?" murmured Rita, catching a word.

"Yes, Mama. The Chilhowee sandstone started out as sand in the Cambrian Age, 550 million years ago, when this land was covered by a warm, shallow ocean. You can find fossils in it—things like trilobites, which don't even exist anymore."

"Just because something is dead doesn't mean it doesn't exist. I recall—"

"Good point," said Charlotte quickly, forestalling another family story. "I had a fossilized one on my desk at the university. I should have said that there are no *live* ones, and there haven't been for millions of years. But you do find their remains as fossils."

"Your dad used to find arrowheads every time he tilled the garden for spring planting."

"Arrowheads are only a couple of hundred years old," said Charlotte, fighting the urge to say what had first come into her mind: *Which dad?* "You know what made these mountains, Mama? Two hundred and fifty million years ago, two continents crashed into each other, creating a thrust fault that moved up to seventy miles—"

"I wonder where the family was then," mused Rita. "Our ancestors, I mean. Back in Europe?"

"Our part of Europe was *here*," said Charlotte. "It was one of those continents I told you about that bumped into one another."

"We-ell," said Rita. "I reckon they could have just stepped off right then, and saved their great-grand-young'uns the trouble of taking the boat."

Charlotte Pentland sighed. She didn't want to have to explain *what* her mother's beloved "ancestors" might have consisted of in that far-off Cambrian age. That was a few million years before *fish* existed, much less dinosaurs, mammals, or the Scotch-Irish forebears her mother considered the first rung on their evolutionary ladder. Why didn't the ancestors just get on when the continents touched? What a hoot. She could tell it back at the department, if she didn't let on that it was her mother who posed the question.

"Look, Mama, are you sure you want to spend the afternoon doing this?" she asked. "We could drive over to the Lost Sea and take the tour. I could tell you more about those caves than all the guides put together."

"No, thank you, Chalarty. I've got it set in my mind to go up here, and it has to be done."

"Are you sure you'll be able to find the right road?" Charlotte asked. "It's been a long time since you've been up here, hasn't it?"

"I used to go now and again when you were little," her mother replied. "I wasn't used to living in town back then, and I missed the woods. I remember one time I was up there on an overcast day, and I saw a doe looking at me from the laurel thickets. Lord, I sat down on a rock and cried, I was so glad to see her. She looked so lovely, and so lost. I wondered if hunters had taken her man, too."

Charlotte glanced at her. *Too?*

"I was missing your daddy something awful back then. People said it served me right for marrying when the haw bushes were in bloom. Just asking for bad luck, they said, but I didn't ever see things between me and him that way. I just couldn't believe he was gone."

"Well, he was," said Charlotte, hoping to dam this unpleasant flood of recollections. "Maybe you were better off with him gone. He might have murdered *you*."

"No." Rita Pentland shook her head. "I don't say that Harm was a saint. Poor people mostly can't afford to be. And the Sorleys were bold—they were bad to cross. He had been arrested a couple of times for fighting and blockading—"

"For what?"

"Moonshining. At least, that's what the government calls it. It means you were selling whiskey without giving the government their percentage of the profit even though you've done all the work. I guess they'd rather have you get on welfare, so they can spit on you."

Charlotte shivered. These were strange words to be coming from her mother, that timid, colorless woman with her perfectly styled helmet of hair, and her tasteful beige life. Perhaps she shouldn't have agreed to this afternoon drive into the hills. It seemed to be stirring up bad memories and dangerous notions in the older woman's mind. She seemed to have forgotten how lucky they were to have escaped from the mountain poverty, and how grateful they were for the suburban security of Hamelin and Euell Pentland. Charlotte wondered if she should speak to the family doctor about it.

"But Harm was a believer in the Word of God," Rita was saying.

"What about *Thou shalt not kill?*"

"That was between him and Claib Maggard. It was his business, but I wouldn't say that Claib Maggard was an honest man. He was the one that put your grandparents off their farm for the national forest when your daddy was a young'un, so there was bitter blood between them to start with. Now Claib, he wasn't much on fighting, 'cause he'd rather go sneaking to the law to do his dirty business for him, but if your daddy did kill him, there was good reason. He had a temper when he felt he'd been cheated, but I never saw no meanness in him."

"Then why did he do it?"

"I hadn't thought about any of it in years," said Rita slowly. "I'm not rightly sure I ever did know. I remember our cow died that day. Your daddy said he was going off to talk to Maggard about it, but I was busy tending to you, so I didn't pay much attention. You had some kind of stomach flu. Then after the killing, I was too grieved to care."

"What did they say at the trial?"

Rita Pentland shook her head. "Court-appointed lawyer said he couldn't afford to spend a lot of time on a foregone conclusion. Just pleaded your daddy guilty, and asked for a verdict of unpremeditated murder. They convicted him of first degree, though. Nobody ever went into the whys of the matter. And by then, when they locked him away forever, it didn't make no never mind to me, either."

"Yes. You were better off without him." Charlotte had seen awkward, backwoods mountain girls from sixty-student high schools, trying to fit in at the university. She was glad she hadn't grown up to be one of them.

"He did the best he could for us. He was a good daddy to you."

"I don't remember."

"Well, he was. He carved you that cherrywood rabbit you used to keep on your bedroom shelf. And every night at bedtime, he'd carry you off to your cot, and he'd say, 'It's time to hit the—' "

"The Goodnight-Loving Trail," murmured Charlotte. The phrase was so much a part of her that she still thought it to herself sometimes at night when she was very tired, but she couldn't remember who used to say it. Years later, she had been surprised to learn that the Goodnight-Loving Trail was the route of a Texas cattle drive. She supposed that her dad had been a reader of westerns.

"You and him used to sit down by the creek together, trying to catch tadpoles," Rita was saying. "He taught you to sing 'She'll Be Comin' Round the Mountain When She Comes.' "

*She'll be comin' round the mountain . . . We will kill the old red rooster when she comes . . .* Charlotte used to wonder who "she" was, and why the singers were so glad to see her. A long lost daughter, perhaps? When she was four, she had imagined herself getting lost in the woods, and being met with such joy at her homecoming. Now she supposed she saw herself with a Ph.D., returning from far-off universities in academic triumph. *She'll be riding six white horses when she comes.*

It was still a favorite tune of hers. But when had she learned the old song? Charlotte tried to picture herself as a toddler, singing those words. Where was she? Who was with her? But the image would not take shape. She supposed it must have been her real father who taught her the song, though. Euell Pentland said that folk songs and handicrafts were embarrassing reminders of the region's uncouth past. His music of choice was Lawrence Welk and easy listening. She had never heard him sing.

"Mamma, why do you want to go back to the old farm? Are you afraid? You don't think he's hiding out there, do you?"

Rita Pentland was silent for so long that Charlotte began to wish she wouldn't answer, but finally she said, "Chalarty, sometimes you just have to go look at the past before you can figure out where you're going."

Jeremy Cobb wondered how many miles he had come. It was not yet dark, but his feet were radiating pain waves, and a determined squadron of gnats had been flying in formation around his face for what seemed like hours. He decided to pitch his tent and light a campfire, in hopes of driving them away with the smoke.

He had found the stone and wrought-iron archway to Camp AHISTADI without difficulty. The bridge leading to the Iron Mountain Trail was within sight of the road, giving him a feeling of trail mastery that was perhaps unwarranted, but was reassuring nonetheless.

From there it was 12.4 miles to Sandy Gap, which wasn't even on his Tennessee highway map, but his trail directions placed it somewhere between Shady Valley and Mountain City. He located both of those along Highway 421, surmised that they were not so much towns as wide places in the road, and supposed he would emerge somewhere in between them. For now, he wanted to concentrate on the immediate twelve-mile stretch of wilderness.

He walked along level ground into a forest of towering hardwood trees, protected from harsh winters by the encircling mountains. Here the trail paralleled another stream. Half an hour later, as he was climbing a steep ridge, he noticed that the trees were now pines. He tried to clear his mind of all concerns of the present century, and to see the woodland as Katie might have looked at it, but the gnats droning around his head made reverie impossible, and besides, he was beginning to itch from the sweat. He kept walking, and presently his determination was rewarded when the gnats abandoned him, and he reached an outcropping of rock on the ridge that opened onto a panoramic view of green pastures and rolling hills to the east. Jeremy eased off his pack, and sat down on a boulder to steep himself in the silence and sunlight of the mountainside. It was beautiful country, still wild enough in places to convince a traveler that he could be in some other century.

Surely there must have been vistas like this one when Katie Wyler journeyed through these hills. He wondered if she'd had the strength and the sensibility to feel the joy in such a display of nature. Or would she have felt only despair that there was no cabin within sight, no sign of people who could help her? Would she have been too footsore and knotted with hunger to care for pretty scenery? Jeremy liked to think of her standing on this lonely mountaintop, looking out on the glorious world, and giving thanks to God for having brought her safely thus far. She still had a long way to go, though—at least fifty more miles of mountain fastness lay between here and Mitchell County. That meant that he had a long way to go as well, and he'd better get moving if he wanted to cover even five miles before dark.

It was odd how long it took to get anywhere on a trail. He had timed himself walking the one-mile seniors lap in the local mall, and he could manage it in just under twenty minutes. Here he could walk for twenty minutes and hardly be out of sight of where he'd started. Of course, the pack was a hindrance, both in weight and balance, so he could not expect to equal his mile-time at New River Valley Mall. Not at first, anyhow. He was sure his progress would improve as he went along and became accustomed to the terrain.

As long as he had stopped, though, he might as well take off the hot sweatshirt and stow it in the backpack. He could dig out the camera, too. This sprawling valley was worth recording on film. He peeled off the sweatshirt, which was living up to its name, and began to plow through the contents of the backpack in search of useful items that might come to hand while he worked his way down to the camera. He needed to rearrange things anyhow. One of the beef stew cans kept thunking against his back every time he leaned on a tree to rest. Oblivious now to the view, Jeremy Cobb sat on the flat rock ledge with his pack balanced between his outstretched legs, examining his supplies. He spent a happy quarter of an hour chewing on a granola bar, and contemplating his camping gear. He tried to pull all the books out at once, and found they were too heavy to be lifted with one hand. Interesting. He hadn't noticed that when he'd packed them. He set them beside him, and extracted his camera from the nearly empty canvas.

Now he would photograph the sunlit valley. Perhaps, if the shot turned out well, he could have it made into a slide to use in future lectures about Katie. But when he peered again at the landscape through the viewfinder, he saw that the valley was no longer bright. Towering black clouds were rolling into view from the southwest, blocking the afternoon sun. Around him, the air thickened. The wind picked up, turning up the silvery undersides of the leaves, in anticipation of the coming downpour.

Jeremy realized that a rocky overlook was not the place one wanted to be in a thunderstorm. As the cool wind swirled around him, chilling his sweat-soaked skin, he began to stuff his belongings back into the pack. He decided to leave the tent until last, thinking that the storm might be a good sign to stop for the day. He didn't want to be crossing open ridges while lightning played about his head. Thunder rumbled across the valley, as if in answer to his thoughts.

He began to shove the supplies in faster, without bothering about logical order or conservation of space. As the first droplets of rain pelted his cheeks, he found that it was just as well he hadn't planned to repack the tent, because there wasn't room for it. The tent and a stack of field guides and paperbacks lay on the ground, next to the bulging canvas. His haphazard packing had used more space than the original careful loading of the pack, which had taken him two hours back at his apartment. He would have to rearrange the objects later, once he had set up camp for the night, but his primary concern was getting off the open ridge before the storm struck with full force. He slipped his arms inside the canvas straps and struggled to balance the pack. Since he wasn't going far to camp, he could carry the tent.

As Jeremy stood up, tottering, feeling like a turtle on its back, he noticed the pile of books at his feet. He could wrap them in the tent, he supposed. The raindrops were falling faster now. He tried stooping to pick up the books, found that didn't work, and at last he bent his knees until he reached the ground, and felt for the books with an outstretched hand. The first one he grasped was *The Collected Poems of Walt Whitman*. Jeremy put it back down. He didn't feel like celebrating the open road anymore.

He stuffed the two smaller books into the tent wrappings, rose to his feet, and staggered down the mountain to make camp in the rain.


He was walking on a two-lane asphalt road, heading west. Harm Sorley had left the land of Oz, a failed theme park that had come and gone on Beech Mountain without his ever being aware of it. Now he did not even remember having been there, but a newly built glass and cedar house near the summit had a broken French window, and his gunnysack contained cookies, cheese and crackers, and two bottles of Scotch. The house was new and expensive, with huge windows overlooking the valley, and gleaming hardwood floors.

Chinese porcelain sparkled on the sideboard, and there was a crystal chandelier above the dining room table.

Harm hadn't known where he was, but he knew absolutely that he didn't belong there, and never had. The fancy furnishings didn't interest him much, but he knew that he was hungry, and that there would be food somewhere in this fine place. The Lord had led him here for provisions.

He found the bathroom first, and took a long hot shower with some scented soap he found in a little basket beside the marble sink. The steamy water felt good on his aching muscles, and he'd scrubbed the dirt and sweat from his legs and back without wondering how he had come to be so dirty. He had forgotten to hurry.

The pants and shirts in the adjoining bedroom did not fit him. The waistband gaped around his scrawny middle, and the shirts enveloped him, so he put his old clothes back on, but he added a navy cable-knit sweater from the closet shelf. He remembered being cold sometime or other, and he thought the sweater would come in handy.

He had rummaged through the kitchen cabinets until he had a sackful of supplies, and then he'd eaten cheese and cold cuts and French bread out of the refrigerator, washing it down with stale club soda. He was just beginning to feel sleepy from an unaccustomed full stomach when the man came in. He wasn't any younger than Harm, but he was red-faced and stout, and his eyes behind gold-framed bifocals were close-set and piggy. After the first shock of seeing an intruder in his kitchen, the man had looked triumphant. He stood in the kitchen doorway, arms folded, sneering at the scraggly man feasting at his chrome and glass table. He didn't see anything to be afraid of, just an old thieving drunk after some chow. Really, there were drawbacks to rural mountain retreats, despite the cool summers and the postcard vistas. But the neighborhood fauna were a nuisance. If it wasn't the deer in the tomato plants, or the raccoons in the garbage pails, it was the local riffraff.

He had said all this to Harm, working his way into self-righteous anger, while Harm sat staring up at him, chewing bread and cheese, and wondering if he had ever seen this man before. He wanted to be away from the man's shouting, and his leering face, but as he stood up to go, the man said, "Oh, no, you don't! You dirty hillbilly! You're going to wait right here for the police, and you're going to pay for my window out of your stinking welfare check! Dirty hillbilly!"

The word *police* and the sneering tone in the man's voice brought back feelings if not memories. Harm had the sense that sometime he had heard someone shout at him like that, and look at him with contempt. He felt his muscles tense and his jaw tighten as he looked at the roaring stranger, and he wondered if he ought to recognize this face. Above all, he wanted the shouting to stop. He wanted to wipe the sneering hatred from that fat red face.

When the man shouted "Police!" again, and tried to push past him to get to the kitchen wall phone, Harm picked up the glass club soda bottle and hit the man on the top of the head. It was like christening a ship—he'd seen it in a newsreel once at a Saturday matinee. Lash Larue it had been. Funny, how he could remember the detail of that black and white western, but he couldn't remember a thing about this morning.

The bottle shattered, and he felt his hand vibrate with the shock of the blow. The man went facedown in a heap, topped with blood, bubbly water, and glass splinters. He sprawled on the kitchen floor, without even a moan, but his hand twitched convulsively, perhaps still reaching for the telephone. Harm almost knelt down to help the man, but then he remembered about the police. The man hadn't understood that the Lord had meant for him to have the food. The police wouldn't understand, either. He walked over him to pick up the gunnysack, where he had stashed cookies, cheese, and whiskey. The red-faced man was forgotten before Harm reached the front door.

He had remembered to hurry away after taking the supplies, and when that memory slid out of his consciousness, he kept on hurrying anyhow, out of some vague notion that he wanted to be elsewhere. He was uneasy in these strange hills with too many houses and too few trees. One hill had telephone poles set in pairs all the way to the top, and little chairs suspended on cables between them. It was a strange land.

He wished he could get back home, where the valleys were close together, and the hills were so thick with oak and maple that you could hardly see from one ridge to the next. Folks lived in little frame houses on bottomland, not in glass cages up the mountain. Somewhere over that fold of mountains or the one after, Pharis McCrory would be tending his bees, or saying the blessing over a dinner of boiled beef, pinto beans, and stewed tomatoes. His sons would be out on the porch making fiddle music, and Aunt Bonnie's latest quilt would be draped over her chair, awaiting its final stitching. Where was that valley, the one that was home? If he just kept going, he would find it. If he hiked on a little farther.

When he finally got tired of walking, he left the roadway and ambled across a pasture, still carrying the heavy gunnysack. He leaned back against an oak tree, feeling unaccountably sad, as if he'd awakened from a nightmare that he couldn't quite remember. Only the feelings came with him into the waking state. He thought he might have had a run-in with Claib Maggard, but he couldn't recall any details. He thought he might rest for a while and then head out into the woods a ways.

*"Will there be any boxcars in heaven?* Good evening, neighbors. This is Hank the Yank coming at you. We're taking calls now to see if any of you folks recognized the voice singing that last tune. It's a real oldie. Arvin already guessed Vice-President Al Gore, and he is in the right state—at least I think he is; what do I know?—but he's in the wrong half of the century. You're bound to guess better than that. So if you don't mind giving your age away for a WHTN coffee mug, then you give us a call."

There were no lights yet on the switchboard. Must be a younger crowd tonight, thought Hank. Better think up something else to say while they were trying to remember somebody older than Merle Haggard. "You know, I like that song," he told the listeners. "There's a note of sadness to it when the old boy asks if there'll be any boxcars in heaven, and if some angelic railroad conductor will tell him that he cannot ride—it makes you think, doesn't it, about the poor, the homeless, and those sad folks who've made such a mess of life that they aren't even sure they'll be welcome in the Here-after.

"It made me think of Wake County's favorite felon— Harm Sorley. Two weeks out and homeward bound. Harm, our hearts are with you. In fact, in the spirit of public service, WHTN, the voice of country music in Hamelin, Tennessee, is setting up the Harm Sorley Legal Defense Fund. We don't reckon he'll need it, 'cause they haven't caught him yet, but we want to prepare for every contingency. We may not raise enough to hire a lawyer, but at least we can get old Harm a new suit for the courtroom. Or, if they don't catch him, maybe we could buy him a ticket to Bolivia. Isn't that where Butch Cassidy and the Sundance Kid ended up?

"In exchange for your generous donations to the Harm Sorley Legal Defense Fund, WHTN is offering bumper stickers that say *Don't Shoot—It Might Be Harm!* as a warning to all the nervous hunters and homeowners in our listening area. And we're taking orders for *Harm Sorley Legal Defense Fund* T-shirts, available in extra-large only. Arvin thinks we ought to print up some that say *Harm: The Vanishing American*. You can state your preference when you call. Or think up a better slogan than ours. That shouldn't be hard.

"In addition to our merchandising efforts, we will also be playing a special selection of tunes dedicated to our elusive and elderly Mr. Sorley, beginning with an old folk tune sung by North Carolina's own Betty

Smith, a world-class artist on the dulcimer, from her album *For My Friends of Song*. Here she plays and sings 'The Darby Ram,' also known in the music circles in my neck of the woods as 'Didn't He Ramble?' This one's for you, Harm."

Hank the Yank cued the tape. The audience seemed to like the convict story, judging by the volume of calls. Bumper stickers were going briskly. He'd even seen a few displayed on pickups around town. Harm's success as a folk hero probably owed much to the fact that his crime seemed remote to the majority of listeners; besides, good citizens and roughnecks alike seemed charmed by the idea that an ancient mountaineer could outsmart the high-tech, humorless Tennessee prison system. They had declined Hank's offer of *Harm* bumper stickers for the fleet of prison vehicles at the Northeast Correctional Center.

He wished he could persuade Sheriff Spencer Arrowood to come on the program, but when he called to invite him, the sheriff had said that the manhunt was keeping him too busy for such activities. Hank suspected sarcasm in this reply, but he could do nothing about it.

The case still worried him. It was like a piece of food caught between two molars; you ought to be able to ignore such a minor annoyance, but you can't; and gradually it becomes the focus of all your attention. A couple of days earlier, the clerk in the courthouse had suggested that he apply to law school. For all his efforts, he hadn't uncovered much. He knew that Claib Maggard was a man with enemies, and he knew that Harm Sorley had been in and out of trouble all his life.

But he couldn't quite make the connection between those two facts and an ax murder. He realized that murders are committed every day for the most trivial of reasons, usually with alcohol as a major component, but he didn't want this story to end like that. There had to be a reason.

The song trailed off into an instrumental ending, and Hank stirred from his reverie to see a cluster of lights on the phone bank. "... *rambled till the butchers cut him down,*" he said into the mike. "Ugh. Grisly song, isn't it? That was the unsavory ending of 'The Darby Ram,' folks. We hope it won't be the end of our own Harm Sorley, America's oldest fugitive. Now it's time to go to the phone lines, and see what's on Wake County's minds. I hope this call will be somebody who can identify that singer who asked if there'll be any boxcars in heaven—Hello, caller. What do you think? Will there be any boxcars in heaven?"

"No, there will not." It was an older woman. Hank didn't get many calls from them. "That was Jimmie Rodgers a-singing it, though. I reckon *he's* in heaven."

"Well, if he isn't, *I'm* not going," said Hank. "And you, ma'am, are exactly right. From about sixty years ago, that was the late, great yodeling rambler Jimmie Rodgers who wrote and sang 'The Hobo's Meditation.' Caller, you have won yourself a coffee mug."

"I don't want one," said the woman. "I just happened to know the answer. I really want to call and say that I think it's disgraceful how you harp on that sorry old murderer all the time. He ought to be put back in jail where he belongs."

"Well, ma'am, that's your privilege," said Hank, who

tried not to argue with his callers. An abrasive show soon tired the listeners. He cleared the line, and took the next call, hoping for someone to lighten the mood.

Another woman. "Yes. I want to know why they haven't caught this convict," she said without preamble. "He might be dangerous. My little grandbaby is having nightmares—"

"Well, ma'am, you'll have to take that up with the Tennessee prison system. They assure me they're doing their best to catch him." He disconnected the caller. Why did women always look at issues personally, instead of in the abstract? They couldn't see the old-convict-versus-the-law as a drama in itself, but only in terms of whether his existence might inconvenience them.

"Hank the Yank," he said to the next caller. "What's on your mind?"

"I'd just like to say that the state of Tennessee owes Rita Pentland an apology, and round-the-clock police protection. What if he comes back here and tries to hurt her? If she's listening, I want her to know that we're all concerned about her." It was another woman, of course, threatened by someone who wasn't following their rules.

"Well, Harm, if *you're* out there listening, you heard it here. These good ladies think you broke out of prison in order to menace your ex-wife who is sixty-something. I think that shows so much optimism on their part that I shouldn't even shake their faith, but—if it'll make anybody sleep any easier tonight—I'll confess that if I had been in prison for thirty years, you'd a lot sooner catch me at a Clinton Highway girlie show in Knoxville than sneaking into the bedroom of any old lady, even—maybe especially—my own. Now, if anybody wants a bumper sticker, you give us a call."

Martha Ayers flipped off the radio. Joe LeDonne had just come in the door. "Did you hear that?"

"What?" He hung up his jacket, and headed for the coffeepot in the kitchen.

"Hank the Yank. People were calling in, concerned that Harm might try to contact Rita Pentland, and Hank as much as told them that no man would bother to hunt up a sixty-year-old wife. He said he'd be out chasing tramps."

"Probably," said LeDonne. He sat down in the easy chair nearest the television, looking at the blank screen, not at Martha.

"Well, *I* thought it was a heartless thing to say." Martha stopped. "Is anything the matter with you?"

"No. Just tired." Then, with an effort, he said, "How was your day?"

"Same old, same old," said Martha, determined to keep her voice light. "Paperwork, and a few traffic citations. One interesting thing, though. I saw Nora Bonesteel, that old lady from Dark Hollow. Spencer's mother brought her to town to get canning supplies, and she was coming out of Brenner's as I was headed to lunch. She gave me a lace handkerchief. Said to keep it with me, that I might need it. Wasn't that sweet?" Martha held up a dainty square of lace-edged linen, but LeDonne was sitting back with his eyes closed.

She put the handkerchief down. "You're back awful late, Joe."

"Lost track of time."

He was still looking away. Martha watched him with a thoughtful expression, but she didn't pursue the matter. That would be self-defeating. Besides, she'd had a long day. She'd spent her free time driving the back roads of Wake County, and even over into Mitchell County, North Carolina, looking for places that a fugitive might hole up in. She'd even walked a few miles of railroad track, thinking that the easiest way to travel into Tennessee would be to hop a freight, but she had found no sign of Harm Sorley. She'd asked at all the gas stations at rural crossroads, but no one had seen an old man traveling alone. Next she would have to find out where his old homeplace was, and check there.

She wondered what was bothering LeDonne. He was always moody, but now he seemed to be avoiding her even when he wasn't angry. She'd seen men behave like that before, and it usually meant that they were unhappy, but they weren't ready to let you know about it. When they *were* ready to let you know about it, they'd be packed and on the way out the door, with the motor running. Maybe he was just feeling a little neglected because of her new job. She could baby him out of that. And if that didn't help, then she'd have to see.

She knew better than to question him about it, though. There are some things you have to find out for yourself.

# CHAPTER
# 9

Come on my partners in distress,
    My comrades through the wilderness,
Who still your bodies feel:
    Awhile forget your griefs and fears,
And look beyond this vale of tears
    To that celestial hill.

#663, "Come on My Partners in Distress,"
Charles Wesley

Tennessee Methodist Hymnal, 1885

In his Northface external-frame pack Jeremy Cobb had packed an Irish fisherman's sweater and two college sweatshirts. On this crisp mountain morning he was wearing all of them. Even though late September was still technically summer, and Tennessee was a nominally southern state, the rainy night had chilled him to the bone with temperatures dropping well below forty, and he'd sat in the drooping tent, watching his breath turn into clouds in the gray light of dawn.

After he was caught in the storm on the ridge, the downpour had gone on for hours, forcing him into a grove of trees farther down the mountain, while silver pellets of rain curtained him off from the misted woods, and thunder rolled across the hills above. The cascade of rain in his eyes and down his back hampered his efforts to set up the Eureka Timberline A-frame, turning the instruction booklet into a sodden lump of paper. Finally, he was too waterlogged to care about setting up the tent properly, and he shoved stakes into the mud haphazardly in a shallow depression between two trees, and crawled into the tiny, lopsided space, too cold and weary to try anymore.

He could not start a campfire in such a storm, and the darkness of the tent and the woods in twilight prevented him from figuring out how to set up his Coleman Peak-1 camp stove. It wouldn't have done him any good, anyhow, he thought. Back in Blacksburg Larkin had made him swear solemn oaths never to use his camp stove inside the tent, and he'd gone on about some friend of a friend who'd suffocated when the burning stove used up all the oxygen in his tightly sealed tent, and about a trio of Scouts who had set their tent afire with a camp stove, and died in the flames. These tales made Jeremy respectful, if not frightened, of the two-pound gas stove, and as cold and wet as he was he did not risk lighting it.

Not using the camp stove limited his options for an evening meal. He struggled out of his wet clothes, and pawed through the pack for dry ones, realizing that his world had shrunk to a vision of a pot of coffee and a pan of Dinty Moore beef stew bubbling on the tiny Coleman. Failing that, what could he eat? There were foil packages of vacuum-packed campers' food, but it was too dark to read the labels, and besides, he had been warned not to prepare them with untreated water. He wondered if rainwater would be pure enough, but in the end he was too tired to bother to prepare them at all. He rolled out his sleeping bag on soggy ground, and climbed into it. He ate two granola bars and three ounces of chocolate before fatigue and cold pulled him into sleep.

Jeremy woke up at dawn, wet and shivering, to find that the rain had stopped, but that his sleeping bag was now lying in a puddle of muddy water. The shallow depression and lack of a ground cloth to floor the tent had allowed the rain to collect inside, so that his pack was muddy and his sleeping bag soaked. But the storm was over, and at least he could see in the dim light of the forest morning. He sat in the opening of his tent, bundled in every sweater he had, watching wet leaves shine in a spire of sunshine. On the bare branch of a nearby sapling, a black spider was spinning, catching the light in its web.

He thought about Katie Wyler, sleeping under the trees without even a blanket in the September rain, past hunger and weary with cold, with nothing to sustain her but the nuts and seeds she would find along the way. At least she had been spared the knowledge of what lay ahead for her. Jeremy would write a few lines in his journal, so that he would remember the feeling of cold solitude, the wet silence of the mountain path.

Later, he would find the stream and fill his coffeepot, and make himself a breakfast of stew on the white gas stove. Later, he would discover that his feet hurt.

"It was the damnedest thing," said Charlotte Pentland into the telephone. "We drove all the way out to the back of beyond—some holler where she used to live when I was a kid—and I thought she'd be terrified when we got there. I mean, I thought we were looking for clues as to his whereabouts. You know who I mean . . . uh . . . my natural father."

"By yourselves?" Charlotte's half-brother, Buck, sounded disbelieving. "That doesn't sound like Mommy." He was twenty-two, a senior at the University of

Tennessee, but, as perhaps fitting for the baby of the family, he still called his mother "Mommy."

"She insisted that we go out there alone. And she made me promise not to tell Dad."

"I guess she wanted to reassure herself that the old devil wasn't out there," said Buck. "But it was a damned stupid thing to do. Suppose he had been?"

"Well . . . he's old," said Charlotte. "He's probably harmless."

"No pun intended!"

"Oh. You've been listening to that radio show?"

"A couple of times a month. I like to hear the mountains of home turned into molehills. I didn't hear it the night that creep called in and mentioned Mommy's name, but Sandy Garland was listening, and she made sure I knew about it in class the next day: 'Oh, Buck, they mentioned your mama's name on the radio last night.' "

"I'd have killed her," said Charlotte.

"Careful, hon. You don't want folks to think it runs in the family." Buck was laughing. "Actually, I kind of enjoyed it. I made out as how I came from a dangerous family of murdering hillbillies, and I've been getting all kinds of mileage out of it here at U.T. I wear my suit jacket over a gray work shirt, an old felt hat, and I jazz up my accent. It's done wonders for my sex life."

"You wouldn't think it was so funny if you really were related to him, instead of being one of the respectable Pentlands," said Charlotte. "At the university, I think everybody is looking at me funny, and I wonder if they *know*. It makes me want to go into my apartment and never come out."

"All this celebrity is completely wasted on you, Charlotte. Who cares about being respectable? You want to be a nerd? A goody-goody? See where *that* gets you. These days people want a little spice in their heroes: a president with a love life, an ex-football star turned lawyer, a sixties radical heading up a national corporation."

"Well, I didn't call you for a lecture in public relations. I thought you'd be concerned."

"I sure am worried about Mommy," said Buck. "I know she's not enjoying this one bit. If it weren't for her, I'd be trying to hawk the movie rights. Is she terrified?"

"I guess so. The place was way out to hell and gone, up a winding dirt road to a mountaintop, and then down again on the other side. Lord knows how they made it in and out in the winter. Anyhow, when we got to the farm where they used to live, she got out of the car, and walked around by herself, touching the branches of trees, and looking about her like she was lost."

"What was this place like?"

"It was a cove, which was pretty interesting. It was like a time line, looking at the rocks. The Precambrian rocks had eroded, exposing the Paleozoic limestones and shales, which are younger, and that's what formed the cove. Of course, it's the weathering of the limestone that made the soil so rich, which is why people put farms there in the first place. Not that I'd want to live there."

"Charlotte, shut up about rocks, and tell me what happened to Mommy."

"We liked to never found the cove. It was up a one-lane dirt road that went up, down, and around for miles, and shook my car like a blender. The yard was overgrown with those cedar weed-trees that you see in pastures, and there was the skeleton of an old blue trailer sitting up on concrete blocks, half-hidden by the weeds."

"Maybe she thought he'd be hiding out in that trailer."

"The windows were all broken out of it, and the floor was rotted through. I don't think anybody had been in there in ages. Mama didn't seem to mind, though. She smiled when she saw it. I left her alone, and went walking around to see what else was there. She'd told me I used to play at the creek when we lived there, so I went hunting for it."

"Was it there?"

"Yes. But it didn't look like any place a kid would play. The stream looked okay, but the ground nearby was just bare dirt, and there seemed to be stuff oozing out of the ground."

"What kind of stuff?"

"I don't know. Thick liquids—yellow, dark red."

"Spilled paint?"

"No. It wasn't paint. It looked like syrup, in a nauseating way. I didn't stay around long enough to investigate, though. The place gave me the creeps."

"What did Mommy say about it?"

"She said it hadn't been nearly that bad when she'd lived here. I asked her what it was, but she didn't know. I made her leave then, and as we drove back to town, I showed her the Honaker Dolomite formations that you can see from the road. She seemed real pleased about that."

Buck Pentland laughed. "I'll bet she was! You and your red, red rocks of home. The only rocks you care about are those found in the region you live in."

"That's my area of specialization. In geology you have to specialize."

"Charlotte, you're the only person I know who practices geology as a form of genealogy."

Because she was still worried about their mother, Charlotte ignored this gibe. "Do you think I should have told Daddy about us going out there?"

He thought it over. "Maybe you should," he said. "After all, we're not home. Somebody needs to look after her."

Henry Kretzer had exhausted the resources of the *Hamelin Record,* and now he spent his free afternoons at a table in the courthouse, searching through trial transcripts and old county records. Kitty Washburn, the clerk who had presided over those records since 1971, now kept her extra pencils in a WHTN coffee mug, autographed in magic marker by Hank the Yank. If she had known anything about the Maggard case, she would have told him, but as it was, all she could do was fetch the documents he wanted to examine, suggest others that might also prove useful, and express a motherly concern for the success of his project.

He was sitting at his usual table by the window with record books piled high around him when Kitty Washburn tiptoed past on her way to shelve a deed book, and dropped a note in front of him. The feeling of being whisked back to junior high school almost made him laugh out loud, but he didn't want to offend an ally. He peered at Kitty's penciled scrawl: *That elderly man at the far table is Dallas Stuart, the lawyer. You might see if he knows anything about your case. He's been in practice around here forever.* Hank the Yank slipped the note in his pocket, and nodded his thanks to the clerk.

The only other person present was a distinguished-looking man in a gray tweed suit and tasseled loafers, studying one of the bound record books. A porkpie hat and a carved walking stick lay beside the book. Kretzer thought the man looked too old still to be practicing law, but since no one came to the courthouse for recreational reading (with the possible exception of Henry himself), he supposed that Dallas Stuart was still a working attorney.

He might as well interview the old fellow. Since he and Stuart were the only two visitors to the record room, their conversation wouldn't disturb anyone. Kitty had gone back to reading *A Brief History of Time.* He picked up his notebook and walked library-quiet to the far table.

The old man had a hawk face and eyebrows like comets. He trailed his forefinger along the page of the deed book as he read, moving his lips occasionally when he reached some relevant passage. Henry Kretzer thought he must be at least seventy-five—certainly old enough to recall the Sorley case, although he knew the old man wasn't Harm's attorney of record. That had been one Malcolm Bostic, now deceased, according to Kitty.

"Excuse me, Mr. Stuart?" Kretzer found himself looking into large blue eyes, magnified by thick bifocal lenses. "How do you do? I'm Henry Kretzer—that is, I'm Hank the Yank on WHTN. I understand you're an attorney. Do you have a few minutes to talk?"

"Well, son, this deed isn't going anywhere," said Dallas Stuart, closing the book. "Do you want to go out in the hall and get a Co-Cola? Kitty won't let me bring one in here."

"Sure," said Henry. "I'll buy."

"It's not free legal advice, is it?" the old man asked. "My fees are reasonable, but I'm not *that* cheap."

Henry Kretzer followed him down the hallway toward the vending machines in the stairwell. "No sir," he said, mining his pockets for change. "I don't need a lawyer personally. Not this minute, anyhow. I'd like to talk to you about a murder case that happened in Hamelin back in the sixties."

He piled quarters into the drink machine and motioned for Dallas Stuart to make his selection. "Back in the sixties . . ." the lawyer muttered. "Oh, I see. You're the talk show fellow who's been making such a song and dance about Harm Sorley these past few weeks. Bumper stickers!"

"Uh . . . that's me," said Kretzer.

"So in addition to cheering on the fugitive over the airwaves, you are conducting your own investigation into the case."

"Best I can." Kretzer slid a damp can past the plastic slot lid. "I guess Kitty won't let us back in until we drink these. Is there someplace we can sit down?"

"There's a stone bench in front of the building. It's

usually occupied by Vernon Woolwine, but nobody pays him any mind at all. Come on."

"Who is Vernon Woolwine?" asked Kretzer, pacing his steps so that the old man could hear him as they went down the stairs.

Dallas Stuart stopped and stared up at him. "Where have you been?" he demanded. "I thought all creation knew old Vernon. I'd expected to have to represent him by now in a commitment hearing, but it would be pro bono, because Lord knows Vernon hasn't any money, except his government check, which he must spend entirely on his wardrobe." He opened the screen door and pointed to a figure on a bench near the statue of the Confederate soldier. "Who is Vernon Woolwine? Well, *today* he seems to be Long John Silver."

Henry Kretzer could have sworn that there had been no one on the bench when he went into the courthouse an hour ago, but now sprawled on the bench was a large stubble-bearded man in a red stocking cap, a puffed-sleeve white shirt, and black bell-bottoms. He seemed to be attempting to whittle with a plastic pirate cutlass. Affixed to one burly shoulder was a red and blue cloth parrot, the sort of cheap stuffed animal given away as a carnival prize.

"Vernon is a lot more interesting than Harm Sorley," said Dallas Stuart, nodding toward the pirate. "Why, he's an institution in Hamelin—of course, he also belongs in one, but that's beside the point. Every day, rain or shine, Vernon is out and about in a different get-up, impersonating everything from cowboys to gorillas. I think he's stuck on Halloween myself, but my young partner J. W. Lyon, who has pretensions to culture,

claims that Vernon is a welfare-funded exercise in
street theatre. We've been known to make bets on who
he will turn out to be on a given day."

"Poor guy," said Kretzer, embarrassed to be headed
toward such a sad case. "Is he homeless?"

"No. He's got a trailer. He's happy. He's just not himself. Ever. And there's something odd about his choice
of costumes. You know, sometimes, I could swear he
was trying to tell us something."

"What?"

"Beats me. J.W. is working on a theory. Anyhow,
when Vernon dresses as my distant relation, Confederate General Jeb Stuart, I always buy him lunch." The
old man cupped his hands to the sides of his mouth.
"Hey, Vernon! Permission to approach the bench?"

The pirate nodded solemnly and waggled his cutlass.

"Lawyer joke," Stuart explained to Henry Kretzer. He
dug in his pocket for a couple of dollar bills. "Listen
here, Vernon, this fellow and I need this bench for
about twenty minutes of consultation, so I'm prepared
to make you a handsome offer for it. Do you reckon
there's a hamburger at Dent's Cafe with your name on
it?"

Vernon Woolwine accepted the cash with a mock
bow, and stumped off down the sidewalk on a homemade crutch. Faithful to the role, he had bound one
foot in brown paper and twine to simulate the peg leg
of Long John Silver.

"So you've been checking up on the Sorley case have
you?" Dallas Stuart settled onto the bench, and put his
head back so that he could see past the bank building
to the green mountain beyond. "How's it going?"

"Well, I didn't learn much from the trial transcript. I was amazed at how short it was. I thought trials went on for weeks."

The attorney shook his head. "Not charity cases, son. What else have you tried?"

"I began by reading newspaper accounts of the case from the *Record,* although they weren't exactly informative, either."

Dallas Stuart chuckled. "Son, I can't think of any two volumes less inclined to be informative than a small-town newspaper and a trial transcript. The former is the guardian of its subscribers' sensibilities, and the latter is the record of a chess game. Around here we read the *Record* merely to see who has been caught."

"The editor as much as told me that," Kretzer agreed. "That's why I thought of asking longtime residents. I was hoping you might be able to tell me more about the case."

"That depends," said the old man. "Is this for broadcast on your radio program?"

"I won't quote you, or mention your name, if you don't want me to, but I do need to hear the facts—if you have any."

"I expect I'll be more helpful than your other sources to date, since I will not be constrained to leave out the hearsay and the slander. I keep hoping I'll outlive everybody so that I can write a book about my cases. Once I defended a woman whose defense for murder was that the victim had been in the form of a black dog at the time the stabbing took place."

"Did you get her off with insanity?"

"No. The jury knew the victim, and they couldn't

rule out the possibility. The foreman said: 'She were a bitch anyway. We couldn't agree on color.' So they brought in a verdict of self-defense."

He related this so solemnly that Hank the Yank didn't know whether to nod sagely or burst out laughing. Finally, he said, "You must have an interesting practice."

"It has its moments. But I suppose you'd rather talk about this case you're interested in. Why don't you begin by telling me what you already know."

"I know that Harm Sorley is serving something like seventy years for the murder of Claib Maggard in 1968. According to the trial transcript, the murder weapon was Maggard's own ax, and the two men had been overheard having an argument earlier that afternoon. The newspaper says it was 'just before Maggard was found dead,' but at the trial, the hired man claimed it had been at least an hour earlier. The prosecution said that Harm left the Maggard farm, and then sneaked back to kill Claib. The most incriminating evidence—to me, anyhow—was that Harm Sorley ran. He was found by searchers hiding in a barn someplace, I think. I still don't know what the motive was. Nobody seems to know what Harm and Claib Maggard were arguing about. And I've had some old-timers call in to my show and say that Claib Maggard was a real creep. When he was a young man back in the thirties, he helped the government put people off their land, so that they could establish the Cherokee National Forest. That shouldn't have any bearing on a murder thirty years later, though. Should it?"

"It depends," said Dallas Stuart. "Feuds can last a long time in these mountains. Maybe it's because the same people stay in close proximity for generations, and their behavior doesn't improve; or maybe it's just in the blood—an American version of the Campbell-MacDonald clan feuds back in Scotland. Why, over in West Virginia, the Hatfields and the McCoys became enemies fighting on opposite sides during the Civil War, and they continued the war in private until about 1910. It's possible that the Sorleys and the Maggards might have been old enemies. Personally, though, I doubt it."

"Why is that?"

"Because the Maggards weren't the feuding kind."

"Too respectable?"

The lawyer gave him a sour look. "*They'd* call it that. The rest of the county thought they were too chicken-shit to fight, and that they cared more about money than honor. Leastways, they had more of one than the other."

"Did you know Harm Sorley and Claib Maggard?"

"Not to drink with. I'm a dozen years older than Harm, and two decades younger than Claib Maggard, so we didn't run with the same crowds. After I worked my way through East Tennessee State, I went off to World War II. When I came back in forty-six, I went to law school on the GI Bill. You know why I chose to study law? Because in east Tennessee about the only way for a college-educated man to stay in his home-town is to be self-employed."

"You didn't want to leave?"

"Oh, son, hardly anybody wants to leave. These mountains are more than just a *place* for folks around here. They're part of what we are. You don't think those old boys went up to the Detroit car factories on purpose, do you? They all come back when they hit retirement age."

"But Claib Maggard and Harm Sorley stayed here."

"They did, indeed. Claib managed to insinuate himself into local government, so he got whatever pickings there were from state money, federal projects, and what-all. He wasn't hurting any. He always made sure of that. And Harm? Well, the Sorleys weren't much on holding down regular jobs. They mostly ran moonshine, and took to logging, preaching, mining, or gambling, depending upon their inclinations. Those that lived past forty took up farming. You've heard tell of the Sorley clan, haven't you? There's ballads written about them."

Henry Kretzer shook his head. "I don't know much about Harm's roots. It isn't mentioned in the newspapers I looked in. Is there a ballad about Harm? I'd like to play it on my show."

"Not about Harm," said Dallas Stuart with an impatient sigh. "He's recent. Small potatoes. His uncle Dalton was hanged back at the turn of the century, after killing a few people and constituting a one-man crime wave between here and Bristol. And in the generation before that, a young Sorley—name of Ventriss—was ambushed by Confederate troops on a furlough home from the War. They cut his throat, and tied him to his horse, so that he turned up at his homeplace on the point of death. They say his mother went out to meet him, and he fell off the horse and died at her feet. People used to sing a ballad about him when I was a young'un. I guess I haven't heard it in forty years, though. Time passes. There was another one of the boys, back in the twenties, who killed a girl after he got her pregnant because she was pressuring him to marry her. I believe I know a verse or two of that one." He looked upward at nothing, and sang, *"Poor Lila Jones— How was she found? Stabbed through the heart, a-laying dead on the ground."*

The raspy voice trailed off, and the old man grinned triumphantly at Hank the Yank. "I can't recall how it goes after that. There's a verse toward the end that tells how the killer played a fiddle tune on the scaffold at his own execution. I was a lap-baby when it happened, but my father used to tell it for true. 'Poor Lila Jones'—I hadn't thought about that one in fifty years. Not bad singing for an old feller, was it?"

"The Sorleys sound like an unusual family," said Kretzer, evading the question.

"We shall not look upon their like again. It was a Sorley that saved my life during the Battle of the Bulge. He didn't make it back, but his name's over there." Stuart pointed to the side of the Confederate soldier monument, where a recent bronze plaque listed the county's dead from later wars.

Henry Kretzer decided that it was time to lead the conversation back to the fugitive. "Since you were practicing law here in 1968, I wondered if you had heard anything at the time that might give us a clue as to motive—or other suspects. Maybe you know something that doesn't show up in the written accounts."

"I'm searching my memory, son. Was there something about a cow?"

"A *cow?* I didn't find any mention of it. Whose cow?"

"I don't recall. It might have been another case. Anyhow, one thing I *do* know about this murder: it seems to me that nobody was particularly surprised by the crime. I reckon folks around here figured that sooner or later somebody would up and kill Claib Maggard, because he was the sort of bureaucrat who liked to bully people. The general feeling was that whoever did it ought to bushwhack him with a deer rifle on a country road, and then nobody would try too awful hard to bring the killer to justice. We could all tell ourselves it was a hunting accident."

"But Harm was convicted of first-degree murder."

"Who defended him?"

"Malcolm Bostic."

"Oh. I'll bet he griped like hell about it. Bostic wasn't much on pro bono work. He lit out for Nashville as a state representative and never came back. I believe he's dead now."

Henry Kretzer nodded. "Heart attack in eighty-six. I checked."

"Ah, well. He wouldn't have been any help. I doubt if he cared a rat's ass for Harm's life or liberty."

"Could Harm Sorley appeal his conviction on those grounds?"

"No. Besides, Bostic probably did an adequate job of representing his client. He was always careful about the letter of the law."

"But a first-degree conviction!"

"Well, Harm did take an ax to the man. That's a hard thing to overlook. Besides, he had been getting into scrapes with the law for years. People aren't as tolerant of that now as they were back in Dalton Sorley's day."

"But why? Why would Harm take an ax to his neighbor? Even if that neighbor was a real bastard, there had to be some spark, didn't there?"

"Bound to have been," the lawyer agreed. "But it might have been a tiny one, magnified by the amount of moonshine drunk by the assailant. I'm not sure you'll find a reason to suit you."

"Well, I have to keep trying," said Kretzer, getting up. "My next stop will be the scene of the crime. Kitty found the Maggard farm for me on a county survey map."

"I'll wish you luck then. If I think of anything, I'll let you know."

"I'd appreciate that, sir. Would you like one of my cards?"

Dallas Stuart smiled. "Maybe I'll just call you there on your radio program."

Martha Ayers reckoned she had been to dozens of high school football games in Hamelin's stadium of wooden bleachers, but this one was a novelty. This time, instead of sitting in the stands watching the team and envying the cheerleaders, Martha was a uniformed deputy, in charge of keeping the peace at the game.

Now she watched the stands instead of the field, and found that the action there was considerably more interesting. There was the group of teenagers who kept passing a plastic soft drink cup from hand to hand along the row. She had no doubt that one of them was refilling it from a hip flask, and she wanted to catch him at it, but her attention was also diverted by toddlers playing between the seats, and threatening to fall through the opening onto the gravel below; and by the face of Sabrina Harkryder, with the green and purple bruise from eyebrow to upper lip. She sat alone, staring out at the field, but she didn't seem interested in the game. Martha wondered where Tracy Harkryder was and, more importantly, whether she could get Sabrina to press charges against him. She hoped the baby was still at its grandmother's house.

Martha walked under the bleachers to the gate, where Spencer Arrowood was sipping coffee from a paper cup, and dividing his time between watching the parking lot and keeping track of the game. "How's it going?" he asked her. "Want some coffee? I think I've got another couple of quarters."

"No, thanks," said Martha. "You don't buy coffee; you just rent it. Everything seems peaceful so far in the bleachers, but I'm pretty sure the gang of boys in row W has moonshine in a plastic cup. They're handing it back and forth."

"Okay. I'll take a look." His attention strayed to a fumbled fourth down play, and he smiled.

"Also, Sabrina Harkryder is sporting some new bruises, probably courtesy of her husband. Okay if I ask her about it?"

"Go ahead, but don't be surprised if she says she walked into a door. Some women are like that." He looked past her toward the field, watching the ball arc toward Hamelin's goalposts. "Field goal! We're catching up. Isn't this great, Martha?"

She stared at him. It was two minutes until halftime, and the score was thirteen to three, in favor of the Johnson County Longhorns. "Great?" she echoed. "Not unless you know the players, preferably as parent or loved one. This isn't exactly a high point in the history of the sport, Spencer."

"No, but I like it. There's something *real* about it. I mean, it doesn't look like a television commercial for pickup trucks. The band is a little off-key, and the football players are short and skinny, and the cheerleaders are ordinary-looking kids, not starlets."

"Definitely not starlets," said Martha, eyeing the chunky one on the right. She hoped nobody showed the poor thing a videotape of the cheerleading.

"When we were juniors in high school, Harm crashed a football game. Do you remember?"

"I didn't go to many games that year," said Martha. "I used to baby-sit for extra money."

"Well, you remember the old mascot? The Shawnee brave mounted on that pinto pony borrowed from the Jessups' farm? Well, apparently Harm thought that we were being disrespectful to the memory of the tribe, or maybe he figured that he'd show us how dangerous the old-time Indians really were. Anyhow, before the game he coldcocked Gene Blevins, who was mascot that year, and Harm put on the war paint and rode around the stadium, waving the tomahawk."

Martha frowned. "I suppose he was drunk?"

"Bound to have been. Anyhow, everybody thought it was Gene underneath all that war paint, so they didn't pay him any mind. Then in the middle of the second quarter, old Harm rode past the cheerleaders and scooped up Jenny, and rode off with her, out of the stadium."

Martha studied the sheriff's face, wondering if this

was going to be a sad story. Spencer hadn't mentioned his ex-wife's name in a couple of years. But he seemed happily absorbed in his tale of high school pranks, transported back to a time before things turned bitter between them. "He must have brought her back," Martha said. "I'd have remembered if one of our classmates was kidnapped."

"Oh, he didn't get out of the parking lot with her. It's hard to hold a squirming girl on a running horse. As soon as Jenny realized he wasn't Gene Blevins, she put up a fight and he dropped her and kept going."

"Do you think he meant to rape her?" There were no innocuous pranks for Martha anymore. Women lived dangerous lives.

"I think he just wanted to liven up the football game," said Spencer. "It's the sort of thing the Sorleys have always done. A stylish stunt mixing audacity with clowning. They were a wild family, but they didn't hurt people for no reason. At the time I remember thinking that he was reenacting the Shawnee kidnapping of Katie Wyler."

"Too bad he didn't keep her then," said Martha. Whether she was thinking of Katie Wyler's fate in pioneer days or of Spencer Arrowood's subsequent marriage to Jenny, she didn't say.

# CHAPTER

# 10

Bid me of men beware,
  And to my ways take heed,
Discern their every secret snare,
  And circumspectly tread.

#585, "BID ME OF MEN BEWARE," CHARLES WESLEY

TENNESSEE METHODIST HYMNAL, 1885

The Johnson County Longhorns won, to no one's surprise, and to no one's great disappointment, as far as Martha could tell. She hadn't spent much time watching the game, the one place where people could get hurt without it being her responsibility. During halftime, she waylaid Sabrina Harkryder on her way to the snack bar, and asked her about the baby. "He's at my mama's," said Sabrina sullenly, eyes downcast, fist clenched. Martha let that pass. When she asked about the shining bruises on the girl's face, Sabrina said she'd fallen down the trailer steps. "If you want to press charges, you call me," said Martha, but Sabrina Harkryder shrugged her thin shoulders and hurried away.

The teenagers in the stands had surrendered their whiskey flasks upon the sheriff's demand, and the one fistfight under the bleachers was over a girl, not a game dispute. The combatants ended it with an insincere handshake as Spencer loomed over them, so nobody had to be arrested. The sheriff and Martha ended the evening directing traffic out of the stadium's gravel parking lot, and then headed out to the main highway in the patrol car.

"This is unpaid overtime," the sheriff told her. "But after football games, I like to put in an extra hour or so on the roads, in case anybody decides to go joyriding after the game."

"Fine with me," said Martha. "I doubt if Joe will be worried." She found herself wishing that he would.

They cruised by the local diner to check on the action in the parking lot, looked in on a couple of dead-end dirt roads that served as lovers lanes, and took the main road out of town toward Johnson City. They had driven in silence past several miles of woods and pastures when they caught sight of a weaving car ahead of them, horn blowing, headlights flashing over different parts of the dark landscape as the car careened from lane to lane.

"Shit," said Spencer Arrowood. He flipped on the light bar.

The swaying car shot ahead of them, straddling the yellow line, and peeling rubber at the curves in the narrow blacktop. Spencer hit the siren, and stepped on the gas. "Make sure your seat belt is tight, Martha."

The sirens drowned out the screech of tires against asphalt.

Martha gripped the door handle, and thought how smooth car chases looked in the movies. On screen the cops didn't appear to be riding in a blender, jolted into the door handle as the car took curves too fast. A lifetime of watching those cinematic chase scenes hadn't prepared her for the cold pit in her stomach, a combination of nerves and dizziness from the twisting road. "Do you think it's kids?" she called out to the sheriff.

"It could be anybody. We can't get close enough to

read the license plate, so we can't call in a check," said Spencer, peering out at the red taillights ahead. "When people won't stop for the blue lights, they could be wanted for worse than a traffic violation, or they could be just contrary. Playing macho games. Only way to find out is to catch them. Meanwhile, we assume the worst, and act accordingly."

Macho games. A cold fact rose unbidden in Martha's mind: approximately 50 percent of all officers who were killed in the line of duty each year worked in the Southeast: Virginia, North Carolina, Tennessee, Georgia, Florida. It was a culture where guns and honor mixed to form a lethal combination for all concerned. She thought it might hark back to the Civil War, when the Southern warrior, who prided himself on his bravery and shooting skill, had lost a war to a bureaucratic foe, who won by having more supplies and a vast expendable population of immigrants to throw in the path of Southern gun barrels. The injustice of that defeat still rankled, and some Southern men seemed to feel that Appomattox was the last insult their manhood would ever suffer. They fought authority at every turn, met every slight with clenched fists, and died to prove how brave they were. Some of them were outlaws, and some of them were cops. But almost all of them were male, and Martha thought that all of them were crazy. Gallant, romantic, quixotic, courageous—maybe all of those things—but doubly dangerous for all that, and no less crazy.

The road began to climb as it left the valley, snaking around the ridge of a dark mountain, forcing the pace to slow. Once again the dark car was in the range of their headlights. "He can't be going more than about sixty now," said Spencer.

"He's crazy if he's doing that," Martha replied.

"We're not going much slower. I just hope he has the sense to slow down even more, because these curves get sharper in about a quarter of a mile."

"You're not going to stay in pursuit if he doesn't slow down, are you?" Her words came out staccato, jolted out of her throat by the rocky road. They were well beyond the few streetlights of Hamelin. Martha looked out at the empty darkness, glad that she could not see the blur of trees outside.

Spencer glanced at her and grinned. "C'mon, Martha! I know what I'm doing. Haven't you ever wanted to burn rubber on a back road like they do in the movies?"

"No."

"Oh, lighten up, Martha. Anyhow, we have to finish this. Hold on. He's trying to turn up that dirt road without slowing down." Spencer hit the brakes, and for several seconds their headlights held the fugitive car in an eerie tableau, before the dark shape floated sideways away from the road and the curve of the ridge, and then was gone.

Spencer cut the siren, and stopped the car. "He's gone over the side," he said. "I'll see if we can get the cruiser close enough to the edge to see the wreck."

He climbed out of the car. Martha felt the rolling in her stomach subside, but her heart was still double-timing. They were halfway up a mountain, miles from nowhere. You could see every star in the sky, so dark were the surrounding woods.

Spencer was back. "We can't get any closer," he told

her. "He's in there good. No response to my hailing. You get on the radio. Tell the rescue squad to get out here. Then radio the state police, and find out if they can get a car here in less than an hour. Then come and assist me." He reached for the shotgun, racked a round, and climbed out.

Three minutes later, when Martha reached his side, he was standing on the edge of the hillside, his shotgun cradled on his arm, shining his flashlight into the ravine at a rhododendron thicket, out of which only red taillights were visible. When he saw Martha, Spencer motioned for her to stand behind him. He directed the light toward the driver's side of the car.

"Driver!" he yelled down. "Put your hands flat against the window glass, palms out, and then open the door and come out."

In the ravine, silence. Nothing moved.

"He's still in there," Spencer told her, moving the tiny circle of light up and down the thicket. "The bastard. I guess we have to go get him."

Martha looked at the steep slope that ended in a tangle of bushes, and again at the glow of taillights far below. "What if the thing catches on fire?"

"That only happens on television, Martha." In the darkness she heard him sigh. "What's the ETA on the state police?"

"I gave them our position, and they said it would take them an hour to get a car here. The rescue squad should get here in half that time."

"Yeah, but they can't get near the car until we have secured it."

"What if the guy in there has a gun, and is waiting for us?"

"What if he's badly hurt and we can save him?"

*But he's not worth it,* Martha thought. She didn't say it out loud, though, because she recognized this opinion as unworthy of someone sworn to protect the public. It seemed a given that the two of them were going to walk down into that dark ravine, to a wrecked car that might contain a crazed and armed occupant, and that they were going to risk being immolated in the explosion if the wreck caught fire. For this, they were being paid less than a hundred dollars a day.

Spencer cupped his hands around his mouth. "Driver! Can you hear me? If you can exit the car without help, do so now. Do it slowly. Let us see your hands—palms out!"

They waited, feeling the cold air curl about them. Nothing.

"All right," said the sheriff. "We're going down that hill. Martha, keep your flashlight off until I tell you otherwise, but draw your gun."

She stared at him open-mouthed. He knew she was thinking about tripping over a root on the dark slope, and shooting herself in the head as she fell. "Don't put your finger near the trigger. You have to be ready, though."

"Right." Her mouth was dry. She looked at the red pinpoints of light below them, wondering if she was in the sight of someone's weapon.

"Okay, we're going to walk about twenty feet down that hill and stop, flashlights off. When I get to that first tree, I'm going to take cover behind it, reach my hand out on the other side of the tree and shine the flashlight on the car again. That way, if he shoots at the light, he won't hit me. Never shine the light close to your body."

"Okay. What do you want me to do?" She had taken the Glock pistol out of her holster. It did not have the familiar inanimate feel she knew from her target sessions. Now it felt warm, pulsing—as if it could strike without waiting for her decision.

"I'm going down on the left side of the car—but staying at least ten feet from it at all times. You start down the slope so that you end up on the passenger side. Try always to keep cover between you and the car. Go from tree to tree if you can."

"How am I supposed to see to get down there? Look at that slope. It's steep and it's all underbrush."

She heard a puff of exasperation. "All right, Martha. But remember that a three-mag flashlight puts out a lot of light, and when you use it, you're vulnerable. If you have to use the flashlight, aim it about four feet in front of you—*not* at your feet. And don't keep that light on for more than two seconds, understand?"

"Yeah."

"Good. I don't need an officer down in addition to this other situation here. Do you remember how to see if there's someone in the car?"

"Yes."

"Okay. You know the procedure. I'll be the contact officer. You'll be the cover officer. You don't speak. I'll signal our moves to you with my flashlight. A quick on-off aimed at the car. Got that?"

"I think so."

"Good. Remember—stay behind cover, move slowly, and don't use that light if you can help it."

She clipped the flashlight on her belt, and eased her way down the mountain, pointing the gun at the ground away from her, still thinking that it might somehow have a power of its own. Why did men like guns? Why did they get a thrill from reckless driving on dark, twisting roads? Sometimes she thought that men couldn't see death coming any more than a chicken could.

The slope was covered in a tangle of woody kudzu vines, not yet beaten back by a killing frost. The image of a rattlesnake rose in her mind, but she pushed away the thought: too cold; they'd be burrowed in for the night, at least. There was something to be said for the chilling night air. Martha edged down the hill, moving sideways, picking up first one foot and then the other. She only used the flashlight twice. Once, after she had stumbled on a loose rock, she forgot and shined the flashlight at her feet, but she switched it off almost at once, and zigzagged away from the spot. There were no sounds from the wreck, though. It lay with its hood submerged in the rhododendron bushes, as if it were just another junked car in a holler.

Spencer Arrowood reached the first marker—a maple twenty feet down. He flashed his three-cell mag light on the car, and hailed the driver again. "Come out! Palms up!" Nothing.

For an instant Martha wondered how she would feel if she were trapped inside a car crash, and her only rescuers were approaching inches at a time, guns drawn. *You brought it on yourself,* she thought to the occupant of the car. *You've already risked our lives tonight. Why should we care what happens to you?*

Seconds later they were inching forward again. Now they were level with the car. From the far side of the ravine, she saw a light flash on-off. It was time to see how many passengers they were dealing with. The confrontation would come soon. Martha took a deep breath and felt the cold air sear her throat as it went down. She stepped out from behind the tree and raised her flashlight, ready to shine it at the top corner of the backseat window.

LeDonne had taught her how to shine a light at the top corner of a car window so that the light reflecting down casts an image in the lower half of the window, revealing a fuzzy image of the interior of the vehicle— not much of a reflection, but enough to indicate whether someone was in there: a movement or a color variation was all they'd get, but it would be enough. Martha and LeDonne had practiced the technique in the driveway with the husky in the backseat of the car, repeating the exercise until Martha could get a usable reflection in less than five seconds. She hoped she could do it now.

She slid the switch to On, and positioned herself to look beneath the beam. Ready, now—on!—she steadied the beam toward the upper portion of the glass, and looked for the corresponding reflection: nothing there. The backseat was empty. Kill the light. She had been aware of the crackle of underbrush as she stood there, but it was only afterwards that she realized that Spencer had used the diversion to approach the car. She could see him now in the faint glow of the taillights, crouching beside the back bumper, too low to be hit by gunfire through the back window. A circle of light appeared at the catch of the trunk. He was trying to open it, but it seemed shut fast. One less possible ambush to worry about. Darkness again.

"Driver! Come out of the car now!" Spencer sounded out of breath from plowing through the rhododendron thicket.

Now that they were close to the car, they could see that only the hood was submerged in the bushes. The rest of the vehicle had bent the branches, but had not been engulfed. The windows were clear. A dim shine of headlights made the leaves glow green farther into the thicket. They waited a few more seconds in cold silence, but no sound or movement escaped the wreck. Martha saw the flashlight signal again: on-off. Last phase of the maneuver: check the front seat. She would shine the light from the passenger side, try to see if the driver had a weapon. Spencer would take whatever action was necessary.

Martha crept forward, edging closer to the car, keeping her head below the level of the windows. The driver would know they were coming. Perhaps he could hear the snap of twigs as they moved. If he were conscious. *Maybe it's Harm in there,* thought Martha, to distract herself from the cold sweat in her armpits and the ice water in her stomach. *Yeah, maybe he stole a car and came back to Wake County. We've got him.*

In one smooth motion she straightened up, with the gun in her right hand and her finger poised on the trigger. Her left hand flicked on the light, illuminating the front seat of the wreck. In one bright glimpse she could see a spiderweb of windshield glass, a whiskey bottle on the passenger seat, and a round-eyed face staring back at her. He could only be seeing the light, but it felt as if he were staring into her eyes. It was a kid— maybe seventeen—brown hair, his complexion red spots over paste, and those huge staring eyes. He was holding a pistol level against the side of his head, its black barrel feathering a tuft of hair above his right ear.

Martha froze: light on; weapon trained on suspect. The scene played in slow motion in the black and white glare of a three-cell mag light. She heard herself—*saw herself*— scream "No!" and the sound was echoed in Spencer Arrowood's voice on the other side of the car, and then—then it was over. The kid's fingers moved. Clutched at the trigger. His expression changed from electric terror to a dazed emptiness.

Then Spencer had the driver's-side door open, and was grabbing the gun. He tossed it on the ground, out of reach. *Secure the weapon.* He propped the shotgun against the back door, and she saw him search his jacket pocket.

"You got anything I can use to staunch this wound?" he called out to her.

Martha stood for a dazed moment before the words reached her. Then she opened the passenger door, and pulled a square of white linen out of the pocket of her shirt. She watched Spencer press the handkerchief against the small red hole above the boy's ear. *Direct pressure on the wound.* There didn't seem to be much blood. The delicate lace shone white in the glare of the flashlight. She would not want it back, though.

Martha held the light on the boy, careful not to shine

it in the sheriff's eyes. The kid's hands and feet were still. She saw no sign that he was breathing.

Spencer glanced up at her. "Go back up to the cruiser, Martha," he said. His voice was soft, almost absentminded. "Prop up that light so that I can see, though. Then go. There's nothing you can do here."

"Why did he do it?"

"Radio the rescue squad, and tell them to step on it. You might cancel the call to the state police, too. We don't need them anymore. You wait for the squad up at the car."

The words didn't seem to register. She looked at the still form under the sheriff's hand. "But he just—"

"Go on now, Martha," Spencer said, a little louder this time. "Here, use my flashlight to find your way back up the hill. Take it slow."

She realized then that her teeth were chattering, but she couldn't even feel the cold anymore.

Jeremy Cobb lay in the darkness, far from sleep, listening to the pain in his feet. If he put on the light, he thought, he might be able to see the waves of pain radiating out of blisters, strained muscles, and aching joints. The blisters were the worst. His socks had become soaked, first with sweat, then with drainage from raw wounds mixed with blood. He had brought only two pairs of socks with him—to save pack space—and no gauze bandages. He tried soaking his feet in the creek, but the water felt like snowmelt, and he had seized up with chills almost instantly, forcing him to withdraw from cold comfort. He would give anything for a hot bath. He thought of rigging up the solar shower, but it would only work during daylight, and he couldn't afford to spend a day sitting around camp waiting for icy creek water to warm up. He had to keep moving. He was already behind schedule.

Now he was curled up in his sleeping bag, with his wounds bound in the shreds of a new T-shirt. He was miles from anywhere. In fact, he wasn't sure he knew where he was.

*Why didn't she die?* he wondered. Why didn't Katie Wyler starve to death somewhere in that green emptiness? Why didn't numb, bloodied feet and a cold, shriveled belly make her wade into the creek and never come out? Or just go to sleep under the laurel leaves until the night wind took you off for good. *Cease upon the midnight with no pain.* Jeremy hadn't packed his paperback volume of Keats: that line rose unbidden to tempt him.

He was being melodramatic, and somewhere under the pain he knew he ought to smile at himself. How far could he be from civilization? Four miles? Seven? If the journey became truly unbearable, he could hobble to some backwoods gas station, or some ramshackle farmhouse, and help would come. But he told himself that he could not accept defeat so soon, and so easily.

His daily mileage average had fallen far short of his estimated ten miles a day. That had seemed such a reasonable pace when he planned the trip back in his Blacksburg apartment, but he had reckoned without rocky terrain; bleeding, blistered feet; and the ache in his back muscles from lugging the unfamiliar weight of his backpack. He had overfilled it. That much was clear. The luxuries of civilization seemed less enticing when you were forced to haul them with you, straining your muscles with their bulk every step of the way. Today Jeremy had parted with a six-pack of Coors and two Backpacker's Pantry dehydrated, foil-wrapped selections: the lemon cream pie and the chili mac with beef. True, together they were only half the weight of one of his cans of Dinty Moore, but he could not part with this one familiar comfort, and risk his shriveled stomach to a meal that might taste like library paste. (Why hadn't he tried them back at the apartment? Oh, yes. Because the little foil package of chili mac cost $5.95.) He abandoned one of his cooking pots as well. Carrying two seemed excessive. Larkin had stressed the importance of "packing it out"—that is, leaving no garbage on the trail—, but Jeremy could not bear the weight another step, and he didn't know where "out" was. He reasoned that some other hiker might find the items useful, which made him not a litterbug, but a benefactor.

He had been tempted to discard the solar shower, which was both heavy and bulky, but the thought of a week on the trail, encrusted in his own sweat and body odors, revolted him. Surely he would be able to use it sometime. Make camp early on a warm afternoon, perhaps.

He had pitched his tent, with somewhat more success this time, since there was no downpour to distract him. First he had tended his wounds. Then, after a meal of stew, delayed by his inability to figure out the camp stove on the first six tries, he had lit the Coleman lantern, and devoted mealtime to map study. After he reached a tentative decision about his position (somewhere southwest of Mountain City), he had leafed through his field guides, recognizing nothing that resembled the birds and plants he'd noticed on the day's trek.

Finally, when fatigue outweighed the ache of blisters and muscles, he had settled in to sleep, his head cradled on the burlap bear bag into which he had carefully packed his foodstuffs and deodorant. Jeremy Cobb, nineties pioneer, slept.

By the time the rescue squad arrived, Martha had stopped shaking, and the urge to cry or throw up or both had left her.

As she'd sat in the dark cab of the cruiser waiting for them, she realized that Spencer had sent her up the hill in order to keep her focused on something, so that she wouldn't have time to think about what had just happened. The boy—whoever he was—wouldn't make it, whether the rescue squad hurried or not. He was gone before she got halfway up the hill, maybe before that. She thought she had seen the moment when he changed from a terrified adolescent to an empty husk of flesh.

She huddled in her jacket, wishing that she could have a cup of coffee. Wishing LeDonne would somehow show up, so that she could feel safe. The rescue squad was still fifteen minutes away. She watched her breath hang in the air, and thought about the risk she took every day. Had she really considered it, when she demanded that Spencer give her the deputy's job? It seemed to her a terrible thing that death was a split-second matter. How monstrous that so casual an act as crooking one's finger around a curve of steel, the gesture of an instant, could end something as wondrous as the light of a human soul. She thought about how somber and permanent *dead forever* was, and she tried to imagine what it would feel like. How could the world keep going on, and you not know about it? She wondered if the wide-eyed boy had felt even an instant of regret, before he felt nothing at all. And was there anything they could have done that would have kept him from ending like that?

When the rescue squad arrived, she scrambled out of the car to meet them. They asked who the victim was, but Martha didn't know. She led the squad members down the slope, and stood by with the flashlight while they examined the body of the boy. Spencer Arrowood, who appeared as tired as she'd ever seen him, walked away from the car. He had spent twenty minutes sequestered with a dead boy, and he looked every minute of it.

"Here's his wallet," he told her. "His name was Patrick Allan Kendrick. He went to my church. He was seventeen."

"Did you know him?"

"He was at the game tonight. You mean, did I know him socially? Knew his name. That's about it. He was an honor student, though. Eagle Scout."

They moved aside as the rescue squad went past, trundling the blanket-covered form up the hill. The thicket was dark now. They let the silence sink in.

Finally Spencer said, "We'll have to notify the family. I'm going to wait until morning to call the wrecker for the car. It's too dark and steep to worry about it until daylight."

Martha looked at her watch. "That will be in about four and a half hours," she told him.

"You may still be up to see it in," said Spencer, turning to climb out of the ravine. He motioned for Martha to follow. "We're going on to the hospital after this."

"But the boy is dead."

"Not until Graybeal says he's dead. That's the law. It's the coroner's call. And after we get the official notification of death, the boy's parents have to be told."

"They'll want to know why he died," said Martha. "Do we even know?"

"I know." Spencer sat down in the driver's seat of the cruiser, and leaned his head back, eyes shut. "Remember when I broke up that fight under the bleachers?"

"Vaguely. I think I was talking to Sabrina Harkryder at the time."

"Patrick Kendrick was one of those boys. They were fighting over a Hamelin cheerleader."

Martha heard herself ask: "Which one?"

"The chunky one on the end—her name's Brandy. She just broke up with Patrick, and he was taking it hard."

Honor again. Martha shivered. "But you said he was a good kid. Scouts. Honor roll."

"Yeah. He was. But tonight he was just a hurt seventeen-year-old who had more pain than he could handle. There was a whiskey bottle on the seat beside him."

"I saw it."

"He got wasted, so he wouldn't feel so bad, and then

he started driving like he didn't give a damn. But this just wasn't his night. We spotted him."

"He only made things worse," said Martha, failing to see the logic in this masculine reasoning. "He's upset about his girlfriend. He loses a fight over her. He gets drunk. Then he gets in trouble with the law."

"He didn't *plan* it, Martha. One thing led to another. It ends with him sitting in a wrecked car at the bottom of a ravine, with two angry cops coming after him. But I figure that all he can think about is his parents. The good boy with the good grades is suddenly in major trouble: no girlfriend, wrecked car, maybe a night in jail. And then the parental wrath. And the gun is lying there on the seat, and he just says, 'to hell with it.' Because he can't take any more grief tonight."

"We could have talked him out of it," said Martha.

"I wish he had let us try. Death isn't a decision you should make in a split second. That's the trouble with guns: they make it too easy." He stifled a yawn. "Let's get to the hospital. It's still a long time 'til morning."

Harm Sorley was supping with sorrow. As he lay down beneath the laurels near a rocky stream, his mind turned to the past, and he knew himself to be missing Rita and baby Chalarty, but he knew, too, that there were cobwebs in his remembrance. It seemed like such a long time since he'd seen them, but, of course, it couldn't have been, since he was just coming back from the logging camp. He couldn't get a ride, so he was walking most of the way, but—shoot—that didn't bother Harm. In his thirty-eight years of living he must have walked every foot of these mountains twice over.

But it took time to hike these hills, and he felt that he had been gone too long already.

He knew it was late September. The bull thistles were flowering purple in the clearings; tiny white wood asters shone like stars on the forest floor; and stalks of Queen Anne's lace dappled the abandoned fields, ready to be picked for their roots: wild carrot. He had dug and eaten half a dozen as he walked along. There were hickory nuts strewn along the forest path, and wild fox grapes ripe on the vines that curled around trees. He'd added those to his sack, even though the grapes wouldn't taste sweet until after the first frost. The scattered acorns under the burly oak trees he left alone: acorns were too bitter to fool with, unless you were flat out starving, which he wasn't. The Lord would provide better than that. He had.

Late that afternoon as Harm was walking along a footpath fringed with possum haw, he'd found two silvery packages placed neatly on the path in front of him. The writing on one of them said "chili mac", and in fine print on the back, he'd seen the words *light weight food*. Apparently, you just added water to this stuff, and you had a meal. The Lord had dropped it there for him to find—manna from heaven in a shiny package.

"Now how am I supposed to fix this with no bowl to mix it in?" Harm said aloud, in case there were angels hovering nearby among the laurels.

But before he'd gone another twenty paces, there it was a few feet from the trail: a little saucepan, good as new, with just one little dent in the side, but not a single hole or a speck of rust. He deposited it in the sack with the rest of the provisions. Walking was a hungry way to travel. Harm was getting so scrawny, he thought he could suck in his stomach and feel his backbone.

He had forgotten the saucepan and the silver packages by the time he found the next gift from heaven: six metal beer cans—unopened—just sitting there on the ground beside a rock. The label said "C-O-O-R-S," which didn't mean anything to Harm, but if it was beer, it suited him down to the ground. He'd sat down then and there, and said a blessing over the heaven-sent bounty, and then he'd downed three of the beers in quick succession. They made him feel swimmy-headed, like somebody who wasn't used to putting it away, but Harm reckoned he must have drunk stronger than that by the pintful in the logging camp. Maybe he was just weak from walking. He didn't know how long he'd been walking. Every time he tried to grab hold of a memory, it turned fuzzy, like fine print in dim light.

He began to feel sorrowful right soon after he'd finished off the third beer. He'd found himself a laurel thicket—folks up home called it *ivy*, but it was mountain laurel to everyone else. He curled up under the gnarled branches, and pined for Rita and the baby, wishing they had a telephone up home so he could hear their voices. If it weren't for missing them so much, he'd be a happy man in these woods. If he had a gun so's he could hunt, he'd be king of the mountain. He'd build him a shelter, and live free: no forms to fill out, no payments to make, and no rules but God's. It was paradise up here, and he would have to leave it like Adam did—for a woman.

He reckoned he had to get home, one way or another, because his womenfolk needed him, and that was a covenant the Lord intended for him to keep. So he would go back to Rita, quick as he could find his way through the hollers, but that didn't mean he couldn't savor the wonder of it along the way.

When the woman in the torn blue dress walked through the clearing, Harm tried to crawl out of the laurels to ask her the way, but his legs felt wobbly, and his head ached. He fell back into the shelter of the leaves and into sleep, and the vision of the running woman sank into his mind like a stone, making soft ripples that faded into black.


Martha could see gray clouds above the black shapes of trees. The long night was over at last. She was driving her own car now, nearly home. Her back ached, and her stomach swirled with the acid of too much coffee, taken in gulps to calm her and later to keep awake as they waited for Patrick Kendrick to be pronounced officially dead.

Spencer and Martha had driven to the Kendrick home in silence. What they had to say needed no rehearsal. A couple of sentences would do it. After that, they would talk on, but the Kendricks would not hear. The pain of their loss would drown out the words of consolation. Ellen Kendrick kept saying that it could not be Patrick. Not *her* son Patrick. He was an honor student. Honor students don't wreck cars on lonely roads, and then shoot themselves in the head. Surely they understood that?

Finally they left her, because her husband, who had hardly spoken, nodded to them that he would take care of things. First a doctor for Ellen Kendrick, and then

Graybeals to see to the burying of Patrick. No, Mr. Kendrick said, he didn't want coffee. He just wanted for them to—please, God—leave.

Spencer offered to take her home, but she wanted her own car. The drive back alone through graying streets would clear her mind, and distance her from the images of last night. Martha wanted to talk to Joe LeDonne. He had lived through such nights many times, in Vietnam as a young soldier, and here in Wake County, as deputy. She wanted to know if the images ever faded. If you stopped replaying the scene, trying to change the ending. And she had to ask LeDonne if that mountain road would be forever haunted in her mind; if she would always see the wide eyes of an adolescent in the glare of a flashlight whenever she passed that way, day or night. Joe had nightmares. Maybe once a month he would wake her, struggling and crying out in his sleep, the sheets soaked in cold sweat. Was this the stuff of his dreams, and would they now visit her as well?

She pulled into the driveway of her duplex, leaden-eyed and numb. The sky was a lighter gray now, so that the first tinges of color brightened the shadows. She wondered if the coffee could have worn off so fast, or if her fatigue had finally overruled the stimulant. It took her a moment in the stupor of fatigue to realize that LeDonne's Volkswagen wasn't parked in its usual place. He must be at his place, then. Lately, he'd taken to staying home a couple of nights a week, when one or the other of them was too tired to make the effort to be sociable. She knew that she should let him sleep, because he had to be at work in a few hours, but she knew that she wouldn't be able to let go of the night's events until she talked to him. He would understand. She had been there for him often enough.

She drove the few blocks to his place, thinking of how she would wake him, and wondering if they would make love before they talked. Would it make her feel any better, or was she only considering it as a perfunctory thank-you for making him share her pain?

She slowed down on the curve at the boxwood hedge, and turned into LeDonne's driveway, cutting her lights. There were two cars parked under the tree in the side yard. One was LeDonne's old Volkswagen with its *Tennessee Sheriffs Association* bumper sticker. The other was a white Chevy Nova, maybe an '87, with a bumper sticker that said: *Don't Shoot—It Might Be Harm!* The Nova had a vanity Tennessee license plate: CRYSTLS.

Martha looked at it for a long time, trying to fit the information into her brain. She was dazed with sleep, almost past feeling anything except to register the fact that there was a strange car in Joe's yard. Wearily, she heard herself thinking Ellen Kendrick's protest: Not him . . . Surely you understand?

Martha backed out of the driveway, and drove three blocks back to the Methodist Church parking lot before she called in the license check to the Highway Patrol.

# CHAPTER
# 11

We, while the stars from heaven shall fall,
   And mountains are on mountains hurled,
Shall stand unmoved amidst them all,
   And smile to see a burning world.

#690, "THE GREAT ARCHANGEL'S TRUMP,"
CHARLES WESLEY

TENNESSEE METHODIST HYMNAL, 1885

"Good evening, folks. This is Hank the Yank coming at you on WHTN—Hamelin, Tennessee, your electronic neighborhood watch program. We're still monitoring sightings of Wake County's own geriatric fugitive, Harm Sorley, three weeks out of the Northeast Correctional Center in Mountain City, and now residing in the Twilight Zone. We're giving WHTN coffee mugs to the five callers with the best theories as to his whereabouts. It's not much of a reward, as bounties go, but it's a lot less work than tracking fugitives with a bloodhound, and besides, our budget wouldn't be spending money for a gerbil, so don't complain about it. Don't think of it as a coffee mug; think of it as a ceramic tribute to your creativity.

"We're going to play some old-time country music between call-ins, and we're going to do some ruminating tonight on Tennessee justice. Just how good is it? We're talking about the legal system that ordered Harm Sorley to prison until he was a hundred and four years old for one murder that *may* have been unpremeditated, or *may* have been self-defense, or *may* have been committed by someone else entirely. What kind of system keeps people locked up until they're a hundred?

"What's that, Arvin?—Well, folks, Arvin says that if Harm Sorley could manage to escape from prison in Mountain City at the advanced age of sixty-three, then the state might have the right idea, after all." Hank the Yank chuckled appreciatively.

"Arvin, that's cold. By any chance, were any of your ancestors on jury duty over in Erwin in September 1916? That was another fascinating example of Tennessee jurisprudence, you know. That's when they hanged the elephant.

"That's right, Arvin. *They hanged an elephant over in Erwin, Tennessee, in 1916.* If I'm lying, I'm dying. Now I bet there are a lot of new people out there in our listening area who think I'm putting them on about this, but I'm not. It's the gospel truth, folks. They hanged an elephant in these parts, nearly eighty years ago. So if you're ever charged with murder here in Tennessee, don't plead *elephant*. It is not a valid defense.

"Her name was Mary, this elephantine felon. She was a pachyderm with a traveling circus called Sparks World Famous Shows. The circuit of traveling shows used to travel by railroad, and around here they'd hit all the towns along the Clinchfield line. They went from St. Paul, Virginia, to Kingsport, Tennessee, and the next stops would be Johnson City and Erwin. The circus had a new trainer, a drifter by the name of Eldridge who had joined the show in St. Paul, and apparently he didn't know enough about handling five-ton females. All circus elephants are females, you know. They tried using males in the early days, but they proved to be unruly. One bull called Hannibal killed seven people. Personality-wise, Mary took after him.

"The fatal incident happened during the circus parade along Center Street in Kingsport. This fella Eldridge was sitting on Mary's back, leading the five-elephant procession, when the big gray lady spotted a melon rind on the street. She started to sniff it with her trunk, and her trainer prodded her with his stick. Hey, she was holding up the parade, all right? She reached for the rind again; he poked her again.

"That did it. That big gray trunk snaked up over Mary's head, snatched Eldridge off his perch, and cracked him like a bullwhip. Then she flung him into the air, and he crashed headfirst into a wooden refreshment stand by the side of the road. Before anybody could do much more than gasp and stare big-eyed at the fallen man, Mary walked over to where he lay in the dirt, and she put her big rough front foot on top of his head, and then she pushed down, until his head went squish like a cantaloupe. People were screaming and running to get away from the rogue elephant. The other elephants were trumpeting and backing away, and the local blacksmith charged out of his forge and fired five bullets at Murderous Mary. They just bounced off—which left the people of Kingsport and the state of Tennessee with another dilemma: what do you do with a murderer if it happens to be an elephant?

"I'll tell you what the circus would like to have done: change the elephant's name, and sell her cheap to one of the other dozen or so traveling shows of that era. That's what they usually did. More than a few people suspected that Mary had killed before, someplace else under some other name.

"What's that, Arvin? Yes, that is correct. An elephantine *serial* killer. Quite a problem for local jurisprudence. Mary went ahead and performed that night at the Kingsport show, but the mayor of Johnson City had heard about Eldridge's death, and he wasn't going to let the matter drop. He declared that the circus couldn't play Johnson City unless they got rid of Mary.

"Now the circus was in a pickle. They had to choose between sacrificing an eight-thousand-dollar elephant—that was Rolls-Royce money in 1916, folks—or missing play dates in Johnson City and Rogersville. And the newspaper had fired folks up so that they were screaming for her blood. It doesn't appear that anybody considered Mary's feelings in the matter. Was she a victim of abuse under a cruel and inexperienced trainer? Did she consider her actions self-defense? Did she understand that her actions would result in the man's death?

"Those are nineties questions, neighbors. Nobody asked them in 1916. The circus owner reasoned that he couldn't afford to lose money from missing show dates, and after all the notoriety occasioned by Eldridge's death, he didn't think he could get any other show to buy her. Apparently, he decided that the only way to profit from the experience would be to reap some free publicity by staging a spectacular public execution.

"That's where Erwin comes in. I mean, how are you going to kill an elephant? Poison? How many *pounds* would it take? Electrocution? I wouldn't want to be around if you miscalculated the lethal dosage and pissed her off. But Erwin, population in 1916 two thousand, was the site of the repair shops for the Clinchfield Railroad. It offered the circus owner a solution. Why not hang the beast on a one-hundred-ton railroad derrick? That's the equipment they used to lift railroad cars. A five-ton animal would pose no problem at all for such a contraption.

"Arvin is making faces at me here, neighbors. I think he was hoping that I'd tell him Mary got herself Clarence Darrow for an attorney, and that he'd got her off with life. Arvin was picturing Old Mary over there in Mountain City to this day, pressing out license plates with her trunk. 'Fraid not, Arvin. Absolute justice can be a terrible thing.

"They marched Mary down to the railroad yard after the matinee performance, and she was nervous about it, too. Elephants are big, ungainly looking creatures, but they aren't stupid. She knew something bad was happening. The circus people put a chain around her neck and hoisted her right up off the ground. It took them two tries, but they finally succeeded in killing a rare and intelligent creature, that maybe had no business being enslaved in a sideshow anyhow. Maybe she even preferred a quick death to a life of servitude. I don't claim to be an expert on the opinions of elephants.

"I do know this: sometimes the law seems more concerned with shutting up mobs who are too dumb to be reasoned with than they are with dispensing justice. Maybe you're wondering what all this has to do with one old man who took an ax to his prosperous neighbor a quarter of a century ago. It's just a feeling I have, folks. Something tells me that Harm was just as much a pawn as Mary was. I think there's another side to both stories, and while we're never going to hear the truth in Mary's case, I'm still hoping that it can be uncovered for Harm Sorley.

"The switchboard's lighting up now. It must be time to start giving away those coffee mugs."

Jeremy Cobb ran his finger along the map, trying to match the trail lines to Larkin's written instructions. He figured he was at least halfway there. He had passed Highway 421 day before yesterday, marking the end of the Iron Mountain Trail. Then he had entered the Flint Mill Scenic and Primitive Area, heading south, with more than twelve miles of trail to his credit, and the blisters to prove it. On 421 he had resisted the urge to stick out his thumb, and cadge a ride to Mountain City for an all-you-can-eat meal and an all-the-hot-water-you-can-soak-up shower in a cheap motel room. As if any motorist would pick him up, the way he looked. At least he couldn't smell his own body odor. He could make it a few more miles, he told himself, and in a few more miles the tempting highway had vanished between the hills, and he was safely enveloped in timeless forest.

He had found the U.S. Forest Service sign at Camp Tom Howard Road. This, too, was paved, but it had soon become a gravel road, so he walked in the grass alongside it to ease the pain in his feet. He hoped the wetness in his boots was sweat. He decided that finding out for sure would serve no useful purpose. The graveled road connected to the Flatwoods Horse Trail at a gated road on the left, and he'd followed that to the Flint Mill Trailhead, and down past Holston High Knob, and into what should be the Laurel Branch Wilderness. Maybe he should have followed the Appalachian Trail. At least that was contiguous. This business of hopping through civilization to find the next link in the pathway was disconcerting. It broke the mood. How could he hope to find his way into the mind of an eighteenth-century woman if his journey was punctuated by the buzz of passing cars every ten miles or so?

In the Big Laurel Wilderness, he had been instructed to pick up the Appalachian Trail. Larkin had no other recommendations. But Jeremy decided that he valued solitude more than safety. The thought of other hikers, wanting to swap trail stories and scolding him for his foolishness, made him determined to avoid the road most traveled. He thought he had hiked enough to take risks. He had a compass and besides, according to the map, there was a huge man-made lake in the territory, and he should be able to navigate by that. It was a long, narrow body of water, made to control the flooding of the Watauga River. If he could keep Watauga Lake in sight as he traveled, he would stay on course. He knew that the name Watauga was an Indian word meaning "broken waters," and he wondered what the Cherokees had meant by it. Rocks in the riverbed making white water, perhaps? The lake was less than fifty years old. Katie would have found a river here, leading her south toward home.

By the time he made camp for the night, Jeremy was still searching for a glimpse of blue water through the trees. Perhaps his compass reading was off. There was no lake in sight. He would keep heading south and hope he found it.

He looked at the shrubs and grasses around him, wondering which of them would be good to eat. Could you boil them into a soup, and would it be dangerous to try? He was a bit low on food. By now he had discarded his solar shower, the rest of the canned goods, all his books, and his fishing rod. He discovered that his electric razor had been damaged somehow—perhaps it had been at the bottom of the pack, and was slammed too hard against the ground in one of his frequent unburdenings. Anyhow, it wouldn't hold its charge anymore, and was now a heavy and useless hunk of metal. Seventy dollars; a Christmas gift from his folks. He threw it into the weeds. The pack would be lighter now, and he would make better time. He kept the gun, though.

In the gray light of dawn, Martha had sat in the church parking lot shaking with cold. The engine was idling, the car's heater on full blast, and still her teeth were chattering, and her hands shook too badly for her to drive. At first she thought that she had come down with the flu from spending a cold night on the mountain. Later she realized that she was in shock, maybe a delayed reaction to watching Patrick Kendrick blow his brains out, but she doubted that he was the cause. The cold and fatigue had hit her within minutes after she ran the license check on the car in LeDonne's driveway. Crystal Stanley, female, white, single, age twenty-three, resident of 1016 Forest Trail, Hamelin, Tennessee. No outstanding warrants.

When she was able to drive again, she drove to the truck stop out on the highway. She drank three cups of black coffee to deaden her nerves and to jolt the fatigue out of her system, and then she drove to the office. There were things she needed to check on, but she had to be out of there before LeDonne showed up.

Martha considered sleep and decided against it. LeDonne was covering the day shift, which meant that Martha ought to be at home in bed, resting up for her turn on night duty, but she knew that she would only lie dry-eyed in the dim curtained bedroom, playing out endless scenes against the white ceiling. She could not surrender to the torments of solitude—much better to keep busy.

At the office, Martha kept the door closed and the blinds drawn, so that no early risers would drop in to pass the time of day. After a quick glance around for messages, she checked the fax machine. Nothing urgent. A convenience store robbery two counties away; a stolen car from Sullivan. The NECC had passed along a report of an assault case in Beech Mountain, North Carolina, with an APB for a suspect resembling the escaped convict Harm Sorley, but the identification was not positive. Martha glanced at the map. Beech Mountain. Maybe forty miles east of here; about the same distance south of Mountain City. Martha put her finger on the spot for Beech Mountain on the map. "It's him," she said.

She reread the report. There weren't many details. The victim of the attack was a sixty-five-year-old retiree, resident of a resort community on the site of the old Land of Oz theme park. He had returned home to find that a derelict had broken into his home, and was helping himself to supplies in the kitchen. The man had attempted to frighten off the intruder, but he had been hit on the head with a glass bottle. He had made his statement from the local hospital, where his condition was listed as serious, but not life-threatening. "You got off lucky, buddy," Martha said to herself. "Good thing you didn't keep an ax around the kitchen."

How long ago had the incident occurred? A couple of days. He was getting close. Martha knew that Spencer and LeDonne believed that Harm was a senile old man, more of a danger to himself than to anyone else, but this report proved them wrong. He was out there, and he was violent. She touched the butt of the Glock, holstered at her side. She was ready.

It was getting late—nearly 7:00 A.M. Shafts of autumn sunlight were filtering in through the blinds, making dust motes dance above the wood floor. LeDonne would be in soon. She would search his desk for any further evidence of CRYSTLS, and then she would head for the backcountry, the ridges near the North Carolina line, and search for Harm Sorley. Let them think she was home asleep with the phone unplugged. While she walked the hills, she could think about what to do about that other matter. About whores who thought that any man was fair game.

For the first time since he began his footsore journey, Jeremy Cobb found himself thinking about his parents. At first he had tried to block out all memories of the twentieth century, to will himself into Katie Wyler's wilderness, but that hadn't worked. Each stab of pain from a blistered foot sent his thoughts scurrying back to Blacksburg—to the salve and bandages section of University Mall's Super-X drugstore, or to the Virginia Tech student infirmary, where he could lie in sedated oblivion while his wounds healed.

Despite his reverie of civilization, he was still determined not to turn back. He pictured his father's face, no less sneering for its mask of concern, saying: "You should have known you couldn't make it, Jeremy. Remember when you were nine, and you wanted to camp out in Stevie Fezer's backyard? How long did you last— three hours? Said the Fezers' trees looked liked a giant cat playing a fiddle with a godzilla monster dancing beside it." That was Dad—do something right, it's a fluke; screw up, and it's an indelible character trait that you bear for the rest of your life. Jeremy's father didn't like him much, but since he was an only child, they both pretended otherwise.

His mother considered this trek through the Smokies a great and perilous adventure—but to a timid woman like Joyce Cobb, what wasn't? Every telephone conversation he could remember began with her saying "How are you?" in anxious tones, as if he were calling from beneath an oxygen tent in intensive care. The call always ended with the warning "Be careful!" She'd been afraid that he'd drown in swimming class at the YMCA, that he'd die in a fiery wreck with his learner's permit, and that graduate school would jockey him into a nervous breakdown. He wasn't sure this concern constituted love, either. She never seemed interested in anything he actually said or did. He felt himself to be a priceless but unlovely porcelain egg entrusted to her care. She felt the responsibility of him, without any joy of possession.

Back in the history department, his death would be a nine days' wonder, but a source of no real grief to anyone. It would not even stir the pity and imagination of strangers, as Katie Wyler's death had done to him. No one, decades hence, would walk these hills in memory of Jeremy Cobb, seeker of knowledge. There is no tragedy in avoidable stupidity.

It was past dawn now, but the sun was not yet high enough to burn off the morning fog that drifted through the hollows. It was hunger, not daylight, that had awakened him. He had made another evening meal of candy bars and water, because he was too cold and weary to contend with the camp stove. He couldn't go on like that, burning up many more calories than he was taking in, especially since he wasn't even sure where he was. Soon he would weaken so much that he would be unable to carry his pack, or even to continue on the trail, and then he would die of exposure. And everyone would say how silly he had been to attempt such a stunt. There would be no sympathy in their thoughts of him, only a solemn smugness over the guy who wouldn't listen to reason.

He was shivering now. Nights were so cold on the mountain. The leaves hadn't even fallen yet, and already it felt like the dead of winter. He didn't want to leave his sleeping bag, but he knew that he had to get going. Any more delay would only cost him another night on the trail.

He put on more soiled clothes over the ones he had slept in, and stumbled down to the stream to get water.

The stubble on unshaven face itched, and his back ached from carrying the heavy pack. He splashed his face in the bone-chilling water, but he felt no inclination to bathe. He might have brushed his teeth, if he had remembered to bring along his toothbrush, but it didn't seem worth a trek back uphill to retrieve it. He didn't bother with the water purification kit, because he was going to boil all of it anyhow. Sixteen ounces for tea, and the rest to be added to three packages of instant oatmeal. He wished he had brought another six boxes of instant oatmeal, instead of all those cans of beef stew he'd had to discard because he didn't have the time to backtrack the previous day's trail to find where he dropped his can opener.

When he got back to his campsite with the plastic jug of creek water, he found four small apples and a cluster of dark berries piled at the entrance to his tent. Jeremy looked around, but there was no one there.

Martha wondered if weariness would overtake her as she drove, forcing her back to her bed. Surely she must be tired, after being up and under combat stress for more than twenty-four hours, but she felt no easing of tension. The muscles in her neck and shoulders ached from the strain of maintaining composure, and she felt a thousand miles away from sleep. She had been talking the whole way, a monologue of poison addressed to LeDonne, who was not present either in person or on the police band radio. Martha had turned off the communication system. It was just her and the demons, out for a spin. She would say it all, here in the privacy of an empty car.

"Just who the hell do you think you are, anyway?" she said, glancing back at the cloud of road dust in her wake. "Do you think it's been easy putting up with you? Think you're such a prize with your fucking nightmares, and your flashbacks, and your goddamn self-centered moodiness all the time! I went to a damned *support group* with you! And I wasn't sick. And after all the love and loyalty I've given you, in spite of everything, you go and do this."

She spun tires on curves that she usually took at twenty-five, but the road was dry, and she knew where the bends were, so she stayed on the tarmac. She wanted to get as far away from Hamelin as she could, out to where you could look across miles of rolling hills and see not a trace of man. Except that she was bringing sorrow with her, trapped in a litany in her head. Damn, damn, damn Joe LeDonne.

"Is that all you want, you bastard? I take care of you, and I make love to you, and then I try to better myself so you'll be proud of me, and instead of being supportive and respecting me for my efforts—I get *this*? You go out and find some dumb teenage cunt who can't even *spell* Vietnam. You want some slack-jawed waitress who thinks you're hot because you've got a gun on your hip? A worshipful moron: is that what it takes to prop up your manhood? Do you have to feel superior to get it up? Why didn't you just buy a sheep, Joe?"

She had thought that she would drive out to the farthest hill in the county, sitting up on an outcropping of rock, and cry into the granite until she felt nothing, but where there should have been tears, there was only a tightness in her chest. She could not cry. She could not keep her mind on the tracking of the escaped convict, either. So now she couldn't do her job right. Was LeDonne going to cost her that, too? Had he, in fact, taken up with this bitch to punish Martha for daring to compete with him?

"What did you want, Joe?" she said aloud. "A woman who'd stay barefoot and pregnant? Did you think you could hurt me so bad that I'd stop trying to play with the big boys? Well, Mr. War Hero with the night sweats, you don't know what tough is. How would you like to see your whore's guts trailed through every room in her stinking house? They say people have miles and miles of guts inside them. Wonder how many times it would go around a room?"

Odd that she could think such a thing without shrinking away from the brutality of the image. Her mind should automatically repudiate this urge to violence as un-Christian, uncivilized, unworthy of a peace officer. She felt none of those things. She was fascinated by the imagined scene: a cheaply furnished living room streaked with gore and ropes of flesh, leading back to the eviscerated corpse of a bleached blond with a sharp chin and ferret teeth. Was she insane to let her mind linger on such visions? Would the scene haunt her until she was compelled to act it out so that she could stop imagining it?

She wondered if she ought to tell anyone what she knew and how she was reacting to it, but there didn't seem to be anyone that she could confide in. Spencer Arrowood would side with LeDonne, because men always stick together, and somehow all this would become *her* fault. Her family would offer no comfort.

Martha had two failed marriages behind her: it was obvious to the Ayers clan that she just couldn't hold a man, so it was only natural that LeDonne should have strayed. Martha clenched her teeth. She hadn't done anything wrong, except maybe to try to become more than she had been. It wasn't right to get punished for trying to better yourself.

Her thoughts kept veering back to CRYSTLS, and she found that most of her anger flowed in that direction. Her rage at LeDonne was tempered by the fact that she loved him, and he was all she had; but CRYSTLS was a stranger, of whom she knew nothing but ill. There was no reason not to hate her. She should be made to suffer for putting Martha through all this pain.

She forced herself to cover the back roads, check the hunters' cabins for signs of break-ins, and stop the occasional south-bound backpacker to see if they'd encountered any strange old men on the Appalachian Trail. She walked all the way out to Tamson's Ridge and sat on the prow of rock overlooking the long valley of the Little Dove River, watching for wisps of campfire smoke, or for some other sign of the fugitive. Nothing. Martha thought she was doing a pretty good job of going through the motions of police work. Inside, she was still shuttling scenes of carnage across her mind's eye, but at least she was functioning. She figured she'd stay out in the woods, watching and looking for Harm, until it was time for her to go back on duty. By the time she finished her shift, it would be midnight, and her body would surely give out by then. She would have to be too exhausted to hunt down CrystalS—that's how the name stuck in her mind now; she wasn't just Crystal, she was *CrystalS*. It wouldn't work forever, but maybe she could distract herself until the rage burned down low enough to live with.

Harm Sorley knew that he had been drinking again. He couldn't remember what he'd had or how he got it, but he knew that wobbly feeling, and the sense of being once-removed from everything around him. Still, that didn't explain about the trees. Harm wondered what was wrong with the trees. These big red spruces on the highest ridges looked like they were dying. Their needles were brown, and the branches, when he touched them, snapped off dry as kindling. It was like somebody had watered them with poison, but these were wild trees, out on a cliff in the deepest woods. Nothing would touch these trees but wind and rainwater, and what could be purer than that?

The image of the dying trees reminded him of something else, but he couldn't quite remember what. Something nagged at the back of his mind, but he couldn't drag it up to the surface. Something about dead land. He had been angry about it, like it had something to do with him. He had been someplace—was it recently? Standing on dead land, and feeling sorrowful. He strained to catch an image. No. The thought was gone.

Harm knew that he was in the woods somewhere between Watauga Lake and home, and he felt he'd been out here for some time. His beard itched, and his clothes were rank and muddy. His teeth felt like mossy rocks in a creek bed. He had a burlap sack, but no rifle. Had he been hunting and lost his weapon? It was autumn; the leaves were bronze in the sunlight.

He felt annoyance and a stab of fear at his confusion. He wished he could recall what he was doing out here. He stumbled over an outcropping of rock. Pulling a drunk, most likely, he reckoned. Maybe he had been visiting somebody's still. But they didn't ought to have left him to go off by himself in the wild. He reckoned he ought to head downhill and find him a creek to follow to civilization, so he could get on home to Rita.

"You don't want to go home."

He turned around. She was a bony woman, but she looked young. Except for her eyes. And her dress, blue and raggedy underneath the dirt, looked too big for her. She had twigs in her hair and a briar cut on her cheek, but she didn't seem afraid. Her voice was gentle, sad. "You don't want to go home," she said again.

Martha was two minutes early for the evening shift, because two minutes of Joe LeDonne was about all she thought she could stand right now. She wanted to go on duty and get away from him as fast as she could. While they were both in uniform or at the sheriff's office, their personal lives could not be an issue: they would have to be working professionals putting the good of Wake County before anything else. Martha had thought all this out on the groggy drive back to town. No matter how great the temptation to rage at the faithless LeDonne, she would have to swallow her wrath, and wait. At first, Martha thought she would explode if she tried to bottle up her feelings, but when she walked into the office and saw LeDonne doing paperwork at his desk, she knew she could wait. Waiting was better. Then she would be past ready, and he would be flat-footed. Besides, she wanted to deal with CrystalS before Joe realized there was trouble.

The fatigue had finally hit her. It showed in her face. There were dark circles under her eyes, and she had the washed-out look of someone coming down with the flu. She dabbed on some lip gloss in the parking lot, because she didn't want him to suspect that anything was wrong. Her movements were slow, and she had to think them through. It was like being drunk on exhaustion. Eight hours to go.

She stood in the doorway watching him. Usually, she spoke first, asking him how he was, and burbling whatever news she had that might interest him. Not now. She stood, arms crossed, pistol on her hip, and watched expressionless while he wrote.

Finally LeDonne looked up. "You're back," he said. "I heard about last night. The Kendrick boy. Too bad."

Martha shrugged. "There's worse things," she said. *Like picturing you and that bitch together naked. I could put a bullet in my own brain to make that vision go away.* She didn't say anything, though. Just looked at him, the way Spencer had taught her to look at people she was about to arrest: cool, appraising, wary.

"Yeah." LeDonne seemed puzzled by her attitude, but he wouldn't ask questions. "Well, there was some excitement on day watch, too. Spencer's coming in tonight, because it's still not settled."

"What is it?" asked Martha after a pause. She would discuss department business with him, and be civil about it. She kept standing, though, and she didn't go any closer to him. "Something else about the Kendrick boy?"

"No. A missing persons alert." LeDonne shrugged. "Maybe it will prove you had the right idea about that escaped convict after all, Martha. Rita Pentland is missing."

# CHAPTER
# 12

The world can never give
  The bliss for which we sigh:
T'is not the whole of life to live,
  Nor all of death to die.

#676, "O, Where Shall Rest Be Found,"
Montgomery

Tennessee Methodist Hymnal, 1885

With the help of Kitty Washburn at the courthouse, Henry Kretzer had figured out exactly which dirt-road holler had been home to Harm Sorley at the time of the Maggard murder. He had a photocopy of the map, written directions from several lifelong residents, and a full tank of gas. It was time to visit the scene of the crime. The only other piece of the puzzle that he hadn't tried was to talk to Rita Pentland, the former Mrs. Sorley, but he knew that the interview would be unpleasant and perhaps painful. Henry Kretzer was incapable of staging confrontations. As Hank the Yank he might have been able to interview the woman—he thought of her as *the widow*—on the air, but in his private persona, he could not seek her out to reopen old wounds. This lack of killer instinct had kept him out of hard news, and would probably keep him in backwater AM stations for the rest of his so-called career, but Kretzer didn't mind. If he had to choose between getting rich and staying sane, he'd opt for the latter.

Now he was driving his ancient Gremlin up the two-lane road that ended up in North Carolina, six mostly vertical miles from Hamelin. It wasn't too far from

Nora Bonesteel's place on Ashe Mountain, and the scenery looked about the same, too. He didn't care much for the solitude. Although the occasional glimpses of distant valleys were scenic enough, Hank wasn't much of a sightseer. He could talk up the landscape for the listeners, but it was a country of the mind. He could talk with ardor and conviction about tulip poplars and grasshopper sparrows without having the least idea what either one looked like.

The Sorleys' bit of scrubland had bordered Claib Maggard's farm, but you reached it by a different road. The juncture of the sprawling Maggard farm and Sorley's meager acres had been at the back, along a cold stream that came from up in the hills, and there was no right of way through Maggard land. To get to the Sorleys' holler you went much farther from town, finally ending up on dirt roads that led back behind the ridge. The Maggard land was rented out now to a retired Eastman Kodak executive from over in Kingsport. The Maggard descendants were long gone: some people said Ohio, others said Florida. Maggard's widow had died out in some rest home near her daughter twenty years back, and the one witness called at the trial—a stockman, said to be simpleminded—had died of pneumonia, working as a hired man on someone else's place over in Virginia.

There wasn't anyone else left to talk to about the past. Only people like Dallas Stuart and the call-ins to the radio show, people who half remembered facts heard secondhand. And if Sheriff Arrowood could be believed, even Harm Sorley was brain damaged and incapable of recalling that day. Hank the Yank wouldn't be mentioning that fact during his Neighborhood Watch commentaries. The hint of tragedy would spoil both the humor and the bravado of the old man's jail-break.

He found a dirt track leading off to the right: two ruts divided by a grassy mound. Surely that couldn't be the old logging road indicated in Kitty Washburn's directions. It was, though. One good rain would turn this lane into an impassable mudhole. He hoped the car's suspension system would keep the chassis high enough to drive over it; otherwise this jaunt was going to cost him the whole exhaust system. Well, it would add color to his broadcast account of the adventure when he described it for tonight's listeners.

He took the road at a crawl, peering at the underbrush that scraped the doors on either side, half expecting to see the leering face of a bear looking back at him. He was climbing higher on this tiny road, corkscrewing around the mountain, sometimes with nothing but some matchstick pine trees between him and a half-mile drop. Why did people choose to live in places like this? Where did they find out about them? He couldn't imagine such a remote parcel of woods ever attracting the notice of a realty company. Maybe it was family land. Maybe the Sorley clan claimed these woods at a time in the distant past when most of the roads in the world looked like this one.

When he reached the crest of the trail, he revised his opinion. The view was certainly first rate: miles of field and forest spreading out below him, like the view from a commuter plane. If this landscape were in Vermont, it would be all right. Say, three hours from Boston; a nice postcard view. Five hundred K in roadwork, and it would be inhabitable.

The Sorleys hadn't lived up here, though. Maybe the wind blew too cold to make a mountaintop hospitable year-round for poor folks, or maybe you just couldn't get water up there. Whatever the reason, the Sorleys had planted themselves on the other side of that ridge, another brake-burning mile down into a cove, shrouded by oaks, and nestled up against the mountain's skirts, so that you could barely see in. He put the car in low gear, and began to ease his way down the steep grade. A dozen yards farther down a doe skittered across the road and disappeared into the underbrush. "Great!" said Hank the Yank aloud. "A damned deer! Can bears and snakes be far behind?"

"When we get to the Pentlands' house, I'll let you do the questioning," the sheriff told Martha. "Like you said, women are better at talking to people in domestic matters. I'm just going along to show the extent of our concern."

"Just what extent is that?" Martha asked. "I haven't noticed you expressing any interest in capturing the escaped convict who's probably responsible for her disappearance."

"Martha, before you appoint yourself judge, jury, and executioner, don't you think you ought to at least question somebody?" Spencer's tone was mild, a little joking, but Martha could see that he was disappointed in her.

She felt like hell. Her head seemed to be full of cotton batting, and she was snapping at everything Spencer said. When he gets back to LeDonne, there'll be remarks about PMS, Martha thought. She had to force herself to concentrate on Rita's disappearance. Sometimes she would wonder why she felt such anguish, and then she would remember about CrystalS. So Rita was missing. Maybe her ex-husband killed her for running out on him. Served her right. Loyalty should be enforced. In her heart, Martha knew that it was her pain talking, but she couldn't summon up an ounce of charity, not even for a meek old woman who had gone missing.

"Are you all right, Martha? You're not still upset about last night, are you?"

"Last night?" Oh, he meant the Kendrick boy. She had almost forgotten him. "I'll be fine," she said.

"Don't let the pressure of this job get to you," Spencer said. "You have to learn not to take it home with you. If you need to talk to anybody about stress or anything, let me know."

"Sure." She kept staring out the window. The Pentlands' house had just come in sight, as neatly kept as ever. The extra cars in the driveway meant that the family had gathered together to face their loss. Good. They could question everybody in one visit, and not have to chase around three counties to find people.

"Okay, Martha. Listen up. We're just going to hear what the Pentlands have to say. We're not going to offer them any theories about Mrs. Pentland's absence. Got that?"

"I expect they've worked it out for themselves," said Martha. She wondered if he'd dismantled the alarm system before he went in and got her. Had she screamed? She'd know soon.

"And we're not going to jump to conclusions about the outcome of this case and upset those grieving family members. Understood."

"Ten-four," said Martha wearily.

She followed him up to the house, hoping that somebody would have the presence of mind to offer them coffee.

Jeremy Cobb was hiding in an ivy thicket in the woods somewhere south of Watauga Lake. He had finally found the long valley of water, nestled in among the ridges, and he had kept it in sight as he traveled. That and his compass had kept him going until his next point of reference: Roan Mountain. He had just caught sight of it towering ahead, when the ripple of voices sent him scurrying for cover.

Hikers were walking twenty yards away from him on a well-marked trail, but he didn't want to be seen by them. They looked young enough to be his students, but worse than that: they looked like day-trippers. The pair were clean, well dressed, and laughing, whereas he was stinking, unshaven, and ragged. He would not have believed that a few days out of civilization could reduce him to such a state of savagery. He had lost most of his supplies now—either he'd used them up, dropped them, or discarded them deliberately to lighten his burden. The field guides and works of literature were long gone. Maslow's hierarchy of needs had certainly proved right on that point: hungry, pain-racked, shelterless creatures have no need of poetry or philosophy.

He had used up all his bandages, and thrown away the deodorant and other toiletries as silly affectations from a world he no longer lived in. Today he had eaten purple berries from a tree-coiling vine without even bothering to wash them first, and he had drunk deep from a fast-running brook before he remembered about the water purification kit. Katie Wyler must have eaten worms, tree buds, and even the carcasses of putrid animals she'd found dead along the way. Anything to survive. His feet were wet from having forded a small creek a mile back, and his bruised toes squished against the soggy leather, sending chills up his legs.

He was no longer sticking to any marked trail. He was heading south-southwest, knowing that soon he would be in Katie's home country. He felt certain that he would know when he reached it, as if telling the tale a hundred times in a classroom had made the experience somehow a part of his own past.

Jeremy came out of the thicket for a better look at the strange hikers, but they did not glance in his direction. He felt contempt for the city rats as they strode past, giggling at some private joke. Why weren't they aware of his presence? This wasn't a shopping mall. Didn't they know to be watchful in the woods? A few moments later it occurred to him that if he had stopped those happy wanderers from civilization and asked them for help, in an hour he would be encased in a fast-moving car, glassed off from the wilderness, and headed back to the comforts of his technocage. He let himself think of pizza and hot tubs, of bacon double cheeseburgers and electric blankets. But they were gone now, too far down the trail for him to totter after them with the remnants of his supplies. Besides, he couldn't face them: the laughter or the pitying revulsion with which they would look at him. *Poor fool,* they would think, *People don't have to do this anymore. We beat Mother Nature, didn't you know?*

It couldn't be far now. He was at least two-thirds of the way there, now that Roan Mountain lay up ahead. The thought of great bald Roan, its rolling summit crowned with rhododendron bushes, had kept him going when he thought he was too weary to walk another step. So many times had he seen that glorious mountain on calendars and local postcards that he felt no stranger to it. It was a great grassy treeless peak towering more than six thousand feet above sea level; scientists still argued about why the crest had no timber. Some of them said that the Indians had burned the mountaintop to make grassland, but Jeremy thought that couldn't be right, because the Cherokees themselves had legends about the balds of Roan. They told of a giant wasp called *Ulagu* that had menaced the tribe, and, in answer to the people's prayers, the Great Spirit had struck the creature with lightning. The blast of divine fire had left the mountain forever bare of trees. Jeremy wondered if wasps frequented the top of Roan to gather nectar from the rhododendron flowers and from the wild blackberry bushes. He believed that all myths began with a kernel of truth, if one could only discover it amid the chaff of embellishment.

He'd also heard that the *Nunnehi*, the Cherokees' spirit people, lived at the summit of the balds. They were said to help warriors in battle or lonely travelers, and they appear as mortals when they allow themselves to be seen. Most of the time they wear fairystones, staurolite crosses of a natural crystalline formation found in the southern mountains, which render them invisible. Jeremy hoped that they would stay invisible. He wanted to meet no one on his journey now. But he did want to look at the land from the mountaintop. The day was cold, but clear. You would be able to see for miles from the top of Roan: vistas that hadn't changed much since Katie's day.

Thoughts of the prophet Moses flickered through his mind: stand on the mountain and gaze at the promised land. He hoped there wouldn't be hordes of tourists cluttering up the landscape. He was almost done with the twentieth century: there was just the sleeping bag, the P-32 pistol, and a few other items. He'd ditched the camp stove when he ran out of things to cook on it.

He braced himself for another upward climb, wondering if there was anything else in the pack that he could do without, now that he was nearing journey's end. He felt his stomach gnawing with hunger, but the sensation pleased him. He felt that he was becoming one with the wilderness.

Henry Kretzer stopped the car in the middle of the road, and got out to look around. His palms were wet, and he felt uneasy looking at the narrow path through the trees. He hoped more Sorleys hadn't come to take up residence. These people didn't appear to like strangers. He followed the footpath from the road through a short stretch of woods, and came out in a barren field fringed with brown grass and scraggly pine seedlings that testified to the land's neglect. He wondered why nothing was growing in the field. Had someone tilled it for next season's planting? It didn't look like it, but then, Hank the Yank didn't know much about farming.

At the far end of the field, Kretzer could see an old trailer set up on cinder blocks. The sun glinted on shards of broken glass in the trailer windows. There was no sign of life.

Of course, if you were an escaped convict, you wouldn't want to advertise your presence. He'd better check the place out. He glanced about him at the dark thickets of trees at the far end of the field. It wasn't hunting season yet, was it? You'd never get out of here with a bullet in you, not over that cow path they called a road.

He crossed the field as quickly as his suede shoes allowed, dodging the occasional mudhole. The mud looked funny. In the slanting autumn sunlight, he could see streaks of orange that definitely weren't red clay. Here and there were swirls of green and red in stagnant puddles. It was pretty, he thought—like a reflection of autumn leaf colors from the earth itself. But *nothing* was growing. Not even weeds. The dirt was smooth, unplowed.

He made a mental note to ask somebody about the funny colored field. A runoff from strip mining, maybe? But, whatever it was, it had nothing to do with the convict.

The trailer was ancient: eight feet wide at best, and not more than forty feet long. Kretzer wasn't very good at guessing such things; all he could say for sure was that it looked small enough to be a doghouse. The idea of living here with a wife and baby made him shudder. He wondered who owned the land, and why they allowed this junk heap to disintegrate here, instead of hauling it away.

The door opened easily, much to his relief. He hadn't liked the idea of crawling through those narrow windows, still studded with shards of dirty glass. The plywood floors sagged where they had rotted through, and stalks of dry grass poked through the cracks. He wondered what the smell was. Dead possum under the floorboards?

Kretzer stood still and listened. The place felt empty, but just to make sure, he decided to check the tiny bedroom that must lie beyond that doorway against the main room's back wall.

He walked carefully, steadying himself against the wall, in case more floorboards should give way under his weight. He reached the door, and turned the metal handle, lurching a bit to avoid another patch of rotted wood. *I might as well check the whole place,* he was thinking to himself as he pushed his way in.

He had thought it was too late in the year for flies, but apparently the brisk autumn weather hadn't killed them off yet, because there seemed to be hundreds of them swarming around the very still form sprawled on burlap sacks in the corner. He couldn't see the face even if he wanted to, which he definitely did not. But the rest of the body was small and shrunken, clad in a beige pantsuit of polyester. One bone-colored shoe protruded from the burlap. The corpse was female, and she might have been there hours or days, but certainly not years. Shaken by the sight of untidy death, Kretzer's powers of reasoning took him no further.

Henry Kretzer stood five feet from the death scene, and thought that the humane thing to do would be to make a perfunctory—though futile—check for signs of life, try to determine identity, and then find a blanket and cover up the remains, but before he could will himself to do so, several of the flies detached themselves from the deceased and began a wobbly dive in his direction.

Hank the Yank slammed the door and ran.

The Pentlands looked more bewildered than grief-stricken, an attitude that Martha considered denial in the face of Rita Pentland's disappearance. Charlotte Pentland, the missing woman's daughter, sat on the beige sofa with a county map spread out before her on the coffee table. "She didn't take her car," the young woman kept saying. "She couldn't have got far."

"She could have," said Spencer Arrowood quietly. "She could have taken a bus, or even hitchhiked to the Tri-Cities airport. But we'll need more information before we can make any good guesses about where she went and how she got there."

"Can't you just call the airport and the bus station?" asked Buck Pentland. He looked embarrassed, whether from the red-rimmed eyes that betrayed his tears or from unease at his mother's capricious behavior, Martha couldn't tell.

"There's no point in doing that," said the boy's father. Euell Pentland's red-faced self-importance had given way to a pale ferocity. "We all know what's become of my wife, so why don't we just say it, and be done with it!"

"What's that, Mr. Pentland?" asked the sheriff, as calmly as before.

"Why, that escaped convict has kidnapped her. Made away with her, just like we feared! And you people didn't do a damned thing to prevent it. Not even a guard to watch the house! You'd better believe I'm reporting this to the state authorities!"

"Fine, but let's get some facts first. Who discovered that your wife was missing, and when?"

"I guess I did," said Euell Pentland, glaring at the officers. "I came home last night and she was gone."

"What time was this?"

"Six o'clock, I guess. I went back out, though. I had a council meeting at eight. I figured she had gone out shopping or some such fool thing, but when I got back at nine-something, she still wasn't home."

"But her car was here, so surely she couldn't have been shopping?"

"She might have been off with Charlotte. I was certainly angry that she hadn't left a note, but Rita could be thoughtless at times. Her class doesn't observe the social niceties."

Martha, who had been taking notes, looked up quickly when he said this. She glanced at Spencer, but the sheriff was nodding encouragement, apparently unperturbed by this slander of the victim.

"But you didn't call us to report her missing?"

"No. I went out and drove around."

"You were trying to find her yourself?"

Euell Pentland hesitated. "That may have been in my

mind," he said. "Also, I was so angry at her for worrying me that I needed to get out. I find driving very soothing. I didn't go anywhere in particular. Just drove around the back roads."

"So last night you didn't think that your wife had been abducted?" Spencer Arrowood sounded innocent, not accusing. Martha thought he was being more patient than she could ever be with such a bully.

"I suppose not," muttered Pentland. "I see now that I should have called you in sooner."

"But now you think that Mrs. Rita Pentland was kidnapped, and you suspect the escaped convict. Now, were any windows broken here in the house? Any sign of forced entry?"

"None that I could see." Pentland reddened. "He could have picked a lock. Or tricked her into opening the door."

"We'll take a look at the doors and windows," said Spencer. "Martha, I wonder if you and Miss Charlotte Pentland would take a look through her mother's belongings? See if anything is missing."

Martha got up quickly, before Euell Pentland could think too much about the implications of the sheriff's request. She thought it was a waste of time, but she knew better than to argue. Among outsiders, cops were always in perfect agreement. "Come on," she said to the pale young woman who was still paging through her maps. "You can help me."

"Do you think he might have stolen things as well?" asked Charlotte, as she led the deputy down the beige-carpeted hall. Their footsteps made squeaking echoes on the plastic runner.

"I don't know," said Martha. "We just like to be thorough."

The bedroom was as colorless as the rest of Rita Pentland's house. It was decorator-correct, and spotless, but Martha could get no feel for the personality of anyone who slept there. She slid back the doors of the walk-in closet, and glanced at the row of pastel polyester outfits.

"Could you tell if anything was missing?" she asked.

"Probably not," said Charlotte. "Mama's clothes tended to be pretty much the same. The suitcases should be on the top shelf, though. There are two of them. I'll look in her jewelry box."

Martha stood on tiptoe, and pushed sweaters aside on the closet shelf until she touched the cold shell of a suitcase. There were two bags: beige Samsonite. "They're here," she said.

Charlotte Pentland had opened a white vinyl jewelry box, the kind that discount stores sell at Christmas for six dollars or so. "She didn't have anything worth taking," she said. "Mama wasn't one for being flashy. She used to say that she thought Dolly Parton was gorgeous, but that she wouldn't have the nerve to go around dolled up like that. She used to let me play dress-up with her jewelry when I was a kid. This stuff is just phony gold chains to wear with her Sunday dresses, and a couple of brooches that Buck or I had given her for Mother's Day, and suchlike."

Charlotte Pentland looked up at Martha, and shivered. "*And suchlike,*" she said. "I'm *talking* like her. I never thought I'd do that. I just can't believe she's gone."

"We'll hope for the best," said Martha.

"What if you can't find her? Do you think you'll broadcast an appeal for the kidnapper to bring her back?"

"It's not up to me," said Martha. She was thinking that escaped convicts who hide out in the woods don't listen to the news much.

"I could do it," said Charlotte, twisting her hands. "It would be humiliating, of course, for everyone at college to know that I'm connected to this, but I'd do it. He might listen to me. He's my daddy, you know."

"I'd heard," said Martha, sliding wire coathangers along the wooden rack.

"We never went to see him in prison. Never wrote or anything. Euell was ashamed of us being connected to him, and he thought I'd be better off just pretending he didn't exist. So we just acted like he was dead. Guess I can't blame him if he's mad at us over it." Her voice quavered. "I just hope he doesn't take it out on her. It's not like she could help it."

"I suppose not." Martha was hardly listening. The dark closet made the tiredness slide over her like a soft quilt.

"I'm getting a master's in geology. The first college graduate in the family *ever*. You'd think he'd be proud of that. At least *I* won't be poor or dependent on some man all my life. You'd think he'd be glad that we managed to survive without him."

"We don't know anything about your mother's disappearance for sure yet," murmured Martha. "Try not to meet trouble halfway." So far she had found a raincoat, walking shoes, and imitation-leather gloves stuffed in the pocket of an old car coat. "Are these all your mother's coats?"

Charlotte inspected the shabby coats. "No," she said. "I made Daddy get her a tan London Fog for Christmas last year. We even put her initials on the lapel. I gave her navy gloves to match. It wasn't hanging in the front hall, so if it isn't in the closet, I guess she took it."

Martha nodded.

"Maybe he didn't want her to get cold," said Charlotte. "I guess he still loves her."

"Maybe." Martha stifled a yawn. She was thinking that it was more likely that Harm had abducted his former wife to punish her for her faithlessness, but it wouldn't do to say that to the victim's daughter. This train of thought led her back to CrystalS, and she felt her throat muscles tighten. It was hard to keep her mind on the case at hand, with fatigue and her own problems pressing down on her. She should be glad that the convict had proved her instincts right. Maybe Spencer would listen to her from now on.

"There are some things missing from this jewelry box," said Charlotte, who had resumed her search.

"What things? Something valuable?"

The young woman shook her head. "Not really. I gave her a serpentine necklace for Christmas last year, because—well, I don't guess you want to know that."

"I'd better hear it," said Martha, sitting down on the bed. "At this stage we don't know what's important."

"Serpentine is a light green rock, sort of like jade. There's a vein of it that runs all the way along the Appalachians from Georgia up through eastern Canada. Then it stops. But if you look in the mountains of Scotland, you find it again. See, it's a *connection*. It's how the mountains used to fit together before continental drift tore them apart."

"And that's why you gave your mother a serpentine necklace?"

Charlotte nodded. The light of excitement left her eyes. "Yes. I'm a geologist, and that serpentine chain is one of the things I'm studying. I thought it made a nice gift, because it was connected to what I do. A conversation piece, I guess. And I was trying to help her understand my work."

"Was she interested in geology?"

"No. But she cared about what I did. That made it important to her."

"Then maybe she would have taken the necklace. Was it valuable?"

"No. It cost me thirty dollars at the Smithsonian. My budget doesn't run to expensive gifts."

"Mine either," said Martha with an encouraging smile. "My mother would've had to take six baths a day to use up all the dusting powder she got over the years. Now, you said something else was missing?"

"Yes. A narrow wedding band of plain gold. It probably didn't cost more than twenty buck new. It was from her marriage to—to my daddy."

"Harm Sorley."

"Yeah. I wonder why she'd take that? Or maybe she didn't. Maybe she finally threw it away. It's been ages since I looked in here."

Spencer Arrowood appeared in the doorway. "We have to go, Martha," he said quietly. Something in his tone made her look up. She knew they had to get out

of there calmly, pleasantly, reassuringly, but *fast*. Someone had found her.

Jeremy Cobb thought that he could hear someone *singing* somewhere deep in the underbrush. He had
thought he was alone on the trail. There had been no
signs of other hikers for more than an hour. Thoughts
of the *Nunnehi* rose unbidden in his mind, but not
even New Age spiritualism could persuade him that
Cherokee fairyfolk would be singing "She'll Be Comin'
Round the Mountain When She Comes." The voice
was a reedy tenor, not unpleasant, but by no means
that of a professional singer.

The sounds didn't seem to be coming any nearer to
him. Jeremy's first impulse was to hurry away, before
the interloper spotted him and trotted out to compare
camp stoves or some such nonsense. He had encountered one of those pests a few days back, and he had
felt like an utter fool in the face of Camping Man's
technical expertise. Besides, the chatter had broken his
tenuous tie with his wild surroundings for at least an
hour after they had parted. He did not want to risk another spell-breaking confrontation, especially since he
felt several degrees more distant from civilization than
he had at the beginning of his journey.

He kept walking, sometimes holding on to shrubs to
keep from falling when the ground was steep, feeling
like a turtle in the unwieldy knapsack. He thought it
might be cheating on the purpose of his journey to
climb Roan for the pleasure of it, but he told himself
that Katie might have done this as well. He didn't know
that she *didn't*. There was only Andrew Wyler's second-

hand account of his sister's journey to go by, and as he'd only heard it once, in childhood, most of the details were left out.

"Howdy," said a voice behind him.

Jeremy turned so quickly that he lost his balance, and the metal-framed backpack toppled him over into a thorn bush. He could feel the blood beginning to seep out of tears on his cheeks and hands, as he peered out to see who had accosted him. The man had stepped out from between the branches of two rhododendron bushes. Their leaves were touching, but there was space between them to walk, if someone pushed his way through.

The man looked too old, too seedy to be a hiker. He was unshaven and dirty, with ill-fitting clothes, and a burlap sack instead of a backpack. Jeremy wondered if homeless people ever wandered out on the Appalachian Trail. The old fellow was smiling at him. He didn't look threatening. He was about five-foot-eight and lean, with streaks of gray in hair that had once been black. Jeremy wondered if he ought to offer him some money.

"Was that you singing?" he asked.

"I believe it was," said the stranger after a moment's hesitation. "It was 'Lead On, Oh King Eternal,' wasn't it? I dearly love that old hymn."

Jeremy frowned. "I heard 'She'll Be Comin' Round the Mountain.'"

"Oh, that one. My little girl is partial to that tune, so I like to sing it every chance I get. She's just a lap-baby, but she loves to get sung to."

"Is she with you?" There seemed to be no one else in

the shrubs behind him. Were they camping somewhere? Occupying National Forest land as squatters?

"No, the young'un's up home with her mommy. I sure do miss her, though. Seems like I went home not too long ago, but I disremember seeing her." He grinned. "Guess I been hitting the shine again."

"Do you work out here?" Jeremy didn't see any tools or other indications that the man might work for the Forest Service.

"That's right," the man smiled. "I'm a logger."

"In the National Forest? Oh, that's right. The government does some tree harvesting as part of the forest management, don't they?"

The old man smiled. "What about you? You lost out here?"

"Off and on," Jeremy admitted. "Actually, I'm a historian. I'm looking for the old Wyler homeplace over in Mitchell County, North Carolina."

"You want something to eat?" asked the man as if he hadn't heard. "I think I must have something in here."

Jeremy glanced at the sack, hoping that a dead rabbit wasn't about to be proffered. "Well . . ."

He watched while the wizened woodman thrust his hand into the muddy sack. He pulled out two shiny foil packages. Backpacker's Pantry products. Just like the ones Jeremy had discarded along the way. "Sure," he said. "Why not? Let me go down to the stream. You have to add boiling water to those entrées before you can eat them. I'll be right back."

The man sat down on a rock and pulled out a tattered leather Bible, leafing through it without another glance at Jeremy, who took this for permission to leave.

He unshouldered his backpack, and set it on the ground. "I'll just get out my water jug, and leave this stuff here with you," he said. "I don't guess I'll need the purification kit, since we're going to boil the water anyhow. Oh, what the hell. Better take it!"

The man ran his finger along the lines as he read, squinting at the fine print, and holding the book so that sunlight fell on the page.

Jeremy scurried away through the rhododendrons, down the hill. He had passed the creek a ways back, and now without the encumbrance of his supplies, he could make it down and back in fifteen minutes or so. He did not resent the intrusion of the old fellow. There was no taint of civilization about *him*, either. The Bible-reading was a little odd, Jeremy thought. He hoped he hadn't run into a crazed fundamentalist, but the man had seemed friendly enough. Besides, he seemed to be a local, so perhaps he would have information about the old Wyler farm. He hadn't reacted to the name, but Jeremy planned to tell him the story of Katie, and see if that jarred any recollections.

He was running now, giddy with the momentum of his downhill passage, and glad to be free of the weight of the knapsack. His feet seemed to hurt less when he ran. It would be good to rest and eat.

The walk back up the hill was slower. With a full plastic jug of water, gripped by the handle with thumb and forefinger, Jeremy's light step became a determined march, and finally a trudge as he retraced his steps, stumbling over outcroppings of rock and dodging prickles in the nameless weeds that barred his way. By now he had remembered that he had discarded his camp stove somewhere a few miles back, and he wasn't going to retrace his steps to retrieve it. Maybe they could build a fire in a clearing. The man was a Forest Service employee; surely he would be able to suggest something. Now faced with the prospect of food, Jeremy felt his hunger as a pain in his gut.

Despite the chill wind, he was sweating by the time he reached the little boulder where he'd left the Bible-reading stranger.

Two packs of Backpacker's Pantry chili mac lay on the stone, but there was no one in sight. The woods were silent. The man and his testament were gone. So was Jeremy Cobb's backpack.

# CHAPTER
# 13

Watch, 'tis your Lord's command;
   And while we speak he's near,
Mark the first signal of his hand,
   And ready all appear.

#594, "YE SERVANTS OF THE LORD," PHILIP DODDRIDGE

TENNESSEE METHODIST HYMNAL, 1885

"Wake up, Martha. We're there."

Martha Ayers awoke with a shudder and a momentary disorientation before she realized that she was in the sheriff's patrol car, and that it was not moving. The long jolting ride over the mountains in twilight had combined with her fatigue to lull her to sleep.

She saw that it was nearly dark, which meant that she had been asleep about forty minutes. Behind them, the mountain was a dark shadow against graying sky. Spencer parked the car at the side of the dirt road, next to a battered Gremlin. A slight, bespectacled man in jeans and a sheepskin jacket stood next to the car, and was waving his arms to attract their attention. Beside him, Deputy Joe LeDonne looked as grim as ever.

It took Martha a moment to recall why she felt a pang of grief when she looked at him. An instant later, fully awake, she remembered CrystalS, and seeing the strange car parked in his driveway at dawn. It seemed like weeks ago now, distanced from her by exhaustion and the jumbled events of the past twenty-four hours. She wondered why she felt only sadness toward Joe LeDonne, and only anger when she thought of CrystalS. *Because if I hate him, I'm left with nothing,* Martha thought. She had written her family off long ago. Now there was just Joe, which was why no matter how moody he became, how bad the nightmares, she had always held on, thinking she could ride out the bad times. *I just want things to go back the way they were before.* They never would, of course. Martha had been in enough relationships to know that no matter what you try to glue them with, the cracks always show.

"According to Jennaleigh, the volunteer firemen ought to be here soon with their spotlights," Spencer Arrowood was saying. "Just once, I wish somebody would die in broad daylight."

"Are we handling this on our own?"

"No. We put a call in to the TBI. They'll be along sooner or later, if they don't foul up the directions."

"That guy next to Joe—is he the one that found her?"

"That's him, Martha. Hank the Yank in person. You can talk to him while LeDonne and I do the crime scene. Do you ever listen to his show?"

"Sometimes, while I'm running. What was he doing way out here?"

The sheriff smiled. "Martha, why don't you ask him?"

He left her then, taking his camera and crime scene kit out of the trunk of the cruiser. He and LeDonne ambled off through the field toward the ruins of a trailer at the edge of the woods. Martha wished she had been alert enough to ask Spencer more procedural questions. The first one that came to mind now was: can I let this guy leave after I've finished questioning him? She didn't see why not, though. She looked at LeDonne's retreating back, and realized with satisfaction that her senses were too dulled for much of the pain to reach her. Later. She would think about him later.

She took out her pen and approached Hank the Yank.


Joe LeDonne circled the body, punctuating his movements with bursts of light from the camera's flash attachment. "He tore her up pretty bad, didn't he? The identification is going to be hell to handle; her relatives having to see her like that."

"I'll put Martha on it," said Spencer, and the two officers smiled at each other.

"How's she doing?"

"Better than I expected. I shouldn't joke about her. That business with the Kendrick boy shook her up pretty bad, I think. She's been a little spacey this evening. I don't think she got any sleep between shifts."

"She'll learn to quit doing that," said LeDonne.

"Yes, but she didn't have hysterics, I'll give her that." Spencer Arrowood knelt by the body, brushing flies away with his notebook. "Get another close-up of her face. Quick before the flies land again. This is a mess, isn't it? I can't tell a damned thing about what actually killed her. I'll just let the medical examiner tell me when he's ready."

"It is Rita Pentland, though, isn't it?"

"Far as I can tell. Her wallet is in the handbag here. It still has money in it." He placed the black vinyl purse into a plastic evidence bag. "The hair color, height, and body type all match that of Mrs. Pentland.

I'd say she died sometime last night, but we'll let the M.E. make that call, too."

"I wonder how she got all the way out here without a car."

"I'd say she walked part of the way," said Spencer. "Look at her shoes." He pointed to scuff marks, and the worn heels on her bone-colored pumps.

"Why would she come all the way out here?"

"No telling. Maybe to get away from old Euell. If it was me, I'd walk at least this far to get away from him, the condescending bastard."

"He was a stinker all right, but they had been married for—what?—twenty-five years? She should have been used to him by now."

Spencer had gone into the living room, and was checking for bloodstains or other evidence of the second person at the crime scene. "Either she was resigned to Euell, or else she had no place to go," he said.

LeDonne bent down for a closer shot at the fake wood paneling on the trailer's back wall. Rust-colored flecks spattered the weathered wallboard. "I'd say she was killed here, wouldn't you? But with what?"

The sheriff came back in, looked at the stains, and shrugged. "Depends. I can't tell if these battering wounds are postmortem or not. A rock, maybe, if she was bludgeoned to death. We can check around outside for that. I haven't found anything in the other room to fit the bill. Did the deejay mention anything about seeing a weapon?"

"Old Hank? He's still shit-green from shock. I think he got out of here at warp speed. Don't count on any

brilliant observations from him. At least he was too
scared to monkey with the evidence, so he didn't do
any harm."

"*Harm,*" echoed Spencer.

"I know what you mean," said LeDonne. "Who
would have thought it?"

They were sitting in the front seat of Henry Kretzer's
Gremlin, because with sunset it had become too cold
in the mountain's shadow to talk in the open air. Hank
shone Martha's flashlight on the page of her notebook
as she took down his answers in careful printing.

"So you were just out here playing detective, and you
stumbled on a body?"

Hank the Yank looked flustered. "It sounds stupid
when you put it that way," he said. "Actually, I had become fascinated with the Sorley case when I featured
the escaped convict story on my show."

"I heard," said Martha.

"Yeah, it's been a popular topic, but there haven't
been any new developments, so I thought I'd look into
the murder case itself. This was just a long shot. There
aren't any living witnesses to talk to about the Maggard
case except—well, I guess there aren't any witnesses
now."

"You recognized Mrs. Pentland?"

"Oh, God, no! Her own mother wouldn't—well, no."
He managed a smile. "I'm afraid that statement was me
playing detective again. I just *assumed* that the body
was that of the convict's wife. At the time of the
Maggard killing, the Sorleys used to live here."

"Go on. So you drove out here looking for the escaped convict yourself?"

"No! If I'd thought there was a chance he'd be out here, there's no way I would have come. I wanted to look at the setting of the old crime, that's all. First I wanted to see where Harm had lived, and then I thought I would retrace his steps to the Maggard farm. I don't know what I expected to learn from that, but it seemed worth a try."

"Did you see any signs of Harm Sorley? Anything to indicate that he'd been here?"

"Just—her."

"Why are you so interested in Sorley's past?"

"I don't know. At first it was a joke, but then I got interested. It seemed incomplete somehow. Something about that original case just doesn't make sense to me."

"After what you found in the trailer over there," said Martha, "I guess it makes sense now."

Henry Kretzer shrugged, and glanced at his watch. "Are we finished? I have to be on the air in an hour or so."

"I know where to reach you," said Martha. "If you remember anything else, let us know."

"Can I mention this on my show tonight? It's news."

"Wait until tomorrow's program," said Martha. "We'd like to notify the family first. It isn't something you want to find out on a talk show."

Hank the Yank shivered. "God, no."


LeDonne had finished photographing the body, and had joined the sheriff in a search of the trailer, but it was not completely dark outside, and the flashlight did not provide enough illumination for a thorough investigation. They would have to wait for the state's crime lab people, who would be bringing better equipment. The door to the tiny bedroom was closed, and the frail body lay alone in the darkness, covered by the sheriff's first-aid blanket.

"I appreciate your staying on," Spencer Arrowood told his deputy.

"No problem," said LeDonne, gruffly. Kindness made him shy.

"I know you've got time off coming, but I may need you tomorrow, too. When word of this gets out, the department's phone will ring off the hook. People will be seeing escaped murderers under their beds."

The deputy smiled. "The hardware store should do land-office business in padlocks and shotgun shells."

"I don't think anyone else is in danger, but there's no point in trying to put that point across to a hysterical citizen. I'm sure the TBI will organize a manhunt now, and that'll be the end of the convict scare. Meanwhile, when the county residents hear a noise outside and call us in a panic, we'll make house calls and run the raccoons out of their garbage."

"Martha won't be fit to live with after this," said LeDonne. "We'll never hear the end of her bragging about how she knew the convict was dangerous."

"Maybe so." Spencer Arrowood was staring at the floor, not listening. "Something bothers me about this crime scene, though. You think she was killed here, don't you?"

"Bloodstains match. Spatter patterns point to that conclusion. I'd say this is the murder site. Why?"

"Because we haven't found any evidence of captivity. No discarded rope or chain. No marks on her wrists and ankles. No gag in her mouth, or evidence that one was used. And I'm willing to bet she wasn't raped. We'll have to wait for the medical examiner's report to know for sure, but there's not a doubt in my mind that sexual assault did not take place."

"I wonder how he got her here without being seen," mused LeDonne. "For that matter, why did he bother? Why not just kill her at home?"

They heard someone fumbling with the metal handle of the trailer door, and then it swung outward, and Martha Ayers peered in at them. "Mind if I join you?" she asked.

"Come on in," said the sheriff. "It's getting cold out there. Is your witness gone?"

"Yes. He wasn't much help. I made him promise not to announce the murder on his talk show, though."

"Good. That ought to postpone the panic 'til morning, anyhow," said Spencer Arrowood. He noticed that his two deputies were studiously avoiding each other. *Whatever fresh hell this is, it can wait until this case is solved*, he thought. Martha looked terrible, though. He wondered if it was lack of sleep or more shock from dealing with a second death at close quarters.

He had expected Martha to talk about the murder, maybe gloat a little, but she was rubbing the knuckles of her hand, and staring at nothing in particular. "I guess we just wait for the TBI now," she said.

"Shouldn't be too long. Why don't you go on back and tell the Pentlands that we might be needing them to identify the remains? I don't guess they'll want to wait until morning."

"I wouldn't," said Martha. "I like to take bad news straight." She was looking at LeDonne.

"Right," said Spencer. "Okay, tell them I'll call them when we get back to town. Probably between ten and midnight. Don't give them too many details, though. You can take One-Alpha, and I'll ride back with LeDonne. Break it to the family gently, will you?"

Martha nodded. "Okay. Is there anything else you want me to do?"

"After you talk to the Pentlands? Yes. Go home and get some rest. Your eyes look like two burnt holes in a blanket."

"Won't you need me, Spencer?"

"I don't think there'll be any more excitement to-night. Get some rest."

"Okay." She stifled a yawn. "I guess I'll go then."

Joe LeDonne said, "What's that on your shoes, Martha?"

Charlotte Pentland had gone to her room to keep from screaming at her stepfather and Buck. Neither one of them would shut up about Mother's disappearance, and Charlotte couldn't stand to hear another half-baked theory from either of them. She was alone now, in her old room that looked just as she had left it when she went off to college: chenille bedspread, stuffed animals on the top bookshelf, and frilly curtains edged in pink. The only addition was her mother's sewing machine and a row of paperback romance novels on the night-stand. Charlotte tried to remember what it felt like to be the girl who lived here. Her mother had kept the shrine carefully preserved, as if that laughing teenager were expected to return. Charlotte had never told her mother how silly and tasteless she thought it now, perhaps because a part of her felt comforted that her past was cherished by someone, in case she ever needed such a retreat from life's increasing complexity.

She wondered what would become of the room now. Euell would no doubt sweep it away in cardboard boxes to make himself a home office, or perhaps some new young wife would obliterate all traces of her predecessors. She was not Euell's daughter, only a burden acquired by marriage. She doubted if he liked her enough to preserve the bond between them for its own sake. He always treated her like an acquaintance who had dropped in unannounced. Now Charlotte wasn't safe anywhere, and she would have to find some other place to picture in her mind when she said the word *home*.

She was sure that her mother was dead, but nothing could have made her voice that thought. She wouldn't listen to speculation about Rita's fate from Euell and Buck. All the same, she knew. That strange, anxious look on the sheriff's face when he left that afternoon had told her that wherever they were going, it was to meet bad news. Now they would have to wait to be told the details.

Someone was tapping at the bedroom door. She wanted to yell for them to go away, but it might be the news, the end of the waiting. "Come in," she said.

Euell Pentland came in, stiff and dry-eyed, as if they were strangers. "I know you're upset," he said, eyeing her nervously.

"What is it? Do they know anything yet? I didn't hear the phone."

"No. Still waiting. I came to see how you were."

"I'm worried half out of my mind," said Charlotte, sitting back down on the bed. "But I guess you are, too. Can I do anything for you? Make coffee?" Euell never lifted a finger around the house. The first thing he would miss about Rita would be the maid service. But Charlotte felt sorry for him. He wasn't a cruel man. She would make him coffee if that would help.

He looked relieved. "Coffee would be fine, Charlotte. I guess the waiting is the worst of it."

"Is it? As long as we don't know for sure, she's alive."

"I think you should be prepared for bad news if it comes, Charlotte. False hopes will only hurt you later."

"Where's Buck?"

"Asleep." Euell was leaning against the bedroom door, but he was careful not to close it. He hadn't hugged her since she was twelve. "Buck had a long drive, and then he drank a couple of beers while we talked. I guess the strain got to him. He might as well sleep while he can. I thought I'd see how you were."

"I won't sleep. I guess it's worse for me," she said. "Not only is my mother missing, but if she's dead, my daddy killed her."

"Don't say that, Charlotte." The remark seemed to upset Euell Pentland more than anything else so far. "He's not your daddy anymore. I raised you. You have an education, and you speak properly. You're not a Sorley. You're not the towheaded hillbilly baby he left behind. Don't you think it. What he's done has got nothing to do with you."

Charlotte was crying. "So he is coal and I'm a diamond? We're still kin."

"Let it go, Charlotte. I came to tell you that you have a home with me as long as you want one. No matter what your mother has done."

She heard the tightness in his voice and wiped her eyes. "No matter what she's done? What do you mean by that?"

"I mean, she may not have been kidnapped. She may have asked for what she got."

"You think she went looking for him?"

"I don't know, Charlotte dear. It's a tragic business best not dwelt on. Let's see what the law enforcement people can tell us. That's not important. Right now I just wanted to reassure you. You need to know that whatever happens, you're still welcome."

"I'll make the coffee now," said Charlotte. She wondered if there was anything here that she would want to take when she left. She didn't think so.

Martha put her pistol on the nightstand beside her bed. There were more things she'd like to have done tonight, but she'd have to trust them to Providence. She was too tired to be driving mountain roads in the dark. Tomorrow she would try to find time to warn some of the cove dwellers about the danger. Many of them did not have telephones. She'd have to ride up to see Nora Bonesteel on the top of Ashe Mountain. Martha didn't think it likely that the convict would get all the way up there, but an old woman living alone had to be cautioned. For a moment she even thought about cautioning the Harkryders, and that made her smile. If any escaped murderer blundered into the Harkryder camp, she figured he'd end up wishing he'd stayed in prison.

It was nearly midnight, finally time to relax. A hot bath had loosened her muscles and eased the headache that she knew came from tension and fatigue. She'd stayed on duty longer than Spencer had asked her to, because, despite her own exhaustion, she had found she couldn't leave the Pentlands.

When she arrived to tell them about the body at the old trailer, they had insisted that she stay, plying her with coffee and offers of cold cuts and potato salad brought by neighbors. She had expected a barrage of questions, but they seemed shy to press her for details. Martha explained that human remains had been found, and that the sheriff would be calling them for an identification within the next few hours. It was an awkward speech. She had rehearsed it in the car on her drive back to town, but she hadn't been able to find a way to sound sympathetic and yet detached. She couldn't give the family false hopes, because she knew that it was almost a certainty that the body was Rita's, but it wasn't Martha's place to tell them so.

As she drank cups of Mr. Coffee coffee, and watched the gray faces of the grieving family, she wondered why they wanted her to stay. They made small talk about the weather, and asked her polite questions about her job in general, like strangers in a waiting room, avoiding unpleasant facts. Euell Pentland was a man who could not sit still. He paced, and rambled on about sports and county business in a tone of forced cheerfulness that made everyone else ill at ease.

Euell Junior, whom the family called "Buck," had

driven over from U.T. in Knoxville for the vigil. He was the silent one. Martha wondered if he had been drinking. When she first broke the news to them, he'd stared at nothing. After that, he leafed through an old *Reader's Digest* without ever stopping at one page long enough to read a sentence.

Charlotte Pentland had a dazed look and red-rimmed eyes, but she was calm enough for someone who had just lost her mother in the worst of circumstances. It was on Charlotte's behalf that Martha stayed until the call came. Euell Pentland insisted on going alone, and Martha agreed with him. That body was not a sight for two grieving young people, no matter how grown-up and sophisticated they thought they were. She told Pentland to go to the mortuary, and promised that she would stay with Buck and Charlotte until he returned.

They sat mostly in silence after Euell left. Martha offered to make more coffee, but none of them wanted it. It was late when Euell got back, but they were still sitting there, staring and waiting. He didn't say anything—just stood in the doorway and bowed his head, and the room became quieter still. Martha waited a moment before she got up. She whispered, "I'm sorry," and patted Buck and Charlotte on the shoulder. "If there's anything I can do . . ." She was gone before the full impact of the news had hit them.

Now she had to sleep. The real work would begin tomorrow. Now that she had been proved right about the danger of the escaped convict, the net would begin to close.

* * *

Harm Sorley had built himself a fire. The night had come in crystal cold, with the glittering pinpoints of stars that you see clearest in winter. He knew from the trees that it wasn't winter yet, but it was headed that way. Still, the fire would keep him warm, and it would last the night, because he knew how to make a proper fire. He did it just like the old song said to: *Build you a fire with hickory. Hickory and ash and oak. Don't use no green or rotten wood: they'll get you by the smoke.* He'd known that moonshining tune all his life, which was about how long he'd known about fire building. It was the only heat they had up home when he was little. You either learned your way around fire, or else you froze.

He looked around to get his bearings. He was out in the woods, somewhere high on a ridge, and he was leaning against a crumbling log, staring into a dancing fire. He seemed to be roughing it, judging from his burlap sack and his worn shoes. He had a pistol, too, but that puzzled him. It was hunting season, dead leaves underfoot, but this was no proper weapon to take out hunting.

It wasn't even much of a pistol, to his way of thinking, and Harm knew guns. People liked to say, *Why, I cut my teeth on guns*, and it was just a manner of speaking, but with Harm it was quite literally true. Back in 1931, when Harm was a lap-baby, his daddy had owned a nickel-plated .38 with a rubber pistol grip. To hear Uncle Pharis tell it, little Harm used to reach that gun down from the wall, thinking it was a shiny play-pretty, and he'd ease his itching gums on that red rubber grip until it had tiny toothmarks all up and down the sides. Now this here gun he had resting on his lap was a tin-pot .32, made out of some cheap lightweight metal that sure as hell wasn't steel. He'd bet it wouldn't stop hot butter unless you were good and close, and you hit a soft spot. What was he doing with such a puny firearm?

Why was he out here at all?

He felt the familiar clutch of panic tighten his throat, and he looked around for clues about where he was and why. That's when he saw her, not much more than a shadow, on the other side of the campfire. He leaned forward, thinking it must be Rita, but it wasn't, not with that curly black hair down about her shoulders, and those sharp cheekbones. He squinted into the darkness for a closer look, but just then a puff of wind blew some smoke in his direction, and he had to lean away again. This woman was young, but rail thin, and she had a familiar look about her, but Harm couldn't place her. He didn't wonder why she was out here in the wilderness. Harm seldom wondered about anything anymore: the question always left him before he could find an answer, so he gradually stopped trying to make sense of things. To Harm Sorley, things just *were*. The woman he didn't know was staring into the fire, not paying him any mind.

"I sure am hungry," he said, by way of making conversation.

The dark lady in the firelight nodded gently. "I chew birch bark when I can't find nothing else," she said.

Harm nodded in agreement. "I'd rather have a slab of ham, though," he said. "Ham and grits and red-eye gravy sure would hit the spot."

The silence went on for a while, and his stomach

cramped on emptiness, so he said, "You ever catch a fish with just your hands the way a bear does?"

"Mayhap," the woman said. "Not at night, though. You can't be too particular at night when you're hungry. That rotten log you're a-leaning against—have you felt around inside? It might have grubs in it."

Harm shook his head. "I believe I can last," he told her. "I'm awful tired."

"You eat when you're tired all the same, or else you won't go any farther. You eat weeds, bugs, and dead things—the leavings of the turkey buzzards. Else you'll just lay here 'til the wolves feed on your carcass."

He half smiled at her foolishness, because there hadn't been any wolves in these mountains for a hundred years and more, but he knew she was right about keeping up strength. He could feel the tiredness creeping over him. Wherever he was, it was a long way from home. He wasn't sure how he knew that, but he felt it was so.

"I've been out here a long time," he said, and he thought he saw a flicker of a smile through the firelight.

"It won't be much longer now," said the woman in her soothing voice. He felt peaceful just listening to that calm whisper, as soft as laurel leaves rustling in the wind. "Not much longer."

Harm felt himself drifting away, lulled by the warmth and the weariness that felt like a soft coverlet pushing down on him. "Where are we going?" he murmured, over the crackle of the fire.

"I reckon we have to go home," she said, and her voice was sad.

# CHAPTER
# 14

I have lived in the darkness for so long,
   I am waitin' for the light to shine,
Far beyond horizons I have seen,
   Beyond the things I've been,
Beyond the dreams I've dreamed . . .
   I am waitin' for the light to shine.

"Waitin' for the Light to Shine," Unknown

"Did you see Vernon Woolwine this morning?" asked Joe LeDonne.

"Can't say that I noticed. This double-shifting wears me down," said Spencer Arrowood. "Why? What's the matter with him?"

"Nothing. It's the damnedest thing. He's over there at the courthouse on his bench as usual, but he's wearing a dark suit—cheap and shiny, but a suit nonetheless—a white dress shirt, and a black-and-gold-striped tie that I'd swear wasn't a clip-on. If it was anybody but Vernon, I'd say they were going to a job interview."

"Or a funeral," said Spencer.

"That's a thought. But I've never seen Vernon at any weddings or funerals, have you?"

"Not that I recall." The sheriff shrugged. "Maybe the outfit is just another costume. Maybe it's Vernon's day to be a lawyer. Did you ask him what the occasion was?"

"No. Since I was in uniform, I thought it might worry him if I approached. And I don't want to discourage this new trend toward respectability. Maybe he'll make a habit of this."

"Not Vernon. I'm always afraid he'll turn up in a deputy's uniform, and then what will we do?"

"I just hope he doesn't turn up this week in that black-and-white-striped convict suit he wears sometimes. Some nearsighted old lady will probably catch a glimpse of him out her car window and go berserk. Besides, with all those law enforcement people coming through here with the search parties, Vernon could get in a world of trouble."

Spencer smiled. "I think Vernon is the least of our worries. We have the Pentland case on our hands and, as you said, half of Tennessee coming over for a manhunt. Did you know they're sending a helicopter?"

"Is that so? You don't want me to go up in it, I hope?"

"No, I thought I might take a ride if they don't mind. I love the view of these mountains from up there. Even with the trees nearly bare, it's pretty. Silver branches catching sunlight on the ridges. Sure you don't want to go?"

"I had enough of that in 'Nam. I guess I'll stay on the ground and take the Pentlands. Unless you want Martha on that."

They were sitting in Spencer's office. In the main room, Jennaleigh was already at the switchboard, checking for overnight messages. Spencer glanced at the half-open door to satisfy himself that she wasn't listening. "Martha on the Pentlands? No. That's the last place I want her. I'm sending her to get that crud analyzed from the Sorleys' field, and then I thought I'd send her off to talk to the rural residents. Warn them to keep an eye out for our wandering boy, while I keep down the panic around here." He set down his coffee mug and glanced at the clock. Five past eight. "If she ever gets here, that is. Was she running late this morning or what?"

LeDonne studied the hunting scene on the wall calendar, English setters nosing a pheasant into flight. "I don't know," he said. "I haven't seen her."

Spencer noticed his uneasiness. "Everything's all right, isn't it?" he said in the tone that's meant to close the subject.

"Sure. It'll work out." The deputy reached for his hat and leather jacket. "Well, I guess I'd better get a move on. I need to see what the TBI can give me from their bag of tricks. Maybe drop by the hunting supply place on the highway and remind them about the waiting period for gun purchases. I expect there'll be some anxious customers today wanting some fast protection from the bogeyman. If you need me, you know my number. Beta-Two."

"You think it's okay to send Martha out on the manhunt, then?" asked Spencer as he turned to go.

Joe LeDonne smiled. "In Harm's way? I think it's the safest place she could be. What do you think?"

"Poor old Harm Sorley," said the sheriff. "I hate to see it come to this. I just hope they take him alive."

"It doesn't much matter, does it?"

"I guess not."

Martha waited until LeDonne's patrol car drove past Dent's window before she picked up her raisin biscuits and left the cafe. She couldn't keep dodging him forever, but until she had time to think things over, avoiding him seemed the best course of action. She wondered if Spencer knew what was going on. She knew that men always stuck together, but she hoped that wasn't the case this time. You can't work with someone you don't trust—not in law enforcement, anyhow, because your life depends on their loyalty. She was glad she hadn't been partnered with LeDonne, because she knew that whatever happened between them personally, she would never completely trust him again.

She found Spencer still at his desk, making lists of things that needed to be done today. He always made lists of objectives, and checked them off as he did them. When he saw her come in, he smiled, but she could see a wary look in his eyes, and she wondered whether anything besides Rita Pentland's murder was worrying him.

"Coffee?" he said by way of greeting. "You just missed LeDonne."

"Thanks. I stopped at Dent's and got some. I figured you could spare me for ten minutes, since I didn't go off duty until nearly midnight."

"Midnight? I thought I told you—"

"I couldn't leave them," said Martha.

"Well, that was conscientious of you, but you can't wear yourself out in this business. Crime doesn't stop to let us catch our breath. How did it go last night at the Pentlands?"

"As well as can be expected. They didn't say too much. I think they were prepared for the worst. Have you got the autopsy report yet?"

"Not the complete workup. I know how she died, though. Manual strangulation, with antemortem battering injuries to the face and upper body. She'd been dead at least eighteen hours when we found her." When she took out her notebook and pen, Spencer added, "LeDonne is covering this one, Martha."

For a moment he thought she would argue, but then she shrugged and said, "Okay. I guess it'll be mostly paperwork, anyhow. What's my assignment?"

He handed her a plastic evidence bag. "Run that over to Carter Biological for testing. Tell them to bill the department. Then, if Jennaleigh hasn't radioed you different instructions, go on your regular patrol. You can do it alone today." He sighed. "I'll be out contending with the electric posse."

"Okay if I stick to the rural areas, to let people know about Sorley?"

"I figured you would, Martha," said the sheriff. "Just don't get all gung ho about this, okay? Don't shoot some poor deer hunter in an excess of zeal."

"The wanted man is a convicted murderer, his ex-wife has been beaten and strangled, and you're worried that *I* might be dangerous?"

"Yes, Martha. That's exactly what I'm worried about."

Jennaleigh appeared in the doorway carrying a pink message slip. "Pearl's Beauty Shop just called, Sheriff. They'd like someone to escort them to the bank between four and five this afternoon when they deposit the day's receipts."

"All forty-two dollars," said Spencer, crumpling the message and tossing it at the corner wastebasket. "Damn. The panic has started. They won't be the last business to make that request today. Damn it all! Jennaleigh, get me the radio station on the phone."

* * *

"Hello, WHTN neighbors. This is Hank the Yank coming to you at broad daylight for a change, so don't think you've overslept by ten hours just because you hear my voice. I'm in your ear this morning. Arvin has brought me what passes for coffee here. I think he runs his breakfast grits through the oil filter in his Hyundai and claims they're coffee grounds. So I am wide awake, neighbors. Either that or it's rigor mortis setting in early.

"Guess I shouldn't joke about that, though.

"You see, the reason I'm up and broadcasting so early is because there are startling new developments in the Harm Watch, and I felt that I had to be the one to bring it to you. It won't be in the *Johnson City Press* today, because it happened last night, so for once, let me tell you something you don't already know. It's sad news, folks.

"The body of Mrs. Rita Pentland of Hamelin was discovered last night in an abandoned trailer in the Painter Cove section of Wake County, an apparent murder victim. It's quite a story, and I'll be telling it sooner or later, because I'm the one that found the poor lady's body, but the sheriff's department doesn't want me to give out too many details at this time, because officially the case is unsolved. I don't want my big mouth to get in the way of justice around here. I mean that.

"The one thing that everybody in this county seems to already know about the case is that the victim, the late Mrs. Rita Pentland, was once the wife of Wake

County's own geriatric felon: Harm Sorley. Now that was thirty years ago, but there's no getting away from it.

"So I guess I'll be receiving a lot of calls from the more belligerent segment of my listeners, all wanting to gloat about what a fool I've been to make light of the escape of a dangerous convicted murderer. I know I'm going to get those calls. I can hear your dialing fingers out there tapping right now."

Lights were blinking on the telephone, and in the control room Steve Huang, aka Arvin the Terrible, was pointing toward the instrument, but Hank the Yank shook his head and went on talking.

"Yes, neighbors, I see your call lights, but you know what? I'm not abashed for befriending Old Harm from afar. Not a bit of it. Because, friends, what I say is this: a man is innocent until he is proven guilty, and sometimes he keeps on being innocent even after that, but here's my point: we don't know for sure that Mrs. Pentland was killed by our boy Harm. Why, the autopsy isn't even in yet, so the sheriff tells me, so it's a little early to convene a kangaroo court. If some of you out there insist on trying the case with your mouths anyhow, then you can count me in as the kangaroo attorney for the defense.

"Now, Sheriff Spencer Arrowood may be a little shy about coming on radio talk shows, but he's a good man, and I don't hold it against him. He called me this morning, and asked me to appeal to your better natures for calm and reason. Consider it done, Sheriff. See, Mr. Arrowood is afraid that there's going to be a panic here in Wake County, with panic-stricken people stalking around the woods toting M-16s, loaded for convict.

Maybe they'll be drunk, too, for the occasion. Won't that be delightful? Give me a woods full of convicts any day, if they're all sober.

"Now the sheriff, he's figuring on getting his own share of calls this morning, mostly from people who hear two raccoons in their garbage cans, and think they're under attack by crazed, homicidal felons. And what we're saying here, people, is that we'd all be better off if you stayed calm, took some sensible precautions—like staying *out* of the woods and not picking up any hitchhikers—but otherwise just go on about your business as usual.

"Let the law take care of it. Yes, there is a search party. In a little while, Sheriff Arrowood tells me, you'll hear the buzz of a helicopter flying over the valley, and he'll be in it himself, trying to spot the escaped prisoner from the air. So something is being done to catch this man, and then we can worry about what to do with him.

"Tennesseeans, what I'm saying to you this morning is: *Don't hang the elephant again.* Think on that a while. Back in 1916, a frightened and angry group of citizens executed a defenseless animal for causing a death—manslaughter, perhaps, but they never bothered to look for another side to the story. It was easier to kill the offender than to think too much about the crime. Don't let it happen again. Please give this poor old man his day in court.

"I'm going to play an old gospel song called 'I Am Waiting for the Light to Shine' for you now. Well, actually, I'm kind of thinking of Old Harm, which is why I selected it. Before you go telling yourself that the old man out there in the woods hasn't got a prayer, let me assure you that he has mine. And he ought to have yours, too, if you call yourself a child of God. So we'll call the Lord in on the case here. Then we'll go to news, and try to talk about something else. You folks have a good one."

Jeremy Cobb heard the sound of a huge winged thing flying over the ridge, and he told himself that the droning creature was Ulagu, the giant wasp of Cherokee legend, come to claim more victims. "Ulagu," he said aloud, as if that would make it so, but the spell of the wilderness was broken, and the sound annoyed him. He wanted to throw rocks at the clacking monster, to drive it back into its own century, because out here on the ridge, in the endless ripple of mountain and forest, he had almost willed it to be 1779. Katie's time. He was very near.

And now this. A helicopter, for God's sake. It wasn't enough that he'd had to dodge hikers. Hikers with boom boxes. Hikers accompanied by dogs wearing bandannas around their collars. Hikers with video cameras. Why were these clowns walking the Appalachian Trail, anyway, instead of grooving through Disney World?

He strayed farther from the trail, and finally abandoned it altogether, following instead the Toe River. Here was the oldest and best trail, the river itself. The one that had guided Katie. He was very near now. He had almost reached the end of the journey, and he was ready to meet it. Each day was colder than the last, and he knew that his strength wouldn't carry him for many more days. Soon it would be time to return to the twentieth century, but for now he felt he had almost attained that state of liminality described by Victor Turner in *The Ritual Process*. Here in the wilderness, devoid of temporal landmarks, he sometimes managed to find himself betwixt and between Katie's world and his own. Sometimes he could forget to think the thoughts of the modern world, and he could force his mind in the narrower patterns of that simpler time. He could never hold that focus for more than a few moments, but each time he succeeded even for an instant, he felt triumphant. The hunger helped, of course. It allowed his mind to slip the bonds of flesh. And, when he had finally got away from trails, the enveloping forest had become a liminal eden, swallowing the years in its green silence. He moved through it as an ant might cross a featherbed, alternately engulfed and disgorged, but leaving no sign of passage.

All his camping gear was gone, the shiny marvels of his own era, the epoch that saw nature through plate glass. All his high-tech toys had been stolen by the strange man, or discarded along the way: tent, vacuum-packed foodstuffs, solar shower, canned goods, first-aid kit. Gone, all of it. He should have kept the water purification kit. The cramps in his abdomen were not from hunger, and his bottom was raw from frequent scrapings with whatever rough leaves came to hand in the thrice-hourly call of nature. The diarrhea must stop soon, he thought. Surely his insides were empty of food by now. He had eaten very little in the past day. Only some berries and nuts, and an occasional rotting apple fallen from an old tree, perhaps part of a long-abandoned orchard. Surely the pain in his gut would stop soon. There had been blood on the last clump of leaves he'd used to clean himself. He resolved not to look again.

He might have a fever. Certainly he no longer felt cold. Under a brush of week-old beard stubble, his lips were cracked, and his thirst was never slaked, not even after he drank deep from the cold running streams. He could not bring himself to drink river water, but he knew that before many hours had passed, he would probably abandon this last reserve and do so.

What was that damned helicopter circling for? Was this an attempt to spot marijuana fields in the national forest? He had heard that such illegal plantations existed, cruelly booby-trapped by the drug dealers with sharpened stakes in pits and other maiming traps gleaned from jungle warfare. Jeremy hoped that no such nuisances lay in his path. His concern was with an older crime, and he knew that he was very near.

Somewhere along the banks of this river, young Andrew Wyler had hid in the tall grasses, waiting for his chance to slip away upstream to summon help for his family. Jeremy had long since discarded his field guides, and even his water-logged journal, but he needed no reference for this part of the journey. What little there was to know about Katie Wyler's return, Jeremy knew by heart. He had told the story many times, to crowded lecture halls full of indifferent students to whom Katie Wyler was one more answer on a forthcoming quiz, to be forgotten by the end of the chapter. Once in a great while, Jeremy had succeeded in bringing Katie to life for some student whose imagination held the right tinder, but the majority of his listeners sat unmoved.

What did those stolid students matter? Now he was out here alone, and the conjuring trick was for his benefit alone. He must stand in the fields where the cabin had once been, and then he must retrace Andrew's steps to the Greers' farmstead: the final scene in Katie Wyler's life.

She had made it all the way home. Three hundred miles and more through mountain wilderness: without supplies or compass, without anyone to help her along the way, with nothing to shelter her, with rag-wrapped feet bruised into calloused husks, and with nothing to eat except wild roots, insects, and carrion. He had always imagined her clean and beautiful, but he knew better now. The weeks in the wilderness would have taken that.

Jeremy tried to think of something that would make him embark on such a journey, but there was nothing and no one that would move him to such sacrifice. True, he had spent a week tracing part of the original trek on a trail that he knew he could exit anytime he chose. If there is a way out, there isn't total commitment. But to retrace Katie's steps entirely? From the broad Ohio at the far end of West Virginia all the way across the mountains to the cloud-veiled Smokies of western North Carolina? He would not make such a pilgrimage to save his mother's life, nor to prove his devotion to any of his past lovers, if you could dignify his few tepid sexual encounters with so exalted a word as love.

Had Katie Wyler loved Rab Greer? Or did she simply

feel that as his betrothed it was her bounden duty to return to him if she possibly could? Or was she running not *to* him, but *away* from the harsh, alien Shawnee? Did she simply have nowhere else to go? He had thought that the journey would tell him that, but there weren't any parallels in his own life to judge by. If love had fueled her long walk home, he envied her that. Even though her love had been wasted, he envied her the strength of it. He would never love anyone so much; that was no longer possible in a crowded world of pretty people who were too easily replaced, and who in the final analysis always remained strangers. The love of Katie's era was in his own century as diminished as her wilderness, now carefully trammeled.

Jeremy watched the sun glint on the blades of the chopper as it tilted and swirled out of sight behind a piney-wood ridge. He was alone again in the silent woods, with only his footsteps for sound, and only his frosted breath for warmth. He would reach the end soon, and then he would have to admit that he had learned all he could from the land, and he would have to let Katie go.

While Spencer was out with the high-tech posse, Le-Donne made the rounds of Hamelin to reassure the county citizens that the department was on the job. The streets were as quiet as usual, although he did notice that gates were locked on the houses with chain-link fences, and more dogs than usual were pacing their yards. He had just checked on ammunition sales at the hardware store, and was walking back to the patrol car when he saw Crystal Stanley at the door of the cafe, motioning for him to come over. LeDonne felt a flicker of annoyance at the distraction, but he ambled over.

"Good morning," he said with a faint smile. "You're up early for a night owl."

Crystal's lank hair looked stringy in daylight, and he could see a tinge of brown at the roots. She was built like Martha—scrawnier, maybe—but Martha didn't wear turquoise bell-bottoms and fake-fur coats. He supposed that Crystal needed flashy outfits for her job at the bar. She had a lot of them. In her cramped little brick house on Forest Trail, Crystal had stacks of cardboard boxes filled with clothes for herself. Maybe she got them at yard sales or at Goodwill in Johnson City. He wondered if she owned anything that didn't look cheap and out of style. She was, however, a great piece of ass. She'd be better if her breath didn't smell like nicotine when he kissed her. LeDonne hated the stink of cigarettes. He'd told her so often enough, but she'd laughed at him and said that she'd get fat if she quit.

She lifted her hand, and he saw the curl of smoke as she took another drag on a Marlboro. "Breakfast at the cafe. I hate to cook. Besides, I don't need much sleep," she drawled, peering up at him through greasy black lashes. "Good thing, huh, Joe?"

"I guess."

"Want to come in and eat?" She smiled up at him. "Or have you already had your breakfast Pepsi?"

"An hour ago. I'm on duty now."

"So, you coming by tonight?" She was standing very close to him now, leaning her body toward him suggestively. LeDonne glanced out at the street to see if anyone noticed.

"Tonight? It's hard to say. We have a murder investigation going on."

She turned her head to breathe out smoke. "I heard. It's made me kinda nervous, an escaped convict and all."

"I wouldn't worry about it, Crystal."

She raised her eyebrows. "Don't worry? But they're saying he killed a woman near here."

"You're not in danger."

"Did he—you know—rape her?"

"No."

She fixed her lips in a mock pout. "Well, I'm still nervous. Maybe you ought to come over and protect me after I get off work tonight. I bet I could make it worth your while."

She was being coy, not frightened. If she had been afraid, LeDonne might have felt an urge to look after her, but flirting games bored him. Besides, there was an edge to her teasing that made him wary: the sound of desperation in the current of her voice. Crystal wanted somebody bad; she wanted out of the Mockingbird Inn even worse. Sex was the only bait she had. Still, he reasoned that Martha, who seemed to be trying to out-macho him lately, would be working or exhausted as usual, and he might well be horny again by the time Crystal finished work for the night, so he said, "I'll see what I can do."

She hid her smile behind the cigarette. "You told that other deputy about us yet? The one you're so pissed at?"

"No," said LeDonne. "No, I haven't."

"Well, I don't see what's holding you back. Like, it's your life, you know. If you're not happy with her, why don't you just leave?"

LeDonne shrugged.

She touched the sleeve of his jacket. "I'm your friend, Joe. I hate to see you unhappy."

"Yeah, well, I have to go, Crystal. I'm on duty. We'll talk about it later."

"Well, you be careful when you're out there today. You know I worry, honey. Doncha?"

He stood still while she kissed him, holding his breath against the odor of nicotine and stale perfume. Crystal was twenty-three. In a couple of years she would look forty. He left her on the porch of Dent's Cafe without looking back.

By three that afternoon, Spencer Arrowood was back in the office, checking for reports on convict sightings from the adjoining counties. At this point, Harm Sorley seemed to be the convenient solution for a host of rural incidents from dog poisonings to hubcap theft. Sifting through the reports, Spencer doubted that Harm was connected to any of them. The other officers probably agreed with him, but at this point they were pooling all unsolved incidents, because you never knew what could turn out to be significant.

A new wanted poster had come by express mail, bearing a grainy prison photo of Harm, probably years out of date. So now the hunt would begin in earnest, and he supposed that as an elected official, he couldn't very well oppose it. He wished he could stop feeling sorry for the old man, though. There was Harm, who killed the county's worst son-of-a-bitch, and who would have been out of prison in eight years if he hadn't also committed the crime of being poor. As it was he'd lost everything: home, family, and—thanks to his mental condition—even the future. And now criminal investigators from Nashville to Boone and everywhere in between were out hunting poor Harm with tracking dogs and tear gas. They were hunting him on land that had once belonged to his people. He was a Sorley. His people went back two hundred years in these mountains. He belonged here; but then so had the buffalo, and they were wiped out, too. Spencer had looked at the old court records of Harm's first trial, and he wouldn't have called that jury an assembly of Harm's peers: new people, townfolk, people transferred in by the TVA and the Forest Service, who saw the land as a playground and vacation site for quality folk, once you cleared out the rabble. In 1830 the local rabble had been the Cherokee nation; now it was the rest of them. Harm was caught in the crossfire, and there wasn't a thing Spencer could do about it, except to tell everybody he could that the suspect was a sick old man, and to ask them to take him alive. It was not much for a man who had lost everything, but it was the best he could do.

"Sheriff? Somebody's here." The new dispatcher Jennaleigh appeared in the doorway, looking more anxious than he'd seen her yet. This couldn't be from fear of disturbing him. He motioned for her to close the door.

"What's wrong?"

"There's a young woman out there to see you. Well,

a teenager, really. She looks kind of upset—or angry. I don't know." Jennaleigh kept glancing at the door behind her, as if she expected the visitor to barge in unannounced.

"I'll come out." Spencer straightened his brown tie and pushed a strand of pale hair off his forehead. He wondered if this would turn out to be the first visit of a panicked citizen. Raccoons in the garbage already? But when he opened the office door, he saw Sabrina Harkryder, sullen and shivering in a chair near the furnace duct. She was wearing an old plastic parka with split seams, and her gloveless hands were red from the cold. He wondered how far she'd had to walk. Surely not from the clan's encampment up the mountain.

"Good afternoon, Mrs. Harkryder," he said with careful politeness. "How can I help you?"

She scowled at his attempt at civility, perhaps taking it for sarcasm. He saw that her eyes were red-rimmed, and her lip had been bleeding. "Sheriff," she said. "That there convict stole my baby. I want you to shoot him down like a dog. He stole my baby."

Before Martha Ayers set off for the biological testing office in Johnson City, she drove down a side street off Ashe Lane, and turned left onto Forest Trail. It was a street of mostly one-story wooden houses, built in the fifties for working-class people. They must have cost about fifteen thousand dollars apiece back then. Now the rundown dwellings, mostly rental property, would go for forty, maybe, because of inflation, but they would always be shabby dwellings in a neighborhood most people wanted out of. Crystal's house, 1016 Forest Trail, was next to last, a squat brick box with steep front steps and a new wooden deck at the side. Idly, Martha wondered if LeDonne had put any time or money into that deck. It looked like a renter's house: no trees or flower beds, no little touches of landscaping to mark one's ownership. Probably no alarm system, either. What could CrystalS own that anyone could want? Well, one thing, maybe, but she seemed to give that away pretty freely. Martha thought the porch light ought to be red.

She turned around in the last driveway, and headed for the road to Johnson City. Now she knew where the bitch lived. Now she could picture the house when she had time to think about Crystal, while she tried to decide what to do about her. Martha wasn't ready to think about LeDonne yet, because that rage was tempered by grief. She couldn't allow herself to feel that pain yet, because it would hinder her in her work, which was to hunt down Harm Sorley. As soon as her errand was completed, she would be out on the back roads, looking for traces of the wanted man.

The others hadn't wanted to catch him at first. They'd made jokes about the poor addled convict. Now every officer in Tennessee wanted to be in at the death, but Martha reckoned he was hers. He was her ticket to a permanent position as deputy. Catching him would be the consolation prize owed her by Providence, because she had lost everything else.

# CHAPTER
# 15

Watchman, tell us of the night,
    What its signs of promise are.
Trav'ller, o'er yon mountain's height,
    See that glory-beaming star.
Watchman, does its beauteous ray
    Aught of hope or joy foretell?

#765, "WATCHMAN, TELL US OF THE NIGHT?,"
SIR JOHN BOWRING

TENNESSEE METHODIST HYMNAL, 1885

for a moment, listening and watching the trees on the

Sabrina Harkryder sat silent in the passenger seat of the patrol car, and Spencer Arrowood occupied his mind by working out a speech to the county commissioners for extra funding for the sheriff's department. "All right, we do average only two murders a year," he pictured himself saying to the half-circle of old men in their green padded chairs. "But from time to time all hell breaks loose, and three people have to try to be everywhere at once." Today would be the perfect example. The woods were full of trackers looking for an escaped convict; Martha was running evidence to the lab; LeDonne was taking statements from the victim's family; and now this—a missing baby. He wished to God he had some backup on this, but with a child's life at stake, he couldn't afford to waste time waiting for LeDonne. He'd left instructions with Jennaleigh to try the radio, and if that failed, call the Pentlands, and send LeDonne up to Painter Cove at once.

He wanted LeDonne for the search and questioning. If Sabrina had been distraught, he would have summoned Martha as well, but there had been no hysterics from the teenage mother of little Dustin Allison

Harkryder. She sat tight-lipped and pale on the seat beside him, staring out at the sweep of trees and road dust as hostile and silent as a shoplifter.

"Where is the baby's father?" he asked. There were questions to be covered, and he might as well not waste the long drive. He could write down her answers later.

Sabrina shrugged. "Out with his buddies, I guess. It's where he usually is."

"You haven't seen him since you discovered that the child was missing?"

"No." She rolled her eyes at his foolishness. "I mean, like he *cares* or anything."

"In most child abduction cases, the victim is taken by a parent or other relative. Now we know that you and your husband had been having some problems. Is there a chance that he left you, and took the baby with him?"

"Yeah. Right." Heavy sarcasm for the naivete of this dumb cop. "I don't think Tracy would have bothered to take Dustin Allison if the damned trailer had been on fire."

"We'll need to talk to Tracy real soon, Sabrina."

She made a face. "Good luck finding him sober."

The sheriff decided to return to a safer subject before he lost his rapport with the young wife. "So, let's get back to the facts of the disappearance. You said that you put the baby to bed last night. Was that in your room?"

"No. He sleeps in a little bedroom next to the bath. In a wicker clothes basket; just fits him. It's still there."

"And you didn't hear the baby cry at all in the night."

"No."

Spencer hesitated for a moment before he said, "Well, wasn't that odd?"

"What do you mean?"

"I thought babies always woke up a couple of times a night. Don't you have to feed and change them?"

"I didn't hear him. I was too tired to care. It's not like anybody helps me or anything. I take care of him round the clock, you know." Her voice rose in anger, or perhaps grief at her loss.

"Okay," said Spencer. "Okay. Take it easy. So you woke up this morning, and you found the basket empty. And you didn't hear anything last night? The dogs didn't bark."

She gave him a level stare. "Dogs?"

He remembered their last meeting: the pools of antifreeze and the stiffening bodies of the Harkryder hound pack. No, there had been no dogs to bark. Sabrina had seen to that. They were beginning the steep climb up from the river's edge toward the trailer encampment on Painter Cove. The trees were bare now, and between their branches he could catch glimpses of the valley below. He thought about the young woman's story.

"Are you and your husband getting along any better these days?" he asked, keeping his voice neutral and his eyes on the road.

"We get by," she said. "There hasn't been any more hitting."

"That's good." The thought of an infant trapped in that armed camp of a marriage made him sad. Little Dustin's death could be hardly more tragic than his fate

had he lived: another ill-fed, unschooled Harkryder, going nowhere.

"So you asked the other Harkryders about the baby?
To make sure no one came and got him during the
night?"

"They never have before," said Sabrina. "But, yeah, I
asked around. Tracy's stepmother and two of his aunts
helped me look around in the woods. Then one of
them brought me to town on her way to work, so I
could report it."

"Well, we'll look some more," the sheriff promised
her. "My deputy will be along soon, and we can radio
some of the other searchers to come and help us."

"The other deputy that's coming—would that be the
lady cop?"

"No. She's on another case. Would you like to talk to
her?"

"I don't know." She was twisting the edges of her
coat with nail-bitten hands. "Maybe."

"I may be able to get her to come later in the day,"
said Spencer. If the girl trusted Martha, they might get
further if she handled the questioning. "One more
thing I need to ask about the break-in, Sabrina," he
said. "Was anything else taken?"

"No." She glanced at him, and closed her mouth
quickly. "I don't know. I didn't really check."

"Well, when we get there, that's the first thing you
need to do, Sabrina. You go right inside your trailer, and
check your belongings. Especially food, clothes, and
blankets. Will you do that?"

"I guess so."

"That's fine." He didn't want her with him when he

opened the trunk of the patrol car and got out the shovel.

Joe LeDonne welcomed Euell Pentland's anger. Anger he could deal with. It was grief, real or pretended, that made him sweat. He had arrived early at the Pentland house, saying that he had come to give them a progress report. He hoped that the family would be too upset to notice that he asked more questions than he answered.

Euell Pentland came to the door in a brown bathrobe that reminded LeDonne of a monk's habit. His red face was unshaven, and tufts of uncombed white hair stuck out about his ears. Only his anger kept him from seeming foolish.

"Just one of you?" he said, glaring at the deputy. "Is that all a death is worth to your department?"

"The rest are involved in the manhunt," said LeDonne, stepping across the threshold and closing the door behind him.

"I should hope they are. If you people had organized that manhunt a good deal earlier, my wife might still be alive, Deputy."

"I expect that's so," said LeDonne. He almost smiled, thinking that Euell Pentland wouldn't hear the irony in his ostensible agreement. "I have the autopsy report."

"If there are photographs in it, keep them away from us." The old man padded back to the dining room table where a mug of coffee waited beside a congealing fried egg. "Still, I suppose that's good news. I suppose you'll release the body now so that we can go ahead with the funeral."

"Don't you want to know how she died?" asked LeDonne.

Euell Pentland froze, the mug hovering near his lips. "My wife is dead, Mr. LeDonne. For me that fact overshadows the rest."

"I want to know," said a voice from the hallway. Buck Pentland, in wrinkled jeans and a faded U.T. sweatshirt, stood in the doorway of the living room. "She was murdered. We know that. Did she suffer?"

LeDonne met the young man's gaze. "The death itself was quick," he said. "She was strangled—manually. We have a thumbprint bruise from the side of her throat."

"But—that's all?"

"No," said LeDonne evenly. "She was beaten around the face and upper body. We think she lost consciousness quickly, though. I don't suppose she knew what was happening after the first couple of seconds." It would have been longer than that, but LeDonne saw no point in adding to the family's grief.

Rita Pentland's son looked embarrassed. He stared down at the floor. "No, officer. I meant—"

"Oh." LeDonne nodded his comprehension. He was asking about rape. All male relatives of victims wanted to know that. Some of them seemed to think that being raped was worse than being murdered. "No, sir, Mrs. Pentland was not molested in any way."

Buck Pentland looked relieved, as if the killer had conferred some mercy on his victim by merely beating her and strangling her to death, but sparing her intercourse. LeDonne knew that strangling *was* a form of intercourse to some sexual psychopaths, but he didn't see any point in mentioning it. He didn't think it applied in this case, anyhow.

Buck Pentland's father had turned away in disgust at the question. "Well, that's a blessing, anyhow," he said. "I mean, we can all be thankful that she was spared that."

*You* were spared that, thought LeDonne, but he said nothing.

Buck said, "Poor Mommy. Have you got enough evidence to convict that monster who did it?"

"We're still conducting the inquiry," said LeDonne. "We don't know everything yet. I hope you'll cooperate with us in the investigation."

"What does that mean?" asked Euell Pentland.

"Fingerprints, for one thing, Mr. Pentland." Seeing the look of outrage on the old man's face, LeDonne added, "We have to know which ones to disregard." It wasn't strictly true, but it would smooth the path of the investigation, which was reason enough to say it.

"Does Charlotte know that Officer LeDonne is here, Dad?" Buck Pentland was turning to go back down the hall. "You know she'd want to be told of any developments."

Euell Pentland scowled. "I don't think the deputy's report is a fit subject for your sister's ears, boy. Women have to be protected from such filth as this."

"I'll need to speak to Miss Pentland as well," said LeDonne. "I'll try not to upset her."

As Buck Pentland hurried down the hall to summon his sister, LeDonne said, "The problem with this case is that we can't put together a scenario that makes sense."

Euell Pentland gave him a red-faced stare. "Meaning?"

"Mrs. Pentland, who hadn't heard from Harm Sorley in thirty years, is found dead at the place they used to live. Now the popular assumption is that her ex-husband kidnapped her, seeking revenge."

"Of course he did."

"But we can't find any evidence of forced entry. Nothing to substantiate the kidnapping."

"She was gone, wasn't she? There's your proof."

"Possibly. But how would Harm Sorley know where to find her?"

"He asked someone. Depend on it, Mr. LeDonne, these people stick together. Some of his trashy kin have been helping him. Why do you think you haven't caught him?"

"Well, I'll talk to the neighbors. Maybe someone saw something the night she disappeared. But there's also the possibility that your wife left of her own accord. Now, do you have any idea why she would do that?"

"She wouldn't," said Euell Pentland. His teeth were clenched, and he appeared to be one breath away from shouting again.

"There was no trouble between the two of you?"

Before the old man could react, Buck reappeared in the doorway. "Charlotte's gone!"

"What do you mean, gone?" Euell Pentland hurried to the window and peered out. "Her car's not here. I thought she was still asleep. Well, maybe she went back to her apartment, Buck. Have you tried phoning her there?"

"She left a note." He held up a folded sheet of yellow

legal paper. "She says he's her father, no matter what he has done, and that she's going to find him."

"May I see that?" asked LeDonne, reaching for the note.

"She's gone after that convict?" murmured Euell Pentland to no one in particular. As he turned away from the window, he let the curtain fall. "Charlotte?"

"Can you find her?" asked Buck. "If the old man's crazy, he might kill her, too."

LeDonne had finished scanning the note. "I can't force her to come back here," he told them. "But I don't want her out in those hills with a manhunt going on." He sighed. "Let me make some calls."

Before the search party arrived, Spencer Arrowood had time to search the battered trailer, still a dark warren of dirty clothes and cast-off furniture, stinking of sour milk and fouled diapers. He wondered how Sabrina could tell if anything were missing, and what could induce anyone to enter the place of their own free will.

Sabrina Harkryder had led him from room to room, in her usual sullen silence. She did not apologize for the condition of her living quarters, and she made no effort to pick up discarded towels or scattered glasses as they proceeded. He found no sign of forced entry, but Sabrina had told him that the trailer was never locked. Indeed, the back door latch was so bent that it was hard to keep it closed. The temperature was barely higher than outdoors, but at least it was dry. He saw small kerosene space heaters in several rooms. Those heaters turned trailers into death traps, but he supposed that the Harkryders would consider it worth the

risk if the heaters could make the place warmer. It was
all the heat they could afford, he knew, and it was better than nothing.

"Can I go to my mama's house when you're done
here?" asked Sabrina, as he searched the baby's room.

"We'll have to see," said the sheriff, his mind elsewhere. "Don't you want to wait for your husband?"

The girl shrugged. "Won't do no good," she said. "I
just want to get shut of this place for good. I wish I'd
never taken it into my head to marry Tracy."

"It's rough when you're both so young," said Spencer.
"Are there any blankets missing?"

Sabrina came forward and examined the pile of thin
cotton receiving blankets. They were thin and faded
with many washings; yard-sale baby items, a quarter
apiece. It would take all of them to keep an infant
warm in this autumn chill. The temperature had
dropped twenty degrees since they'd found Rita
Pentland's body covered with flies. It was a changeable
season. Tomorrow could be a day of sixty degrees and
sunshine, but it might just as easily snow. You never
could tell. The search today had to be as thorough as
time and daylight would allow.

"I don't see the one with the merry-go-round horses,"
she said. "Maybe it's dirty, though. I'll—" She stopped
and listened. "Car's coming."

It was another thirty seconds before Spencer's ear
could detect the whine of engines climbing the steep
road to Painter Cove. The search party hastily summoned by Jennaleigh had begun to arrive. Spencer
went out into the yard to meet them, gesturing for
them to park their four-wheel drives in the brown grass

in front of the trailer. He had already walked over that patch of ground; the soil was undisturbed. "Park there."

Four trucks churned up the dirt road from the valley, bringing nine volunteers to search the woods. Spencer nodded to short, gray-haired Millie Fortnum, a mainstay of the rescue squad, and she gave him a brief smile. "It's a sad business, Sheriff," she said.

"When you and I meet, it usually is," Spencer reminded her.

The others were volunteer firefighters from Hamelin, or just ordinary folks stirred by the news that a baby had been taken. Millie Fortnum was the only woman among them. The others looked like deer hunters, clad in thick, colorless jackets with ear-flapped caps and muddy work boots. One of them came out of his truck with a rifle in the crook of his arm, but Spencer told him to put it back. "We're a search party, not a posse," he told them.

Sabrina Harkryder did not come out of the trailer to meet them, but an old woman came out of one of the other trailers and asked who was in charge. Spencer came forward.

Her lank hair was iron gray, and her face was quilted with fine lines around the eyes and mouth. She had lost some teeth. She looked sixty; Spencer doubted if she was much past thirty-five. "It's a pitiful shame about that baby," she said. "Tracy didn't ought to never have married her. I'll help you'uns look." Her offer ended in a cough, smothered into her cold-reddened fist.

Spencer looked at her shapeless polyester coat and her ragged high-top sneakers. He could see his breath in the air between them. "Could you make us some coffee instead?" he asked. "That would keep us going longer."

She nodded. "I'll boil water. Rap on the door when you're in need of a cup."

Spencer watched her trudge back to her home. "Wait!" he called after her. "You could help just now by telling us if you know anything about the baby's disappearance. Did you see a strange man lurking around the place? Hear anything?"

The faded woman shook her head. "I seen nothing. But I can't say I'm surprised. When that Sabrina planted parsley in her garden plot, I told her she ought not to do it, because parsley in a yard invites death into the house, and she was pregnant then, but when I warned her, she just back-talked me, and went on planting. It was a sign; I knowed right then it was. That poor little baby. You won't find h'it alive."

Spencer thanked her and turned away. He gave perfunctory instructions to the searchers. Most of them had been through it many times before, searching for lost hunters, wandering old folks, or missing hikers. They knew the drill as well as he did, but they listened respectfully, huddled together in the bare yard, making breath clouds and stamping their feet, waiting to begin the sad task. He didn't tell them anything about suspects or motives. That wasn't their concern. For now it was enough to find the child; affixing the blame would come later.

The searchers fanned out, some along the road or up the mountain, and others into the sloping woods behind the Harkryders' place, looking for bits of cloth on bushes, or broken twigs that might indicate the abductor's path. If this search failed, they would bring in dogs. Spencer Arrowood walked slowly, watching the leaf-packed ground for signs of disturbed earth. He tried to move silently, stepping over dead branches and dry leaves, as he listened for a sound he had no hope of hearing: a baby's cry.

Jeremy Cobb wondered if the river had changed much since Katie's time. He was following it now, as she had done, but as he thought about the great gulf of years between their separate journeys, he knew that he had little chance of finding her homeplace. Forty years is time enough for a tree to grow twenty feet tall. It had been five times that long since the Wyler family had carved a meadow out of the forest. By now the forest would have reclaimed its own many times over. Even the stones of the cabin's chimney would most likely be unrecognizable. The chimney would have toppled, and the stones might be half-buried in dirt or tangled in vines. He doubted if Katie herself could find the place now.

It was a miracle that she found it in her own time, traveling so many miles alone through the autumn woods. Because he knew that he could not have made such a journey himself, his awe for Katie was even greater. It sharpened the sorrow of knowing that she had done it all for nothing.

She had escaped from the Shawnee village when everyone was asleep, and by daylight she had put six miles between her and her captors. She never looked back. She had no supplies, and her cloth shoes didn't

last more than a few hours on the rocky trails. Forty
days of cold starvation in the wilderness, and then she
must have begun to see the familiar sights of her home
country. Bald-topped Roan Mountain with its crown of
laurels welcoming the victor. The Roan highlands
would have been white with mayapple and phacelia
when she'd passed that way a captive, and now the
meadows were brown and the leaves falling, but she
was free. Going back to burly, fiddle-playing Rab Greer,
to present herself as a miracle: Eurydice back from the
dead.

Jeremy pictured her homecoming. The ragged girl,
gaunt and dirty, stumbles out of the forest at dusk and
approaches the Greers' cabin. She hellos the house,
calling out in a hoarse voice for Rab, for Andrew. She
is weeping. The Greers go out and half carry her into
the cabin, holding a tallow candle up to her face to see
who she is. In his memoir, Andrew writes of bringing
her bear meat from the stewpot, and she tears off
hunks of the marbled dark flesh with her fingers, filling
her mouth until her cheeks bulge, with tears still
streaming down her cheeks. The Greers crowd around,
peppering her with questions about her escape, her
time with the Shawnee, but Rab Greer hangs back,
watching her sullenly from the chimney corner. The
fatty, greasy meat is too much for her shriveled stomach. When she hears the fate of her parents and
brother, she clamps dirty hands over her mouth and
runs outside to heave all that she's eaten into the
weeds.

They make her eat again but less this time—bits of
leaner meat and corn mush—and they all take wooden

plates themselves and have their dinner, talking among themselves so as not to upset her again. Rab is still quiet, but he comes and sits at the table with the others. After supper, Rab gets up and says he is going for a walk down by the river. He motions for Katie to come, too. Walking in woods must surely be the last thing that Katie Wyler would have wanted to do, gaunt and footsore as she was from doing nothing but that for forty days and nights, but he was her betrothed, and she went.

They were gone a long time, Andrew Wyler later wrote. He said the moon was as high as the bare branches of the sycamores, and the fire was burning low before Rab Greer returned alone.

Martha Ayers's pistol lay on the seat beside her as she drove. She wanted to have it ready so that she wouldn't have to fumble with a holster in case of emergency. She supposed it wasn't likely that she would see the fugitive strolling down a country road, but stranger things had happened. She drove slowly, looking for barn doors not quite closed, or open cattle gates. She watched for a ripple of movement in the rhododendron thickets along the road, and for signs of occupation in vacant houses. Each time she stopped at a farm, she would put the Glock back in its holster before she approached the house.

She never stayed long anywhere. At each stop she would warn the household of the escaped convict, inform them briskly that Rita Pentland had met her death in a solitary hollow far from town, and she'd ask them to call the sheriff's office if they saw anything suspi-

cious. Some people were frightened. She could hear
them locking their doors as she turned to go. Others—
the old-timers—laughed and said that Harm Sorley
wouldn't hurt anybody unless he had a reason. Martha
wasn't sure they'd call if they spotted him, but none of
them had acted nervous enough to be concealing information.

She had begun her canvassing on the far side of the
mountain, the area she reached first on her way back
from running the test samples to Johnson City. Now
she was heading for the hollers around Ashe Mountain,
the place she most expected Harm Sorley to turn up:
near the scene of the murder, his old home. Talking to
folks there might take another hour, and then she
might hunt up one of the search parties and offer her
services. Martha had got over the satisfaction of being
proved right about the threat posed by the old fugitive.
Now she just wanted it to be over.

The radio crackled, and Jennaleigh's voice said,
"Martha, are you there?"

"Ten-four, dispatcher," she said crisply. "Adam-One
reporting in."

"Where are you?"

" 'State your position, Adam-one,' " said Martha with
a sigh. Jennaleigh was making progress in the dispatcher's job, but she tended to lapse into ordinary speech
when she became excited. "To answer your question, I
am proceeding in a southwesterly direction on the Ashe
Mountain Road. Over."

"Listen, I have stuff to tell you, and I haven't worked
out all the numbers, so can I just say it?"

"People might be listening in on this frequency. Over."

"Well, Marth—uh, Adam-One—do you want to go to a phone booth and call me back? Over."

Where did Jennaleigh expect her to find a phone booth on the Ashe Mountain Road? Martha scowled at the radio. She couldn't afford to stand on procedure in an emergency. She had to know what the message was, risky or not. "Go ahead, Jennaleigh, but watch what you say. Over."

"The sheriff has gone up to the Harkryders for a 10-96. No, that's not right. A 10—well, Sabrina Harkryder's baby is missing, and she says the convict stole it. Sheriff Arrowood went back up there with her, and he had me send the rescue squad and some volunteers to join the search."

"Ten-four. Does he want me to join them?"

"No. I mean, negative, One-Alpha. At least he didn't say so. I have another message for you from Deputy LeDonne."

"What?" said Martha. It had better not be personal, she thought. She felt her hands tighten on the steering wheel.

"He said for me to tell you that Charlotte—do you need me to say her whole name?"

"Negative. Don't say the name again. What about her?"

"She's run off. Apparently she left a note, saying she was going to find her father. That would be—"

"Don't say it. I know. Do they know where she's headed?"

"Negative. But he said that her car is gone. It's a

1991 red Dodge Shadow. Two-door. Vanity license plate: C-R-O-C-K-C-T."

Martha tried to picture the letters in her head. She couldn't very well jot them down while she was driving. "Say again. What's that, Jennaleigh? *Crockett?*"

She heard the dispatcher chuckle. "No. I wrote it down, and even then it must have taken me five minutes to get it, but then I remembered that Charlotte Pent—I mean, you-know-who—is a geology major at ETSU, and then I saw it. It's *See Rock City.* Get it?"

Martha sighed. *See Rock City.* That phrase had been part of the regional consciousness for the past sixty years. Most people who read the phrase wouldn't know that Rock City was a ten-acre garden with spectacular views atop east Tennessee's Lookout Mountain, but anybody who had driven any distance in the Southeast had seen the slogan in billboard-sized letters. By offering five dollars and a free paint job, the park owners had arranged for *See Rock City* to be painted on red barns along highways in eighteen states. Martha had never been to Rock City, but the painted barns had been part of the landscape of her childhood; like the Burma Shave road signs, it was a case of the ad outselling the product.

"See Rock City," she said into the radio. "That ought to be easy to spot. Any idea when she might have left?"

"Negative, Adam-One. Subject was discovered missing early this morning."

She probably left at first light then, Martha thought. And if I were going out looking for my wandering convict dad, I'd start at the last place he's known to have been. The old homeplace. "Ten-four, Jennaleigh," she said. "Tell the sheriff I have this one covered. Will report back in thirty minutes unless I hear from you first."

"Where are you going, Martha?"

"To the crime scene, Jennaleigh. Adam-One out."

Spencer Arrowood had sent most of the searchers downhill from the Harkryder settlement. The slope that led to the mountain's crest seemed too steep for anyone to have attempted with an abducted infant. Besides, he knew that in most wilderness missing persons cases, the subject could be found downhill from the PLS—the place last sighted. He had directed the searchers to keep to within a two-mile radius of the trailer for now. The experts with air-scent dogs could widen the parameters if today's investigation failed.

He had started at the front door of the trailer and walked into the woods, looking for signs that someone had passed that way. An hour's search of that patch of woods turned up nothing more than a few old tires and some broken beer bottles that had probably been used for target practice.

He returned to the trailer and began a new path, this time from the back door, the one closest to the child's room, and not within sight of the other Harkryder dwellings. He tried to imagine carrying a sleeping child, fifteen pounds or so, in his arms. Where would he go? Away from the buildings as soon as possible so that there would be less danger of the child's cries alerting the family. But suppose that were not an issue? Suppose you just wanted to get rid of a fifteen-pound burden on a cold dark mountain?

He walked into the patch of woods on level ground behind the trailer. The underbrush had been thinned by the recent cold snap, and there weren't many places that a body could be concealed, even a small one. He checked each clump of bushes anyhow, in case the child had been wrapped in cloth of a concealing color. One pile of rags made his heart tighten, but it was only an old shirt discarded or lost long ago. When he picked it up, the cloth disintegrated in his fingers.

He was about to turn back when he saw the log. A fallen locust tree, about thirty inches in diameter, lay to the right of the thicket, and it didn't look right. The sheriff stared at the log for nearly a minute before he realized what was wrong with it. There was no moss on the top, and no leaves blown up against it. He knelt down to examine the log more closely. The bark on the top side of the locust was damp, although it hadn't rained in the last twenty-four hours. It was also rotting away from the wood. Clumps of discolored bark peeled away at his touch, but the bark on the sides of the logs was still firm and dry.

Until a few hours ago, the rotting part of the log had been the underside, pressing against the damp forest earth, perhaps for years. Someone had brushed away the leaves, rolled it over, and then shoved it back into place. Spencer Arrowood put his hands on the side of the log and pushed hard. When he had succeeded in moving the log a foot from its original resting place, he saw what it had been intended to conceal: a two-foot rectangle of broken soil.

He began to dig with his bare hands, guessing that what he sought would not be far from the surface. The wet loam clung to his fingers, blackening the nails, but it came away easily as he dug. He could feel the dampness seeping through the knees of his trousers, and every deep breath brought the cold into his body. His fingers touched something that wasn't dirt, and he stopped and began to scrape away the soil, holding his breath like wet cotton in his throat, until he saw the pale roundness of a tiny fist beneath his hand.

# CHAPTER
# 16

Faithful 'til death, said our loving Master,
  A few more days to labor and wait,
Toils of the road will then seem as nothing,
  As we sweep through the beautiful gates.

"FARTHER ALONG," TRADITIONAL HYMN

Spencer Arrowood came out of the woods empty-handed. He would have to summon the other searchers, and with Millie's help, he would photograph and measure the site. First, though, he had to see Sabrina Harkryder, who had not joined in the search for her missing child.

He tapped on the back door of the battered trailer, but no one came to open it. Within all was silent. He waited a few more moments and then went around to the front. Perhaps the girl was asleep after the strain of the day's events. As he rounded the trailer hitch, he heard someone shout, "There he is! Hey, Sheriff!"

Spencer saw six members of the search party clumped together. Their expressions ranged from shock to anger. The man who yelled was running toward him now; the others trailed behind, murmuring among themselves.

"What is it?" said Spencer. He had found the body, but the others were upset. Strange.

"She stole my car," said the flannel-jacketed man, gasping cold breaths between words.

"Stole your car? Who?"

"The baby's mother. While we were back from the road searching, she took off in my car. We saw her whiz past us down the mountain."

The others had caught up to them now, and were nodding in agreement. Spencer ran his hand over his hair. "Okay," he said. "I should have figured it. Describe the car, and I'll put out the APB to the state police."

Millie Fortnum stepped forward and put her hand on the sheriff's coat. "When you came around the trailer, you weren't ground searching anymore, Spencer."

"No, Millie." He looked away. "I found him."

Charlotte Pentland hadn't expected to come back to her old homeplace so soon. She had driven up in the gray light of morning thinking of the day she had taken her mother back to look at the old trailer. It had been a happy journey, and she remembered telling Rita about the rock formations along the way, and hearing in return endless stories about kin and neighbors in the coves. Her derelict first home set in untended fields had awakened no memories in her, but perhaps it had been different for her mother. The old woman had seemed reluctant to leave, even as the light faded into early evening. Charlotte wondered if there had been some sign of her father's presence that she had missed seeing that day?

Why had Rita Pentland gone back? Charlotte supposed that her mother's reasons must be the same as hers: to see Harm Sorley, thirty years distanced from their lives, but now back from the dead.

She had stopped her little red car on the logging road that led over the mountain from the paved two-laner.

The rusting trailer lay in the field below, shadowed by the mountain. Even on such an overcast day as this, the view from the mountain was exhilarating. Ordinarily she would have treated this excursion as a lab exercise, her face near the ground, poring over rock formations and collecting samples for further study, but today she was content to gaze out at the green-and-brown patchwork below.

She was sitting on a boulder overlooking the valley, her legs dangling into space. Beside her was the knapsack that she took on field trips, but it did not contain her usual gear. Today she had brought food, a first-aid kit, and matches. She couldn't see the trailer from here, which was just as well, because the sight of the trailer would have destroyed the peace of the landscape. Charlotte didn't want to think of her mother's last hours, or the reason that armed men were now combing the area in search of the fugitive who was her half-forgotten father.

She did know that if she had any family left, it was that ailing old man lost in the mountains. She gazed down through shifting cloud-shapes at the dun fields, and the fading woods, losing leaf cover with each night's frost. He couldn't stay out there much longer. She wanted him to come in alive, so that she could talk to him, even if it was only for a minute, for the last time. She wanted to know what happened, and she wanted to hear it from him. Those men out there with their rifles and their walkie-talkies must not allow Harm Sorley to take his secrets to the grave. She left the car on the steep side of the logging road, and began to walk down to the valley to look for her father.

* * *

Jeremy Cobb thought that he might just survive if it didn't get any colder. That morning he had found a cluster of marble-sized purple berries frozen by the night frost, and when he tasted one, he had found it sweet, like a wild grape, which perhaps it was. Jeremy didn't know much more about wood lore now than he had going in, and he had seen no more wildlife than a few rabbits and from time to time a glimpse of a fleeing deer, but he had learned that human beings—except for the very young, the very old, and the infirm—are not easy to kill. They can survive on mouthfuls of food, untreated water, and sleep in a leaf pack if they have to, but barring despair or illness, they will survive.

The irony was that all along the journey, he had taken pains to avoid civilization, feeling tainted by the sight of a house or a paved road in the distance, but now, when he was cold and starving, broken by the elements and longing to call it quits and go home, he could find no trace of salvation. He would have given himself up to the loudest, drunkest hunters, or to an encampment of Girl Scouts. It was all one to Jeremy; he was done with the wilderness. But now he was lost. The valleys were twisting and narrow here, with steep-sided wooded mountains that all looked alike, and they seemed to go on forever, one forested hollow leading into another with no discernible change. He had left the river, and tried climbing one of the mountains in hopes of spotting a farm, but the underbrush blocked his path, and the clustered pines and low-hanging clouds kept him from seeing out. That's why they call these mountains the Smokies, he thought. He could see why they were sparsely populated. The majority of settlers had stopped at the piedmont around Morganton or Statesville, or else skipped over to flatlands west of Johnson City and on to the Midwest. Those that settled the steep, inaccessible wilderness in between had come early, and stayed put, far from the cities and the luxuries of any century. Jeremy, to whom one suburb was much like another, wondered what spell the land could cast that could keep its inhabitants imprisoned for centuries. He wondered if its call would draw him back to the mountains after he had escaped to his stone-walled office in technocratic Blacksburg. Then he wondered if he would ever make it out at all.

He wasn't even sure that the stream he had been following was the Toe, or if he were in Tennessee the Nolichucky River, or neither. Rivers were as narrow and shallow as creeks up here. Its banks were choked with bushes, and after a few miles of open marsh—perhaps a flood plain—the forest had closed in alongside its course, so that he lost all hope of orienting himself.

He thought of turning back, but he knew that miles of national forest land lay behind him, and he thought that surely if he kept traveling south-southwest, he would find Bakersville, or perhaps Flagpond, or Hamelin, depending on how far he had come.

Now he was again walking along the banks of a creek, because he reasoned that creeks ought to lead somewhere. Settlers used to put their homesteads as near water as they could, sensibly enough, and he thought that if he could only follow water downhill, it would take him to some human habitation. Then he realized that he had not worked out this bit of survival lore for himself. Before he set out on his hike, that student of his—Larkin? it seemed so long ago now—had told him what to do if he became lost. Odd that it should come back to him now.

He thought the day was colder than yesterday, with no hint of sun in the gray pall overhead. He had learned to ignore the pain in his feet, the roughness of his cracked and scaling lips, and the knotting of his stomach by thinking: *Any minute now, I will see someone, and I will ask them for help, and all this will be over.*

He had been expecting such a deliverance, even willing it to happen. But when he saw the dark-haired girl standing on a narrow dirt road across the field, he thought for a moment that he had imagined it.

It took Martha Ayers nearly half an hour to reach the logging road that led to the crime scene. As she turned off the paved road, she pulled over to the road's edge, and called Jennaleigh to report her position. "I am proceeding on the Sorley Cove Road," she said into the microphone. "No activity to report yet. Are there further instructions?"

"Negative, Adam-One," Jennaleigh's voice crackled through static. "Except that the sheriff has issued a BOLO for a stolen vehicle."

"Much better, Jennaleigh," said Martha. The girl had obviously been studying her vocabulary lists. "Give me details."

"The stolen vehicle is a 1988 blue Ford Tempo. Tennessee license number XZK-786. Last seen driving down the mountain from Painter Cove."

"What was it doing in Painter Cove?"

"Sabrina Harkryder came in this morning and said that the convict stole her baby, so the sheriff went up there to investigate, and he told me to send a search party up to help."

"The convict stole the baby?" Martha was still trying to make sense of the message. "And he stole a car?"

"Negative, Adam-One," said Jennaleigh, remembering protocol. "My information is that a female suspect took off in a car belonging to one of the rescue squad members."

"Do you have a description of the suspect?"

"Affirmative, Adam-One."

"Well?"

"She looks a lot like Sabrina Harkryder."

"Meaning that she *is* Sabrina Harkryder?"

"Affirmative, Adam-One."

"What about the baby?" There was no point in using code if you had to stop and explain every sentence to Jennaleigh anyhow.

"The baby." There was such a long pause that Martha thought she'd lost the connection, but then Jennaleigh said, "Oh, Adam-One, the sheriff was so upset. The baby—well, the baby is not Code J."

Martha took a deep breath, and hit her fist gently against the steering wheel. She thought about her first emergency call: Sabrina Harkryder and the baby. If she had been more hardnosed about the incident, would things have turned out differently? "All right. Any instructions?"

"Just keep an eye out. And check in with me regularly for updates. Okay?"

"Affirmative," whispered Martha. "I'll finish this as quick as I can, and then I'll help."

Martha started the car again and headed up the mountain. The logging road was a red-rutted switchback that followed the contour of the mountain, with very little solid ground left on the slope side. Winter snow or spring's heavy rains would render it impassable, but in early autumn there was no view more beautiful than the sprawling landscape spread out beneath the crest of the road. Recent years had given Martha little time or inclination to pursue scenic wonders. This time she barely glanced out at the valley, concentrating instead on avoiding rocks in the road to protect the patrol car's shock absorbers. The rest of her concentration centered on Harm Sorley, who was proving more demonic than even she would have believed. Why didn't the prison warn them that he was violent?

She caught a glimpse of the red car just as she was turning the last bend in the upward climb, and as soon as the road leveled out, Martha parked the patrol car on a patch of dry grass, and took her shotgun out of its scabbard. They might be together, father and daughter. She scrambled into the jacket, picked up the weapon, and began to creep toward the car, using pine trees and boulders for cover as she went. At ten yards she switched to an angle that enabled her to see the license plate: CROCKCT. Charlotte Pentland's car.

Martha wondered if she would find the pair of them waiting for her at the scene of Rita's murder, and, if so, would Charlotte be there as an avenger or as an accomplice? The car was locked and empty. Martha stood still for a moment, listening and watching the trees on the slope above the dirt track. She decided that there was no one nearby.

Martha locked the patrol car. If Charlotte's car was here, she couldn't have gone far. Martha thought she would have a better chance of finding her on foot. She put her pistol back in the holster on her belt, but she took the shotgun with her. Surely the convict hunters would turn up soon. All she had to do was locate Charlotte Pentland, and keep them both from getting killed until help arrived.

Jeremy Cobb's first words to the dark-haired girl were: "Please don't scream. I know what I must look like, but I need help."

The girl had backed up against a tree, staring at him with brown eyes round with alarm. She did not make a sound, but by her expression Jeremy could gauge his dirt-caked ferocity, the croaking hoarseness of his voice, and his sweat-brewed stench. She looked like one of his students—perhaps even younger. She was wearing a cheap, oversized coat, and white boots of imitation leather. She seemed repelled by the tattered apparition from the woods, but not particularly frightened. He wondered what she was doing out in the woods alone. Not hunting, surely.

"My name is Jeremy Cobb. I'm a hiker," he told her breathlessly. She looked as if she might bolt any second now. "I've been on the trail for a week or so. Actually, it seems like about six years, because I got lost, and I managed to ditch all my equipment, so it's been pretty rough."

She was still staring at him wide-eyed.

"So could you tell me where I am?" He tried to force his cracked lips into a smile. "Please?"

"Tennessee," she said. She was a local; she packed the whole dialect into that one word.

Jeremy looked around. They were standing in a dirt track on the edge of the clearing he had just come through. He could see no sign of civilization except this one mooncalf of a girl. He tried again. "I'm sure I need medical attention, miss. What's your name?"

She scowled and looked at the ground for a full minute before she mumbled, "S'brina."

"Sabrina. What a nice name. English folklore." He was babbling from desperation to communicate and sheer relief at no longer being alone. He couldn't remember ever wanting so much to talk to another living soul. "Well, Sabrina, do you live around here?"

"No."

"Is there a farmhouse? A ranger station? Somewhere that would telephone a hospital?"

She shrugged. "I don't think so."

"Well, what are you doing out here?"

"Looking for somebody." She looked away, answering his questions sullenly, like a kid being questioned by the principal.

He forced himself to stay calm, despite the pain in his feet, and the numbing cold that touched each one of his aching muscles individually. His desperation seemed to amuse her, or at least to stir her curiosity. She looked up at him, and touched a fresh briar cut on his cheek. "What are you doing out here, anyhow?" she asked.

"I told you: I was hiking."

"You?" She smiled and shook her head.

"I was, honest. But not for fun. I mean, I'm a history professor, and I came out here looking for Katie Wyler's cabin. Or at least the place it used to be."

"Who's Katie Wyler?"

"Look," said Jeremy, impatient with weariness. "It's getting colder by the minute. Do you have a car or something?"

"Yeah. It's back a ways over the hill. I kinda got it stuck, though. I never came this way before—not driving, anyhow." They were walking now, with Jeremy following her lead, back—he hoped—to her car.

"Why were you driving out here? I know—looking for somebody. Is your dad out here hunting? I hope you were bringing him his lunch."

"No. I was looking for a lady deputy. I think she's out here and I wanted to talk to her, so I took this shortcut that ought to come out near Maggard's farm. It's the quickest way from my mama's house to Painter Cove. We used to do it in the summer when the roads weren't muddy. It's ten miles farther if you take the paved roads."

"I see." Jeremy nodded. "But your car is stuck in the mud."

"Yeah. I got too far over on the left, and I hit a deep puddle, where the bank kind of slid away into the ditch." She brightened. "Hey, maybe you can get it out for me."

"I doubt it," said Jeremy. "In a ditch? Sounds like you'll need a wrecker to get out of that."

"Maybe." The hopeful look on her face was gone.

Now the girl did not seem concerned with the fate of her car. "It doesn't matter."

"Well, which way is the nearest house?" asked Jeremy, whose endurance seemed to have lessened with the prospect of rescue. Suddenly he did not want to walk another step. "Is it quicker to go back toward the car, or to keep walking the other way toward that farm you mentioned?"

"On to the farm, I reckon," said Sabrina. "Just keep taking that road." She pointed to the ridge behind them, and turned away.

"Wait a minute. Aren't you coming with me?"

"What for?"

"Because I don't want to get lost again. How far is it?"

"Five or six miles, I reckon."

"Please come. We'll find the farm, and I'll get them to call the rescue squad, and we'll call a wrecker for your car. Or, better yet, we'll call that deputy you're looking for."

"How? She's out in the woods."

"She probably checks in every so often with her office. We'll call them and leave a message. How about it? Doesn't that sound better than trudging through the cold trying to find one person in all this wilderness?"

She shrugged. "I guess."

"Believe me, you can't do it. I've just nearly killed myself trying."

Charlotte Pentland hadn't meant to look in the trailer, but when she came down the hill and saw it, battered and empty, at the end of the field, she began to walk toward it. There was no one in sight. The sheriff's department had finished all their photography and crime scene investigation, and now the place looked as abandoned as ever. She had expected to see yellow tape, bearing the inscription *Crime Scene—Do Not Cross,* but there was no sign of a warning that someone had recently died here.

I have to see it, thought Charlotte. Imagining it would be worse. How ironic that her mother's life should have ended here in this hovel that she had escaped from for so many years. Charlotte felt her nose tingle and her eyes sting with unshed tears. Last night the sheriff had said that he thought her mother's death had been quick and painless, but she doubted if he would have said otherwise.

She quickened her pace. The trailer, rusty and without wheels, seemed to be disintegrating into the earth. How could they have lived here? She stood on the concrete block that served as a step, and tried the handle. When she pushed harder, it turned, probably rusted open years ago from neglect. Charlotte took a deep breath and went in.

The tiny front room with its broken windows and layers of dirt seemed unchanged from the last time she had seen it. She stood still and waited, half expecting to hear a cry of pain, or to feel some sense of her mother's presence. She felt nothing but the cold. This was not the room in which it had happened, though. The sheriff said she'd been found in the bedroom, that empty cubicle barely big enough to hold a bed. Charlotte pushed open the narrow door and ducked into the room. Her mother's belongings had been taken away when the body was removed, and the room was as empty as before. The floor was stained with rust-colored patches, and there were splashes of it on the wall near the tiny window.

Charlotte knelt down to look at the streaks of dried blood, and then she saw the flies. Dozens of them, hatched during the warm spell a couple of days back, had died in the cold. She ran from the room, forcing images of flies and blood from her mind.

She shouldn't have come. It had never occurred to her that the police did not clean up crime scenes, and since they didn't, she wondered if she should attempt it out of respect for her mother. She was outside now, sweating, although the wind blew cold against her. She looked back at the battered trailer, uninhabitable before, and now likely to become a draw for the curious, a haunted house for thrill-seeking teenagers. Her eyes narrowed. Perhaps the aluminum ruin ought to be torched, a sort of funeral pyre in memory of her mother.

She pulled up handfuls of dried grass and began to throw them through the open door. Some of the plywood paneling was beginning to come off the living room wall. That would burn, too. So would an old orange crate she had seen in the weeds. The pile of tinder grew until it made a mound nearly three feet high in the center of the front room. *Now light the dried grass and close the door.* The muddy field in front of the trailer would keep the fire from spreading to the woods. *Why not?*

She stood on the concrete block and leaned into the trailer. She took the book of matches out of her knapsack and struck a match, tossing it into the dry grass on the sagging plywood floor. Then another. And another. When the brown grass was blazing, Charlotte pushed back on the concrete block to brace herself, and slammed the door. The block toppled over, and she fell into the dirt beside the front door, cutting her cheek on rock.

Charlotte got up on her hands and knees, shaken but unhurt. She decided to move the block step, in case anyone should appear and try to fight the fire. As she shoved the block away from the trailer, she saw an edge of plastic sticking out from beneath it. She squatted and with both hands pushed over the block. There in the hard, damp earth beneath the block lay a plastic sandwich bag containing an envelope. Charlotte could already feel the heat from within the metal walls as she bent down to pick it up.

"You were going to tell me about that woman you were a-hunting in the woods," said Sabrina, tugging at the sleeve of Jeremy Cobb's jacket.

Jeremy was more interested in finding out what this pale young girl was doing looking for a sheriff's deputy in the winter woods, but he knew that he had very little chance of finding out unless he could make her trust him. "Katie Wyler was a pioneer woman back in the 1700s," he said. "She wasn't much older than you are when she was kidnapped by Indians, and taken hundreds of miles from here."

"Lucky her," said Sabrina. She was trudging a little ahead of him, and although she was listening to his story, her eyes never stopped watching the woods on either side of the dirt track.

"No," said Jeremy. "They killed her parents, and one of her brothers. She saved the younger one by sending him down to the river. The Shawnee took Katie with them, but I assure you that she didn't want to go. To her they were murdering savages. Besides, she was engaged to a fellow here named Rab Greer, and she didn't want to leave him."

"So what happened to her?"

"The Indians took her all the way to the other end of West Virginia, but she escaped and followed the rivers back here. It took her more than a month, living on whatever she could find along the way."

Sabrina turned to look at him; a faint sneer played over her lips. "So you thought you'd do like she did, huh? Mr. Tough Guy. Figured you could do it."

Jeremy nodded. "That's right. I was lucky to have lasted a week. How about you? What brings you out in the cold?"

"It ain't so bad out here," said Sabrina. "I'm used to cold. We don't have no central heating up where I live."

"Where's that?"

"You didn't finish your story. What happened to that girl that the Indians took?"

"She made it home, all right, but on the very night she got back she went out walking with her fiancé, and apparently they had some sort of quarrel, and he killed her. Nobody knows for sure what went wrong between them."

"He never said?"

"No. He wasn't even tried for the murder. These

mountains were so isolated back then that the nearest court would have been sixty miles in any direction."

"Then how do you know what happened?"

"Years later, when he was an old man, Katie's younger brother Andrew wrote his memoirs. As a child Andrew went to live with the Greers, after his parents were killed in the raid that took Katie. Some sixty years later he wrote about his sister's return. He said they all welcomed her, and asked her questions as she ate her first real meal for many weeks. Andrew said that Rab Greer hung back while the others talked to his fiancée. He looked troubled, but Andrew didn't know why. Later he asked Katie to go out walking with him, and a few hours later he came back alone."

"Maybe he didn't kill her," said Sabrina. "Maybe she had a heart attack or a wolf got her."

"Andrew says he killed her. He said there were thumb bruises on her neck, and deep red marks on Rab Greer's wrists and hands, where she'd clawed him with her fingernails. Katie was a fighter. But Andrew was a young boy, and he knew better than to accuse one of his hosts of murder, so he didn't say anything about it. The Greers were long dead when he wrote his memoirs."

"So why did her boyfriend kill her?"

"At first I thought she might have been raped by the Shawnee, and that he killed her for being 'unfaithful.' Men had weird ideas about sex back then."

Sabrina's look was scornful. "Like they don't now?"

Jeremy sighed. "I hear that from my students, too. Anyhow, I don't think that was it. Everything I've read on Indian captivity indicates that the Indians didn't go in for that sort of thing. If you were willing to voluntarily become some man's wife, that was fine, but they weren't into violence. Now if Katie had willingly married a Shawnee man, she wouldn't have tried to escape, and if she had been unwilling, sources say that she would not have been assaulted. I always thought that she must have really loved Rab Greer to go to all that trouble to get back to him."

"Choices aren't always that simple, mister."

Jeremy smiled indulgently. "What do you think happened?"

"I think people can get caught between a rock and a hard place, and then there's no right answers without somebody getting hurt." Jeremy started to answer her, but she grabbed his arm and pointed up ahead. "Do you see smoke over yonder?"

The trail wound around for more than a mile across the top of the mountain before it spiraled down the opposite side in a long series of loops and sharp turns, following the contours of the ridges. More than once Martha was tempted to retrace her steps and take the patrol car down the other side, but she had no way of knowing how far Charlotte Pentland had gone, or in which direction. She spent twenty minutes following a side track to a dead end—probably a hunters' trace, or the remnants of an old logging venture. She found no sign of Charlotte or the fugitive.

Martha had never been afraid of the woods. As a child she had always played in the fields and forest around the homes of various relatives, and once, when she was seven, her daddy had even taken her deer hunting. It was different, though, when you were out there alone with a gun in your hand, and one slung over your shoulder. It was different when there was a killer hiding out there somewhere. Martha decided that she'd have to be crazy not to be afraid, but she wasn't going to turn back. The convict was an old man; the pursuing deputy was a woman. That was fair odds, she thought. And there was always the chance that by being sympathetic, she could talk him into surrendering. She decided that it was better for her to track down Harm than for Spencer or LeDonne to get into some kind of macho showdown with the fugitive. Her way seemed less likely to end in bloodshed. She hoped she found the old man before Charlotte did.

You could see for miles through the gaps in the pines on the mountaintop, and there was not a house in sight. For a moment she thought about bringing CrystalS out here. No one could hear her scream. Martha pictured herself sitting on a rock, pistol in hand, forcing the bitch to strip, and then throwing her clothes off the mountain. Watching them ride the currents of air far down into the woods below. Then getting back in the car and driving off—alone. For CrystalS it would be a long cold walk back out. She'd have plenty of time to think about her future moral obligations. Martha found herself thinking: *But what would it accomplish?* She turned her thoughts back to the matter at hand, before the pain could spoil her fantasy.

Martha had just rounded a curve that cut the crest of the mountain when she saw the curls of black smoke swirling up from the valley. Too much smoke to be a chimney fire. Martha looked over the bank for a shortcut, and then decided that it would be safer to take the road. She checked the safety on her weapon, and took off downhill at her jogging pace.

Harm knew these woods, and the saddle shape of the mountain ridges against the clabbered sky. He wasn't sure where he had been or why he was footsore. He didn't know why his cheeks felt hollow in a face that he knew to be lean and hawklike, or why the cold wind seemed to pass through him as if he were insubstantial. He had little interest in the thought of food, except to sense that he hadn't had much of it in a while. But he knew this country now, and the joy of that filled him with more warmth than the heartiest stew. He felt like a man gaining his footing again after a precipitous drop.

He could not recall where he had been or why, but whatever had happened to him, he was nearly home. He felt as if he had just awakened from a nap, or perhaps he'd been hit on the head and was just now coming out of the concussion. He might have been drunk, of course. Rita would mind about that. She didn't want him traipsing out in the woods to where the blockaders worked, transforming corn and sugar into tax-free bourbon. He knew them all and was kin to some, but sometimes they shot before they got a good look, and Rita worried that he might not come home.

He took stock of himself and his belongings. He found no bullet holes or knife cuts. His limbs were a cross-stitch of ordinary scrapes and bruises, testimony to time spent in the wild, but he did not think he had been badly hurt, wherever he had been. His torn trousers were dirty, and the mud-caked sweater miles too big for his bony frame. Even in their present state, the clothes looked expensive—like nothing he could remember owning. They didn't look like his usual hunting gear.

He glanced around the clearing for his hunting rifle, but didn't find it. In the burlap sack at his feet, though, he discovered a fancy pistol. He wouldn't have been out hunting with that piece. He might have won it in a card game, though. Or he could have been up to meanness with it. He wondered if anybody was a-hunting him.

Rita might know. He would go on over the ridge to home, and see what she could tell him, and if the charge was too bad, he could light out again for the woods like Dalton Sorley did all those years ago, when he'd laid low and tricked the law into thinking he was dead.

The snug little trailer wasn't more than a mile or two along the ridge now. Wherever he had been, whatever he had done, at least he was sober now and almost home. Rita would be tearful glad to see him, and baby Chalarty would wrap her little arms around his legs and hug like a kudzu vine. Maybe he could take the young'un for a walk by the creek before supper time.

Harm slid the pistol into his jacket pocket and slung the burlap bag over his shoulder. His steps quickened. He hoped Rita was cooking pinto beans and taters for supper tonight. It seemed like forever since he'd had a square meal, but it wasn't the food he wanted as much as the sight of her smiling at him across the table, pushing the plate of cornbread at him, as if love was butter. He smiled to think of it.

He kept the ridge in sight, dodging past trees as he hurried now for the first time in his journey. He was nearly home. Each time he looked down at the ground or over into the brush, and the memory started to slide away, he had only to look ahead again to feel the joy of discovery anew. Each glimpse of the ridge called him home.

He was hurrying through an abandoned field, littered with weed cedars and rocks. He had just passed the tumbled-down chimney stones of the old settlers' cabin when he saw the pall of smoke hanging above the bare branches of the maples. It was a black plume drifting up from the holler, rising to the level of the first bend in the mountain road. There was only one thing in that holler that could be afire.

Harm Sorley began to run.

# CHAPTER
# 17

O may we view with dauntless eyes,
   The last tremendous day,
When earth and seas, and stars and skies,
   In flames shall melt away.

#854, "AFTER A FIRE," PHILIP DODDRIDGE

TENNESSEE METHODIST HYMNAL, 1885

The sheriff's office was a patchwork of sheepskin and plaid flannel jackets, so packed with strangers that Henry Kretzer stood with his hand on the doorknob, blinking uncertainly at the prospect of going in. He could be relatively affable with four or fewer strangers, or with several thousand listeners at the other end of the radio signal; it was the numbers in-between that gave him trouble.

After a moment's pause, he regained enough composure to realize that he had encountered the search party, which had apparently called it a day and was now congregating on Spencer Arrowood's premises, drinking coffee out of Dixie cups and arguing about what to do next. He closed the door behind him. One more interruption for the sheriff couldn't matter in this melee.

He knew that he should be relaxed and effusive—the local celebrity offering to lend a hand—but Henry Kretzer could never make Hank the Yank come to life off-air. He would have to be his meek, unassuming self, and hope that the sheriff would hear him out. He threaded his way through a crowd that reminded him of the grandstands of local football games. As he passed one knot of people, he heard someone say, "If she doesn't radio in soon, we'll have to go back out there."

He knew Spencer Arrowood on sight: the Wake County sheriff had the chiseled features and slight, sturdy build that would keep him looking thirty-eight until he was seventy. He was listening to uniformed officers detail their search, punctuating their accounts with gestures and finger-drawn lines on the framed county map. He looked tired and grave; not the amiable politician that Kretzer expected to find working the room, but a solemn man whose thoughts seemed to be elsewhere. Rather than interrupt, the disc jockey simply stood close by, waiting, until the sheriff noticed his stare, and came over to speak to him.

"Spencer Arrowood," the fair-haired man said, as if the badge were not introduction enough. He held out his hand. "Were you out there today?"

"No, sir. You may not remember me, but we've met. I'm Henry Kretzer." The answering smile showed no recognition. "WHTN. Hank the Yank."

The sheriff's smile dimmed a bit, and he sighed. "Didn't recognize your voice at first. I hope you're not here for an interview, Hank, because today has just been a bear. And I won't be able to issue any statements until tomorrow at the earliest."

Hank the Yank shook his head. "I didn't come to get a press release, Sheriff. I came to ask if you think Harm Sorley is guilty."

"I'm sorry. I just can't comment on that. We still have an officer in the field, and the suspect has not been apprehended."

"I just want your opinion, off the record, on whether you think he killed his ex-wife, and if you people do think he's guilty, then I guess I want to volunteer to join the posse tomorrow."

Spencer Arrowood smiled a little. "The—posse," he mused. "And why would you want to do that, Hank?"

Kretzer edged away from the elbow of a burly hunter. "I guess I want to do what I can to make sure that Harm Sorley comes out of those woods alive."

"Why? You think you can do a jailhouse interview for your show? Sell some more bumper stickers?"

"No." Kretzer reddened, but he stood his ground. "Okay, fair enough, I thought Harm was pretty much of a joke when this thing started, and I did ride it on my show, but then I got interested in him, and I've been doing research into the original case. I don't think he got a fair shake thirty years ago, whether he was guilty or not, and I guess I'd like to see him get another chance."

"And you think if you're not in the search party, we'll shoot him on sight?" The friendliness was gone from Spencer Arrowood's voice.

"No, I guess not, but—"

"Look, Mr. Kretzer. You have no training in search and rescue. You don't know the terrain. And you don't know the individual we're searching for. I don't think you'd exactly be an asset out there."

Henry Kretzer nodded, and turned to go.

"Wait," said the sheriff. "I know you want to help, and I'm willing to believe that you feel sorry for that old man. I know about the Maggard case, too. I think the best thing you can do is to tell people how you feel on your show tonight. Keep people calm. I've been listening to your program, and I appreciate what you've been saying about not hanging the elephant again."

"You listen?"

"Now and again." The sheriff smiled. "Maybe I'll even come on the show one of these days."

"You want me to broadcast. But what can I tell people? Is he a dangerous man?"

"He's an escaped convict."

"Did he kill Claib Maggard?"

Spencer Arrowood hesitated. Then he shrugged. "Oh hell. I think so. Yes. But I wouldn't have called it murder in the first degree. It might even have been self-defense. We may never know."

"Do you know why he did it?"

"I think so. It's not something I can talk about just yet, though."

"But even if he was guilty then, that was thirty years ago. He's past sixty. Is he dangerous now?"

The sheriff shook his head. "That's a tough call. You know about his mental problems?"

Kretzer nodded. "If he's as bad off as the prison reports say, I'm surprised he hasn't been captured before now."

"I know. So maybe he's saner than the NECC thinks, or maybe he's a psychotic killer. In fugitive cases, we can *never* afford to say that a suspect is not dangerous, because then some gung ho civilian will try to make a citizen's arrest brandishing his pocketknife and get himself killed. On the other hand, I don't want terrified residents in fear of their lives, shooting any bush that moves. I think if everybody stays home, nobody will get hurt."

One of the civilian searchers had overheard this last exchange. "What about the Harkryder baby, Sheriff? Shouldn't people be warned about that?"

Spencer Arrowood saw the stricken look on the face of Hank the Yank. "Oh hell," he said.

Jeremy Cobb called out again for the girl to slow down. He was trying to run, but every time he landed with his weight on his right foot, waves of pain went through him. He felt tears sting his eyes. Finally, when he simply stopped, squatting under a tree, gulping breaths of cold air, Sabrina turned and came back for him.

"It's not far to the fire now," she said. "You can make it. It'll be warmer there, anyhow."

"My feet hurt." He sat in the brown grass, tugging at his boot.

"In this weather it's when they stop hurting that you'd better worry." Her voice was matter-of-fact, without sympathy. "Now come on if you're coming."

She did help him up, though, and she slowed her pace to accommodate his limping stride. They rounded another bend in the road, and saw the burning trailer nestled in the shadow of the mountain. Only a metal outline of the structure remained, sagging in the blaze. The air around the fire was blurred with heat.

"Does anybody live there?" asked Jeremy as they walked toward the flames.

"I don't think so. Wonder how it got started."

"Arson, I expect," said Jeremy. "Drunken hunters or teenage vandals. It doesn't look like it's spreading, though. The trees are far enough back from it. Good thing this field is bare. It stinks, though. Watch where you step. What is this muck on the ground?"

Sabrina shrugged. "Oil or something, looks like."

They came to a stop about ten yards from the burning trailer, close enough to feel the heat. Except for the soaring flames, all was still. "Wonder if anybody's reported the fire," said Sabrina.

"Not in this godforsaken place," said Jeremy. "I guess it's up to us. How do we get to the nearest house from here?"

Sabrina pointed to the ridge above. "Climb that mountain."

"I thought you said that deputy you're looking for was out here."

"Somewhere. I don't think we can afford to sit here and wait, though. Besides, she'll be pleased if I report the fire. A good turn, like."

"Why?" asked Jeremy, looking down at her with all the severity that he could muster in his weariness. "Why do you need to do a good turn?"

Sabrina looked away. "Something bad happened."

Jeremy waited a long minute for her to go on, but she kept staring into the flames, unconscious of the silence. Finally, he shrugged. *What the hell,* he thought. *Maybe she skipped school.* Aloud he said, "Come on then, Sabrina. We'd better get started on that mountain."

When they turned away from the fire, Jeremy stopped, open-mouthed. A man had come up behind them, and he was staring at them with a look of outrage. He was the scruffy old devil Jeremy had met on the trail, now looking more wild and gaunt than ever. His eyes were red-rimmed, but he did not speak. He was holding the pistol that had been in Jeremy's backpack, and he had it aimed at Jeremy's chest.

Charlotte Pentland had not wanted to watch the trailer burn. She wanted it gone from the landscape, because its existence offended her, and so that ghoulish locals would not congregate around it, inventing tales of her mother's ghost flitting past the broken windows. She had thought she was doing her mother a service by obliterating the last trace of a past from which they had escaped.

When flames engulfed the sagging ruin, Charlotte ran up the dirt track that led over the mountain. She would put height and distance between herself and the fire, and then she would read the letter. She climbed the first steep grade of the mountain, and stopped to sit on a boulder at the edge of a narrow overlook. A vista of pine forest and dark hills beyond lay before her, encompassing the southern end of the valley, ending at Ashe Mountain. Somewhere under all those trees and soil, a serpentine chain wound its way north, an eternal reminder of the mountain's beginnings. Charlotte wondered if her mother's serpentine beads had been destroyed in the fire, or if they were with her belongings at the sheriff's office. Or perhaps she was her mother's serpentine chain, entrusted with remembering their past.

She turned her back to the spiral of smoke hanging over the ridge she had just crossed. The sun was low in the sky now. She shivered a little, and drew out of the plastic bag the square green envelope with the single word *Hiram* penciled on it in her mother's handwriting.

Her mother must have hidden the letter the day that she had insisted that Charlotte take her there. Had it been when she had walked down to the creek, leaving her mother alone at the trailer? Charlotte opened the letter, reading the few lines again and again in the cold twilight.

She was still sitting there, holding the letter and staring out across the fading landscape, when someone shouted her name. Charlotte turned toward the upland grade of the dirt track, and saw Martha Ayers of the sheriff's department running toward her. She shoved the letter into the pocket of her jeans and stood up.

"Are you all right?" asked Martha. She set the stock of the department issue Mossberg shotgun on the ground while she caught her breath.

Charlotte nodded. "I had to come out here," she said.

"Is your half brother out here, too?" Martha kept glancing down the road toward the trees. "Or your stepfather?"

"I came alone. Why? Have you found my father?"

"He's down at the trailer," said Martha. "It's on fire. I spotted him just now from the ridge above. I think he's armed. But if you're here alone, then who's he got down there with him?" Martha picked up the shotgun and turned to go.

"Wait!" said Charlotte. "I have to talk to you!"

"Later!" called Martha, already picking up stride.

"Then I'm coming with you! I won't let you shoot him!"

Martha turned to look back at her. Her face was lined with weariness and cold. "Come on then," she said. "We'll try talking first."

The old man's gaze was unwavering. He stood still, his face streaked with tears, with the pistol aimed at the chest of Jeremy Cobb.

"I told you," said Jeremy, straining to keep his voice from rising in fear. "We didn't do this."

At his side Sabrina Harkryder was murmuring, "That's the escaped convict my deputy friend was a-hunting. He's a killer."

"We've met," said Jeremy to the stranger, trying to smile. "Out in the woods, remember?"

"I never seen you before."

"Sure you have. I offered you something to eat. In fact, that's my gun you're holding."

Harm Sorley said, "Where's my wife and baby?"

Jeremy looked around him. "We haven't seen anybody."

"They live in that trailer!" the old man shouted.

"It's been deserted for years," said Sabrina, raising her voice a little so that he would look at her.

"They live there," said Harm Sorley. "I just left them there."

"How long ago?" asked Jeremy.

The old man blinked, as if he were trying to remember, but the answer eluded him. The gun shook in his hand. "Couple of days. Not long." He took aim again at Jeremy. "Now what happened to 'em? Who burned my home? Are you some of Claib Maggard's people? Did he kill them?"

"He's crazy," whispered Sabrina. She stood calmly beside Jeremy, watching the gunman with no sign of fear. "He's a dead man."

"Look, sir," said Jeremy. "We don't know anything about you or this fire. We're just lost here in the woods, looking for help, okay?"

But Harm Sorley wasn't listening. He was sobbing now, looking over their heads at the dancing flames, and then back at them with renewed anger. "They were all I had in this world. If I don't find them—"

"Would you like us to help you search for your family?" Jeremy persisted.

The gun wavered in the old man's hand. He was looking past them, across the barren field and up at the mountain road, and he began to smile. He turned away from Jeremy and Sabrina, kicking aside the burlap sack at his feet. "Well, there she is, a-coming toward me!" he murmured to himself. "There she is right now!"

His hand fell to his side, and he began to run across the field without a backward glance at his captives. Jeremy turned around and saw two people running down the dirt track. One of them was in uniform and carried a weapon; the other, a young light-haired woman, was holding out her arms. She was shouting something, but he couldn't make out the words.

He felt Sabrina grab his arm. "Come on," she whispered. "He's distracted. Let's go!"

They ran for the cover of the trees at the far end of the barren field. Jeremy paused for a moment behind the branches of an evergreen to look back, but no one was following. He heard no shots. Sabrina tugged at his arm again, and he stumbled after her, keeping his head low, as she did, and trying not to step on twigs or piles of dry leaves.

"Where are we going?" he asked.

But she put a finger across her lips and shook her head. Then she pointed back the way he had come, toward the river. The shadows were deepening in the woods now, and the color was leaching out of the landscape. A crash in a thicket behind them sent them sprawling. It might have been a deer startled by their presence, but they ran anyhow, dodging fallen branches and bramble bushes, staggering on until the woods thinned, and they saw a field strewn with pines and weed cedars, gray in the twilight.

"The river's to the left, I think," whispered Sabrina. "Across this old field."

Jeremy stopped, listening. "What was that?"

She shook her head. "I didn't hear anything. What did it sound like?"

"A shot, maybe."

He followed her across the field, through the brown stubble of dead grass, past a crumbling mound of riverstone and clay. Now that the danger had lessened, Jeremy's foot had begun throbbing again, and the cold pierced his lungs. "Can we rest?" he called out.

Sabrina pointed to the trees on the left side of the field. "Nearer the river," she mouthed, and plodded on. He watched the thin figure in her shapeless coat stumping on across the field, and it shamed him into motion. "Do you do much hiking?" he asked breathlessly, reaching her side. "Or camping?"

Sabrina rolled her eyes. "Don't know jack-shit about that stuff," she said softly. "You do what you have to."

They had reached a cluster of hemlocks, affording more shelter than the leafless hardwoods beyond. "Rest," said Jeremy, squatting down on the pine needles, and tugging at his wet boot. Sabrina sank down with her back to him, warming her cupped hands with her breath, her eyes closed, listening.

Jeremy heard faint sounds coming from the meadow. He caught his breath, tensing every muscle, straining to hear: hoarse shouts, words he couldn't make out, the whinny of horses, and the high, wavering screams of a woman in terror. At first he thought he was hearing the people back at the trailer, but the sound was too close to be them, and the shouting voices were male. He could see no one.

Then from the direction of the abandoned field there came the smell of fire, and the crackle of flames, and more shouts, all sounding close, but in the dusk no fire light matched the sound of burning, and no smoke drifted up from the graying heath. The field was empty, a grassland whose only trace of human habitation was the square cairn of gray rocks, the ruins of an ancient chimney put together with red clay and stones from the nearby river. In the twilight the green of the scrub pines and cedars faded to black, and the colorless grass was still. They could no longer see the distant smoke from the burning trailer, and there was no wind to carry sounds so far. Jeremy strained to see shapes in the twilight, but nothing moved in the empty meadow.

They huddled together in the cluster of hemlocks, motionless and silent, waiting. In a little time, the rough voices faded, and they heard the rustle of dry grass parting before running feet. The soughing sound came toward them, closer and closer, but the grass was still. The rustling stopped. They saw no one, but there was a smell of sweat, blood perhaps, and something else that Jeremy couldn't put words to, but it made him think of cooking. He heard the swish of unseen cloth brush the leaves. Close to his ear, a woman's voice spoke softly: "Try to make it to the river. Go quick. And don't you look back."

The air was crisp, and the light was slanted, and the birds were still.


"Don't go any closer," Martha Ayers called out. "Can't you see he's got a gun?"

Charlotte did not break stride. Without looking back she said, "He's my father."

"He won't know that. Keep back."

But the old man was smiling at Charlotte now, pistol hanging limply at his side, as if he had forgotten it. He didn't seem aware of the deputy behind her, still holding the Mossberg shotgun and waiting. He was walking toward her with a look of joyful recognition.

Charlotte stood still and waited for him. "You keep back," she hissed at Martha. "Let me talk to him." She tried to stand still and to smile, despite the tightness in her throat. When he was a few yards away, she said softly, "Hello, Daddy."

Harm Sorley smiled back. "Hello, Rita," he said. "I missed you something awful." He was close enough to embrace her now, but a spurt of flames from the trailer caught his attention, and he looked again at the blazing ruin, experiencing anew the shock of his home's destruction. "A-Lord, Rita," he whispered. "What happened?"

His daughter took a deep breath. "It just caught fire," she said.

"Was it set on purpose? Did you see who did it, Rita?" He coughed a little as tendrils of smoke reached them. "Was it some of Claib Maggard's people? I wouldn't put it past him, not after I caught him dumping that poison on our field."

The deputy stiffened at these last words, and the old man noticed the movement. He looked at her for a long minute: a grim, uniformed woman holding a shotgun. He looked back at the short blond woman at his side. "Who is that, Rita?" he asked softly.

"It's all right," said Charlotte. "She came about the fire."

Martha stepped forward, unsmiling, the shotgun cradled in the crook of her arm, aimed at the ground. "We're here to help you, Mr. Sorley," she said. "Give me the pistol now."

He wasn't listening. He stepped closer to Charlotte and cupped her chin in his free hand. "Rita, you look changed. Your hair is lighter, and those clothes. You don't dress that-a way. What's been happening here?" His voice was gentle with bewilderment.

Charlotte was crying now, and Harm Sorley looked with alarm from the scowling deputy to the weeping woman. He turned and saw his home wreathed in flames. He cried out, "Chalarty!" and began to run toward the blaze.

Martha watched for a frozen second as the old man

ran stumbling toward the trailer. His daughter, Charlotte, had sunk to the ground, her face buried in her hands. Martha looked down at the weeping young woman and then back at the spindly figure of the county's last desperado, racing toward the flames to save a long-vanished child. She set down the Mossberg shotgun and went after him.

She wished she had on her jogging shoes instead of regulation black leather lace-ups, but she had her running practice and twenty years' advantage in age, which compensated for the old man's determination to reach the trailer in time to rescue his daughter. She pounded across the hard crust of the barren field, heedless of the red seepage that oozed from cracks in the soil in spots. She would not have caught him but for the fact that he stopped, wavering with a second's indecision, midway between where they had stood and the flames.

An instant later Martha was at his side, trying to edge her body between him and the burning trailer. "She's not in there!" she shouted. "She's not there!"

Harm Sorley looked at Martha with puzzled eyes, and then over her shoulder at the blond woman, struggling to her feet. "Come back, Daddy!" she was screaming. "I'm Chalarty! I'm your little girl."

"Your wife is dead, Mr. Sorley," said Martha, quietly now. "You've been very ill. You've suffered memory loss. You are disoriented. You need to understand that the woman over there is your daughter, Charlotte, grown up. Thirty years have passed since you lived here. You're sixty-three. Now please come away from the fire."

Harm saw the truth of it in her face, and her words took half his lifetime. He was old.

"Come away from the fire, Mr. Sorley," Martha said again. "I'm placing you in custody."

He looked as if he understood. If he had looked away from the burning trailer and the two anxious women for even a few moments; if he had stared instead at the ripple of dark mountains against a buttermilk sky; if he had thought of something else, he might have forgotten her words. But he stood staring at her, silent. Then he took a step backward from Martha's upraised hand, and smiled. "I have to go," he said, and began to walk slowly toward the fire.

She reached for his shoulder, but he shook her off and kept walking. "Don't make me shoot you, ma'am."

He was still holding the pistol, walking slowly toward the blaze.

Martha ran back to the place under the trees where Charlotte Pentland sat. Martha barely glanced at the weeping woman. She picked up the shotgun. It was an inexpensive, department-issue Mossberg loaded with double-aught pellets of approximately .32 caliber. Martha raised the weapon to her shoulder and racked a round.

A few yards across the field Harm Sorley heard the unmistakable sound of a shotgun being prepared to fire. Martha knew that it is one of the most chilling sounds on earth: it means there is no time to get out of the way. The old man stood still. As Martha took aim, she could see him flinch, but he did not look back.

"Don't kill him!" screamed Charlotte.

"Shut up," said Martha, and fired. She hoped that

the shot would hit hard ground. It was a chance in a thousand.

As she watched, Harm Sorley clutched at his legs and fell.

"You shot him!"

"Not exactly." Martha had set down the shotgun and was already running toward the injured man, with Charlotte laboring to keep pace with her. "I aimed for the ground about five yards in front of him," she called out as she ran. "The discharge struck the hard-packed clay, and the pellets ricocheted off, kept going about a foot above the ground, and hit his legs." Martha and LeDonne had practiced the maneuver a few times, but trying it now was a last resort. There was no other way to stop the old man. She was too far away to use the Glock, and aiming directly at him with the shotgun blast likely would have killed him. Martha hoped that she and Charlotte could drag him away from the fire and get him off the mountain alive.

"He's getting up!"

Martha stopped. A few yards from the blaze, Harm Sorley was struggling to his feet. From his knees to his ankles, his trousers were blood soaked and tattered. He swayed as he regained his footing, staggering the last few feet toward the burning trailer.

"Stop him," said Charlotte softly.

Martha shook her head. "I can't."

Dark smoke billowed out of the ruins, enveloping the last of the outlaw Sorleys. They could no longer see him, but they stood there, not speaking, until the roof collapsed and the metal frame of the trailer curled downward in the heat, until there was nothing left but the scorched remnants of a shell. There was no sign of the old man.

"I never got to talk to him," Charlotte whispered. "I never got to tell him anything."

"I'm sorry," said Martha. "I did everything I could to stop him. More than I should have, really. I'll have to do a lot of explaining to the sheriff about discharging the shotgun. But I think your father made his decision. He knew what he wanted."

"I should have stopped him."

"He had a gun," said Martha. "Besides, what was left for him? Prison? Since he'd murdered Mrs. Pentland, they'd never let him out."

"He didn't kill my mother," said Charlotte. She handed Martha the faded letter that began: *Hiram, My darling Husband* . . .

It was a starless night by the time they followed the river to the next ridge, and then crossed that to the valley of Wake County's other river, the brackish Little Dove, flowing west from North Carolina's paper mills. There they saw a light like a single star on the brow of a dark hill above them, and they found the path to take them toward that light, a footpath leading over Ashe Mountain. Isolated from each other by cold, hardly speaking, they had trudged upward through the gathering darkness until a break in the trees gave them another glimpse of the light. They saw that the light belonged to a small white house in a meadow on Ashe Mountain. They were almost there.

In the hours that had followed their escape, they had said nothing about the occurrence in the empty field near the Toe River, but Jeremy had thought of little else since then, and the memory of it kept him going, humming through him louder than the pain in his body. He tried to remember the timbre of the voice, and whether the accent had sounded British or Southern, but the details were already blurring in his mind. All he knew for certain was that he had found her—that the journey was over, and he would never pass this way again.

Ahead the lights blazed in uncurtained windows, and through an expanse of glass, Jeremy could see a wooden loom and the shine of polished oak in a sitting room with a fireplace. He must have imagined the smell of baking bread that fit so perfectly with the cozy scene before him. This was so like civilization as he wanted it to be, and as he had never found it, that at first he thought it was a mirage, conjured up by his own fatigue as he froze to death on a dark mountain.

As Jeremy and Sabrina approached the house, a figure holding a kerosene lantern appeared on the back steps. He could see the lined face of the tall old woman who was waiting for them. She was wrapped in a crimson shawl, and a knitted tam covered all but a few tendrils of her hair. "You'd better come in," she called out. "You've come a long way."

"How did she know we were out here?" muttered Jeremy.

"Probably saw us," said Sabrina, pointing to an outside light mounted on a twenty-foot pole. "That's Nora Bonesteel." She looked as if she wanted to say more, but they had reached the steps by then, and the old woman was asking if they were all right.

Nora herded them into a pine-walled kitchen where

a kettle was boiling, and white china mugs were set out on a gingham tablecloth. Jeremy sank into a ladder-back chair. "I made it back," he said to no one in particular.

Then he smiled up at Nora Bonesteel and said, "Have you ever heard of Thomas Wolfe, the novelist? I've been thinking about him some as we walked here. You know, he lived not fifty miles from here, and he wrote once about the unfound door, the lost lane-end into heaven."

Nora Bonesteel smiled back. *"Which of us is not for-ever prison-pent,"* she quoted. *"Which of us is not forever a stranger and alone?"*

Jeremy stared. "You've read him?"

Nora nodded. "I had kin in Asheville. Now sit back and rest yourself. You've had a cold day for walking. Are you any the worse for it?"

"I need a doctor," said Jeremy. His hands shook as he lifted his mug of coffee. "I think it might be infected." He raised his swollen foot.

"I don't have a telephone," said Nora Bonesteel. "But we'll send for help. Is it walking sores? Take off your boot, and let me have a look."

"You have no phone?" Jeremy repeated. "How can you get help then?"

Nora Bonesteel turned to Sabrina. "If you'll put your coat back on and go out into the front yard—through that door—you'll see a cast-iron bell mounted on a pole up the hill near the front gate. Just give that rope about six hard pulls. That will let the folks down the mountain know to send someone up to see about me. They'll be here directly." As the girl stood up to go, Nora

Bonesteel added, "Come right back in when you're finished. The hawk is flying low tonight."

"The *hawk*?" said Jeremy.

Sabrina sneered. "She means it's cold."

When the girl was gone, Nora Bonesteel took a pan of hot water and a box of first-aid supplies, and sat down in the chair next to Jeremy. "You'll not want to think too much about this foot of yours while I'm seeing to it," she told him. "Why don't you close your eyes and talk about your journey while I work?"

"All right. Listen, don't you think we'd better—" She had loosened the bootlace now, and was tugging gently on the leather. Jeremy swallowed hard and closed his eyes. "I was looking for Katie Wyler," he said.

"You came to the right place," murmured Nora Bonesteel. "I'm going to cut this sock off. What's left of it. Now how is it that you came to find Katie?"

He told her about his dissertation, and about his efforts to follow her path, and, failing that, to duplicate the experience of part of her journey through hardship and solitude. "Her story has fascinated me for such a long time," said Jeremy. "I wanted to know what she was *like*."

Nora Bonesteel nodded toward the front door. "Like your young friend there, like as not."

"That girl?" Jeremy opened his eyes, caught a glimpse of his purple foot, and shut them again. "But she's a—"

"A hillbilly?" The old woman smiled thoughtfully. "Yes. Not much education. No manners to speak of. Nothing much in the way of looks or charm. Just a hard life that'll see her through just about any trouble

that comes. Katie all over again. She was a scrawny little thing, too, all hair and eyes—and backbone, Katie
was."

"You talk as if you'd seen her."

"They say she still walks here now and again," Nora
said, dipping a cloth into the pan of hot water. She began to clean his injured foot. "You spoke of visions. Is
that what you saw behind the unfound door?"

"Didn't see anything," Jeremy's voice was unsteady
with pain. "Just heard." In fragments, punctuated by
sharp intakes of breath, he told her what had happened
in the meadow near the river, and what the voice had
told them. From the darkness outside they heard the
iron bell clang eight times.

"She spoke to you," said Nora Bonesteel, looking
thoughtfully at the front door. "We-ell."

Sabrina Harkryder came in. "Hope I rang it loud
enough for them to hear," she said. "Everybody will be
indoors in this cold."

"They'll come," said Nora Bonesteel. "Sit by the fire
and get warm. There's a pot of stew that will be ready
directly."

Sabrina went back to the table for her coffee. "Were
y'all talking about the escaped convict?" she asked.

"I forgot all about him," said Jeremy.

"Harm Sorley? You saw him out there?" Nora
Bonesteel was spreading a white salve on the blisters.
She looked at Sabrina for confirmation.

"Yeah, we saw him. He pulled a gun on us, but the
lady deputy showed up, and we lit out of there. I hope
he's dead," said Sabrina Harkryder. "That murdering
devil killed my baby."

Jeremy stared at her, trying to take in the fact that this runaway schoolgirl was herself a mother. "He killed your child?" He stammered. "But you never said anything at all while we were out there. When? How?"

The sullen girl took a long swallow of coffee. "He broke into the trailer last night," she said tonelessly. "When I woke up the baby was gone. He's took and killed it."

Nora Bonesteel was watching her with mournful eyes. "Oh, child," she said softly. "Out there in the meadow, did you hear Katie Wyler, too?"

"You mean that voice that told us to head for the river? Yeah, I heard it. First we smelled smoke and heard a lot of yelling, then we heard somebody come up and tell us to run. It didn't bother me. I know about spirits and such. I'm Melungeon, you know."

The old woman nodded solemnly. "I see now. Yes, I see why she came to you. I reckon it was the bond between you that did it."

"What bond?" said Jeremy. "With me, because I was thinking about her?"

"No." She was still watching the dark-haired girl, crouched before the hearth, hugging herself for warmth. "The bond with Sabrina. Katie Wyler killed her baby, too."

Sabrina Harkryder looked back, white with anger, but Nora Bonesteel met her gaze with a look of calm sorrow, and finally the young girl turned away. "All right!" she shouted, her voice echoing in the narrow room. They did not reply.

After a minute she went on, quietly now, with the detachment of one who can feel nothing more. "I didn't exactly mean to!" she said, staring into the fire. "I just had to get away from there. I'm still a kid myself. I felt like a prisoner having to stay trapped up there in Painter Cove, missing my own people, and Tracy never paying me no mind. And it just kept crying all the time, day and night, crying, crying. I thought if I could just get shut of this kid, things could go back to being like they was before, and I'd be free to leave. I could go back home to my mama, maybe even go back to school. I never thought I'd miss it, but I did. That lady deputy will understand. I know if I can just talk to her, she'll make it all right."

Jeremy Cobb hardly heard her. He was thinking of Katie Wyler. "Rab Greer's baby?" he whispered. "Was she pregnant before she was even captured?"

Nora Bonesteel nodded. "It wasn't the kind of thing anybody would write in the history books, but the people in these mountains always knew. The women did, anyhow. I had it from my grandmother long ago."

"It was born while she was with the Shawnee. She killed it so that she could escape. It would have died anyway on the journey, wouldn't it?"

"She couldn't have nursed it, no more than she had to eat. There's some would say it was kinder not to let it starve."

"And when she got back to Mitchell County, and Rab asked her about the child, she told him the truth. And he—"

Nora Bonesteel patted his ankle and stood up. "I put some Balm of Gilead salve on that foot of yours," she said briskly. "I think the doctor will tell you it'll be all right. Now you rest a spell, and let me see to that poor young'un over there. No Balm of Gilead can help her." She added to herself, "Tracy Harkryder mustn't be let into the jail to see her."

# CHAPTER
# 18

Through many dangers, toils, and snares,
   I have already come:
'Tis grace has brought me safe thus far,
   And grace will lead me home.

#654, "Amazing Grace," John Newton

Tennessee Methodist Hymnal, 1885

Spencer Arrowood folded the letter and set it on his desk. "We figured it had to be something like that," he said.

"She loved him all along." Martha was shivering now, although it was warm in the sheriff's office. She scooted her chair closer to the electric baseboard heater. It was the first time she had relaxed in hours. When she left the burned-out trailer, she had radioed in to the department to be told by Jennaleigh that LeDonne was transporting Euell Pentland to the jail facilities in Erwin, and that Spencer was on his way up Ashe Mountain to pick up an injured hiker and Sabrina Harkryder. Martha's orders were to leave the death scene, and to break the news to Charlotte Pentland about the arrest of her stepfather. Martha dreaded another outburst from her, but Charlotte took the news calmly. After reading her mother's letter, she had worked it out for herself.

"Do you want me to take you home?" Martha had asked her.

Charlotte shook her head. "I'm going back to my

apartment and catch up on some work. There is something you could do for me, though."

Martha blinked. The sheriff had just asked her something. "I'm sorry. I guess it's all catching up with me. What did you say?"

"I asked if you were all right. Not going into shock, are you?"

"No. I was just remembering. Charlotte Pentland asked us to check her mother's belongings. There's a green necklace that she'd like returned."

Spencer pointed to his desk drawer. "It's in the manila folder with the other items. How did she take the news about her stepfather?"

"She pretty much knew when she found the letter under the trailer step, and learned that her mother was planning to run away with Harm Sorley. I guess Rita put it there when she visited the place with her daughter, hoping Harm would check there if he made it back to the county."

"Then she got tired of waiting, and decided to go out there herself," said Spencer. "We found the neighbor who gave her a ride part of the way. Rita had told her that she was going up into the hills to surprise her daughter on a geology field trip."

"After all these years, Rita was going back to Harm." Martha's smile was bitter. "You wouldn't catch me going back to my first husband. But I remember now that when we questioned Rita Pentland, she never really said she was afraid of Harm. She always asked how he was. I thought now that she'd bettered herself, she'd have wanted to forget about him."

"Bettered herself?" said Spencer. "I'm sure Euell reminded her of that often enough. You heard how he talked to her. It can't have been easy spending her life being grateful and walking a social chalkline. She didn't leave Harm Sorley, you know. He was put in prison, and she was left with a child to fend for. Maybe Euell was the only choice she had."

"He wouldn't have been my choice," Martha admitted. "I always thought he was a pompous fool, but how did you come to suspect him?"

"Harm Sorley's mental problems were so severe that he seemed incapable of the crime. How would he find her after all these years? And how would he even recognize her if he saw her? Remember, he was still back in the sixties."

"I wish I were," said Martha. "Back then I believed in happy endings."

"I guess if you're happy, it isn't the end," said Spencer. "By the way, we never did find the note she left Euell."

"That's what made him go after her, I suppose." Martha shivered again. "He couldn't believe that she'd leave him for a convict."

"Yeah. He was a bully, all right, but he confessed fast enough today. LeDonne is not impressed by bullies, so I left them to it. I was up at Painter Cove searching for the Harkryder baby."

Martha sighed wearily. "I blew that one, Spencer. I should have taken that baby away from her the first time we went up there."

He shrugged. "Wouldn't have mattered. Social Services would have given it back the next day. When I took the girl to jail, she cried all the way to Erwin. I think she'll get off with a couple of years, although I'm not sure how I feel about that. She kept asking to see you, by the way."

Martha looked uneasy. "I'll try to get over there tomorrow. I mean—depending on what you want me to do."

"We'll be busy enough. One of us will go back to the trailer with a medical examiner to recover Harm's remains, and I'll be questioning Sabrina Harkryder's bastard of a husband about the baby's death. Sometime you and I need to talk about shotguns, departmental procedure, and such." He frowned. "But starting tomorrow, Martha, I want you to take some time off."

She hung her head. "I understand."

"No you don't," he said. "I'm worried about you. It's standard procedure for deputies who have been through what you have. You may need to talk to somebody to sort out your feelings about job stress. While you're off, you also need to look into taking the law enforcement training."

Martha almost smiled. "I passed probation, huh?"

"You'll do, Deputy."

"What about Godwin?"

"No word from the doctors yet. If he recovers, I'll try to find the money to hire him back, too, but that won't affect your job. You'll stay on." Spencer looked at his watch. "Joe should be back soon. It's nearly eleven, though, and there's one more security job that we promised to do tonight." He yawned. "Guess I'm stuck with it."

Martha stood up, zipping her jacket. "I'll take care of it," she said.

"You sure, Martha? You've had a hell of a day."

She smiled. "It will be my pleasure, Sheriff."

" 'As all things eternal and primordial reappear, so all things mortal return to the earth. Honor, old age, probity, justice, constancy, virtue, and gentleness all are gathered into the cold tomb.' " Henry Kretzer was once again Hank the Yank, master of the electronic closet. He reared back in his swivel chair, notecards in hand, and addressed the microphone. "Francis Quarles, who said that in 1635 in *Emblems, Divine and Moral*, has been gathered into the cold tomb himself, neighbors, but the truth of his observation remains. We are ephemeral, but the mountains endure, and when they are finally worn away to dust by wind and water, new mountains will rise up in their place. I'm not sure I find the stability of nature comforting, though. The mountains will be back, but none of us will pass this way again. That makes it all the sadder when any one of us goes.

"I guess most of you have heard that our escaped convict drama is over now. Old Harm, the last outlaw of the infamous Sorley clan, is dead, and the world is a little bit tamer now, a little more bland. I'm sure somewhere people are rejoicing over his demise. They're the same sort of people who drove the wolves to the brink of extinction. Said they were too dangerous to be left alive. Now, a naturalist will tell you that there has not been one single documented case of a North American wolf *ever* killing a human being, but you try telling that to the safety fiends. They'd pave the planet, and tell us it was for our own protection. They're the folks who hanged the elephant.

"The naturalist David Brower said, 'The wild places are where we began. When they end, so do we.'

"Hearing about Harm Sorley's death tonight got me to thinking about wolves, I guess, because, like them, he got a bum rap. I don't think that old man was any more dangerous than a wolf is. Oh, we heard a lot of alarming reports about his exploits: how he'd killed his ex-wife and a little baby, but you know what, folks? He didn't do it. I'm serious, now. This isn't just my opinion. Sheriff Spencer Arrowood himself told me that someone else has confessed to the murder of the infant, and that Euell Pentland has been charged with the murder of his wife. So much for the crime wave.

"The sheriff called me to request a song, which has to be a first in the history of this show. He wants me to play 'Someday Soon,' and he said to check around for old Judy Collins albums, but I can do better than that, Mr. Arrowood. I've got a recording of 'Someday Soon' by Ian and Sylvia. Ian is the fellow who wrote it. When I was growing up in New England, Canadian country and folk music was a passion of mine, and I guess Ian Tyson was my poet laureate. The sheriff asked me to dedicate 'Someday Soon' to the memory of Rita Sorley Pentland, and I guess if you listen to the words, you can figure out why. *Going with him,* the song says. Sometimes love is just as strong as those things primordial, no matter what we civilized folk do to kill it. Here's your song, Sheriff Arrowood. Thanks for asking."

* * *

The cardboard sign on the door of the Mockingbird Inn was turned to *Closed* and the building was dark, but the brown patrol car pulled into the space closest to the entrance and stopped, idling with its headlights and motor still on. The door to the beer joint opened wide enough for a skinny young woman in a fake-fur parka to dart out. With a wave at the car, she turned, hunching over the doorknob to make sure the place was locked. That done, she smiled into the glare of the cruiser's headlights, hurried to the passenger side, and slid in.

"Hello, darlin'!" she said to the uniformed officer.

"Good evening, Ms. Stanley," said Martha Ayers. "I believe you needed an escort to the bank."

The arch smile stretched into a rictus. "Where's Joe?" Her hand groped for the door handle, but this deputy was already pulling out of the Mockingbird's parking lot and building up speed.

"Officer LeDonne couldn't make it tonight, Ms. Stanley," said Martha over the roar of the engine. "He and the sheriff are finishing up a couple of homicide cases, so I volunteered to take care of you." There was a slight emphasis on the word *you*.

"Did Joe—I dunno—say anything?" Crystal Stanley fumbled in her purse for a crumpled pack of cigarettes.

Martha glanced at her. "No. He was preoccupied. Please don't smoke in this car, Ms. Stanley. I came out because I thought it was time we got acquainted."

"What do you mean?" She was staring out the window, watching the blur of dark fields fall away as they sped along the country blacktop. Her voice was strained, and she kept her fingers wrapped around the door handle.

"Seems like we have a lot in common," said Martha.

The girl craned her neck, peering into the darkness for landmarks. "Where are we going? I don't see any lights."

"Johnson City," said Martha, easing around a curve at straight-away speed. She remembered Spencer Arrowood saying to her: *Haven't you ever wanted to burn rubber on a back road like they do in the movies?* At the time she had thought he was crazy, but, yeah, now she did want to. Like a bat out of hell. Aloud she said, "Isn't that where your bank is? Johnson City?"

Crystal Stanley wasn't listening. "You won't hurt me," she said. "You're a cop."

"Not a full-fledged one," said Martha. "Besides, I've already watched two people die this week. I'm getting kind of used to it."

"You're kidnapping me!"

Martha shrugged. "I'm just giving you a ride to the bank."

"I'll tell Joe what you done. Threatening me."

"You do that," said Martha. "He hasn't got a lot of sympathy for cowards, but you can give it a shot. Remember, though, that I'm a deputy, too, and from now on, I'll be on you like white on rice. You have a taillight burned out on your car? I'll be there. You sell beer to a minor at the Inn? Expect to see me. Go thirty-*six* miles an hour through town, and I'll pull you over. You'll be seeing me a lot."

"Can you do that?"

"Try me."

The girl sneered. "You think that will stop me from seeing Joe?"

"No," said Martha. "I think he'll take care of that. I don't think you mean much to him, anyway. And you don't strike me as the patient type. So I figure that in a couple of weeks or months, you'll hang it up. He's not easy, you know. Have you sat through one of the nightmares yet? He has flashbacks of Vietnam and wakes up screaming about some guy named Parnell. He'll never talk to you about it, though. Don't bother asking. Then there's the night sweats, and the times a noise will send him rolling under the bed for cover, dodging a rocket that burned out in 1968. Have you seen one of his depressions yet? He sits in a chair and stares at the wall for hours at a time, with Doors tapes blasting away on the stereo. And sometimes he won't show up for a couple of days, and then he'll be back with no explanation. Oh, and one more thing about his depressions. Do you know how to unload a .45 automatic? That's something you'll need to learn."

Crystal Stanley was staring at Martha open-mouthed. "Shit," she said. "What do you want him back for?"

Martha shook her head. "You wouldn't understand."

Jeremy Cobb was sitting on Nora Bonesteel's flowered sofa, drinking chamomile tea. When the sheriff came to get Sabrina Harkryder, he hadn't wanted to take Jeremy with them, so Nora offered to put him up in her guest room, and the neighbors had promised to come back for him in the morning and take him to town to be picked up by Linley from the Virginia Tech history department, who would drive down from

Blacksburg to get him. They had talked a little about Sabrina, but soon Jeremy's attention drifted back to Katie Wyler.

"I actually found her," he said to Nora Bonesteel, who was weaving on her loom. "She spoke to me. I wish I could say so in my dissertation."

"No, I don't suppose your college would care much for that," said Nora. "But you could tell people about the child, I think. Explain why she died. I'll be your reference."

"I guess I could. Oral history from the region." He stood up to set his teacup on the table and winced.

"Foot still troubling you?"

"I need to stay off it."

"We'll try the salve again in the morning."

"Thank you. I'd like the recipe for my notes, if you wouldn't mind." Jeremy rubbed at his bandaged ankle. "I may end up on crutches for a week when I get back, but the trip was worth it."

Nora Bonesteel nodded. "Next time you'll know to travel light on the trail, and take it slowly."

He stared at her. "*Next* time? You think I'd ever do this again?"

She smiled and went back to her weaving. "Back in Mitchell County, at the fork where the North and South Toe rivers come together, there's a place called Kona. You'll be wanting to visit there, I expect."

Jeremy pulled a quilt up over his legs. In the firelight his eyes shone. "Why?" he asked. "What happened there?"

"It's an old story," said Nora. Her voice rose and fell above the soft, rhythmic clatter of the loom, and in the firelight Jeremy listened, caught in an old enchantment.

One o'clock in the morning, and the only light on in Martha's kitchen was on the hood above the stove. On the round oak table, an ashtray overflowed with stubbed-out cigarettes. Martha sat at the table, still in uniform, staring into an untouched cup of coffee, and trying to will herself to sleep. It wasn't working. She kept replaying the scene at the burning trailer, trying to think up some way to make it turn out differently, but she couldn't see that any changed behavior on her part would have affected the outcome. She wondered which was worse: brooding about it awake, or risking nightmares when she tried to sleep. Spencer was right. She ought to talk to somebody before the stress of the job engulfed her.

She heard a sound at the back door, and she had half risen from her chair to reach the pistol on the countertop when the door opened and Joe LeDonne stepped in.

"Mind if I talk to you?" he said, leaning against the door.

Martha shrugged. "What is there to say?"

"I heard you had a rough time out there today. Spencer said you had to fire at the suspect."

"I was trying to save his life," said Martha. "I fired the shotgun at hard ground like you taught me, and the low-flying pellets brought him down. It worked."

"Well, that's good, Martha. Sounds like you acquitted yourself well for a rookie."

"He still died."

"He was a lost cause. His tombstone ought to say 1968. The point is nobody else got hurt. That's mostly what we're there for."

She sat with her back to him, saying nothing. After a moment's silence, LeDonne went on. "I was worried about you this afternoon, when you didn't call in for so long."

"Yeah, right." She reached for another cigarette, the last of a pack she'd found in the back of a drawer from back when she smoked.

"I owe you an apology," he said. He pulled out the chair across from her and sat down. "There was a message from Crystal on my machine when I got home."

She shrugged. "So?"

He shifted uneasily in his chair. "I didn't know you smoked, Martha."

"I guess there's a lot we didn't know about each other." There was no emotion in her voice, but she looked down at her cup, not at him.

"There was a lot I didn't even know about myself," said LeDonne. "I didn't realize how much of my ego was tied into being the lawman in the—family." He stumbled over the word. "I didn't tell you, but when Spencer made you a deputy, it stuck in my craw."

"You didn't tell me. Since when have you ever told me anything?" she said bitterly. "It bothered you. Why?"

"Because—I don't know—I guess I wanted somebody who'd be impressed by what I was doing, not somebody who was competing with me, matching my war stories with ones of her own."

Martha turned to look at him, her eyes narrowed. "Is

that your idea of a relationship, Joe? Quarterback and cheerleader?"

"I thought it was." He spoke slowly, thinking out each phrase. "Maybe it made me feel important."

"So you decided to punish me for daring to compete with you?" She filled her lungs with smoke, holding her breath so the tears wouldn't come. "Did humping that piece of trash make you feel special, Joe?"

"No." He sounded tired. "I impressed the hell out of her, but I can't say I respected her judgment. It was nice, though, to feel wanted while you were busy."

"I wasn't out drinking Mai Tai's on the Clinton Highway, LeDonne. I was working sixteen-hour days, trying to become something more than a jumped-up secretary. Trying to be somebody whose judgment you could respect."

He winced at the sarcasm in her tone. "I screwed up, Martha, all right? I've certainly done enough of that in my life. You should be used to it by now."

"What do you want from me?" she asked wearily.

"I've told Crystal it's over. There wasn't much to it, anyway, but I won't see her again. I guess I want to work things out between us."

Martha shrugged. "Meaning what?"

"Like it was. I'm no good at this kind of talk, Martha. You know."

"I know," she said. "But you're going to have to get better at it, because I'm not going to be shut out again while you indulge your own pain. You treat me as a friend first, a woman second. Got that? I may not have a penis, LeDonne, but I sure as hell have a gun. That ought to count for something."

He smiled a little. "Ma'am, yes, ma'am," he said.

"I'm making no promises, either," she said, ignoring his smile. "I'll never trust you again, ever. And someday you might just find me gone. That's how it is. No promises. Now, circumstances being what they are, why the hell would you want to stay?"

"I reckon I love you, Martha."

It was the first time he had ever said it. In the near darkness, Martha swallowed her tears. "It's a start," she said.

Hank the Yank had dimmed the lights in the sound booth, so that the control panel shone like an electronic Christmas tree. "I'm going to play another Ian Tyson song in a minute, folks," he told the microphone. "And I'm dedicating that one to Harm Sorley, the last outlaw. It's called 'The Renegade' and it's Tyson's song about a Canadian Indian, but it kept running through my head these past few days when I thought about that poor old man stuck out there in the past. In the refrain of the song, the renegade says that he'll hunt his own knowledge, and drink his own whiskey, and he'll sing until morning the old-fashioned songs. The old ways—he just can't let them go. Of course, the Indian dies at the end of the song. 'The Renegade' by Ian Tyson, coming up soon from Hank the Yank on WHTN.

"Was Harm Sorley a renegade? Oh yes. He committed that first murder all those years ago. The sheriff finally convinced me of that. But at least we know why now. Seems that when the peace officers were out there checking out the crime scene, which had been the Sorley residence in 1968, they found some kind of crud oozing out of the ground. I saw it myself when I was out there detecting. The sample is at the lab, but Spencer Arrowood told me he'd seen something like it before. It's toxic waste, folks. Industrial chemicals dumped in a poor man's field. I got to thinking about the fact that on the day Claib Maggard was murdered, Harm Sorley's cow died.

"And Claib Maggard was a high muckety-muck with the county back then, remember? The EPA will probably be all over that site, trying to figure out what it is and how to clean it up, and who to bill for their trouble. I'll bet they find out that Claib Maggard arranged for that dumping, and pocketed the money from whatever company unloaded it. What did he care? It wasn't his cow. Or his family living next to the poison.

"Did that justify killing him? Maybe not, neighbors. But it makes me wonder if Claib Maggard's grasping, ruthless life was worth thirty years of time in the penitentiary for Harm Sorley. That's what I'm wondering. I guess it doesn't matter now. Maybe it never mattered. Maybe Harm never had a chance anyhow. The people who settled this land, and loved it too much to leave it, were being pushed back then by the government interests, and the corporations, and the tourists, and the city people with their vacation homes. Thirty years hasn't changed any of that, either. We've got the pollution, and condos, and barbed wire around ski resorts to prove it. They got rid of the wolves a long time ago. Guess the hillbillies will go next.

"We'll lose something precious when that happens, neighbors." Hank the Yank took out a paperback book, and opened to a dog-eared page. Pressing his face close to the words in the dim light, he said, "I guess we're having an electronic wake here, my friends, so let me finish up with an epitaph for Harm Sorley. It's from a long poem called 'John Brown's Body' by Stephen Vincent Benet, and here he's talking about the people of these mountains. Listen up.

> *"When the last moonshiner buys his radio,*
> *And the last, lost, wild-rabbit of a girl*
> *Is civilized with a mail-order dress,*
> *Something will pass that was American*
> *And all the movies will not bring it back."*

He closed the book. "I guess I'm done now," he said.

# ACKNOWLEDGMENTS

My thanks to the naturalists, historians, law enforcement people, fellow writers, and my colleagues in Appalachian Studies for their help and encouragement in the writing of *She Walks These Hills*. Special thanks to Charlotte Ross and Becky Councill for hearing me out as the project took shape; to Appalachia's distinguished poet James Still, whose poem "Heritage" was an inspiration; to poet Clyde Kessler for sharing his knowledge of the plants and animals of the region; to fellow author and Knox County Deputy Sheriff emeritus David Hunter for technical assistance; to Dot Jackson, for her tale of the long-dead Indians who can still be heard crossing the Big Santeetlah; to Mark Schoenberg, M.D., for help in understanding Korsakoff's syndrome; to Sgt. Joe Niehaus, Kettering, Ohio, P.D.; to Bill Elliott of NECC; to David Fryar; to Appalachian Trail guide Harry Smith; to Linda Arnold of the Virginia Tech history department; and to Joan Hess, Barbara Michaels, and Park Overall for their encouragement and friendship.

In addition to hymns, family legends, mountain lore, and tales gathered from people I know, I also consulted the following works, listed here for the benefit of those who want to "hunt their own knowledge":

*Traces on the Appalachians: A Natural History of Serpentine in Eastern North America,* by Kevin T. Dann, Rutgers University Press, New Brunswick, NJ, 1988.

*The Highland Geology Trail,* by John L. Roberts, Strathtongue Press, Tongue by Lairg, Scotland, 1990.

*Wilderness Trails of Tennessee's Cherokee National Forest,* edited by William H. Skelton, University of Tennessee Press, Knoxville, TN, 1992.

*News from Pigeon Roost,* by Harvey J. Miller, The Foxfire Press, 1974.

*Crimes, Criminals and Characters of the Cumberlands and Southwest Virginia,* by Roy L. Sturgill, Bristol, VA, 1970.

*The Appalachian Trail Backpacker's Planning Guide,* by Victoria and Frank Logue, Menasha Ridge Press, Birmingham, AL, 1991.

*The Day They Hung the Elephant,* by Charles Edwin Price, Overmountain Press, Johnson City, TN, 1992.

*Touring Western North Carolina Backroads,* by Carolyn Sakowski, John F. Blair Publishers, Winston-Salem, NC, 1990.

*Follow the River,* by James Alexander Thom, Ballantine Books, New York, 1981. (This is a novel about Mary Draper Ingles, one of the pioneer women on whom Katie Wyler is based.)

*Mountain Ghost Stories and Curious Tales of Western North Carolina,* by Randy Russell and Janet Barnett, John F. Blair Publishers, Winston-Salem, NC, 1988.

*A Roadside Guide to the Geology of the Great Smoky*

*Mountains National Park,* by Harry L. Moore, University of Tennessee Press, Knoxville, TN, 1988.

*Strangers in High Places,* by Michael Frome, University of Tennessee Press, Knoxville, TN, 1966.